IT HAD TO
BE YOU

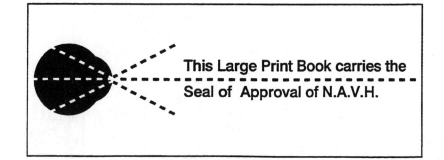

This Large Print Book carries the
Seal of Approval of N.A.V.H.

IT HAD TO
BE YOU

Susan Elizabeth Phillips

G.K. Hall & Co.
Thorndike, Maine

Published in 1996 by arrangement with
Avon Books, a division of the Hearst Corporation.

G.K. Hall Large Print Romance Collection.

The text of this Large Print edition is unabridged.
Other aspects of the book may vary from the original edition.

Set in 16 pt. News Plantin by Rick Gundberg.

Printed in the United States on permanent paper.

Library of Congress Cataloging in Publication Data

Phillips, Susan Elizabeth.
    It had to be you / Susan Elizabeth Phillips.
        p.   cm.
    ISBN 0-7838-1659-6 (lg. print : hc)
    1. Large type books.   I. Title.
    [PS3566.H522I85   1996]
    813'.54—dc20   95-52456

---

*To Steven Axelrod, who's been around from the
beginning with a good head, a strong shoulder,
and a high tolerance for crazy authors.
This one had to be yours.*

ACKNOWLEDGMENTS

This book would not have been possible without the gracious assistance of the Chicago Bears' organization. A special thanks to Barbara Allen for opening doors and answering questions. Go Bears!

I am also deeply indebted to the following people and organizations:

The National Football League

The Dallas Cowboys' and Denver Broncos' organizations

The public relations staff at the Pontiac Silverdome and the Houston Astrodome

Linda Barlow, Mary Lynn Baxter, Jayne Ann Krentz, Jimmie Morel, John Roscich, and Katherine Stone, for brainstorming, answering questions, providing perspective, and, in general, bailing me out of trouble

The wonderful reference librarians at Nichols Library

Claire Zion, for years of guidance and support

The people at Avon Books, especially my enthusiastic and helpful editor, Lisa Wager.

A special thank you to my husband, Bill Phillips, who, since my writing career began, has planned golf tournaments, designed computers, and spent the past year managing a professional football team. This book truly would not have been possible without his help.

Susan Elizabeth Phillips

1

Phoebe Somerville outraged everyone by bringing a French poodle and a Hungarian lover to her father's funeral. She sat at the gravesite like a fifties movie queen with the small white poodle perched in her lap and a pair of rhinestone-studded cat's-eye sunglasses shielding her eyes. It was difficult for the mourners to decide who looked more out of place — the perfectly clipped poodle sporting a pair of matching peach satin ear bows, Phoebe's unbelievably handsome Hungarian with his long, beaded ponytail, or Phoebe herself.

Phoebe's ash blond hair, artfully streaked with platinum, swooped down over one eye like Marilyn Monroe's in *The Seven Year Itch*. Her moist, full lips, painted a delicious shade of peony pink, were slightly parted as she gazed toward the shiny black casket that held what was left of Bert Somerville. She wore an ivory suit with a silky, quilted jacket, but the outrageous gold metallic *bustier* beneath was more appropriate to a rock concert than a funeral. And the slim skirt, belted with loops of gold chain (one of which sported a dangling fig leaf) was slit at the side to the middle of her shapely thigh.

This was the first time Phoebe had been back in Chicago since she'd run away when she was eighteen, so only a few of the mourners present had ever met Bert Somerville's prodigal daughter. From the stories they'd heard, however, none of them were surprised that Bert had disinherited her. What father would want to pass on his estate to a daughter who'd been the mistress of a man more than forty years her senior, even if that man had been the noted Spanish painter, Arturo Flores? And then there was the embarrassment of the paintings. To someone like Bert Somerville, naked pictures were naked pictures, and the fact that the dozens of abstract nudes Flores had executed of Phoebe now graced the walls of museums all over the world hadn't softened his judgment.

Phoebe had a slender waist and slim, shapely legs, but her breasts and hips were plump and womanly, a throwback to an almost forgotten time when women had looked like women. She had a bad girl's body, the sort of body that, even at thirty-three, could just as well have been displayed with a staple through the navel as hanging on a museum wall. It was a bimbo's body — never mind that the brain inside was highly intelligent, since Phoebe was the sort of woman who was seldom judged by anything except appearances.

Her face wasn't any more conventional than her body. There was something off-kilter about the arrangement of her features, although it was difficult to say exactly what since her nose was straight, her mouth well formed, and her jaw strong. Perhaps it was the outrageously sexy tiny black mole that sat high on her cheekbone. Or maybe it was her eyes. Those who had seen them before she'd slipped on her rhinestone sunglasses had noted the way they tilted upward at the corners, too exotic, somehow, to fit with the rest of her face. Arturo Flores had frequently exaggerated those amber eyes, sometimes painting them larger than her hips, sometimes superimposing them over her wonderful breasts.

Throughout the funeral, Phoebe seemed cool and composed, despite the fact that the July air was heavy with humidity. Even the rushing waters of the nearby DuPage River, which ran through several of Chicago's western suburbs, didn't provide any relief from the heat. A dark green canopy shaded both the gravesite and the rows of chairs set up for the dignitaries in a semicircle around the black ebony casket, but the canopy wasn't large enough to shelter everyone attending, and much of the well-dressed crowd was standing in the sun, where they'd begun to wilt, not only from the humidity but also from the overpowering scent of nearly a hundred floral arrangements. Luckily, the ceremony had been short, and since there was no reception afterward, they could soon head for their favorite watering holes to cool off and secretly rejoice in the fact that Bert Somerville's number had come up instead of their own.

The shiny black casket rested above the ground on a green carpet that had been laid directly in front of the place where Phoebe was sitting between her fifteen-year-old half sister, Molly, and her cousin Reed Chandler. The polished lid held a star-shaped floral spray of white roses embellished with sky blue and gold ribbons, the colors of the Chicago Stars, the National Football League franchise Bert had bought ten years earlier.

When the ceremony ended, Phoebe cradled the white poodle in her arms and rose to her feet, stepping into a shaft of sunlight that sparked the gold metallic threads of her *bustier* and set the rhinestone frames of her cat's-eye sunglasses afire. The effect was unnecessarily dramatic for a woman who was already quite dramatic enough.

Reed Chandler, Bert's thirty-five-year-old nephew, got up from his chair next to her and walked over to place a flower on the casket. Phoebe's half sister Molly followed self-consciously. Reed gave every appearance of being grief-stricken, although it was an open secret that he would inherit his uncle's football team. Phoebe dutifully placed her own flower on her father's coffin and refused to let the old bitterness return. What was the use? She hadn't been able to win her father's love while he was alive, and now she could finally give up the effort. She reached out to give a comforting touch to the young half sister who was such a stranger to her, but Molly pulled away, just as she always did whenever Phoebe tried to get close to her.

Reed returned to her side, and Phoebe instinctively recoiled. Despite all the charity boards he now served on, she couldn't forget what a bully he had been as a child. She quickly turned away from him, and in a breathless, slightly husky voice that fit her chicky-boom body almost too perfectly, she addressed those around her.

"So nice of you to attend. Especially in this awful heat. Viktor, sweetie, would you take Pooh?"

She held out the small white poodle to Viktor Szabo, who was driving the women crazy, not just because of his exotic good looks, but because there was something hauntingly familiar about this gorgeous hunk of a Hungarian. A few of them correctly identified him as the model who posed, hair undone, oiled muscles bulging, and zipper open, in a national advertising campaign for men's jeans.

Viktor took the dog from her. "Of course, my darling," he replied in an accent that, although noticeable, was less pronounced than that of any of the Gabor sisters, who had lived in the States many decades longer than he had.

"My pet," Phoebe purred, not at Pooh, but at Viktor.

Privately Viktor thought Phoebe was pushing it a bit, but he was Hungarian and inclined to be pessimistic, so he blew a kiss in her direction and regarded her soulfully while he settled the poodle in his arms and arranged his posture best to display his perfectly sculpted body. Occasionally he moved his head so that the light caught the sparkle of silver beads discreetly woven into the dramatic ponytail that fell a quarter of the way down his back.

Phoebe extended a slim-fingered hand whose long, peony-pink nails were tipped with crescents of white toward the portly U.S. Senator who had approached her and regarded him as if he were a particularly delectable piece of beefcake. "Senator, thank you so much for coming. I know how busy you must be, and you're a perfect honey."

The senator's plump, gray-haired wife shot Phoebe a suspicious look, but when Phoebe turned to greet her, the woman was surprised at the warmth and friendliness in her smile. Later, she would notice that Phoebe Somerville seemed more relaxed with the women than the men. Curious for such an obvious sexpot. But then it was a strange family.

Bert Somerville had a history of marrying Las Vegas showgirls. The first of them, Phoebe's mother, had died years before while trying to give birth to the son Bert craved. His third wife, Molly's mother, had lost her life in a small plane accident thirteen years earlier on the way to Aspen, where she was planning to celebrate her divorce. Only Bert's second wife was still living, and she wouldn't have walked across the street to attend his funeral, let alone fly in from Reno.

Tully Archer, the venerable defensive coordinator of the Chicago Stars, left Reed's side and approached Phoebe. With his white hair, grizzled eyebrows, and red-veined nose, he looked like a beardless Santa Claus.

"Terrible thing, Miss Somerville. Terrible." He cleared his throat with a rhythmic *hut-hut*. "Don't believe we've met. Unusual not to have met Bert's daughter, all the years we've known each other. Bert and I go way back, and I'm going to miss

14

him. Not that the two of us always agreed on things. He could be damned stubborn. But, still, we go way back."

He continued shaking her hand and rambling on without ever making eye contact with her. Anyone who didn't follow football might have wondered how someone who seemed on the verge of senility could possibly coach a professional football team, but those who had seen him work never made the mistake of underestimating his coaching abilities.

He loved to talk, however, and when he showed no intention of running out of words, Phoebe interrupted. "And aren't you just a *dear* to say so, Mr. Archer. An absolute *sugarplum*."

Tully Archer had been called many things in his life, but he had never been called a sugarplum, and the appellation left him temporarily speechless, which might have been what she intended because she immediately turned away only to see a regiment of monster men lined up to offer their condolences.

In shoes the size of tramp steamers, they shifted uneasily from one foot to the other. Thousands of pounds of beef on the hoof with thighs like battering rams, they had thick, monstrous necks rooted in bulging shoulders. Their hands were clasped like grappling hooks in front of them as if they expected the national anthem to begin playing at any moment, and their freakish, oversized bodies were stuffed into sky blue team blazers and gray trousers. Beads of perspiration from the midday heat glimmered on skin that ranged in color from a glistening blue-black to a suntanned white. Like plantation slaves, the National Football League's Chicago Stars had come to pay homage to the man who owned them.

A slit-eyed, neckless man who looked as if he should be leading a riot at a maximum security prison stepped up. He kept his eyes so firmly fixed on Phoebe's face that it was obvious he was forcing himself not to let his gaze drift lower to her spectacular breasts. "I'm Elvis Crenshaw, nose guard. Real sorry about Mr. Somerville."

Phoebe accepted his condolences. The nose guard moved on, glancing curiously at Viktor Szabo as he passed.

Viktor, who stood only a few feet from Phoebe, had struck his Rambo pose, a feat not all that easy to carry off considering the fact that he had a small white poodle cradled in his arms instead of an Uzi. Still, he could tell the pose was working because nearly every woman in the crowd was watching him. Now, if he could only catch the attention of that sexy creature with the marvelous derriere, his day would be perfect.

Unfortunately, the sexy creature with the marvelous derriere had stopped in front of Phoebe and had eyes only for her.

"Miz Somerville, I'm Dan Calebow, head coach of the Stars."

"Well, *hel-lo,* Mr. Calebow," Phoebe crooned in a voice that sounded to Viktor like a peculiar cross between Bette Midler and Bette Davis, but then he was Hungarian, and what did he know.

Phoebe was Viktor's best friend in the entire world, and he would have done anything for her, a devotion he was proving by agreeing to act out this macabre charade as her lover. At this moment, however, he wanted nothing more than to whisk her away from harm. She didn't seem to understand that she was playing with fire by toying with that hot-blooded man. Or maybe she did. When Phoebe felt cornered, she could haul an entire army of defensive weapons into action, and seldom were any of them wisely chosen.

Dan Calebow hadn't spared Viktor a glance, so it wasn't difficult for the Hungarian to categorize him as one of those maddening men who was completely close-minded on the subject of an alternative lifestyle. A pity, but an attitude Viktor accepted with his characteristic good nature.

Phoebe might not recognize Dan Calebow, but Viktor followed American football and knew that Calebow had been one of the NFL's most explosive and controversial quarterbacks until he had retired five years ago to take up coaching. In midseason last fall Bert had fired the Stars' head coach and hired Dan, who had been working for the rival Chicago Bears' organization, to fill the position.

Calebow was a big, blond lion of a man who carried himself with the authority of someone who had no patience for self-doubt. A bit taller than Viktor's own six feet, he was more muscular than most professional quarterbacks. He had a high, broad forehead and a strong nose with a small

17

bump at the bridge. His bottom lip was slightly fuller than his top, and a thin white scar marked the point midway between his mouth and chin. But his most fascinating feature wasn't either that interesting mouth, his thick tawny hair, or the macho chin scar. Instead, it was a pair of predatory sea-green eyes, which were, at that moment, surveying his poor Phoebe with such intensity that Viktor half expected her skin to begin steaming.

"I'm real sorry about Bert," Calebow said, his Alabama boyhood still evident in his speech. "We surely are going to miss him."

"How kind of you to say so, Mr. Calebow."

A faintly exotic cadence had been added to the husky undertones of Phoebe's speech, and Viktor realized she had introduced Kathleen Turner to her repertoire of sexy female voices. She didn't usually shift around so much, so he knew she was rattled. Not that she'd let anyone see it. Phoebe had a reputation as a sexpot to uphold.

Viktor's attention returned to the Stars' head coach. He remembered reading that Dan Calebow had been nicknamed "Ice" during his playing days because of his chilling lack of compassion for his opponent. He couldn't blame Phoebe for being unsettled in his presence. This man was formidable.

"Bert surely did love the game," Calebow continued, "and he was a good man to work for."

"I'm certain he was." Each prolonged syllable she uttered was a breathlessly delivered promise of sexual debauchery, a promise Viktor knew all too well Phoebe had no intention of keeping.

He realized how nervous she was when she turned and held her arms out to him. Guessing correctly that she wanted Pooh as a distraction device, he stepped forward, but just as she took the animal, a maintenance truck that had entered the cemetery backfired, startling the poodle.

Pooh gave a yap and leapt free of her arms. The dog had been restrained too long, and she began a wild dash through the crowd, yapping shrilly, her tail wagging so wildly the pom-pom looked as if it might fly off at any moment and whistle through the air like Oddjob's hat.

"Pooh!" Phoebe cried, taking off after her just as the small white dog bumped against the slender metal legs that supported a towering arrangement of gladiolus.

Phoebe wasn't the most athletic of creatures under the best of circumstances. Further hampered by her tight skirt, she couldn't reach the dog in time to prevent disaster. The flowers teetered and toppled backward, knocking into the wreath jammed next to them, which, in turn, upset a massive spray of dahlias. The arrangements were packed so closely together that it was impossible for one to fall without knocking into another, and flowers and water began to fly. The mourners who were standing nearby jumped away in an effort to protect their clothing and knocked into more of the floral tributes. Like dominoes, one basket tipped against another, until the ground began to look like Merlin Olsen's worst nightmare.

Phoebe whipped off her sunglasses to reveal her exotically tilted amber eyes. "Stay, Pooh! Stay, dammit! *Viktor!*"

Viktor had already rushed to the opposite side of the casket in an effort to head off the rampaging poodle, but in his haste he knocked over several chairs, which, in turn, flew into another group of floral arrangements, setting off a separate chain reaction.

A Gold Coast socialite, who fancied herself an expert on small dogs since she owned a shiatsu, made a leap for the frenzied poodle only to draw up short when Pooh dropped her tail, bared her teeth, and snapped at her like a canine Terminator. Although Pooh was generally the most congenial of dogs, the socialite had the misfortune to be wearing Calvin Klein's Eternity, a fragrance Pooh had detested ever since one of Phoebe's friends, who had been drenched in it, had called her a mutt and kicked her under the table.

Phoebe, whose side-slit skirt was showing far too much of her thigh for respectability, shot between two defensive linemen. They watched with open amusement as she gestured toward the poodle. "Pooh! Here, Pooh!"

Molly Somerville, mortified by the spectacle her half sister was making, tried to hide herself in the crowd.

As Phoebe dodged a chair, the heavy gold fig leaf dangling from the links of her belt bumped against the part of her that fig leaves had been designed to shield. She began to grab for it before she was permanently bruised, only to have the slippery leather soles of her pumps hit a batch of wet lilies. Her feet shot out from under her, and, with a whoosh of expelled breath, she fell.

At the sight of her mistress sliding across the ground on her rear, Pooh forgot about the menacingly perfumed socialite. Incorrectly interpreting Phoebe's actions as an invitation to play, the dog's yips grew delirious with excitement.

Phoebe tried unsuccessfully to scramble to her feet, giving both the Mayor of Chicago and several members of the rival Bears' organization a generous view of the top of her thigh. Pooh dashed between the legs of a pompous network sportscaster and shot under the graveside chairs just as Viktor came toward her from the other side. The dog loved to play with Viktor, and her yips grew more fervent.

Pooh made a quick jog, but braked sharply as she realized she was blocked by overturned flower baskets and a large patch of sodden grass — a formidable barrier for an animal who hated getting her paws wet. Cornered, she leapt up onto one of the folding chairs. When it began to teeter, she gave a nervous yip and jumped to another and from there up onto a smooth, hard surface.

The crowd gave a collective gasp as white roses and streamers of sky blue and gold ribbon went flying. Everyone fell silent.

Phoebe, who had just managed to get to her feet, froze. Viktor cursed softly in Hungarian.

Pooh, always sensitive to the humans she loved,

21

cocked her head to the side as if she were trying to understand why everybody was looking at her. Sensing that she had done something very wrong, she began to tremble.

Phoebe caught her breath. It wasn't good for Pooh to get nervous. She remembered the last time it had happened and took a quick step forward. "No, Pooh!"

But her warning came too late. The trembling dog was already squatting. With an apologetic expression on her small, furry face, she began to pee on the lid of Bert Somerville's casket.

Bert Somerville's estate had been built in the 1950s on ten acres of land in the affluent Chicago suburb of Hinsdale, located in the heart of DuPage County. In the early twentieth century the county had been rural, but as the decades slipped by, its small towns had grown together until they formed a giant bedroom for the executives who boarded the Burlington Northern commuter trains that took them into the Loop each day, and also for the engineers who worked in the high-tech industries that sprang up along the East West Tollway. Gradually, the brick wall that bordered the estate had been enclosed by shady residential streets.

As a child Phoebe had spent little time living in the stately Tudor home that sat among the oaks, maples, and walnut trees of the western suburbs. Bert had kept her in a private Connecticut boarding school until summer, when he sent her to an exclusive girls' camp. During her infrequent trips home, she had found the house dark and oppressive, and as she climbed the curving staircase to the second floor two hours after the funeral, she decided that nothing had happened to make her alter her opinion.

The condemning eyes of an elephant illegally bagged during one of Bert's African safaris stared down at her from the maroon-flocked wallpaper at the top of the staircase. Her shoulders slumped dispiritedly. Grass stains soiled her ivory suit, and the sheer nylons that sheathed her legs were dirty and torn. Her blond hair stuck out in every direction, and she'd long ago eaten off her peony-pink lipstick.

Unbidden, the face of the Stars' head coach came back to her. He was the one who had picked Pooh off the casket by the scruff of her neck. Those green eyes of his had been cold and condemning as he'd handed the dog over to her. Phoebe sighed. The melee of her father's funeral was another screwup in a life already full of them. She had wanted everyone to know she didn't care that her father had disinherited her, but as usual, she had gone too far and everything had backfired.

She paused for a moment at the top of the stairs, wondering if her life might have been different if her mother had lived. She no longer thought very much about the showgirl mother she couldn't remember, but as a lonely child she had woven elaborate fantasies about her, trying to conjure up in her imagination a tender, beautiful woman who

23

would have given her all the love her father had withheld.

She wondered if Bert had ever really loved anyone. He'd had little use for women in general, and none at all for an overweight, clumsy little girl who didn't have a high opinion of herself to begin with. For as long as she could remember, he had told her she was useless, and she now suspected that he might have been right.

At the age of thirty-three, she was unemployed and nearly broke. Arturo had died seven years ago. She had spent the first two years after his death administering the touring exhibits of his paintings, but after the collection went on permanent display in Paris's Musée d'Orsay, she'd moved to Manhattan. The money Arturo had left her when he'd died had gradually disappeared, helping to pay the medical expenses of many of her friends who had died from AIDS. She didn't regret a penny. For years she'd worked in a small, but exclusive, West Side gallery that specialized in the avant-garde. Just last week, her elderly employer had closed the doors for the last time, leaving her at loose ends while she looked for a new direction in her life.

The thought flickered through her mind that she was getting tired of being outrageous, but she was feeling too fragile to cope with introspection, so she finished making her way to her sister's bedroom and knocked on the door. "Molly, it's Phoebe. May I come in?"

There was no answer.

"Molly, may I come in?"

More seconds ticked by before Phoebe heard a muted, sullen, "I guess."

She mentally braced herself as she turned the knob and stepped inside the bedroom that had been hers as a child. During the few weeks each year when she had lived here, the room had been cluttered with books, food scraps, and tapes of her favorite music. Now it was as pin-neat as its occupant.

Molly Somerville, the fifteen-year-old half sister Phoebe barely knew, sat in a chair by the window, still dressed in the shapeless brown dress she'd worn to the funeral. Unlike Phoebe, who had been overweight as a child, Molly was rail thin, and her heavy, jaw-length dark brown hair needed a good trim. She was also plain, with pale, dull skin that looked as if it had never seen the sun and small, unremarkable features.

"How are you doing, Molly?"

"Fine." She didn't look up from the book that lay open in her lap.

Phoebe sighed to herself. Molly made no secret of the fact that she hated her guts, but they'd had so little contact over the years that she wasn't certain why. When Phoebe had returned to the States after Arturo's death, she'd made several trips to Connecticut to visit Molly at school, but Molly had been so uncommunicative she'd eventually given up. She'd continued to send birthday and Christmas presents, however, along with occasional letters, all of which went unacknowledged.

It was ironic that Bert had disinherited her from everything except what should have been his most important responsibility.

"Can I get you anything? Something to eat?"

Molly shook her head and silence fell between them.

"I know this has been tough. I'm really sorry."

The child shrugged.

"Molly, we need to talk, and it would be easier on both of us if you'd look at me."

Molly lifted her head from her book and regarded Phoebe with blank, patient eyes, giving Phoebe the uneasy feeling that she was the child and her sister the adult. She wished she still smoked, because she was in desperate need of a cigarette.

"You know that I'm your legal guardian now."

"Mr. Hibbard explained it to me."

"I think we need to talk about your future."

"There's nothing to talk about."

She pushed a wayward blond curl behind her ear. "Molly, you don't have to go back to camp if you don't want to. You're more than welcome to fly to New York with me tomorrow for the rest of the summer. I've subleased an apartment from a friend who's in Europe. It has a great location."

"I want to go back."

From the pallor of Molly's skin, Phoebe didn't believe her sister enjoyed camp any more than she had. "You can if you really want to, but I know what it's like to feel as if you don't have a home. Remember that Bert sent me to school at Crayton, too, and packed me off to camp every summer. I hated it. New York is fun during the summer. We could have a great time and get to know each other better."

"I want to go to camp," Molly repeated stubbornly.

"Are you absolutely sure about this?"

"I'm sure. You have no right to keep me from going back."

Despite the child's hostility and the headache that was beginning to form at her temples, Phoebe was reluctant to let the issue pass so easily. She decided to try a new tack and nodded toward the book in Molly's lap. "What are you reading?"

"Dostoyevski. I'm doing an independent study on him in the fall."

"I'm impressed. That's pretty heavy reading for a fifteen-year-old."

"Not for me. I'm quite bright."

Phoebe wanted to smile, but Molly had delivered the statement so matter-of-factly that she couldn't. "That's right. You do well in school, don't you?"

"I have an exceptionally high IQ."

"Being smarter than everyone else can be as much a curse as a blessing." Phoebe remembered the trauma of her own school days when she'd been brighter than so many of her classmates. It had been one more element that had made her feel different from everyone else.

Molly's expression never altered. "I'm quite grateful for my intelligence. Most of the other girls in my class are dolts."

Despite the fact that Molly was acting like an obnoxious little prig, Phoebe tried not to judge her. She, of all people, knew that Bert Somerville's daughters had to find their own way of coping with life. As an adolescent, she had hidden her insecurities behind fat. Later, she had become outrageous. Molly was hiding behind her brains.

"If you'll excuse me, Phoebe. I've reached a particularly interesting section, and I'd like to get back to it."

Phoebe ignored the child's obvious dismissal and made another attempt to convince her to come to Manhattan. But Molly refused to change her mind, and Phoebe eventually had to concede defeat.

As she got ready to leave the room, she stopped at the door. "You'll call me if you need anything, won't you?"

Molly nodded, but Phoebe didn't believe her. The child would eat rat poison before she'd come to her disreputable older sister for help.

She tried to shake off her depression as she headed back downstairs. She heard Viktor on the living room telephone with his agent. Needing a moment alone to collect herself, she slipped into her father's study, where Pooh was asleep in one of the armchairs that sat in front of a glass-fronted gun cabinet. The poodle's fluffy white head shot up. She sprang from the chair, her pom-pom tail wagging, and raced across the carpet to her mistress.

Phoebe sank to her knees and gathered the dog

to her. "Hey, sport, you really did it today, didn't you?"

Pooh gave her an apologetic lick. Phoebe began to retie the bows that had come undone at the dog's ears, but her fingers were trembling, so she abandoned the effort. Pooh would just work them loose again anyway.

The dog was a disgrace to the dignity of her breed. She hated bows and rhinestone collars, refused to sleep on her doggy bed, and wasn't the slightest bit picky about food. She detested being clipped, brushed, or bathed and wouldn't wear the monogrammed sweater Viktor had given her. She wasn't even a good guard dog. Last year when Phoebe had been mugged in broad daylight on the Upper West Side, Pooh had spent the whole time rubbing against the mugger's legs begging to be petted.

Phoebe buried her hair in the dog's soft topknot. "Underneath that fancy pedigree, you're nothing but a mutt, aren't you, Pooh?"

Abruptly, Phoebe lost the battle she had been fighting all day and gave a choked sob. A mutt. That's what she was. All dressed up like a French poodle.

Viktor found her in the library. With more tact than he usually displayed, he ignored the fact that she'd been crying. "Phoebe, pet," he said kindly, "your father's lawyer is here to meet with you."

"I don't want to see anyone," she sniffed, searching futilely for a tissue.

Viktor extracted a plum-colored handkerchief

29

from the pocket of his gray silk jacket and handed it to her. "You'll have to talk with him sooner or later."

"I already did. He called me about Molly's guardianship the day after Bert died."

"Maybe this has to do with your father's estate."

"I'm not involved with that." She blew noisily into the handkerchief. She had always pretended that being disinherited didn't bother her, but it was painful to have such clear and public proof of her father's scorn.

"He's quite insistent." Viktor picked up the purse she had left in the chair where Pooh had been sleeping and opened it. It was a gently used Judith Lieber clutch he had found in a consignment shop in the East Village, and he gave Phoebe a disapproving glance as he spotted a Milky Way nestled at the bottom. Pushing it aside, he pulled out her comb and restored her hair to order. With that done, he extracted her compact and lipstick. While she repaired her makeup, he took a moment to admire her.

Viktor found the off-kilter features that had inspired some of Arturo Flores's best work far more appealing than the puffy-lipped faces of the anorexic models he posed with. Others had, too, including the famous photographer Asha Belchoir, who'd recently done a photo session with her.

"Take off those torn stockings. You look like you belong in the chorus of *Les Mis*."

While she reached under her skirt to do as he said, he returned her makeup to her purse. Then he straightened her fig leaf belt and walked her to the door.

"I don't want to meet with anybody, Viktor."

"You're not going to back down now."

Panic filled her amber eyes. "I can't pull this off much longer."

"Then why don't you stop trying?" He brushed his thumb over her cheek. "People may not be gloating as much as you think."

"I can't tolerate the idea of anyone feeling sorry for me."

"You'd rather have everyone dislike you?"

She forced a cocky smile as she reached for the knob. "I'm comfortable with contempt. It's pity I can't stand."

Viktor took in the clothes that were so inappropriate to the occasion and shook his head. "Poor Phoebe. When are you going to finish inventing yourself?"

"When I get it right," she said softly.

2

Brian Hibbard shuffled the papers in his lap. "I apologize for barging in on you so soon after the funeral, Miss Somerville, but the housekeeper informed me that you were planning to fly back to Manhattan tomorrow evening. I hadn't realized you'd be returning so soon."

The lawyer was short and plump, in his late forties, with ruddy skin and graying hair. A well-cut charcoal suit didn't quite hide the slight paunch that had formed around his middle. Phoebe sat across from him in one of the wing chairs positioned near the massive stone fireplace that dominated the living room. She'd always hated this dark, paneled room presided over by stuffed birds, mounted animal heads, and an ashtray cruelly made from a giraffe's hoof.

As she crossed her legs, the thin gold chain encircling her ankle glimmered in the light. Hibbard noticed, but pretended he hadn't.

"There's no reason for me to stay any longer, Mr. Hibbard. Molly's returning to camp tomorrow afternoon, and my flight leaves a few hours after hers."

"That's going to make this difficult, I'm afraid. Your father's will is a bit complicated."

Her father had kept her well acquainted with

the details of his will, even before the final six months of his life, when he had been diagnosed with pancreatic cancer. She knew he had set up a trust fund for Molly and that Reed was to inherit his beloved Stars.

"Are you aware of the fact that your father had some financial setbacks these past few years?"

"Not the details. We didn't speak very frequently."

They had been completely estranged for almost ten years, from the time she was eighteen until she had returned to the States after Arturo's death. After that, they'd met occasionally when he came to Manhattan on business, but she was no longer a timid, overweight child he could bully, and their encounters had been angry ones.

Although her father kept mistresses and married showgirls, his own impoverished childhood had made him crave respectability, and her lifestyle mortified him. He was violently homophobic, as well as being contemptuous of the arts. He hated the newspaper and magazine stories that would occasionally appear about her and declared that her associations with "fruits and flakes" made him look like a fool in front of his business associates. Again and again he ordered her to return to Chicago and take over as his unpaid housekeeper. If it had been love that had motivated his offer, she would have done as he'd asked, but Bert had merely wanted to control her, just as he'd controlled everyone else around him.

He'd remained tough and uncompromising to

the end, using his terminal illness as a bludgeon to remind her of what a disappointment she had been to him. He hadn't even let her come to visit him in Chicago when he was dying, saying he didn't want any goddamn vigils. In their last telephone conversation, he'd told her she was his only failure.

As she blinked her eyes against a fresh surge of tears, she realized that Brian Hibbard was still speaking. ". . . your father's estate is not as large as it was during the eighties. He directed that this house be sold, with the proceeds making up your sister's trust find. His condo isn't to be put on the market for at least a year, however, so you and your sister can have the use of it until then."

"A condo? I don't know anything about that."

"It's not far from the Stars Complex. He — uh — kept it for private use."

"For his mistresses," Phoebe said flatly.

"Yes, well — It's been vacant for the past six months, ever since his illness. Unfortunately, those are the only properties not connected with the Stars that he held on to. His financial situation isn't entirely bleak, however."

"I wouldn't think so. His football team must be worth millions."

"It's quite valuable, although it, too, is having financial difficulties." Something in her expression must have given away her feelings because he said, "You don't like football?"

"No, I don't." She had spoken with too much intensity, and he was regarding her curiously.

Quickly, she gave an indolent wave of her hand. "I'm more the uptown-gallery-dinner-at-Le Cirque-before-an-evening-of-experimental-theater type. I eat tofu, Mr. Hibbard."

She thought the remark was pretty darned cute, but he didn't even smile. "It's hard to believe that Bert Somerville's daughter doesn't like football."

"Scandalous, I know," she said breezily. "But there it is. I'm allergic to perspiration — mine or anyone else's. Luckily, my sainted cousin Reed has always sweated copiously, so now the family's football dynasty can live on."

The lawyer hesitated, looking distinctly unhappy. "I'm afraid it's not quite so straightforward."

"What do you mean?"

"Several months before your father's death, he executed a new will. For the short term, at least, Reed has been disinherited."

Several seconds ticked by as she absorbed this startling piece of information. She remembered how calm her cousin had seemed at the funeral. "Reed obviously doesn't know about this."

"I urged Bert to tell him, but he refused. My partner and I have the unenviable task of breaking the news when we meet with him this evening. He's not going to look kindly on the fact that Bert is temporarily passing the team on to his daughter."

"His daughter?" And then she thought of the teenager who was reading Dostoyevski upstairs and began to smile. "My sister's going to make professional football history."

"I'm afraid I don't follow you."

"How many fifteen-year-old girls own their own NFL team?"

Hibbard looked alarmed. "I'm sorry, Miss Somerville. It's been a long day, and I'm not making myself clear. Your father didn't leave your sister the team."

"He didn't?"

"Oh, no. He left it to you."

"He did *what?*"

"He left the team to you, Miss Somerville. You're the new owner of the Chicago Stars."

That night as Phoebe wandered through the rooms of her father's ugly house, she tried to say prayers for the dead animals hanging on the walls. She tried to say them for herself as well because she was afraid she might be turning into one of those cynical people who hug old bitterness like a treasured bone to be gnawed over forever.

Why did you do this to me, Bert? Did you need to control me so much that you even had to bend me to your will from the grave?

When Brian Hibbard had announced that Bert had left her the Stars, she'd experienced a moment of such incredible happiness that she couldn't speak. She hadn't thought about the money or the power or even the fact that she hated football. She'd simply rejoiced that after so many years of animosity, her father had proved that he did care about her. She remembered sitting dazed while the lawyer told her the rest.

"Quite frankly, Miss Somerville, I don't approve of the terms your father has put on your inheritance of the Stars. Both my partner and I tried to change his mind, but he refused to listen. I'm sorry. Since he was definitely of sound mind, neither you nor Reed can successfully challenge the will."

She had stared at him blankly. "What do you mean? What terms?"

"I told you this inheritance was temporary."

"How can an inheritance be temporary?"

"Setting aside the legal language, the concept is quite simple. For you to retain ownership of the team, the Stars have to win the AFC Championship this coming January, something that is highly unlikely. If they don't win, you'll get one hundred thousand dollars and the team reverts to Reed."

Even the news that she might receive such an enormous amount of money couldn't keep her joy from fading. With a sinking heart, she realized this was another of her father's manipulations.

"Are you saying that I'll only own the team until January, and then Reed will get it?"

"Unless the Stars win the AFC Championship, in which case the team would be yours forever."

She pushed her hair back from her face with a trembling hand. "I — I don't know anything about football. This championship game? Is this the Super Bowl?"

To his credit, Hibbard launched into a patient explanation. "It's one step away. The National

Football League is split into two conferences, the American Football Conference, the AFC, and the National Football Conference. The two best teams in each conference play for their conference championship, and the winners of those games meet in the Super Bowl."

She wanted to make certain she understood. "For me to retain ownership, the Stars would have to win this AFC championship game?"

"That's right. And frankly, Miss Somerville, their chances of even getting close are practically nil. They're a good team, but most of the players are still young. Two or three years from now, they may do it, but not this season, I'm afraid. Right now, the AFC is dominated by the San Diego Chargers, the Miami Dolphins, and, of course, last year's Super Bowl champions, the Portland Sabers."

"Bert knew that the Stars wouldn't be able to win this year?"

"I'm afraid he did. His will states that you cannot receive the one hundred thousand dollars unless you show up at the Stars Complex every day for work, for as long as you own the team. You would, of course, have to move to Chicago, but you don't have to be concerned about not being prepared to run a professional football team. Carl Pogue, the Stars' general manager, would do the actual work."

A dull ache spread through her chest as her father's intent became clear. "In other words, I wouldn't be anything but a figurehead."

"Carl doesn't have the authority to sign legal

papers. That's the owner's responsibility."

She couldn't quite keep the misery from her voice. "Why would Bert do something like this?"

That was when Hibbard had handed her the letter.

Dear Phoebe,

As you know, I regard you as my only failure. For years, you've publicly humiliated me by running around with all those fags and fairies, but I'm not going to let you defy me any longer. For once in your life you're going to do what I tell you. Maybe this experience will finally teach you something about responsibility and discipline.

The game of football makes men out of boys. Let's see if it can make a woman out of you.

Don't fuck this up, too.

Bert

She had read the note through three times while the lawyer watched, and each time the lump in her throat had grown larger. Even from the grave, Bert was determined to control her. By removing her from Manhattan, he thought he could reshape her into the person he wanted her to be. Her father had always loved to gamble, and he had apparently decided she couldn't do much damage to his precious team in a few months. Now he would finally have exactly what he wanted. Reed would end up with the Stars, while she danced to her father's tune.

39

She wished she could force herself to believe that his motivations were based on love and concern. Then she might have been able to forgive him. But she understood too well that Bert knew nothing of love, only of power.

So she wandered the halls of her father's house that night saying prayers for the souls of dead animals and unloved little girls, while she counted the hours until she could run away from this place where she'd known so much unhappiness.

Peg Kowalski, who had been Bert's housekeeper for the last eight years, had left a single light burning in the large family room that stretched across the back of the house. Phoebe walked over to the windows that looked out on the grounds and tried to find the old maple that had been her favorite hiding place when she was a child.

Generally she tried to avoid thinking about her childhood, but tonight, as she stared into the darkness, that time didn't seem so long ago. She could feel herself being pulled back into the past, to that old maple tree and the dreaded sound of a bully's voice. . . .

"There you are, Flea Belly. Come on down. I've got a present for you."

Phoebe's stomach did a flip-flop at the loud intrusion of her cousin Reed's voice. She looked down to see him standing beneath the tree that was her haven during those few times when she was at home. She was supposed to leave for summer camp the next morning, and she had so far managed to avoid being caught alone with him, but today she had let down her guard. Instead of staying in the kitchen with the cook or helping Addie clean the bathrooms, she had escaped to the solitude of the woods.

"I don't want any present," she said.

"You'd better come down here. If you don't, you'll be sorry."

Reed didn't make idle threats, and she'd learned long ago that she had few defenses against him. Her father got mad at her if she complained that Reed teased her or hit her. Bert said she was spineless and that he wasn't going to fight her battles for her. But at twelve, Reed was two years older than she was and lots stronger, and she couldn't imagine fighting him.

She didn't understand why Reed hated her so much. She might be rich while he was poor, but his mother hadn't died when he was four like hers had, and he didn't get sent away to school. Reed and her Aunt Ruth, who was her father's sister, had lived in a brick apartment building two miles from the estate ever since Reed's father had run off. Bert paid the rent and gave Aunt Ruth money, even though he didn't like her that much. But he loved Reed because Reed was a boy, and he was good at sports, especially football.

She knew Reed would climb up after her if she defied him, and she decided she'd feel safer facing him on solid ground. With a sinking sense of dread, she began descending the maple tree, her plump thighs making an ugly swishing sound as they rubbed together. She hoped he wasn't looking up her shorts. He was always trying to see her there, or touch her, or say nasty things about her bottom, not all of which she understood. She dropped awkwardly to the ground, breathing hard because the descent had been difficult.

Reed wasn't unusually tall for a twelve-year-old, but he was stocky, with short, strong legs, broad shoulders, and a thick chest. His arms and legs were perpetually covered with scabs and bruises from sports activities, bike accidents, and fights. Bert loved to inspect Reed's injuries. He said Reed was "all boy."

She, however, was lumpish and shy, more interested in books than in sports. Bert called her Lard Ass and said that all those A's she made in school wouldn't get her anywhere in life if she couldn't manage to stand up straight and look people in the eye. Reed wasn't smart in school, but that didn't make any difference to Bert because Reed was the star of his junior high football team.

Her cousin was dressed in a torn orange T-shirt, cutoffs, and battered sneakers, exactly the kind of rumpled play clothes she would have liked to wear, except her father's housekeeper wouldn't let her. Mrs. Mertz bought all Phoebe's clothing in an expensive children's store, and today she had laid out a pair of white shorts that emphasized Phoebe's round stomach and a sleeveless cotton top that had a big strawberry on the front and cut her under the arms.

"Don't ever say I've never done anything nice for you, Flea Belly." Reed held up a piece of heavy white paper just a little larger than a paperback book cover. "Guess what I've got?"

"I don't know." Phoebe spoke cautiously, determined to avoid whatever land mines Reed was laying for her.

42

"I've got a picture of your mom."

Phoebe's heart skipped a beat. "I don't believe you."

He turned the paper over, and she saw that it was, indeed, a photograph, although he flashed it too quickly for her to absorb anything more than the vague impression of a beautiful woman's face.

"I found it stuck in the back of Mom's junk drawer," he said, taking an impatient swipe at the thick, dark bangs hanging in jags to his eyebrows.

Her legs felt weak, and she knew she had never wanted anything in her life as much as she wanted that photograph. "How do you know it's her?"

"I asked my mom." He cupped it in his hand so Phoebe couldn't see it and looked at it. "It's a real good picture, Flea Belly."

Phoebe's heart was pounding so hard she was afraid he would see it. She wanted to snatch the photograph from his hand, but she kept still because she knew from painful experience that he would simply hold it out of her reach if she tried.

She only had one picture of her mother, and it had been taken from so far away that Phoebe couldn't see her face. Her father never said anything much about her except that she was a dumb blonde who'd looked great in a G-string, and it was too goddamn bad Phoebe hadn't inherited her body instead of his brains. Phoebe's ex-stepmother, Cooki, whom her father had divorced last year after she'd had another miscarriage, said that Phoebe's mom probably wasn't as bad as Bert made out, but that Bert was a hard man to live with. Phoebe had loved Cooki. She had painted Phoebe's toenails Pink Parfait and read her exciting stories about real life out of True Confessions *magazine.*

"What'll you give me for it," Reed said.

She knew she couldn't let Reed see how precious the photograph was or he would do something awful to keep her from having it. "I already have lots of pictures of her," she lied, "so why should I give you anything?"

He held it up in front of him. "All right. I'll just tear it up."

"No!" She leapt forward, the protest slipping through her lips before she could stop it.

His dark eyes narrowed in sly triumph, and she felt as if the sharp jaws of a steel trap had just closed around her.

"How much do you want it?"

She had begun to tremble. "Just give it to me."

"Pull down your pants and I will."

"No!"

"Then I'm going to tear it up." He clasped the top between his fingers as if he were getting ready to tear it.

"Don't!" Her voice was shaking. She bit the inside of her cheek, but she couldn't stop her eyes from filling with tears. "You don't want it, Reed. Please give it to me."

"I already told you what you have to do, Lard Ass."

"No. I'll tell my dad."

"And I'll tell him you're a stuck-up little liar. Which one of us do you think he'll believe?"

Both of them knew the answer to that question.

Bert always took Reed's side.

A tear dripped off her jaw onto her cotton top, making an amoeba-shaped smear on the leaf of the strawberry. "Please."

"Pull down your pants, or I'll tear it up."

"No!"

He made a small tear at the top, and she couldn't hold back a sob of distress.

"Pull 'em down!"

"Please, don't! Please!"

"Are you going to do it, crybaby?" He lengthened the tear.

"Yes! Stop! Stop and I'll do it."

He lowered the photograph. Through her tears she saw that he had made a jagged rip through the top inch.

His eyes slithered down over her and settled on the point where her legs came together, that mysterious place where a few strands of golden hair had begun to grow. "Hurry up before somebody comes."

An awful vomit taste rose in her throat. She worked the button at the side of her shorts. Tears stung her eyes as she struggled with the zipper.

"Don't make me do this," she whispered. The words had a wavery sound, as if her throat were full of water. "Please. Just give me the picture."

"I told you to hurry." He wasn't even looking at her face, just staring at the place between her legs.

The bad taste in her mouth got worse as she slowly worked her shorts down over her tummy and thighs and then let them fall. They circled her ankles in a crooked figure eight. She was cold with shame as

45

she stood in front of him in her blue cotton underpants with tiny yellow roses all over them.

"Give it to me now," she begged.

"Pull down your panties first."

She tried not to think about it. She tried just to take her panties down so she could have the picture of her mother, but her hands wouldn't move. She stood in front of him with tears running down her cheeks and her shorts snagged around her chubby ankles and she knew she couldn't let him see her there.

"I can't," she whispered.

"Do it!" His small eyes darkened with fury.

Sobbing, she shook her head.

With an ugly twist to his mouth, he ripped the precious photograph in half, then in half again before letting the pieces float to the ground. He ground them beneath the sole of his sneaker and ran toward the house.

Tripping on her shorts, she stumbled blindly toward the ruined photograph. As she fell to her knees, she saw a set of widely spaced eyes tilted up at the ends just like her own. She gave a little shuddering gasp and told herself it would be all right. She would smooth everything out and tape it all back together again.

Her hands shook as she arranged the four crumpled pieces in their proper order, the top corners first and then the bottom ones. Only after the photograph was reassembled did she see Reed's final act of malice. A thick, black mustache had been inked in just above her mother's soft upper lip.

That had been twenty-three years ago, but Phoebe could still feel an ache in her chest as she stood at the window staring out over the grounds. All the material luxuries of her childhood had never been able to compensate for growing up under the shadow of Reed's cruel bullying and her father's scorn.

Something brushed against her leg, and she looked down to see Pooh gazing up at her with adoring eyes. She knelt to pick her up, then gathered her close and carried her over to the sofa, where she sat and stroked her soft white coat. The grandfather clock ticked in the corner. When she was eighteen, that clock had stood in her father's study. She buried her pink-lacquered fingernails in Pooh's topknot and remembered that awful August night when her world had come to an end.

Her stepmother Lara had taken two-month-old Molly to visit her mother in Cleveland. Phoebe, eighteen at the time, was home packing for her freshman year at Mount Holyoke. Normally she wouldn't have been invited to the Northwest Illinois State football team party, but Bert was hosting it at the house so she had been included. At that time Bert hadn't yet bought the Stars' franchise, and Northwest football had been his obsession. Reed played on the team, and Bert's generous contributions to the athletic fund had made him a highly influential alumnus.

She had spent the day both anticipating and dreading that night's party. Although much of her baby fat had melted away, she was still self-conscious about her figure and wore baggy, shapeless clothing to conceal her full breasts. Her experi-

47

ences with Reed and her father had left her leery of men, but at the same time, she couldn't help but daydream that one of the popular jocks would notice her.

She had spent the early hours of the party standing on the fringes trying to look inconspicuous. When Craig Jenkins, who was Reed's best friend, had walked over to ask her to dance, she had barely been able to nod. Dark-haired and handsome, Craig was Northeast's star player and not even in her wildest dreams had she imagined that he would notice her, much less put his arm around her shoulders after the music ended. She had begun to relax. They danced again. She flirted a little bit, laughed at his jokes.

And then it had all turned sour. He'd had too much to drink and tried to feel her breasts. Even when she'd told him to stop, he hadn't listened. He'd grown more aggressive, and she'd run outside in the middle of a thunderstorm to hide in the small metal shed near the pool.

That was where Craig had found her and where, in the thick, hot blackness, he had raped her.

Afterward, she'd made the mistake so many rape victims make. Dazed and bleeding, she had dragged herself to the bathroom, where she'd thrown up and then scrubbed away the signs of his violation in a tub of scalding-hot water.

An hour later, sobbing and barely coherent, she'd cornered Bert in his study, where he'd gone to fetch one of his Cuban cigars. She still remembered his disbelief as he'd run his fingers through his steel gray crew cut and studied her. She stood before him in the baggy gray sweat suit she'd climbed into when she got out of the tub, and she had never felt more vulnerable.

"You want me to believe a boy like Craig Jenkins was so hard up for a woman that he had to rape you?"

"It's true," she whispered, barely able to squeeze the words through her constricted throat.

Cigar smoke had coiled like a soiled ribbon around his head. He drew his shaggy salt-and-pepper eyebrows together. "This is another one of your pathetic attempts to get my sympathy, isn't it? Do you really believe I'm going to ruin that boy's football career just because you want some attention."

"It's not like that! He raped me!"

Bert had made a sound of disgust and stuck his head out the door to send someone after Craig, who had arrived minutes later accompanied by Reed. Phoebe had begged her father to send Reed away, but he hadn't done it, and her cousin stood at the side of the room sipping from a bottle of beer and listening as she haltingly repeated her story.

Craig had hotly denied Phoebe's accusations, speaking so convincingly that she would have believed him herself if she hadn't known differently. Even without looking at her father, she realized that she had lost, and when he ordered her not ever to repeat the story again, some part of her had died.

She'd run away the next day, trying to flee from

what had become her shame. Her college checking account contained enough money for her to get to Paris, the place where she'd met Arturo Flores, and her life had been changed forever.

Her father's flunkies had visited her several times during her years with Arturo to deliver Bert's threats and order her home. She had been disinherited when the first of the nude portraits had gone on display.

She rested her head against the back of the couch and drew Pooh closer. Bert had finally bent her to his will. If she didn't do as he had dictated, she wouldn't receive the one hundred thousand dollars, money that would let her open a small art gallery of her own.

You're my only failure, Phoebe. My only goddamn failure.

Right then, she set her jaw in a stubborn line. Her father, his one hundred thousand dollars, and the Chicago Stars could go to hell. Just because Bert had set up the game didn't mean she had to play. She'd find another way to raise the money to open her gallery. She decided to take Viktor up on his offer to spend some time at his vacation cottage near Montauk. There, next to the ocean, she would finally put the ghosts of her past to rest.

3

"There's no other way to look at it, Ice," Tully Archer said, speaking to Dan Calebow out of the side of his mouth as if they were Allied spies meeting in the Grunewald to exchange military secrets. "Whether you like it or not, the blond chicky's in the driver's seat."

"Bert must have had his brains in his ass." Dan scowled at the waiter, who was approaching with another tray of champagne, and the man quickly backed off. Dan hated champagne. Not just the sissy taste, but the way those silly glasses felt in his big battle-scarred hands. Even more than the champagne, he hated the idea of that blond bimbo with the drop-dead body owning his football team.

The two coaches were standing in the spacious observation deck of the Sears Tower, which had been closed to the public for that evening's United Negro College Fund benefit. The floor-to-ceiling sweep of windows reflected banks of flowers grouped around trellis arches, while a woodwind quintet from the Chicago Symphony played Debussy. Members of all the area sports teams were mingling with local media figures, politicians, and several movie stars who were in town. Dan hated any occasion that required a tuxedo, but when it was for a good cause, he forced himself to go along with it.

Beginning with his years as the starting quarterback for the University of Alabama's Crimson Tide, Calebow's exploits both on and off the field had become the stuff of legends. As a pro, he had been a bloodthirsty, hell-raising, in-your-face barbarian. He was a working man's quarterback, not a glamour boy, and even the meanest defensive lineman failed to intimidate him, because in any confrontation Dan Calebow assumed he was either stronger than the other guy or smarter. Either way, he planned to come out the winner.

Off the field he was just as aggressive. At various times he had gotten himself arrested for disturbing the peace, destruction of personal property, and, in the early days of his career, possession of a controlled substance.

Age and maturity had made him wiser about some things but not about others, and he found himself studying the newest congresswoman from Illinois as she stood in a cluster of formally dressed people behind Tully. She wore one of those black evening gowns that looked plain but probably cost more than a new set of Pings. Her light brown hair was pulled to the nape of her neck with a flat velvet bow. She was beautiful and sophisticated. She was also attracting a considerable amount of attention, and he didn't fail to note that he was one of the few people at the gathering she hadn't sought out. Instead, a flashy brunette in a tight silver dress came up to him. Turning her back to Tully, she regarded Dan through eyelashes so thick with mascara he was surprised she could still bat them.

"You look lonely over here, Coach." She licked her lips. "I saw you play against the Cowboys right before you retired. You were a wild man that day."

"I'm just about a wild man every day, honey."

"That's what I hear." He felt her hand sliding into the pocket of his jacket and knew she was leaving her phone number. He tried to remember if he'd unloaded his pockets from the last time he'd worn this tux. With a moist smile that promised him everything, she moved away.

Tully was so accustomed to having his conversations with Dan broken into by predatory females that he went on as if there had been no interruption. "The whole thing galls me. How could Bert have let something like this happen?"

What Phoebe Somerville was doing to his football team outraged Dan so much he didn't want to think about it when there was nothing around for him to hit. He distracted himself by looking for the beautiful congresswoman and spotted her speaking with one of Chicago's aldermen. Her aristocratic features were composed, her gestures constrained and elegant. She was a class act from head to toe, not the sort of woman he could imagine with flour on her nose or a baby in her arms. He turned away. At this point in his life, a flour-dusted, cookie-bakin', baby-makin' woman was exactly what he was looking for.

After more years of raising hell than he wanted

to count and a marriage that had been a big mistake, Dan Calebow was in a serious settlin'-down mood. At the age of thirty-seven, he yearned for kids, a whole houseful of them, and a woman who was more interested in changing diapers than taking over Chrysler.

He was on the brink of turning over a new leaf. No more career women, no more glamour pusses, no more sex bombs. He had his eyes out for a down-home woman, the kind who'd enjoy having a toddler mess up her hair, a woman whose idea of high fashion was a pair of blue jeans and one of his old sweatshirts, an ordinary kind of woman who didn't turn heads and make men crazy. And once he'd committed himself, his roaming days would be over. He hadn't cheated on his first wife, and he wasn't going to cheat on his last one.

Next to him, Tully Archer was still gnawing over the subject of Phoebe Somerville. "You know I don't like to speak ill of anybody, especially the fairer sex, but that blond chicky called me 'sugarplum.' Damn, Ice. That's just not the sort of person should be owning a football team."

"You got that right."

Tully's Santa Claus face puckered like a baby's. "She's got a poodle, Dan. Now both of us know the Bears' coaches are always fighting with Mike McCaskey, but damn, at least they're not working for an owner who carries around a French poodle. I tell you, I've been avoiding all of them since that funeral. I'll bet they're bustin' a gut laughing at us."

Once Tully got wound up, it was hard to stop him, and he moved on to the next subject. Dan noted that the congresswoman was gradually making her way to the elevator banks, a cadre of aids surrounding her as she departed. He glanced at his watch.

"This was supposed to be the transitional year for us, Ice," Tully said. "Bert fired Brewster last November and hired you as head coach. We got lucky on Plan B, did better than we expected in the draft, and even won a couple of games at the end of the season. But who could have figured Carl Pogue would quit and we'd end up having Ronald in charge of operations?"

A muscle ticked in the corner of Dan's jaw.

Tully shook his head. "Phoebe Somerville and Ronald McDermitt, the Stars' new owner and acting general manager. I tell you, Ice, even Vince Lombardi's laughing at us, and just think how long he's been dead."

Silence fell between them as both men's thoughts took equally dismal paths. In the six weeks that had passed since Bert's funeral, Phoebe had disappeared, bringing team business to a standstill because no one else was authorized to sign contracts. When she couldn't be located, Carl Pogue, the Stars' general manager, had quit in frustration and subsequently taken a job in the Commissioner's Office. Now, Ronald McDermitt, the man who had been Carl Pogue's assistant, was the Stars' acting general manager, completing the chronicle of disaster.

The terms of Bert's will had been leaked to the

media, leaving all of them stunned. Like everyone else, Dan had assumed Bert would pass the Stars on to Reed immediately, not at the end of the season. Although Reed Chandler had a good reputation in the community, Dan had always found him a bit slippery, and he hadn't looked forward to working for him. Now, however, he would have given just about anything to see Reed sitting in Bert's old office.

"Howie told me you've been trying to get in touch with Ray Hardesty. You're not feeling guilty about finally letting me cut him, are you, Dan?"

Dan shook his head, even though the cut still bothered him. "We had to do it."

"Damn right. He was missing more practices than he was making, and there was no way he was going to pass a drug test."

"I know that." Lyle Alzado's death from steroid abuse hadn't taught guys like Ray Hardesty a damn thing. Dan knew Tully had been right to insist that Ray be cut from the team, and he should have done it when Ray had been picked up for his second DUI arrest of the year. Instead, he'd dragged his heels, giving the Stars' veteran defensive end more last chances than he would have given anybody else. Hardesty had been a great player until his drinking and drugging had gotten out of control, and Dan had wanted to exhaust all of his options. He'd done his best to get Ray into rehab. He'd talked to him until he was blue in the face about showing up on time for practice and at least pretending to follow the rules, but

Ray hadn't been listening to anybody except his street corner pharmacist.

Tully tugged at his collar. "Did you know that Ronald took me aside a couple of days after Carl quit and told me to put more pressure on you to cut Hardesty?"

Dan hated talking about the Stars' acting general manager nearly as much as he hated talking about the new owner. "Why didn't Ronald talk to me in person?"

"He's scared to death of you. Ever since you stuffed him in that locker."

"He made me mad."

"Ronald was never anything more than Carl's gofer." Tully shook his head. "Everybody knows he only got the job because Bert owed his daddy a favor. I know Bert would never have let his daughter get her hands on the Stars if he knew Carl was going to quit. Ronald's a candy ass, Ice. Did I tell you about the time Bobby Tom was foolin' around after practice last season when Ronald came out to the field? You know how Bobby Tom is, just havin' a little fun, says, 'Hey, Ronnie, we're looking for a new wide-out.' And he lobs the ball at him real soft, couldn't have been more than five yards. Anyway, Ronald puts up his arm to catch it and jams his finger. He starts shaking his hand like somebody killed him. Bobby Tom like to bust a gut. How can you respect a general manager can't even catch a lob like that?"

Tully's monologue was interrupted by one of the subjects under discussion, last year's starting wide receiver for the Stars, Bobby Tom Denton. Bobby Tom liked to dress well, and his impeccably tailored black tuxedo was accompanied by a ruffled white dress shirt, glittering silver bow tie, lizard-skin boots, and a big black Stetson.

As far as anybody knew, the only time Bobby Tom took off his Stetson was when he put on his helmet. One of his many girlfriends had told the *National Enquirer* he even wore it when he made love. Her word was suspect, however, since she'd also told the *Enquirer* that Bobby Tom was the illegitimate son of Roy Orbison, a statement that had mightily upset Bobby Tom's mother, despite the fact that anybody who'd ever heard Bobby Tom sing could have figured out it was a lie.

Bobby Tom nodded his Stetson at Tully and Dan. "Coach. Coach."

Dan nodded back. "Bobby Tom."

The wide receiver turned to Tully. "Hey, Coach, what d'ya think? That redhead over there told me all her girlfriends think I'm the best-looking wide-out in the league. What about you? Do you think my profile's better than Tom Waddle's?"

Tully contemplated the wide receiver's profile while he gave the question serious consideration. "I don't know, Bobby Tom. Waddle's nose is straighter than yours."

Bobby Tom tended to get belligerent when anyone challenged his good looks, and tonight was no exception. "Is that so? For your information she said I look like that movie star — what's his name? Christian Slater." Bobby Tom frowned.

"Either of you know who Christian Slater is?"

Neither of them did.

For a moment Bobby Tom looked befuddled. Then he snatched a glass of champagne from a passing waiter and grinned. "Well, I'll tell you one thing about him. He's a damned fine looking sonavabitch."

They all laughed. Dan liked Bobby Tom off the field, but he liked him even better on. One of the best wide receivers Dan had seen in years, he had guts, brains, and hands so soft you couldn't even hear the ball hit when he caught it. What he didn't have was his new contract signed, and that fact was driving Dan to contemplate murdering a certain blond bimbo.

Bert had died just as he'd been finishing the complex negotiations with Bobby Tom's shark of an agent. Now there was no one in the Stars' organization with authorization to sign the final contract except Phoebe Somerville, whose answering service reported that she was on vacation and couldn't be reached.

Bobby Tom wasn't Dan's only unsigned player, either. He had an offensive tackle named Darnell Pruitt, who was so good he was scary, and a young safety who had led the Stars in forced fumbles last season. None of them would be traveling to the Meadowlands that weekend for the Stars' fourth preseason game against the Jets. And if something didn't happen soon, none of them would be in uniform for the season opener in two weeks.

Thanks to the disappearing bimbo, Dan Calebow was in danger of losing three of the most promising players in the league. He understood the way the NFL worked, and it didn't take a crystal ball to know there were a dozen team owners waiting in the wings with open checkbooks and saliva dripping from their jaws just hoping those three players were going to lose patience with a team that was rapidly becoming a joke.

At an early age the sting of his daddy's belt had taught Dan that winning was what counted in life. He'd always been an aggressive competitor, mowing down anyone who got in his way, and right then he made a promise to himself. If he ever got his hands on a certain brainless bimbo, he'd teach her a lesson she wouldn't soon forget.

"Hi, Coach, I'm Melanie."

Bobby Tom's gaze roamed over the shapely young beauty who had eyes only for Dan. The young wide receiver shook his head. "Damn, Coach. You got more women than I do."

"I've got a head start on you, Bobby Tom. You'll catch up." He put his arm around the girl. "Now what did you say your name was again, honey?"

Dan heard the siren just as he reached the point on the Eisenhower Expressway where the East West Tollway split off to the left. He had abandoned Melanie at the reception an hour ago, and as he glanced in the rearview mirror he was glad his heavy drinking days were behind him.

He pulled his red Ferrari 512 TR over. The

car was too small for him, but he put up with the lack of legroom because the Testarossa was the most beautiful driving machine in the world. Still, two hundred thousand dollars was an obscene amount of money to pay for a car when people were sleeping on the streets, and after he bought it, he'd written a matching check to one of his favorite charities. Most years he gave away more money than he spent, which he figured was only right considering how much he was worth.

By the time the trooper approached the driver's side of the car, Dan had his window lowered. The cop had already taken in the Testarossa's distinctive "ICE 11" vanity plates.

He braced his elbow on the hood of the car and leaned down. "Evening, Coach."

Dan nodded.

"I guess you're in a hurry."

"What d'you get me at?"

"You were doing eighty-seven when you passed Mannheim."

Dan grinned and slapped the steering wheel. "Damn, I love this car. I was holding it down, too. There are a lot of fools on the road tonight."

"You can say that again." The cop took a few moments to admire the car before he returned his attention to Dan. "How do you think you'll do against the Jets this weekend?"

"We'll give it our best."

"Bobby Tom signed yet?"

"Afraid not."

"That's too bad." He took his arm away. "Well,

good luck, anyway. And ease up on the gas pedal, will you, Coach? We got some boys on duty tonight who are still nursing a grudge over that sneak you called on fourth and one when you lost to the Browns last year."

"Thanks for the warning."

It was almost one in the morning when Dan pulled back onto the expressway, and traffic was fairly light. He had already removed the jacket of his tuxedo, and as he shot into the left lane, he tugged off his bow tie and unfastened his shirt collar.

Despite a blemished record with the law, he liked cops. They'd stood by him ever since he was a twelve-year-old punk caught stealing beer. And the cops in Tuscaloosa had done a lot more to set him straight when he was playing for the Tide than his old man. One of them had even managed to convince him of the value of a college education one night after the cops had broken up a brawl between Dan and some upperclassmen from Auburn at a bar called Wooden Dick's.

"You got brains, boy. When you gonna start usin' them?"

The cop had talked to him most of the night and made him begin to think about his long-term future. Football was Dan's ticket out of the poverty he had grown up in, but the cop made him realize that he wouldn't always be able to play.

Over the next few semesters, he had gradually replaced his phys ed and industrial arts classes with courses in business, math, and finance. By his junior year he was doing well with a demanding academic schedule, despite too much late-night carousing. His greatest satisfaction at 'Bama was realizing he had a brain and not just athletic talent.

He exited at Cermak Road into the affluent sprawl of Oak Brook and wound through the side streets until he saw the convenience store on his right. He pulled into the lot, turned off the ignition, and got out of the small, sleek car.

There were five people inside the convenience store, but only two of them women. One was a dyed redhead and he dismissed her right away. The other looked too young to be in a 7-Eleven so late at night. She was standing by the Hostess display chewing a wad of bubble gum and contemplating the Ho Hos. Her bangs were teased, but the rest of her hair was pulled back from her face and fastened at the crown of her head with a silver clip. Even though the evening was warm and muggy, she had both hands buried in the pockets of a high school jacket with "Varsity Cheerleader" written in script over her left breast.

She saw him approaching, and her jaw stalled in mid-chew. A short, skintight Spandex skirt peeked out several inches from beneath the school jacket. Her legs were thin and bare, her feet shoved into a pair of black flats. As he stopped in front of her, he noticed she was wearing too much makeup the way young girls sometimes did.

"I know who you are," she said.

"Do you now?"

"Uh-huh." She took three staccato chews —

nervous, but not giggly. "You're the Stars' football coach. Dan — uh — Mr. Calebow."

"That's right."

"I'm Tiffany."

"Is that so."

"I've seen you on television lots of times."

"How old are you, darlin'?"

"Sixteen." Her eyes began to rove over him with a maturity far beyond her years. "You're cute."

"And you look real grown-up for sixteen."

"I know." She worked her gum for a few seconds then looked down at the toes of her shoes. "My folks are gone for the night. You want to come back to my house with me, Mr. Calebow?"

"And do what?"

"You know. Have sex."

"Don't you think you're a little young to pick up an old guy like me?"

"I'm tired of boys. I want to do it with a man."

A video game machine beeped near the doorway.

"I like my women with a few more years on them."

She slipped one hand from the pocket of her school jacket and, moving close enough to him so no one in the store could see what she was doing, brushed upward along the inside of his thigh. "I'll be real good to you." Her hand grew bolder. "Please. I promise. I'll let you do anything you want."

"When you put it like that, doll baby, you make it tough to refuse."

She took her hand away as if she were embarrassed by her brazenness and pulled a set of keys from her pocket. "I'm driving my dad's car. Follow me."

The car was a late model Mercedes. Dan kept the taillights in view as he drove through the quiet, tree-lined streets into an exclusive residential area. The house, an imposing two-story white brick, sat on a wooded lot. As he pulled into the driveway, he saw the muted lights of an elaborate crystal chandelier glowing through the leaded glass fanlight over the front door.

The house had a three-car garage opening off to the side, and the door on the left slid up. She drove the Mercedes in. He parked behind it and got out. When he was inside the garage, she pushed the button that closed the door.

Her little Spandex skirt hugged every curve of her bottom as she walked up the two steps that led into the house. "You want a beer?" she asked as they entered a dimly lit white kitchen with state-of-the-art appliances and a restaurant-sized, stainless steel refrigerator.

He shook his head.

The lights fell softly on her overly made-up face. She set down her purse and kicked off her flats. Without removing her school jacket, she reached underneath her skirt and pulled off her panties. They were light blue.

She dropped them on the white tiled floor. "You want some taco chips or gum or something?"

"Yeah, I want something, all right."

For several seconds she stood completely still.

Then she led him from the kitchen. He followed her through a softly lit hallway into a spacious living room containing whitewashed oak furniture upholstered in rich, gem-colored fabrics. The faux marble walls displayed large canvases of original art and broken stone pediments held several pieces of sculpture.

"Daddy must have some big bucks," he drawled.

"We're Italian. He's with the mob, but nobody's supposed to know. Do you want to see one of his guns?"

"I'll pass on that."

She shrugged and led him into another room, which was dark until she flicked the switch on a small desk lamp with a black paper shade. The light revealed that she'd chosen the study instead of a bedroom. A sleek black desk sat at one end in front of a set of bookcases. More pricey art hung on the walls, and plantation shutters covered the windows. She stopped between a mulberry leather sofa and matching club chair.

"You sure you don't want something to drink, Mr. Calebow?"

"I'm sure."

She gazed at him for a moment, and then her hands went to the row of buttons on the front of her white blouse. One by one, she unfastened them.

"How 'bout you get rid of that gum for me."

She walked over to the desk, her expression sulky, and removed the large pink wad from her mouth. Reaching past a stack of papers, she stuck

66

it in a carved alabaster ashtray. She wasn't wearing a bra, and he saw her breasts as she leaned forward. The glow from the desk lamp gilded her small nipples.

"Sit up on the desk, darlin'."

The Spandex skirt rode high on her thighs as she eased her hips onto the front edge. She parted her legs, keeping the balls of her feet resting on the carpet.

He walked toward her, discarding the cummerbund of his tux. "You're a pretty wild kid, aren't you?"

"Uh-huh. I get into a lot of trouble."

"I'll just bet you do." He slipped his hands beneath the school jacket and then under her blouse, pulling it from the waistband of her skirt. His big hand traveled upward along her spine and moved to the front. He cupped her small breasts and brushed her nipples with his thumbs.

Her hands moved to the slide on his zipper. For a moment she did nothing, and then she shivered. "Tell me what you want me to do."

"You seem to be doing real fine all by yourself."

"Tell me, dammit!"

"All right, darlin'. Open my zipper."

"Like this?"

"Just like that."

"Now what?"

"Reach around a little bit and see if you can find anything that catches your interest."

His breathing quickened as she followed his

instructions to the letter.

"You're real big." She cradled him in her hands as she arched her back so that her breasts were pressed deeper into his palms. "I'm getting scared."

"Oh, I'll take it real easy on you."

"You will?"

"I promise."

"It's okay if it hurts a little."

"I wouldn't want to hurt you."

"It's okay. Really."

"If you say so." He smelled bubble gum on her breath as he caught her by the knees and drew them upward, then braced her heels on the desk top. The skirt bunched across her stomach. He moved between her open thighs and slipped a finger inside her.

"Does that hurt?"

"Oh, yes. Yes! What are you going to do to me?"

He told her. Roughly. Explicitly.

Her breathing grew heavier and he could feel the heat of her skin. He pushed off her school jacket and, slipping his hands beneath her bare buttocks, lifted her from the desk. She wrapped her legs around his hips and ground her breasts against the tucks of his shirt front as he carried her to the big leather club chair. He settled into it and positioned her knees on each side of his hips so that she straddled him.

Her blouse hung open displaying breasts that were rosy from the abrasion of his shirt. Her splayed legs revealed the glistening thicket of curls between her thighs. He was throbbing, and he began to pull her down so she could take him, but she resisted.

"You're not going to spank me first, are you?"

He groaned.

"Are you?" she repeated.

He surrendered to the inevitable. "Did you do something wrong?"

"I'm not supposed to let anyone in the house when my parents are gone."

"I guess I'll have to whale you, then, won't I?"

"No, don't!" Her eyelids drifted closed with excitement.

He was ready to explode and no longer in the mood to play games. Making up his mind not to take long with this, he pushed her down over his lap and shoved her skirt all the way to her waist. With her buttocks bared to his gaze, he smacked the flat of his hand on her soft, round flesh.

He was a powerful man, but he carefully leashed his strength, giving her only a bit more than she wanted. She gasped and writhed beneath his blows, growing increasingly more excited.

As her buttocks took on a faintly rosy hue, he thought of all the trouble his ex-wife was causing him. The late-night phone calls when she ripped his character to shreds, the legal hassles, that newspaper interview.

"Ouch! That's too hard!"

Once again the flat of his hand connected with

her tender flesh. "Are you going to be good, darlin'?"

"Yes!"

"How good?"

"Ouch! Stop!"

"Tell me how good you're going to be."

"Good! I'll be good, dammit!"

He spanked her again. "No nasty little digs in the newspapers."

"All right. Stop!"

"No more late-night harangues on the telephone."

"You're ruining everything!"

He slipped his hand between her legs. "I don't think so." And then he lifted her.

She immediately impaled herself on him. "You son of a bitch."

He drove deep. "That's right, I'm a son of a bitch."

She rode him viciously. The phone on the desk began to ring, but they both ignored it. Harsh moans slipped from her throat as she grabbed his dark blond hair in her fists. He buried his face in her breasts while his fingers dug into her buttocks.

The ringing stopped and the answering machine clicked on.

She threw back her head and yelled as she shattered.

This is Valerie Calebow. I can't come to the phone right now. If you leave a message, I'll get back to you as soon as possible.

The machine beeped and then spoke. "Congresswoman, it's Stu Blake. I'm sorry to be calling so late, but . . ."

The voice droned on.

With a groan, Dan spilled himself inside her. She slumped against him as the message came to an end.

Beep.

4

Dan opened the refrigerator door, pulled out a quart of milk, and unscrewed the cap. Behind him he heard Valerie coming into the kitchen of the house they had once shared. Because he knew it would irritate her, he lifted the milk container to his lips and took a swig.

"For God's sake, Dan, get a glass," she said in that snotty voice he hated.

He took another swig before he screwed the cap back on and returned the container to the refrigerator. Resting the side of his hip against the door, he studied her. She had scrubbed the makeup from her face, revealing her sharp bone structure with a nose that was a bit long but well balanced by a high, smooth forehead. Her light brown hair, free of the silver barrette, fell almost to her shoulders, and her teenybopper clothes had given way to a midnight blue peignoir set trimmed in black lace.

"Where'd you get the cheerleading jacket?"

"My secretary's daughter. I told her I was going to a costume party." She lit a cigarette, even though she knew he hated being around smoke.

"This escapade tonight crossed the boundary into creepy. Sixteen-year-old girls haven't turned me on since I was twelve."

She shrugged and exhaled. "It was different, that's all."

Not so different, he thought. In one way or another, all of Valerie's sexual fantasies tended to lead toward male domination. Pretty damn funny considering the fact that she was a Class A ball buster. Unfortunately, the only person he could share the joke with was Valerie, and he knew she wouldn't laugh. Besides, she got all riled if he criticized any of these weird scenarios she set up, and they already had enough other things to fight about.

Her hand crept to her rear. She rubbed it through the dark blue silk and gazed at him with resentment. "You shouldn't have hit me so hard."

"Honey, I was holding back."

He could tell by her expression that she was trying to make up her mind whether to sink her teeth into him or not. Apparently she decided against it because she walked over to the small kitchen desk and began thumbing through the Filofax she had left there. "I don't have to be in Washington for a few more weeks. How's your schedule for the weekend?"

"I'll be at the Meadowlands. We're playing the Jets." He moved away from the refrigerator and took a banana from a stainless steel fruit bowl that looked like the terminal at Dulles.

She slipped on the pair of half-glasses that were lying on the desk and set her cigarette in a chunky black glass ashtray. "What about Thursday evening before you leave?"

"Meeting. Friday's all right, though."

"The vice president's going to be in town that night, and there's another reception."

"Wednesday night if we make it after midnight."

"That looks like it'll work. Except —" She slammed the book shut. "I'll have my period." Slipping off her glasses, she rubbed the bridge of her nose, took another drag from her cigarette, and said briskly, "We'll work around it. We have before."

"We've been divorced for nearly a year, Val. Don't you think it's time we talked about putting an end to this?"

"There's no need to end it yet. We agreed this would be the best arrangement until one of us finds someone else."

"Or until we kill each other, whichever comes first."

She ignored his crack and showed that rare vulnerability that always got to him. "I just — I just can't imagine how to go about it. I'm attracted to powerful men. How am I supposed to tell someone like that I won't sleep with him until I've seen a complete workup of his blood chemistry?"

He tossed the banana peel in the sink. "Sex in the nineties. It makes for strange bedfellows."

"No one should have to screw an ex-spouse just because that ex-spouse happens to be HIV negative." She stabbed out her cigarette in the ashtray.

"Amen to that." He disliked the arrangement a lot more than she did, but whenever he tried to break it off, she made him feel like a heel. Once he found his baby-makin' woman, however, he was putting an end to this.

"We're both too smart to play sexual roulette," she said.

"And you're crazy about my body."

She didn't have much of a sense of humor these days, and his wisecrack set her off. Her nostrils began to breathe fire, and before long she was accusing him of gross insensitivity, reckless behavior, a bad disposition, not caring about anything but winning football games, and emotional dishonesty.

Since she was pretty much on target, he tuned her out while he polished off the banana. In all fairness, he knew her problem was worse than his, and the fact that he felt sorry for her was one of the reasons he went along with this sick arrangement. As a female member of the House of Representatives, she was judged by a stricter moral standard than her male colleagues. The voters might forgive some hounding around from their congressman, but they sure wouldn't forgive it from a woman. For someone who liked sex as much as Valerie, but didn't have either a husband or a man she cared about, it was a definite problem. Besides, she was one of the few honest legislators in Washington, and he figured it was his patriotic duty.

Not that there weren't some benefits for him. He'd had so much free sex during his early playing days that he'd lost his appetite for promiscuity. He also wasn't stupid, and he had no interest in taking chances with groupies. But despite Valerie's kinky little scenarios, sex hadn't been much fun for a long time.

He knew now that the two of them had been incompatible from the beginning, but they had generated so much sexual heat that neither of them had noticed until they'd made the mistake of getting married. Valerie had been initially fascinated by his rough edges and fierce aggressiveness, the same qualities that had later driven her crazy. And her breeding and sophistication had been irresistible to a kid who'd grown up dirt-poor in backwoods Alabama. But he had soon discovered that she had no sense of humor and no desire for the family life he craved.

Her latest tirade against him was beginning to wind down, and he remembered that he had a score of his own to settle. "While we're airing our grievances here, Valerie, I'm going to dish out one of my own. If you give any more interviews like that one last week, your lawyer's going to get a phone call from mine, and this won't be a friendly divorce any longer."

She refused to meet his eyes. "It was a mistake."

"It's like I tell the team. There's no such thing as mistakes — only a lack of foresight."

He had been intimidating people with his physical size for so long that it had become automatic, and he instinctively moved closer until he was hovering over her. "I don't appreciate public discussions of our breakup, and I'm not crazy about having anybody but sportswriters call me a borderline psychopath."

She began to fiddle with the lace on the front of her negligee. "It was an off-the-record remark. The reporter should never have printed it."

"You shouldn't have made the remark in the first place. From now on when anybody asks you about our divorce, you restrict yourself to the same two words I always use when I get interviewed. 'Irreconcilable differences.' "

"You sound like you're threatening me." She was trying to work up a good lather, but she couldn't quite manage it, so he knew she was feeling guilty.

"I'm just reminding you that a lot of men in this town aren't going to keep voting for a woman that bad-mouths an ex-husband who once completed twenty-nine passes against the 49ers' defense in a single afternoon."

"All right! I'm sorry. I'd just talked to you on the phone, and you'd irritated me."

"Valerie, I irritate you all the time, so don't use that as an excuse to go for my jugular."

She wisely changed the subject. "I heard Bert's funeral was quite entertaining. It's too bad all his old mistresses weren't there so they could have seen that dog pee on his coffin." Valerie smiled in her thin-lipped way. "There is a God after all. And She watches out for Her own."

Dan refused to get into a debate with Valerie about Bert, especially when he knew he was on shaky ground. Men liked Bert, but women didn't. He had been too free with his hands, too quick with the raunchy joke and patronizing comment. That didn't go over well with women like Valerie. It didn't go over all that well with Dan, either, but Bert had been the boss so he'd kept his mouth shut.

"It wasn't funny, Val. A man died, and his daughter managed to turn his funeral into a circus."

"I've heard stories about her. What's she like?"

"A high-class hooker, except not that smart. To tell you the truth, I can't remember the last time I met a person who struck me as being so completely worthless."

"She was Arturo Flores's mistress for years. She must have some redeeming qualities."

"Other than the obvious ones on her chest, I can't imagine what. Bert talked to me about her a couple of times. It embarrassed the hell out of him knowing his daughter's naked body was showing up on the walls of every big museum in the country."

"Flores was a great artist. Don't you think Bert's attitude might have been a bit provincial? Remember that we're talking about a man who wanted to hang gold tassels from the crotches of the Star Girl cheerleaders."

"None of those girls was his daughter. And ticket sales have been real slow."

She bristled. "That kind of blatant sexism isn't funny."

He sighed. "It was a joke, Val. Loosen up."

"You're disgusting. Everything about sex is one

78

big joke to you, isn't it?"

"*I'm* disgusting! Now you correct me if I'm wrong here, but aren't you the one who's been dreaming up all these kinky little sexual scenarios, including tonight's semi-repulsive dip into kiddie porn? And haven't I been warming that butt of yours whenever you decide you want it warmed, even though beating up women has never been high on my list of aphrodisiacs?"

She stiffened. "That's not what I'm talking about, but as usual, you've chosen to misinterpret. I'm talking about your attitude toward women. You've gotten so much free sex over the years that you've forgotten women are anything more than tits and ass."

"Now that's real nice talk coming from a representative of the United States government."

"You won't discuss your feelings. You refuse to share your emotions."

It was on the tip of his tongue to remind her that whenever he'd tried to share his emotions with her, she'd turned it into an all-night discussion of everything that was wrong with him.

"And women let you get away with it," she went on. "That's what's really galling. They let you get away with it because — Never mind. I can't talk to you."

"No, Valerie. Go on. Finish what you were saying. If I'm so terrible, why do women let me get away with it?"

"Because you're rich and good-looking," she replied too quickly.

"That's not what you were going to say. You're the one who keeps telling me I need to be more open in my communication. Maybe you should practice what you preach."

"They let you get away with it because you're so confident," she said stiffly. "You don't seem to have the same self-doubts as everybody else in the world. Even successful women like the security of knowing they have a man like that standing behind them."

Although to another man her words might have been flattering, they had the opposite effect on him. He could feel a red-hot coil of rage burning deep inside him, a rage that went all the way back to boyhood when too much emotion had meant a trip to the woodshed and a walloping from his father's belt.

"You women are really something," he sneered. "When are you going to figure out that God might have made two sexes for a reason? You can't have it both ways. Either a man's a man, or he's not. You can't take somebody whose nature is to be a warrior and then expect him — at your command — to curl up on the couch, spill his guts, and, in general, start acting like a pussy."

"Get out!"

"Gladly." He snatched up his keys and headed toward the door. But before he got there, he threw his final punch. "You know what your problem is, Valerie. Your underwear doesn't fit right, and it's made you mean. So the next time you go to the store, why don't you see if you can buy yourself a bigger-sized jockstrap."

He stormed out of the house and climbed into his car. As soon as he got settled, he jammed Hank Jr. into the tape deck and turned up the volume. When he was feeling this low, the only person he wanted to be around was another hell-raiser.

The Sunday afternoon preseason game against the Jets was a disaster. If the Stars had been playing a respectable team, the loss wouldn't have been so humiliating, but getting beaten 25–10 by the candy-ass Jets, even in preseason, was more than Dan could stomach, especially when he imagined his three unsigned players lounging in their hot tubs back in Chicago watching the game on their big screen TVs.

Jim Biederot, the Stars' starting quarterback, had been injured in their last practice and his backup had pulled a groin muscle the week before, so Dan was forced to go with C.J. Brown, a fifteen-year veteran whose knees were held together by airplane glue. If Bobby Tom had been playing, he'd have managed to get free so C.J. could hit him, but Bobby Tom wasn't playing.

To make matters worse, the Stars' new owner had apparently returned from her vacation, but she wasn't taking any calls. Dan kicked a hole in the visitors' locker room wall when Ronald McDermitt delivered that particular piece of information, but it hadn't helped. He'd never imagined he could hate anything more than he hated losing football games, but that was before Phoebe

Somerville had come into his life.

All in all, it had been a dismal week. Ray Hardesty, the Stars' former defensive end, whom Dan had cut in early August, had driven drunk one too many times and gone through a guardrail on the Calumet Expressway. He'd been killed instantly, along with his eighteen-year-old female passenger. All through the funeral, as Dan had watched the faces of Ray's grieving parents, he'd kept asking himself if there had been something more he could have done. Rationally, he knew there wasn't, but it was a tragedy all the same.

The only bright spot in his week had occurred at a DuPage County nursery school where he'd gone to film a public service announcement for United Way. When he'd walked in the door, the first thing he'd noticed was a pixie-faced, red-headed teacher sitting on the floor reading a story to a group of four-year-olds. Something had gone all soft and warm inside him as he'd studied her freckled nose and the spot of green finger paint on her slacks.

When the filming was done, he'd asked her out for a cup of coffee. Her name was Sharon Anderson, and she'd been tongue-tied and shy, a welcome contrast to all the bold-eyed women he was accustomed to. Although it was too early to speculate, he couldn't help but wonder if he might not have found the simple, home-lovin' woman he was searching for.

But the residual glow from his meeting with Sharon had faded by the day of the Jets game, and he continued to seethe over the loss as he endured the postgame activities. It wasn't until he stood on the tarmac waiting to board the charter that would take them back to O'Hare that he snapped.

"Son of a *bitch!*"

He pivoted so abruptly he bumped into Ronald McDermitt, knocking the acting general manager off-balance so that he dropped the book he was carrying. It was what the kid deserved, Dan thought callously, for being born a wimp. Although Ronald was no more than five-foot-eight, he wasn't bad-looking, but he was too neat, too polite, and too young to run the Chicago Stars.

In pro teams the GM directed the entire operation, including hiring and firing of coaches, so that, theoretically, Dan worked for Ronald. But Ronald was so intimidated by him that his authority was purely academic.

The GM picked up his book and looked at him with a wary expression that made Dan crazy. "Sorry, Coach."

"I bumped into you, for chrissake."

"Yes, well . . ."

Dan shoved his carry-on bag into Ronald's arms. "Get somebody to drop this off at my house. I'll catch a later flight."

Ronald looked worried. "Where are you going?"

"It's like this, Ronald. I'm going to go do your job for you."

"I — I'm sorry, Coach, but I don't know what you mean by that."

"I mean that I'm going to look up our new owner, and then I'm going to acquaint her with a few facts about life in the big bad NFL."

Ronald swallowed so hard his Adam's apple bobbed. "Uh, Coach, that might not be a good idea. She doesn't seem to want to be bothered with team business."

"Now that's just too bad," Dan drawled as he set off, "because I'm going to bother her real bad."

5

Pooh got distracted by a Dalmatian as they were crossing Fifth Avenue just above the Metropolitan. Phoebe tugged on the leash.

"Come on, killer. No time for flirting. Viktor's waiting for us."

"Lucky Viktor," the Dalmatian's owner replied with a grin as he approached Phoebe and Pooh from the opposite curb.

Phoebe regarded him through her Annie Sullivan sunglasses and saw that he was a harmless yuppie type. He took in her clingy, lime green dress, and his eyes quickly found their way to the crisscross lacing at the open bodice. His jaw dropped.

"Say? Aren't you Madonna?"

"Not this week."

Phoebe sailed by. Once she reached the opposite curb, she whipped off her sunglasses so no one would make that mistake again. Lord . . . Madonna, for Pete's sake. One of these days, she really had to start dressing respectably. But her friend Simone, who had designed this dress, was going to be at the party Viktor was taking her to tonight, and Phoebe wanted to encourage her.

She and Pooh left Fifth Avenue behind for the quieter streets of the upper Eighties. Oversized hoops swung at her ears, gold bangles clattered at both wrists, her chunky-heeled sandals tapped the sidewalk, and men turned to look as she passed by. Her curved hips swayed in a sassy walk that seemed to have a language all its own.

Hot cha cha
Hot cha cha
Hot hot
Cha cha cha cha

It was Saturday evening, and affluent New Yorkers dressed for dinner and the theater were beginning to emerge from the fashionable brick and brownstone town houses that lined the narrow streets. She neared Madison Avenue and the gray granite building that held the co-op she was subleasing at bargain rates from a friend of Viktor's.

Three days ago, when she'd returned to the city from Montauk, she'd found dozens of phone messages waiting for her. Most of them were from the Stars' office, and she ignored them. None were from Molly saying she'd changed her mind about going directly from camp to boarding school. She frowned as she remembered their strained weekly phone calls. No matter what she said, she couldn't seem to make a dent in her sister's hostility.

"Evening, Miss Somerville. Hello, Pooh."

"Hi, Tony." She gave the doorman a dazzling smile as they walked into the apartment building.

He gulped, then quickly leaned down to pat

Pooh's pom-pom. "I let your guest in just like you said."

"Thanks. You're a prince." She crossed the lobby, her heels tapping on the rose marble floor, and punched the elevator button.

"Can't get over what a nice guy he is," the doorman said from behind her. "Somebody like him."

"Of course he's a nice guy."

"It makes me feel bad about the names I used to call him."

Phoebe bristled as she followed Pooh into the elevator. She had always liked Tony, but this was something she couldn't ignore. "You should feel bad. Just because a man is gay doesn't mean he isn't a human being who deserves respect like everyone else."

Tony looked startled. "He's gay?"

The doors slid shut.

She drummed the toe of her sandal on the floor as the elevator rose. Viktor kept telling her not to be such a crusader, but too many of the people she cared about were gay, and she couldn't turn a blind eye to the discrimination so many of them faced.

She thought of Arturo and all he had done for her. Those years with him in Seville had gone a long way toward restoring her belief in the goodness of human beings. She remembered his short pudgy body straightening in front of his easel, a smear of paint streaking his bald pate as he absentmindedly rubbed his hand over the top of his head while he called out to her, "Phoebe, *querida,* come here and tell me what do you think?"

Arturo had been a man of grace and elegance, an aristocrat of the old school, whose innate sense of privacy rebelled at the idea of letting the world know about his homosexuality. Although they'd never discussed it, she knew it comforted him to pass her off to the public as his mistress, and she loved being able to repay him in some small way for everything he had given her.

The elevator doors slid open. She crossed the carpeted hall and unlocked her own door while Pooh tugged at the leash, yipping with excitement. Bending down, she unfastened the clip. "Brace yourself, Viktor. The Terminator is on the rampage."

As Pooh shot off, she ran her hands through her blond hair to fluff it. She hadn't blown it dry after her shower, deciding to let it curl naturally for the sexy windblown look Simone's deliciously trampy dress demanded.

An unfamiliar male voice with a distinct Southern drawl boomed out from her living room. "Down, dawg! Down, dammit!"

She gasped, then dashed forward, the soles of her sandals slipping on the checkerboard black-and-white marble floor as she whipped around the corner. Hair flying, she lurched to a stop as she saw Dan Calebow standing in the middle of her living room. She recognized him immediately, even though she'd only had a brief conversation with him at her father's funeral. Still, he wasn't the sort of man one forgot easily, and over the

88

past six weeks, his face had unaccountably popped into her memory more than once.

Blond, handsome, and bigger than life, he looked like a born troublemaker. Instead of a knit shirt and chinos, he should have been wearing a rumpled white suit and driving down some Southern dirt road in a big old Cadillac hooking beer cans over the roof. Or standing on the front lawn of an antebellum mansion with his head thrown back to bay at the moon while a young Elizabeth Taylor lay on a curly brass bed upstairs and waited for him to come home.

She felt the same uneasiness she'd experienced at their first meeting. Although he looked nothing at all like the football player who'd raped her all those years ago, she had a deep-seated fear of physically powerful men. At the funeral she'd managed to hide her disquiet behind flirtatiousness, a protective device she had developed into a fine art years ago. But at the funeral, they hadn't been alone.

Pooh, who regarded rejection as a personal challenge, was circling him, tongue flopping, her pom-pom tail beating out a cadence of lovemelovemeloveme.

He looked from the dog to Phoebe. "If she pees on me, I'm skinnin' her."

Phoebe rushed forward to snatch up her pet. "What are you doing here? How did you get in?"

He studied her face rather than her curves, which immediately set him apart from most men.

"Your doorman's a big Giants' fan. Heck of a nice guy. He surely enjoyed those stories I told him about my encounters with L.T."

Phoebe had no idea who L.T. was, but she remembered the flippant instructions she'd left with Tony when she'd gone to walk Pooh. "I'm expecting a gentleman caller," she had said. "Let him in, will you?"

The conversation she'd just had with her doorman took on a whole new light.

"Who's L.T.?" she asked, while she tried to calm Pooh, who was struggling to get out of her arms.

Dan looked at her as if she'd just been beamed down from outer space. Sticking his fingers in the side pockets of his slacks, he said softly, "Ma'am, it's questions like that are gonna get you in a heap of trouble at team owners' meetings."

"I'm not going to any team owners' meetings," she replied with enough saccharine to supply a Weight Watchers convention, "so it won't be a problem."

"Is that so?" His country boy grin was at odds with the chill in his eyes. "Well, then, ma'am, Lawrence Taylor used to be the team chaplain for the New York Giants. A real sweet-tempered gentleman who'd lead us all in prayer sessions before the game."

She knew she was missing something, but she wasn't going to inquire further. His intrusion into her apartment had shaken her, and she wanted to get rid of him as quickly as possible. "Mr.

Calebow, as much as I adore having uninvited company scare the wits out of me, I'm afraid I don't have time to talk right now."

"This won't take long."

She could see that she wasn't going to budge him until he'd had his say, so she did her best to assume an air of studied boredom. "Five minutes then, but I'll have to get rid of my critter first." She made her way to the kitchen to deposit Pooh. The poodle looked pitiable as Phoebe shut the door on her.

When she returned to her unwelcome visitor, he was standing in the middle of the room taking in the owner's trendy decorating scheme. Frail, twig-shaped metal chairs were juxtaposed with oversized couches upholstered in charcoal gray canvas. The lacquered walls and slate floor emphasized the room's cool, stark lines. Her own more comfortable, and considerably less expensive, furniture was in storage — everything except the large painting that hung on the room's single unbroken wall.

The languorous nude was the first painting Arturo had done of her, and even though it was quite valuable, she would never part with it. She lay on a simple wood-framed bed in Arturo's cottage, her blond hair spilling over the pillow as she gazed out of the canvas. The sun dappled her bare skin from the light that shone through a single window set high in the white stucco wall.

She hadn't hung the painting in the apartment's most public room out of vanity, but because the natural light from the large windows displayed it best. This portrait had been more realistically executed than his later depictions of her, and looking at the figure's soft curves and gentle shadings gave her a sense of peace. A spot of coral emphasized the slope of her breast, a brilliant patch of lemon illuminated the swell of her hip, and delicate lavender shadows were woven like silk threads through the paleness of her pubic hair. She seldom thought of the figure in the painting as herself, but as someone far better, a woman whose sexuality hadn't been stolen from her.

Dan stood with his back to her, openly studying the painting in a way that reminded her exactly whose body was on display. As he turned to face her, she braced herself for a smarmy remark.

"Real pretty." He walked over to one of the twig chairs. "Will this thing hold me?"

"If it breaks, I'll send you a bill."

As he sat, she saw that he had finally been distracted by the curves Simone's clingy dress so blatantly displayed, and she gave a mental sigh of relief. This, at least, was familiar territory.

She smiled as she uncrossed her arms and let him look his fill. Years ago she had discovered that she could control her relationships with heterosexual men far better by playing the sexy siren than the blushing ingenue. Being the sexual aggressor put her subtly in charge. She was the one who defined the rules of the game instead of the man, and when she sent her suitor on his way, he assumed it was because he didn't measure up to all the other men in her life. None of them ever figured out there was something wrong with her.

She added a dash of Kathleen Turner to her naturally husky voice. "What's on your mind, Mr. Calebow? Other than the obvious."

"The obvious?"

"Football, of course," she replied innocently. "I can't imagine that a man like you thinks about anything else. I know my father didn't."

"Now you might be surprised what a man like me thinks about."

His hot-summer-night drawl licked her body, setting off all her internal alarm bells. She immediately hitched her hip onto the corner of a small brushed-nickel console, sending her tight skirt even higher on her thighs. Letting her sandal dangle from her toe, she uttered her lie in a silky voice. "Sorry, Mr. Calebow, but I already have more jockstraps hanging from my bedpost than I know what to do with."

"Do you now?"

She dipped her head and gazed at him through the platinum lock of hair that brushed the corner of her eye, a pose she'd perfected years ago. "Athletes are s-o-o-o exhausting. I've moved on to the sort of men who wear boxer shorts."

"Wall Street?"

"Congress."

He laughed. "You're making me sorry I put my wild and woolly days behind me."

"Too bad. A religious conversion?"

"Nothing that interesting. Coaches are supposed to be role models."

"How boring."

"Team owners, too."

She slipped off the edge of the console, carefully positioning herself so he could take in the inner curves of her breasts showing beneath the gold crisscross lacings. "Oh, dear. Why do I sense a lecture coming on?"

"Maybe because you know you deserve one."

She wanted to wrap herself in her oldest, thickest chenille bathrobe. Instead, she let her tongue drift over her lips. "Yelling upsets me so please be gentle."

His eyes darkened with disgust. "Lady, you are something else. I guess I've got reason to yell, considering the fact that you're ruining my football team."

"*Your* team? Gosh, Mr. Calebow, I thought it was mine."

"Right now, honey lamb, it doesn't seem to be anybody's."

He uncoiled so abruptly from the chair that he startled her into backing away. She tried to recover by pretending she'd been about to sit. The stretchy lime green dress slid high as she sank down onto the couch. She languorously crossed her legs, displaying her thin gold ankle bracelet, but he paid no attention. Instead, he began to pace.

"You don't seem to have the faintest idea how much trouble the team's in. Your father's dead, Carl Pogue's quit, and the acting general manager's

94

worthless. You've got unsigned players, bills that aren't getting paid, a stadium contract that's coming up for renewal. As a matter of fact, you're about the only person left who doesn't seem to know that the team is collapsing in on itself."

"I don't know anything about football, Mr. Calebow. You're fortunate that I'm leaving all of you alone." She toyed with the lacing at her breasts, but he didn't take the bait.

"You can't just walk away from an NFL team!"

"I don't see why not."

"Let me tell you about one of the purest pieces of talent you've got — a kid named Bobby Tom Denton. Bert picked him up as a first-round draft choice out of the University of Texas three years ago, and it paid off because Bobby Tom's on his way to being one of the best."

"Why are you telling me this?"

"Because, Miz Somerville, Bobby Tom's from Telarosa, Texas, and being forced to live in the state of Illinois for even part of the year challenges his idea of manhood. Your father understood that, so he set out to renegotiate Bobby Tom's contract before the kid started to think too much about how he'd like to live in Dallas year-round. The negotiations were completed just before Bert died." He shoved a hand through his shaggy dark blond hair. "Right now you own Bobby Tom Denton, along with a fine offensive tackle named Darnell Pruitt, and a free safety who likes nothing more than to force the bad guys to fumble. Unfortunately, you're not getting your money's worth out of any of them because they're not playing. And do you know why they're not playing? Because you're too busy with all those boxer shorts to sign their goddamned contracts!"

A hot flare of anger shot through her, and she vaulted up from the chair. "I've just had a blazing moment of insight, Mr. Calebow. I've just realized that Bobby Tom Denton isn't the only person I own. Correct me if I'm wrong, but isn't it also true that I'm *your* employer."

"That's true, ma'am."

"Then, you're fired."

He looked at her for a long moment before he gave a curt nod. "All right." Without another word, he began to walk out of the room.

As quickly as it had come, her anger dissipated and alarm took its place. What had she done? Even a fool could figure out that a person who didn't know anything about running a football team shouldn't go around firing the head coach. This was exactly the sort of impulsive behavior Viktor always warned her about.

She heard his firm footsteps hit the marble floor and rushed into the hallway. "Mr. Calebow, I —"

He turned back to her and his drawl oozed like slow poison. "My five minutes are up, ma'am."

"But I —"

"You're the one who set the time limit."

Just as he reached for the knob, a key scraped in the lock and the door swung open to reveal Viktor standing on the other side. He wore a fitted black silk T-shirt with camouflage pants, orange leather suspenders, and motorcycle boots. His dark hair streamed sleek and straight over his shoulders, and he held a brown paper sack in his hands. He was beautiful and dear, and she couldn't remember when she had been so glad to see anyone.

In the tick of a few seconds, his eyes seemed to take it all in — her frantic expression, Dan Calebow's stony one. He turned his beautiful smile on them both.

"A party! I brought you rice cakes and cabbage *kimchi*, Phoebe, along with *chapch'ae* and *pulgogi* for myself. You know how bad the food will be tonight, so I thought we should fortify ourselves first. Do you like Korean food, Coach Calebow?"

"I don't believe I've ever eaten any. Now, if you'll excuse —"

Viktor, with more courage than most men, stepped directly in front of Dan. "Please. I really must insist. We have the finest Korean restaurant in New York barely three blocks from here." He extended his arm to shake hands. "Viktor Szabo. I don't believe we met at that awful funeral, but I am a big fan of American football. I'm still learning, however, and I would welcome the chance to ask a few questions of an expert. The blitz, for example . . . Phoebe, we must have beer! When American men talk football, they drink beer. Miller time, yes?"

Viktor had gradually worked Dan back a few steps into the apartment, but now the coach planted his feet, obviously having gone as far as he intended. "Thanks for the invitation, Viktor,

97

but I'll have to pass it up. Miss Somerville just fired me, and I don't seem to be in the mood for company."

Viktor laughed as he plopped the sack of food in Phoebe's arms. "You must learn when to pay attention to Phoebe and when to ignore her. She is what you Americans call —" He hesitated, searching for the proper phrase. "A fuck-up."

"Viktor!"

He leaned forward and planted a swift kiss on her forehead. "Tell Coach Calebow you didn't mean to fire him."

She batted him away, her pride stung. "I *did* mean to fire him."

Viktor clucked his tongue. "The truth now."

She was going to kill him for this. Holding on to what shreds of dignity she had left, she spoke carefully. "I meant to fire him, but perhaps I shouldn't have done it. I apologize for my short temper, Mr. Calebow, even though you provoked me. Consider yourself rehired."

He turned to stare at her. She tried to return his gaze, but the spicy odors of Korean food were stinging her nostrils and making her eyes tear so she knew she wasn't too impressive.

"The job doesn't hold much appeal for me anymore," he said.

Viktor sighed. "There are still things to discuss, I see, and we will do it over food. One hopelessly stubborn person is all I can deal with at a time, Coach Calebow. Won't you share a meal with us?"

"I don't think so."

"Please. For the greater good of football. And the victorious future of the Chicago Stars."

Dan took his time considering before he gave an abrupt nod. "All right."

Viktor beamed like a proud father, fluffed Phoebe's hair, and nudged her toward the kitchen. "Do your woman's work. We men are hungry."

Phoebe opened her mouth to tell him off, but then clamped it shut. Not only was Viktor her friend, but he was smart about people, and she had to trust him. She sashayed forward, punishing the football coach by putting an extra swing to a pair of hips he'd never get a chance to touch.

As the men entered the navy and white kitchen behind her, Pooh went berserk, but since the dog concentrated her attention on Viktor instead of the coach, Phoebe didn't need to go to the rescue.

Ten minutes later the three of them were sitting on slatted white metal cafe chairs at the matching round bistro table that stood at the end of her kitchen. She served the Korean food on glazed white porcelain plates, each of them painted with a stylized royal blue carp that was the same color as the woven place mats. Only the fact that she had left the beer in bottles so Viktor could get his macho fix ruined the blue and white color scheme.

"*Pulgogi* is the Korean form of barbecue," Viktor explained, after the men had finished an incomprehensible discussion of the blitz. He picked up another thin strip of sesame-marinated meat with his fork. "Phoebe doesn't like it, but I'm absolutely addicted. What do you think?"

"I doubt it's going to put McDonald's out of business, but it's not too bad."

Phoebe had been covertly watching Dan for subtle signs of homophobia and was disappointed when he showed none because he wasn't giving her an excuse to throw him out. She studied his face. He certainly wasn't as good-looking as many of Viktor's friends. There was that small bump at the bridge of his nose, the thin white scar on a chin. But still, she would be lying to herself if she denied that he was an incredibly attractive man. He could even be charming when he tried, and several times she'd had to force herself not to smile at his offbeat sense of humor.

Viktor set down his fork and wiped his mouth with a napkin. "Now, Dan, perhaps you wish to share with me the reasons for your dispute with my Phoebe. I assure you, she is the dearest of persons."

"Must be an acquired taste. Like that Korean meat."

Viktor sighed. "Dan, Dan. This won't do, you know. She is quite sensitive. If the two of you are to work together, you must arrive at some sort of truce."

She opened her mouth to tell Viktor it was hopeless, only to feel her friend's hand clamp down hard on her thigh.

"The problem is, Viktor, we're not going to be working together because *your* Phoebe won't take any responsibility for *her* football team."

Viktor patted Phoebe's arm. "It is fortunate, Dan, that she is leaving you alone. She knows nothing of sports."

The air was so thick with the pollution of male patronization that she could barely breathe, but she held her peace.

Dan nudged Pooh off his right foot. The poodle resettled on his left one. "She doesn't need to know anything about sports. She just needs to fire the current general manager, hire somebody with more experience, and sign the papers that are put in front of her." Briefly, he outlined the difficulties the Stars had been having since Bert's death.

Viktor, who had a good head for business and was notoriously tight with a dollar, frowned. "Phoebe, pet, I'm afraid he has a point."

"You know the terms of my father's will. He left me the Stars only so he could teach me a lesson. I'm not playing his game."

"There are some games you can't walk away from, Miz Somerville, without hurting a lot of people."

"I'm not going to lose much sleep over a bunch of grown men crying in their beer because they aren't winning football games."

"Then how about the staff people who are going to lose their jobs? Our ticket sales are way down from last year, and that means layoffs. How about their families, Miz Somerville. Will you lose sleep over them?"

He'd made her feel like a selfish worm. She'd been so wrapped up in her own feelings that she hadn't bothered to consider the effect her decision to turn her back on the Stars might have on others. If only she could find a way to stay true to herself without hurting anyone else. Several seconds ticked by while she considered her options. Finally, she released an indolent sign.

"All right, Mr. Calebow. You've absolutely devastated me. I'm not going to Chicago, but you can have the papers shipped to me here, and I'll sign them."

"I'm afraid that's not going to work, ma'am. In case you forgot, you fired me. If you want me back, you're going to have to meet a few of my conditions."

"What conditions?" She regarded him warily.

He leaned back in his chair like Big Daddy after a seven-course dinner, except Big Daddy was fat and ugly instead of a hard-muscled athlete with a powerful chest and a lethal grin.

"It's like this. I want you in the Stars' business offices by noon on Tuesday to sign those three contracts. Then we'll sit down with Steve Kovak, your director of player personnel, and discuss qualified candidates for the general manager's job. You'll hire one of them by the end of the week, and from then until the team's no longer your responsibility, you'll show up for work like everybody else and sign the papers he puts in front of you."

Only the warning in Viktor's eyes kept her from emptying the last of the *pulgogi* in the football coach's lap. She could feel her father's net drawing tighter around her, and she thought of those weeks she had spent at Montauk walking on the beach and trying to restore peace to her life. But how could she be at peace with herself if innocent people were going to suffer because of her stubborn pride?

She considered the one hundred thousand dollars. In light of what Dan Calebow had told her, it no longer seemed quite so much like blood money. All she had to do to earn it was endure the next three or four months. When they were over, she'd have a clear conscience and the stake she needed to open her art gallery.

With a sense of inevitability, she gave him a bright, false smile. "You've convinced me, Mr. Calebow. But I'm warning you now. I won't go to any football games."

"That's probably just as well."

Viktor extended his arms and gave them each an approving smile. "There. Do you see how easy life is when stubborn people are willing to compromise?"

Before Phoebe could respond, the telephone began to ring. Although she could have answered it right there, she took advantage of the opportunity to escape and excused herself. Pooh trotted after her as she slipped from the kitchen.

The door closed behind her, and the two men regarded each other for a long moment. Viktor spoke first. "I must have your promise, Coach, that you won't hurt her."

"I promise."

"You spoke a bit too quickly for my taste. I don't quite believe you."

"I'm a man of my word, and I promise that I won't hurt her." He flexed his hands. "When I murder her, I'll do it real quick, so she won't feel a thing."

Viktor sighed. "That's exactly what I was afraid of."

6

"Here we are, Miss Somerville."

The Buick Park Avenue left the highway for a two-lane service road marked with a blue and white wooden sign that read Stars Drive. Annette Miles, the driver who had picked Phoebe up at O'Hare, had been Bert's secretary for several years. She was in her late forties, overweight, with short, graying hair. Although polite, she wasn't particularly communicative, and there had been little conversation between them.

Phoebe was tired from having gotten up at dawn to catch her early flight and she felt tense about what lay ahead. Trying to relax, she gazed out the passenger window at the wooded landscape. Stands of oak, walnut, maple, and pine lay on both sides of the service road, and through a gap in the trees to her right, she could glimpse a cyclone fence.

"What's over there?"

"A regulation-size grass practice field, along with a seventy-yard field. The trees keep the area private from the gawkers." She passed a turnoff with a rectangular blue and white sign marking a delivery entrance. "Your father bought this land from the Catholic church in 1980. There used to be a monastery here. The complex isn't fancy —

not like the Cowboys' or Forty-Niners' facilities — but it's functional, and the Midwest Sports Dome isn't far away. There was a lot of controversy when the dome was put in, but it's brought a great deal of money into DuPage County."

The road curved to the right and up a gentle incline toward an architecturally unimpressive two-story, L-shaped building made of gray glass and steel. Its most pleasant aspect was the way the glass reflected the surrounding trees, softening the building's utilitarian look.

Annette pointed toward a paved lot marked for reserved parking. "I had your father's car brought over from the house as you asked. It's parked by the side entrance. Normally you'll want to use it, but today I'll take you in through the lobby."

She pulled into the visitor's space closest to the front entrance and turned off the engine. Phoebe got out. As she approached the building, she found herself wishing she'd brought Pooh along as a security blanket instead of leaving her with Viktor. She caught sight of her reflection in the double glass doors. This outfit, a pearl gray trouser suit, was the closest thing she had to business attire. She wore an indigo silk shell beneath the short jacket and matching indigo sandals fastened with delicate gold chain T-straps. Her hair curved in sleek blond sickles away from her face. The only frivolity she had permitted herself was a purple and white wooden panda pin on her lapel. And her rhinestone sunglasses.

Annette opened one of the double glass doors

for her. Each door held the team logo of three interlocking gold stars in a sky blue circle. Pushing her sunglasses to the top of her head, Phoebe stepped inside her father's world.

The semicircular lobby, predictably carpeted in sky blue, held gold vinyl chairs and a curved white reception desk with blue and gold stripes. A trophy case sat at one end, along with citations, posters, and a framed display of all the NFL team logos.

Annette gestured toward a chair. "Would you wait here for just a moment?"

"Of course." Phoebe removed her sunglasses and tucked them in her purse. Barely a minute passed before a man came rushing out of the left hallway.

"Miss Somerville. Welcome."

She stared at him.

He was adorable, a short, bookish Tom Cruise with a friendly, deferential expression that went a long way toward settling her nervous stomach. Although he was probably close to her own age, he looked so boyish that he seemed like a teenager. She took the hand he offered and gazed into a pair of glorious Cruise-blue eyes that were on the same level as her own.

"I'm sure you must be tired from your flight." He had the thickest fringe of lashes she had ever seen on a man. "I'm sorry that you haven't had a chance to rest before being plunged into all this."

His voice was soft, his manner so sympathetic, that she experienced her first ray of hope since Dan Calebow had blackmailed her. Maybe this wouldn't be so bad after all.

"I'm fine," she reassured him.

"Are you certain? I know there are a number of people waiting to see you, but I'll do my best to put them off if you'd like."

She wanted to tie a bow around him and put him under her Christmas tree. Her internal radar wasn't sending out any warning signals telling her to vamp him, something that generally happened when she was around good-looking men. His small stature and friendly manner were keeping her from feeling threatened.

She lowered her voice so only he could hear. "Why don't you just stick by my side instead? I have a feeling I'm going to need a friendly face."

"I'll be happy to." They exchanged smiles and she had a comforting sense of connection with him, as if they'd known each other for years.

He led her through an archway into a den of offices decorated with commemorative footballs, pennants, and team cups stuffed with pencils. As they passed through, he introduced her to a number of men, most of whom wore blue polo shirts bearing the Stars' logo and all of whom seemed to have titles: director, manager, assistant.

Unlike his more casually dressed coworkers, her new ally wore a pin-striped charcoal suit, starched white shirt with French cuffs, burgundy rep tie, and polished cordovan wing tips.

"You haven't told me your name."

"Gosh." He slapped his forehead with the heel of his hand and grinned, producing a charming set of dimples. "I've been so nervous about meeting you I forgot. I'm Ron McDermitt, Miss Somerville."

"Please, Ron, call me Phoebe."

"I'd be honored."

They walked through a busy area of staff desks separated by partitions, then turned the corner into the longer back wing of the building. It was decorated as unimaginatively as the lobby: blue carpet, white walls covered with photographs, and team posters in simple chrome frames.

He glanced at his watch and frowned. "We're due in Steve Kovak's office now. He's the director of player personnel, and he wants to get the contracts signed as soon as possible."

"Coach Calebow made these contracts sound like life and death."

"They are, Phoebe. For the Stars, anyway." He stopped in front of a door that bore a small brass placard announcing it as the office of the director of player personnel. "Last season, this team had one of the worst records in the league. The fans have deserted us, and we've been playing in a stadium that's barely half-full. If we lose Bobby Tom Denton, there'll be even more empty seats."

"You're telling me I'd better sign or else."

"Oh, no. You're the owner. I can advise you, but it's your team, and you make the final decision."

He spoke so earnestly that she wanted to throw her arms around him and give him a big smacker right on his cute little mouth. Instead, she walked through the door he had opened for her.

Steve Kovak was a weathered veteran of decades of gridiron warfare. Dressed in his shirtsleeves, he had thinning brown hair, a lantern jaw, and a ruddy complexion. Phoebe found him thoroughly terrifying, and as they were introduced, she wished she weren't wearing slacks.

Since she couldn't flash her legs, she let her jacket fall open as she took a seat across from his desk. "I understand I need to sign some contracts."

"Affirmative." He pulled his eyes away from her breasts and pushed a sheaf of papers toward her. She extracted a pair of reading glasses with leopard-spotted frames from her purse and slipped them on.

The door opened behind her and she tensed. She didn't need to turn her head to know who had come in; there was something in the air. Perhaps it was the subtle citrus scent she had noticed when he had been in her apartment, perhaps simply the atmospheric turbulence of excessive macho. The idea that she still remembered what he smelled like scared her, and she let her jacket fall open a bit farther.

"Real glad to see you could make it, Miz Somerville." A distinct edge of sarcasm undercut his Alabama drawl. Until now, she'd never found Southern accents particularly attractive, but she was forced to admit there was definitely something seductive about those elongated vowels.

She kept her eyes on the papers she was studying. "Make nice, Mr. Calebow, or I'll sic Pooh

110

on you." Before he could respond, her head shot up from Bobby Tom Denton's contract. "*Eight* million dollars? You're giving this man $8 million dollars to catch a football! I thought this team was in financial trouble?"

Dan leaned against the wall to her left, crossed his arms and tucked his fingers under the armpits of the blue Stars' polo shirt he wore with a pair of gray slacks. "Good wide-outs don't come cheap. You'll notice that's for four years."

She was still trying to get her breath back. "This is an obscene amount of money."

"He's worth every penny," Steve Kovak retorted. "Your father approved this contract, by the way."

"Before or after he died?"

Dan smiled. Instinctively, Phoebe looked over at the only man in the room she trusted for confirmation that her father had, indeed, known about this outrageous contract. Ron nodded.

Kovak's chair squeaked as he turned toward Dan, effectively shutting her out of the discussion. "Do you know that the Colts only paid Johnny Unitas ten thousand dollars a year? And that was after he'd led them to two championships."

These men were definitely crazy, and she decided she would be the voice of sanity. "Then why don't you get rid of Bobby Tom Denton and hire this Unitas person? You could triple the Colts' offer and still be a few million ahead."

Dan Calebow laughed. Dipping his head, he kept his arms crossed as his chest began to shake. Steve .

Kovak stared at her with an expression that fell someplace between shock and abject horror.

Her eyes darted to Ron, who had a gentle smile on his face. "What did I say wrong?" she asked.

Leaning forward, he patted her hand and whispered, "Johnny Unitas is retired now. He's — uh — about sixty. And he was a quarterback."

"Oh."

"But if he were still playing and — uh — younger, that might have been an excellent suggestion."

"Thank you," she replied with dignity.

Head still dipped, Dan wiped his eyes with his thumbs. "Johnny Unitas. Jay-zus . . ."

Completely irritated now, she swung her legs toward him while she whipped off her glasses and jabbed them at the unsigned contracts. "Did you make money like this when you were playing?"

He looked over at her, his eyes still moist. "Starting quarterbacks do a little better than that after they've been around for awhile."

"Better than $8 million?"

"Yep."

She slapped the contracts down on the desk. "Fine. Then why don't *you* sign this!" Rising to her feet, she stalked out.

She was halfway down the hall before she realized she had no place to go. An empty office lay off to her left. She stepped inside and shut the door, wishing she'd held her temper. Once again, she'd let her tongue take control of her brain.

Tucking her glasses into the pocket of her jacket,

she walked to the floor-to-ceiling bank of windows that ran behind the desk and looked out over two empty practice fields. What did she know about wide-outs and $8 million contracts? She could converse with art lovers in four different languages, but that wasn't any use to her now.

The door opened behind her.

"Are you all right?" Ron inquired softly.

"I'm fine." As she turned, she saw the concern in his eyes.

"You have to understand about them. About football."

"I hate the game. I don't want to understand."

"I'm afraid you'll have to if you're going to be part of this." He gave her a sad smile. "They take no prisoners. Pro football is the most exclusive boys' club in the world."

"What do you mean?"

"It's closed to outsiders. There are secret passwords and elaborate rituals that only *they* can understand. None of the rules are written down, and if you have to ask what they are, you can't belong. It's a closed society. No women allowed. And no men who don't measure up."

She walked away from the window to one of the file cabinets and regarded him curiously. "Are you talking about yourself?"

He gave an embarrassed laugh. "It's painfully obvious, isn't it? I'm thirty-four years old. I tell everyone I'm five feet ten, but I'm barely five-eight. And I'm still trying to make the team. It's been that way all my life."

"How could it still be important to you?"

"It just is. When I was a kid, I couldn't think about anything else. I read about football, dreamed about it, went to every game I could — playground, high school, the pros, it didn't matter. I loved the patterns of the game — its rhythms and lack of moral ambiguity. I even loved its violence because somehow it seemed safe — no mushroom clouds, no litter of dead bodies when it was over. I did everything but play. I was too small, too clumsy. Maybe I just wanted it too bad, but I could never hold on to the ball."

He slipped a hand into the pocket of his trousers. "My senior year of high school, I was a National Merit Scholar and I'd been accepted at Yale. But I would have given it all up in a second if I could have been on the team. If, just once, I could have carried the ball into the end zone."

She understood his yearning even if she couldn't understand his passion for football. How could this sweet, gentle man have such an unhealthy obsession?

She nodded her head toward the papers he was carrying. "You want me to sign those, don't you?"

He came closer, his eyes gleaming with excitement. "All I can do is advise you, but I think this team has an exciting future. Dan's temperamental and demanding. Sometimes he's too hard on the players, but he's still a great coach, and we have a lot of young talent. I know these contracts represent a fortune, but in football, championships make money. I think it's a good

114

long-term investment."

She snatched the papers from him and quickly scrawled her name in the places he indicated. When she was done, she felt dizzy knowing that she had just given away millions of dollars. Still, it would ultimately be Reed's problem, so why should she worry?

The door opened and Dan came in. He saw the pen in her hand as she returned the contracts to Ron, who gave him a brief affirming nod.

Dan seemed to visibly relax. "Why don't you take those back to Steve now, Ronald?"

Ron nodded and left the room before she could stop him. The office felt measurably smaller as the door once again closed and they were alone. She had felt safe with Ron, but now something dangerous sizzled in the air.

As Dan walked behind the desk and took a seat, she realized this was his office. Unlike other parts of this building, this room had no ego-inflating wall of commendations and photographs. Utilitarian steel bookcases and file cabinets stood on one side opposite a well-worn couch. The desk and the credenza behind it were cluttered, but not disorganized. A television occupied the far corner along with a VCR. She averted her eyes from an ugly hole in the wallboard that looked as if it might have been made with a fist.

She waited for him to start pulling empty beer cans out of the drawers and crushing them in his fists, but he nodded toward one of the blue and chrome side chairs. She took a seat on the couch instead because it was farther away.

The chair squeaked as he leaned back. "I already had lunch, so you don't need to look so scared. I'm not going to eat you up."

She lifted her chin and gave him a smoky smile. "That's too bad, Coach. I was hoping you were hungry."

He smiled. "I'm glad I met you when I was thirty-seven instead of seventeen."

"Why is that?"

"Because I'm a lot smarter now than I was then, and you're exactly the kind of female my mama warned me about."

"Smart mama."

"You been a man-killer all your life, or is it something that happened recently?"

"I bagged my first one when I was only eight. A Cub scout named Kenny."

"Eight years old." He gave an admiring whistle. "I don't even want to contemplate what you were doing to the male population by the time you were seventeen."

"It wasn't a pretty sight." Playing games with this man was nerve-racking, and she searched for a way to change the subject. Remembering the empty practice fields, she nodded toward the window.

"Why aren't the players practicing? I thought you were losing."

"It's Tuesday. That's the only day of the week players have off. A lot of them use it to make community appearances, speak at luncheons, that

116

sort of thing. The coaches do, too. Last Tuesday, for example, I spent the afternoon taping a public service announcement for United Way at a nursery school the county operates."

"I see."

The bantering had disappeared, and he was all business as he slid a manila file folder across the desk toward her. "These are résumés of the three men Steve Kovak and I think are best qualified for the general manager's job, along with our comments. Why don't you look this over tonight? You can let us make the final decision, or you might want to talk with Reed."

"As long as I'm the owner, Coach, I'll be making my own decisions."

"Fine. But you need to move quickly."

She picked up the folder. "What about the current general manager? Has he been fired?"

"Not yet."

When he didn't say anything more, her stomach sank. She couldn't imagine anything worse than firing someone, even a person she didn't know.

"I'm not firing him! I like my men alive and kicking."

"Normally it'd be the owner's job, but I figured you'd feel that way so I asked Steve to take care of it for you. He's probably talking to him now."

Phoebe gave a sigh of relief.

Dan insisted on showing her around the facilities, and their tour of the two-story, L-shaped building took much of the next hour. She was surprised by the number of classrooms she saw and mentioned this to Dan.

"Meetings and watching film make up part of most practice days," he explained. "Players have to learn the game plan. They get critiqued and hear scouting reports. Football's more than sweat."

"I'll take your word for it."

The coaches' conference room had a chalkboard at one end, which was scrawled with words like *King, Joker, Jayhawk,* as well as some diagrams. The weight room smelled like rubber and had an elephant-sized Toledo scale, while the tiny video lab held floor-to-ceiling shelves stacked with expensive, high-tech equipment.

"Why do you need so much film equipment?"

"A lot of coaching involves watching films. We have our own camera crew, and they shoot every game from three different angles. In the NFL, each team has to send their last three game films to their next opponent exactly one week before they play."

She looked through a set of windows into the training room, the only truly orderly area she'd seen on her tour. The walls were lined with cabinets. There were padded benches, several stainless steel whirlpools, a Gatorade dispenser, a red plastic barrel marked "Infectious Waste," and a table that held dozens of rolls of tape in foot-high stacks.

She pointed toward them. "Why so much?"

"The players have to be taped before each practice, usually twice a day. We use a lot."

"That must take a long time."

"We have five tapers at training camp, three during the season."

They moved on. She noticed that the few women they met visibly perked up when they spotted Dan, while the men greeted him with varying degrees of deference. She remembered what Ron had told her about the boys' club and realized that Dan was its president.

In the veterans' locker room, the open lockers were piled with shoes, socks, T-shirts, and pads. Some of the players had taped family snapshots to their lockers. There was a soft drink-dispensing machine at one end, along with several telephones and wooden pigeonholes stuffed with fan mail.

After she promised him she would report back by ten the next morning, Dan left her in the lobby. She was so relieved to have gotten away from him without suffering any major injuries that she had already pulled the keys Annette Miles had given her to Bert's Cadillac from her purse before she remembered that she hadn't thanked Ron for helping her today. She also wanted to ask his advice on choosing the new general manager.

As she headed toward the wing that held the Stars' management, a stocky man carrying camera equipment came toward her.

"Excuse me. Where can I find Ron's office?"

"Ron?" He looked puzzled.

"Ron McDermitt."

"Oh, you mean Ronald. Last door at the end."

She walked down the corridor, but when she reached the end, she decided she'd gotten the instructions wrong because this door held a brass placard marked "General Manager." Puzzled, she stared at it.

And then her heart gave a sickening thud. She flew into a small antechamber, which held a secretary's desk and some chairs. The phone was ringing with all buttons flashing, but no one was there. She experienced a few mad seconds of hope that Ron was some kind of assistant, but that hope died when she rushed over to the doorway of the inner office.

Ron sat at the desk, his chair turned away from the door toward the window behind him. He was in his shirtsleeves, elbows propped on the arms of the chair.

She stepped inside cautiously. "Ron?"

He turned. "Hello, Phoebe."

Her heart almost broke as he gave her a rueful smile. Despite his subdued manner, she permitted herself a flicker of hope. "Have you already — Have you talked with Steve Kovak?"

"Do you want to know if he's fired me? Yes, he has."

She regarded him with dismay. "I didn't realize you were the general manager. Why didn't you tell me?"

"I thought you knew."

"If I had, I would never have let this happen." Even as she said the words, she remembered her agreement with Dan. Part of that agreement had been her promise to fire the acting general manager.

"It's all right. Really. It was inevitable."

"But, Ron . . ."

"I only got the job as assistant GM because my father and Bert were good friends. Your father was never impressed with me, and he would have fired me after six months if Carl Pogue hadn't gone to bat for me."

She sank into a chair. "At least someone was behind you."

"I loved working for Carl. We complemented each other perfectly, which was why Carl didn't want Bert to fire me."

"What do you mean?"

"Carl has good football instincts and he's a strong leader, but he's not exceptionally intelligent. I had the qualities he lacked — organizational ability, a head for business — but I'm a total failure as a leader. Carl and I had worked it out so that I'd do the planning and strategy work and he'd carry it through."

"Are you saying you're the one who was running the team?"

"Oh, no. Carl was in charge."

"Implementing your ideas."

"That's true."

She rubbed her forehead. "This is terrible."

"If it's any consolation, firing me was the proper decision. If a GM in the pros is going to be effective, everyone who works for him — from the office staff right up to the coaches — needs to fear him at least a little bit. The men don't even respect me, let alone fear me. I've got the brains to do the job, but I don't seem to have the personality. Or maybe I just don't have the guts."

"I do." She straightened in her chair, as surprised as Ron that she had spoken aloud the words she had merely been thinking.

"I beg your pardon."

Her mind raced. Bert had wanted her to be a figurehead. He had expected her to spend her days sitting in his old office, obediently signing the papers that were put in front of her and doing what she was told. It would never have occurred to him that she might try to learn something about the job.

She had vowed she wasn't going to play her father's game, and now she saw a way to fulfill the terms of the will but keep her self-respect. "I have the guts," she repeated. "I just don't have the knowledge."

"What are you saying?"

"So far, the only thing I know about football is how much I hate it. If my father had suspected that Carl Pogue would quit, he would never have let me anywhere near the Stars, not even for a few months. I was trapped into doing this, first by Bert and then by Dan Calebow, but that doesn't mean I have to do everything their way."

"I still don't understand —"

"I need to learn something about running a football team. Even if I'm only going to be in charge for a few months, I want to make my own decisions. But I can't do that without having a person I trust to advise me." She gestured toward the papers she still held in her hand. "I don't know anything about these men."

"The candidates for the GM job?"

She nodded.

"I'm certain you can trust Dan and Steve to have picked the best qualified."

"How do I know that?"

"Perhaps your cousin Reed could advise —"

"No!" She forced herself to speak calmly. "Reed and I never got along. I won't go to him under any circumstances. I need you."

"I can't tell you how much your confidence means to me."

She slumped in the chair. "Unfortunately, I promised Dan I'd get rid of you."

"His request wasn't unreasonable. I've been doing a dismal job."

"That's only because he doesn't understand what you're capable of. He doesn't know you the way I do."

"I've known Dan for several years," he pointed out gently. "You and I only met two hours ago."

She had no patience with that sort of logic. "Time isn't important. I have good instincts about people."

"Dan Calebow isn't the sort of man you should think about crossing, and right now, you need him a lot more than you need me. Winning football games is the only thing that counts in his life. I knew that when I convinced Carl to hire him away from the Bears."

"You're the one who hired him?"

By now, she knew Ron well enough to anticipate what was coming.

"Oh, no. Bert and Carl made the final decision."

Based on Ron's hard work. "I need some time to think."

"I don't believe there's much to think about. You gave Dan your word, didn't you?"

"I did, but . . ."

"Then that's that."

Ron was right about one thing, she thought glumly. She didn't like the idea of crossing Dan Calebow.

7

The humid night breeze blew the curtains and ruffled Molly's dark brown hair as she sat in a rocker
by her bedroom window reading Daphne du
Maurier's *Rebecca*. Although Molly knew she was
flying in the face of literary criticism, she thought
Daphne du Maurier was a much better writer than
Fyodor Dostoyevski.

She liked Danielle Steel a lot better than
Dostoyevski, too, mainly because the heroines in
her books survived so many terrible experiences
that they gave Molly courage. She knew that in
real life Danielle Steel had a lot of children, and
when Molly'd gotten the flu at camp, she'd had
wonderful fever dreams in which Danielle was her
mother. Even when she was awake, she'd imagined
Danielle sitting on the side of her bed stroking
her hair while she read from one of her books.
She knew it was a babyish thing to think about,
but she couldn't help it.

She reached for a tissue and blew her nose. The
flu was gone, but she'd been left with a minor
respiratory infection. As a result, the headmistress
at Crayton wouldn't let her have early arrival priv-
ileges. Phoebe had been notified, and Molly had
been forced to come home just a few days after
her sister's return to Chicago. Not that this hor-

rible house felt like home.

She wished Phoebe would leave her alone. She kept making suggestions about renting movies or playing a card game together, but Molly knew she only did it out of duty. Molly hated Phoebe, not just because of the way she dressed, but because her father had loved Phoebe. She knew her father didn't love her. He'd told her more than once that she gave him the "goddamn creeps."

"At least your sister has the guts to stand up to me! You look like you're going to faint everytime I talk to you." He'd told her the same thing whenever she came home. He'd criticized the quiet way she talked, the way she looked, everything about her, and she knew he was secretly comparing her to her beautiful, confident older sister. Over the years, her hatred for Phoebe had settled into a hard shell around her heart.

The distant, hollow sound of the grandfather clock chiming nine made the big house seem even emptier so that she felt smaller and more alone. She went to the side of the bed where she knelt to pull out the object she kept hidden there. Settling back on her calves, she pressed a bedraggled stuffed brown monkey with one missing eye to her chest.

She rested her cheek on a bald patch in the fur between the monkey's ears and whispered, "I'm scared, Mr. Brown. What's going to happen to us?"

"Molly?"

At the sound of her sister's voice, Molly shoved Mr. Brown back under her bed, snatched up *The*

Brothers Karamazov, pushed Daphne du Maurier's *Rebecca* beneath her pillow, and resettled in the rocker.

"Molly, are you in there?"

She turned the page.

The door opened, and Phoebe came in. "Didn't you hear me?"

Molly carefully concealed her jealousy as she looked at her sister's dusty pink jeans and matching crocheted sweater. The sweater had a deep V-neck with a scalloped edge that curved over Phoebe's breasts. Molly wanted to clutch Dostoyevski to her own chest to hide its lack of shape. It wasn't fair. Phoebe was old, and she didn't need to be pretty any longer. She didn't need all that blond hair and those slanty eyes. Why couldn't Molly have been the pretty one instead of a thin, ugly stick with plain brown hair?

"I was reading."

"I see."

"I'm afraid I'm not in the mood for conversation, Phoebe."

"This won't take long. School starts soon and there are a few things we need to discuss."

Phoebe's poodle scampered through the door and bounded over to Molly, who drew back and glared at her sister. "Where did that dog come from?"

"Since it looks as if I'm going to have to settle here for a while, I had Viktor put her on a plane."

Molly moved her feet away from the poodle as it began to attack her fuzzy yellow slippers. "I'd appreciate it if you didn't let it in my room. I'm highly allergic."

Phoebe sat on the edge of Molly's bed and reached down to snap her fingers for Pooh, who came to her side. "Poodles don't shed. They're good dogs for people with allergies."

"I don't care to have animals in my bedroom."

"Are you this unpleasant all the time, or is it just me?"

Molly's lips set in a mulish line. "I'm tired, and I want to go to sleep."

"It's only nine o'clock."

"I've been ill."

Phoebe watched as Molly bent her head over her book, deliberately shutting her out. Once again she experienced the familiar combination of frustration and sympathy that took hold of her whenever she tried to talk to the child. She hadn't even been back in Chicago for a week before Molly had been sent home from camp to recuperate from the flu. If anything, their relationship had grown worse in the past two days instead of improving.

She plucked at the stitching on the bedspread. "This house has to be closed soon so it can be put up for sale. Unfortunately, it seems as if I'm going to be stuck here for the next few months, so I've decided to move into a condo Bert owned that's not too far from the Stars Complex. The lawyers say I can stay there until the first of the year." She was also being provided with a living allowance to take care of her expenses, which was a good thing because her bank account had dipped alarmingly low.

"Since I'll be back at Crayton, I don't see how your living arrangements concern me."

She ignored Molly's sullenness. "I don't envy you going back. I hated it when I was there."

"I don't have much choice, do I?"

Phoebe went completely still as an eerie tingling traveled up her spine. Molly's face was stiff and inexpressive except for a small quiver at the corner of her mouth. She recognized that stubborn face, the refusal to ask for help or admit to any weakness. She had adopted some of those same strategies to survive the misery and loneliness of her own childhood. As she watched, she became even more convinced that the idea she'd been mulling over since yesterday was a good one.

"Crayton is small," she said carefully. "I always thought I'd be happier at a bigger school with a more diverse mix of students. Maybe you would, too. Maybe you'd like to go someplace coed."

Molly's head shot up. "Go to school with boys?"

"I don't see why not."

"I can't imagine what it would be like to have boys in the classroom. Wouldn't they be rowdy?"

Phoebe laughed. "I never went to school with them either, so I have no idea. Probably." Molly was exhibiting the first display of animation she had seen, and Phoebe continued cautiously. "There are some fine public schools in this area."

"A public school?" she scoffed. "The quality of education is so inferior."

"Not necessarily. Besides, anybody with your

IQ could probably educate herself, so what difference would it make?" She gazed at her sister with compassion and said softly, "It seems to me that making some friends and enjoying being a teenager is more important right now than jump-starting calculus."

Molly's protective shell clamped shut. "I have dozens of friends. *Dozens* of them. And I happen to enjoy mathematics. I would never subject myself to an inferior education just to go to school with some silly, adolescent boys, who, I'm certain, wouldn't be nearly as mature as all my boyfriends in Connecticut."

Phoebe had to hand it to her. She was willing to brazen it out right to the end.

Molly's small lip curled. "You wouldn't understand since you're not gifted."

"I hate to disillusion you, Mol, but my IQ isn't anything to sniff at, either."

"I don't believe you."

"Pull out your notepaper then. Let's solve some integrals together."

Molly swallowed hard. "I — I haven't got that far yet."

Phoebe concealed her relief. She hadn't done that kind of math for years, and she didn't remember a thing. "Don't judge a book by its cover, Mol. For example, if people judged you only by appearances they might decide you were unfriendly and a little bit snobbish. Both of us know that's not so, don't we?" She wanted to make Molly think, not to antagonize her, and she tried to take some of the sting out of her words with a smile. It didn't work.

"I'm not a snob! I'm a perfectly nice person with dozens of friends, and —" She gasped.

Phoebe followed the direction of her stricken gaze and saw Pooh pulling a bedraggled stuffed monkey from under Molly's bed. She quickly disengaged the animal from the poodle's mouth. "It's all right. Pooh didn't hurt your toy. See."

Molly's face was scarlet. "I don't ever want that dog in my bedroom again! Never! And it's not mine. I don't play with toys. I don't know how it got there. It's stupid! Throw it away!"

Phoebe had always been a sucker for lost souls, and her sister's rejection of the obviously well-loved stuffed monkey touched her in a way nothing else could have. At that moment, nothing could have made her send this confused, frightened young girl away.

She casually tossed the stuffed animal to the foot of the bed. "I've decided I'm not sending you back to Crayton. I'm going to keep you here in a public school for the fall semester."

"What! You can't do that!"

"I'm your guardian, and I certainly can." Scooping up Pooh, she walked to the door. "We move into the condo next week. If school doesn't work out, you can go back to Crayton for second semester."

"Why are you doing this? Why are you being so hateful?"

She knew the child would never believe the

131

truth, so she shrugged. "Misery loves company? I have to stay here. Why shouldn't you?"

It wasn't until she reached the bottom of the staircase that the full implications of what she'd done hit her. She was already buried under problems she didn't know how to solve, and she had just added another one. When was she going to learn not to be so impulsive?

Trying to escape her troubled thoughts, she made her way to the French doors at the rear of the house and stepped outside. The night was quiet and fragrant with the scent of pine and roses. The floodlights on the back of the house illuminated the fringe of deeper woods at the edge of the yard, including the old maple tree that had been her refuge when she was a child. She found herself heading there. When she reached the tree, she saw that its bottom branches were too high to reach. Leaning back against the trunk, she stared toward the house.

Despite the peacefulness of the night, she couldn't shake off her worries. She didn't know anything about raising a teenager. How was she supposed to overcome Molly's hostility? She slipped her fingertips into the pockets of her slacks. Her problems with her sister weren't all that was bothering her. She missed Viktor and her friends. She felt like a freak when she walked in the door of the Stars complex. And she spent far too much time thinking about Dan Calebow. Why did he have to be so adamant in his refusal to let her rehire Ron?

She sighed. It was more than his attitude toward Ron that kept him in her thoughts. She was much too aware of him. Sometimes when he was nearby, she experienced an emotion that was very close to panic. Her heartbeat accelerated, her pulses quickened, and she had the unsettling sensation that her body was coming awake after a very long hibernation. It was a ridiculous notion. She knew too well that she was permanently damaged when it came to men.

Even though the night was warm, she removed her hands from her pockets and rubbed her arms against a sudden chill. Memories flooded her, and as the night sounds enveloped her, she could feel herself being drawn back to those early months in Paris.

When she'd arrived, she'd located a friend from Crayton and had moved into her tiny, third floor flat in Montparnasse, not far from the gaudy, bustling intersection where the Boulevard du Montparnasse meets the Boulevard Raspail. For weeks, she had seldom left her bed. Instead, she stared at the ceiling while she gradually convinced herself that she had somehow been responsible for her own rape. No one had forced her to dance with Craig. No one had forced her to laugh at his jokes and flirt with him. She had done everything she could to make him like her.

Slowly she grew to believe that what had happened was her own fault. Her roommate, alarmed at her withdrawal, begged her to get out, and eventually it became easier to go along than to resist.

She began spending her evenings drinking cheap wine and smoking pot with the ragtag band of students who frequented the sidewalks and brasseries of Montparnasse. Her misery had destroyed her appetite, and the last of her baby fat melted away, slimming her legs and emphasizing the hollows beneath her cheekbones. But her breasts remained as full as ever, and despite her shapeless clothing, the boys noticed. Their attentiveness deepened her self-hatred. They knew what kind of girl she was. That's why they wouldn't leave her alone.

Without quite knowing how it happened, she punished herself by sleeping with one of them, a young German soldier who had come to Paris to train with UNESCO. Then she let a bearded Swedish art student into her bed, and after him, a long-haired photographer from Liverpool. Lying motionless beneath them, she let them do what they wanted because she knew in her heart that she deserved nothing better. More than their sweating bodies and invasive hands, she hated herself.

Only gradually did she come to her senses. Appalled at what she had allowed to happen, she grew desperate to find a way to protect herself. Men were her enemies. To forget that was to put herself in peril.

She began to observe the pretty young French women who spent their evenings strolling the Boulevard du Montparnasse. She sat in the brasseries and watched them tilt their faces toward their lovers, luring them with bold, knowing eyes. She saw the confident way they walked in their tight blue jeans with hips swaying and breasts thrust forward. One night as she observed a sultry-faced young beauty part her lips so her smitten lover could tip the sweet meat of a mussel shell between them, it all became clear to her. These young French women used sex to control men, and the men were helpless to defend themselves.

That was when she began her own transformation.

By the time Arturo Flores found her working in an art supply store near the Madeleine, her baggy, figure-concealing clothes had given way to tight French jeans and tiny, clingy camisoles that displayed her breasts. Platinum streaks drew men's gazes to the silky long hair that curled over her shoulders. With bold eyes, she issued her sultry, silent assessment of each one of them.

You can look, chère, *but you're not quite man enough to touch.*

The sense of relief she experienced as they flirted with her, only to tuck their tails between their legs when she rejected them, left her dizzy with relief. She had finally found a way to keep herself safe.

Arturo Flores wasn't like the rest. He was much older, a gentle, brilliant, and lonely man who only wanted her friendship. When he asked if he could paint her, she agreed without hesitation, never dreaming that she would find seven years respite with him.

Arturo was part of a close-knit circle of wealthy and prominent European men who were secretly homosexual, and his carefully selected friends became her friends. They were witty, cultured, frequently waspish, generally kind, and the demands they placed on her were not physical. They wanted her attention, her sympathy, and her affection. In exchange, they taught her about art and music, history and politics. She received a finer education from Arturo's friends than her old boarding school classmates were receiving at college.

But they couldn't make her forget. Her trauma was too deeply rooted to be easily conquered, and so she continued to punish the heterosexual men she met with small cruelties: an enticing smile, provocative clothing, a wicked flirtatiousness. She learned she could control all of them by letting her body make promises she would never allow it to keep.

So sorry, Monsieur, Herr, Señor, *but you're not quite man enough to touch.*

As she walked away from all of them, her hips swayed in the rhythm of the French girls who ruled the Boulevard du Montparnasse.

Hot cha cha
Hot cha cha
Hot hot
Cha cha cha cha

She was twenty-six before she'd permitted another man to touch her, the young doctor who attended Arturo during his illness. He was handsome and kind, and his physician's hands had been soothing with their caresses. She had enjoyed the closeness, but when he had tried to deepen the intimacy, she had frozen. He remained patient, but each time his hands slipped beneath her clothing, she was assaulted with memories of the night in the metal pool shed, memories of the young men she had allowed to heave over her. The physician was too much of a gentleman to tell her she wasn't enough of a woman for him, and he disappeared from her life. She forced herself to accept the fact that she was irreparably damaged when it came to sex and resolved not to let herself grow bitter. After the heartbreak of Arturo's death, she found other outlets for her softer emotions.

In Manhattan, she surrounded herself with gentle, gay men, some of whom she held in her arms when they died. These men were the ones who received the love and affection she possessed in so much abundance. These were the men who took the place of lovers who would only have reminded her she was less than a woman.

"Hello, cuz."

She gave a strangled gasp and spun around to see Reed Chandler standing in a pool of light at the edge of the lawn, barely ten feet away.

"Still hiding in the bushes, Flea Belly?"

"What are you doing here?"

"Just paying my respects."

She was no longer a defenseless child, and she

fought against the fear he still inspired in her. During the funeral she had been too numb to note the changes in his appearance, but now she saw that, although his features had matured, he looked much the same as he had during his college days. She imagined that women were still attracted to his gangster's good looks: the thick, blue-black hair, olive skin, and strong, stocky body. But the full lips that his various girlfriends had found so sensuous had always seemed merely greedy to her. That avaricious mouth reminded her of how much Reed had always wanted from life, and how much of what he wanted belonged to her.

She noted that he dressed more like a banker now than a gangster. His blue-and-white-striped oxford shirt and navy trousers looked custom-made, and as he lit a cigarette, she saw the flash of an expensive watch on his wrist. She remembered her father telling her that Reed worked for a commercial real estate firm. At first she had been surprised that he hadn't gone to work for the Stars, but then she had realized that Reed was far too wily to give Bert that much control over his life.

"How did you find me out here?"

"I could always find you, Flea Belly. Even in the dark, that blond hair of yours is hard to miss."

"I wish you wouldn't call me that."

He smiled. "I always thought it was cute, but if you don't like it, I promise, I'll mend my ways. Can I call you Phoebe, or do you want me to address you more formally?"

His teasing was gentle and she relaxed a bit. "Phoebe's fine."

He smiled and held his cigarette pack out to her. She shook her head. "You should give that up."

"I have. Many times." As he inhaled, she was again conscious of those full, greedy lips.

"So how are you getting along? Is everyone treating you well?"

"They're polite."

"If anyone gives you a hard time, let me know."

"I'm sure everything will be fine." She had never been less sure, but she wasn't going to admit that.

"Having Carl Pogue quit was unfortunate. If Bert had realized there was any possibility of that happening, I know he wouldn't have done this. Have you hired a new GM yet?"

"Not yet."

"Don't wait too long. McDermitt is too inexperienced for the job. It would probably be a good idea to let Steve Kovak make the final decision. Or I'd be happy to help."

"I'll keep that in mind." Her voice stayed carefully noncommittal.

"Bert liked manipulating people. He didn't make this easy on either one of us, did he?"

"No, he didn't."

He shoved one hand in his pocket and then withdrew it, looking uneasy. Silence stretched between them. He shifted his weight, took a long drag on his cigarette, and blew the smoke out in a thin, harsh stream. "Listen, Phoebe, I've got something

I need to tell you."

"Oh?"

"I should have talked to you about it a long time ago, but I've been avoiding it."

She waited.

He looked away from her. "A couple of years after we graduated, Craig Jenkins and I were at a party."

Every muscle in her body grew tense. The night suddenly seemed very dark and the house far away.

"Craig got drunk and told me what really happened that night. He told me he'd raped you."

A small exclamation slipped through her lips. Instead of feeling vindicated, she felt raw and exposed. She didn't want to talk about this with anyone, but especially not with Reed.

He cleared his throat. "I'm sorry; I'd always thought you were lying. I went to Bert right away, but he didn't want to talk about it. I guess I should have pressed harder, but you know how he was."

She couldn't bring herself to speak. Was he telling the truth? She had no idea whether he was sincere or simply trying to win her trust so he could influence her decisions while she owned the Stars. She didn't want to believe that her father had learned the truth but never acknowledged it. All the old feelings of pain and betrayal engulfed her.

"I feel as if I need to make this up to you somehow, and I want you to know that I'm here for you. As far as I'm concerned, I owe you a debt. If there's anything I can do to make your time here easier — any help I can give you — promise me you'll let me know."

"Thank you, Reed. I'll do that." Her words sounded stiff and unnatural. She was strung so tightly that she felt as if she would fly apart if she didn't get away from him. Despite his display of concern, she could never trust him.

"I think I'd better go in now. I don't want to leave Molly alone for too long."

"Of course."

They walked in tense silence to the house. When they reached the edge of the lawn, he stopped and gazed at her. "As far as I'm concerned, we're in this together, cuz. I mean it. Truly."

Leaning down, he brushed his greedy lips across her cheek and walked away.

8

A vein bulged at Dan's temples as he screamed. "Fenster! On thirty-two scat left, the tailback goes *left!* Otherwise we would have called it thirty-two scat freakin' *right!*" He slammed the clipboard to the ground.

Someone came up beside him, but he was watching the tailback so intently that several minutes passed before he looked over. When he turned, he didn't instantly recognize the man, and he was about to tell him to get the hell off his practice field before he realized who it was.

"Ronald?"

"Coach."

The kid didn't look like himself; he looked like a South American gigolo. His hair was slicked back, and he wore dark glasses along with a black T-shirt, baggy slacks, and one of those boxy European sport coats with the collar turned up and the sleeves pushed to his elbows.

"Jesus, Ronald, what'd you do to yourself?"

"I'm unemployed. I don't have to dress like a stiff anymore."

Dan spotted a cigarette in the kid's hand. "Since when do you smoke?"

"On and off. I just never thought it was a good idea to do it around the men." He stuck the cig-

142

arette in the corner of his mouth and gestured toward the field with his head. "You're going with the new tailback sweep."

"If Fenster can learn his left from his right."

"Bucker looks good."

Dan was still distracted by the changes in Ronald, not only the difference in his appearance, but his unusual composure. "He's coming along."

"So did Phoebe pick the new GM yet?" Ronald asked.

"Hell, no."

"That's what I figured."

Dan made a snort of disgust. Phoebe'd had a list of candidates since the day she'd arrived more than a week ago, but instead of making a choice, she'd told him she wanted Ronald back. He'd reminded her they had an agreement and told her she'd damn well better live up to it or she could find herself another head coach. When she realized he meant it, she'd stopped arguing. But they had lost their final preseason game last weekend, and with their season opener against the Broncos this Sunday, she still hadn't interviewed a single candidate.

Instead of working, she sat at the desk in Ronald's old office and read fashion magazines. She wouldn't use Bert's office because she said she didn't like the decor. When anybody gave her even the simplest form to sign, the bridge of her nose would pucker and she'd say she'd get to it later, but she never did. Monday, when he'd barged in on her because she'd somehow managed

143

to hold up everybody's paychecks, she'd been painting her goddamn fingernails! He'd gotten mad then, but he'd barely begun to yell before her lip had started to tremble and she'd said he couldn't talk to her like that because she had PMS.

Sometime this week Phoebe had shot right past Valerie in her ability to make him crazy. NFL team owners were supposed to inspire a combination of respect, awe, and fear in their employees. Even seasoned head coaches tread warily around a man like Al Davis, the strong-willed owner of the Raiders. Dan knew he would never be able to hold his head up again if anybody ever found out that the owner of his team couldn't stand any yelling because she had PMS!

She was, without a doubt, the most worthless, spineless, silliest excuse for a human being he'd ever met in his life. At first he'd wondered if she might not be smarter than she let on, but now he knew she was *dumber* than she'd let on, a world-class bimbo who was ruining his football team.

If only she didn't have that drop-dead body. It was hard to ignore, even for someone like him, who'd seen just about everything a woman had to offer before he'd turned twenty-one. He knew the public thought life was one big orgy for professional football players, and they were pretty much right. Even now, when sex was fraught with danger, women lined up in hotel lobbies and stadium parking lots calling out to the players, flashing phone numbers written on their bare midriffs, sometimes flashing more.

He remembered his early playing days, when he'd picked up one, sometimes even two of them, and indulged in long, lost nights of Cutty and sex. He'd done things the rest of the male population had only dreamed about, but as the novelty had worn off, he'd begun to find something pathetic about those encounters. By the time he'd reached thirty, he'd replaced the football groupies with women who had more going for them than a hot body, and sex had once again been fun. Then he'd met Valerie and begun his current downward spiral. But that spiral was about to shift direction now that Sharon Anderson was in his life.

On Tuesday afternoon he'd managed to stop by the nursery school again to watch her with the kids and take her out for coffee after they'd left. She had some stains on her clothes that made him want to hug her: grape juice, paste, a streak of playground dirt. She was quiet and sweet, exactly what he wanted in a woman, which made his physical response to Phoebe Somerville even more aggravating. That female belonged in leather boots and a garter belt, as far away as possible from a bunch of innocent children.

Ronald propped his foot up on the bench and stared out at the practice field. "Phoebe keeps asking me to tell her who the best candidate for the GM job is."

Dan gave him a sharp gaze. "You've seen her?"

"We — uh — spend a lot of time together."

"Why?"

Ronald shrugged. "She trusts me."

Dan never gave anything away, and he concealed his uneasiness. Was Phoebe responsible for the changes in Ronald? "I guess I didn't realize that the two of you were friends."

"Not exactly friends." Ronald took a drag on his cigarette. "Women are funny about me. I guess Phoebe's no exception."

"What do you mean funny?"

"It's the Cruise thing. Most men don't notice, but women think I look like Tom Cruise."

Dan gave a snort of disgust. First Bobby Tom decided he looked like a movie star and now Ronald. But then, as he studied Ron more closely, he couldn't deny there was a vague resemblance.

"Yeah, I guess you do at that. I never noticed."

"It makes women feel as if they can trust me. Among other things." He took a deep drag on his cigarette. "It plays hell with your love life, I'll tell you that."

Dan's instincts for danger were as well developed as a battle-hardened soldier's, and the hair on the back of his neck prickled.

"How do you mean?" he said carefully.

"Women can be quite demanding."

"I suppose I never thought of you as that much of a hound with the ladies."

"I do all right." He threw down his cigarette and ground it out beneath his shoe. "I've got to go. Good luck with Phoebe. She's a real wildcat, and you're going to have your work cut out for you."

Dan had heard enough. Lashing out his arm, he caught Ronald by the shoulder, nearly knocking him off his feet. "Cut out the cute stuff. What the hell's going on?"

"What do you mean?"

"You and Phoebe."

"She's an unusual lady."

"What have you told her about the candidates for the GM job?"

Despite the grip Dan had on him, Ronald's gaze was steady and disconcertingly confident. "I'll tell you what I haven't told her. I haven't told her Andy Carruthers is the best man for the job."

"You know he is."

"Not if he can't handle Phoebe."

Dan slowly released him, and his voice was dangerously quiet. "Exactly what are you trying to say?"

"I'm saying I've got your butt in a sling, Dan, because right now the only person she trusts who knows a damned thing about football is me. And I got fired."

"You deserved to be fired! You weren't doing your job."

"I got her to sign those contracts the first day, didn't I? From what I hear, nobody else has been able to do that much."

"You had time after Bert died to prove yourself, and you blew it. Nothing got done."

"I didn't have the authority to act because Phoebe wasn't returning my phone calls." He lit a fresh cigarette and had the nerve to smile. "But

I'll guarantee she returns them now."

Dan's temper ignited, and he grabbed a fistful of Ronald's fancy European lapels. "You son of a bitch. You're sleeping with her, aren't you?"

He had to give the kid credit. His complexion went a little pale, but he held his ground. "That's none of your business."

"No more games. What are you after?"

"You're not stupid, Dan. Figure it out for yourself."

"You're not getting your job back."

"Then you're in big trouble because Phoebe won't do anything unless I tell her to."

Dan clenched his teeth. "I ought to beat the shit out of you."

Ronald swallowed hard. "I don't think she'd like that. She's crazy about my face."

Dan thought furiously, but he could only come to one conclusion. Ronald had him pinned behind the line of scrimmage and nobody was open. It went against his grain to fall on the ball, but he didn't seem to have a choice. Gradually, he let go of the kid's shirt. "All right, you've got your job back for now. But you'd better control her or I'll have your ass hanging inside out from the yard markers. Do you understand me?"

Ronald flicked his cigarette away and then lifted the collar of his sport coat with his thumbs. "I'll think about it."

Dumbfounded, Dan watched him walk away.

By the time Ronald reached his car, he had sweated right through his jacket. *Dan!* He'd called the coach *Dan* and he was still alive. *Oh, God. Oh, Lord.*

Between the cigarettes and a rapid heartbeat, he'd begun to hyperventilate. At the same time, he'd never felt better in his life. Settling into the driver's seat, he grabbed the phone. After he fumbled with the buttons for a few moments, Phoebe came on the line.

He gasped for breath and pushed the videotape of *Risky Business* she had given him out from beneath his hip.

"We did it, Phoebe."

"You're kidding!" He could envision her wide, generous smile.

"I did exactly what you said." He gasped. "And it worked. Except now I think I'm having a heart attack."

"Take some deep breaths; I don't want to lose you now." She laughed. "I can't believe it."

"Neither can I." He was beginning to feel better. "Let me change my clothes and wash this grease out of my hair. Then I'll be in."

"It won't be a minute too soon. We've got a ton of work here, and I don't have the faintest idea what to do with any of it." There was a short pause. "Uh-oh. I've got to go. I hear an ominous set of footsteps coming my way."

Quickly hanging up, she grabbed her makeup mirror with a shaking hand and lifted her pinky to her eyebrow just as Dan exploded into her office. She caught a glimpse of her secretary's startled face behind him before he slammed the door.

Her office window faced the practice fields, so she should have been used to his aggression by now. She'd seen him throw clipboards and charge onto the field when he didn't like someone's performance. She'd watched him hurl his unprotected body at a player in full equipment to demonstrate some mysterious football move. And once, when she'd been in the office late and all the players had left, she'd watched him do laps around the track wearing a sweat-stained T-shirt and a pair of gray athletic shorts that had revealed a set of powerfully muscled legs.

Swallowing hard, she gazed up at him innocently. "Oh, my. The big bad wolf just blew my door down. What did I do now?"

"You win."

"Goody. What's the prize?"

"Ronald." He grit his teeth. "I've decided I won't stand in your way if you want to hire him back."

"That's wonderful."

"Not from my viewpoint."

"Ron isn't quite the incompetent you seem to think he is."

"He's a weenie."

"Well, you're a hot dog, so the two of you should get along just fine."

He scowled, and then he let his eyes roam all over her with an insolence he had never before displayed. "Ronald sure figured out how to get what he wanted from you. But maybe there's something you should know. Smart businesswomen don't sleep with the men who work for them."

Even though she hadn't done anything wrong, the jab hurt, and she had to force herself to give him a silky smile. "Jealous I chose him instead of you?"

"Nope. I'm just afraid you'll move on to my players next."

She clenched her fists, but before she could respond he had stalked from her office.

Ray Hardesty stood in the shadows of the pines outside the cyclone fence and watched Dan Calebow stride back onto the practice field. Ray had to be at work soon, but he made no move to leave. Instead, he coughed and lit another cigarette, disturbing the butts already on the ground as he shifted his feet. Some of them were fresh, but others had disintegrated in last week's thunderstorms, leaving behind only the swollen, yellowed filters.

Every day he told himself he wasn't going to come here again, but he came back all the same. And every day when his wife asked him where he was going, he said True Value. He never came home with any hardware, but she kept on asking. It had gotten so he could barely stand the sight of her.

Ray rubbed the back of his hand over his stubbly jaw and wasn't surprised when he felt nothing. The morning the police had come to the house to notify him that Ray Junior had died in a car

151

crash, he'd stopped being able to tell the difference between hot and cold. His wife said it was temporary, but Ray knew it wasn't, the same way he knew he'd never be able to watch his son play football for the Stars again. Ever since that morning, his senses had been confused. He'd watch television for hours only to realize he'd never turned up the volume. He'd pour salt into his coffee instead of sugar and not notice the taste until his mug was nearly empty.

Nothing was right any more. He'd been a big shot when Ray Junior was playing for the Stars. The guys he worked with, his neighbors, the boys at the bar, everybody had treated him with respect. Now they looked at him with pity. Now he was nothing, and it was all Calebow's fault. If Ray Junior hadn't been so upset about getting cut by the Stars, he wouldn't have driven through that guardrail. Because of Calebow, Ray Senior couldn't hold his head up any longer.

For months Ray Junior had been telling him how Calebow had it in for him, accusing him of drinking too much and being some kind of goddamn druggie just because he took a few steroids like everybody else in the NFL. Maybe Ray Junior had been a little wild, but that's what had made him a great player. He sure as hell hadn't been any goddamn druggie. Hale Brewster, the Stars' former coach, had never complained. It was only when Brewster had been fired and Calebow had taken over that the trouble started.

Everybody had always commented on how much

he and his son looked alike. Ray Junior'd also had a misshapen prizefighter's face, with a big nose, small eyes, and bushy brows. But his son hadn't lived long enough to get thick around the waist, and there hadn't been any gray in his hair when they'd buried him.

Ray Senior's life had been filled with disappointments. He thought about how he wanted to be a cop, but when he'd applied, it seemed like they wouldn't take anybody but niggers. He'd wanted to marry a beautiful woman, but he'd ended up with Ellen instead. At first even Ray Junior had been a disappointment. But his old man had toughened him up, and by the kid's senior year in high school, Ray had felt like a king as he sat in the stands and watched his boy play ball.

Now he was a nobody again.

He began to cough and it took him almost a minute to get the spasms under control. The doctors had told him a year ago to stop smoking because of his bad heart and the trouble with his lungs. They hadn't come right out and told him he was dying, but he knew it anyway, and he didn't much care anymore. All he cared about was getting even with Dan Calebow.

Ray Senior relished every Stars' loss because it proved the team wasn't worth shit without his kid. He had made up his mind that he was going to stay alive until the day everybody knew what a mistake that bastard had made by cutting Ray Junior. He was going to stay alive until the day Calebow had to eat the dirt of what he had done.

The smell of scotch and expensive cigars enveloped Phoebe as she entered the owner's skybox the following Sunday. She was doing what she had sworn she wouldn't — attend a football game — but Ron had convinced her that the owner of the Stars couldn't miss the opening game of the regular season.

The hexagonal Midwest Sports Dome had actually been constructed in an abandoned gravel quarry that sat at the center of a hundred acres of land just north of the Tollway. When the Stars weren't playing, the distinctive glass and steel dome was home to everything from religious crusades to tractor pulls. It had banquet facilities, an elegant restaurant, and seats for eighty-five thousand people.

"This is an expensive piece of real estate," Phoebe murmured to Ron as she took in the owner's skybox with its two television sets and front wall of windows looking down on the field. She had learned that skyboxes in the Midwest Sports Dome were leased for eighty thousand dollars a year.

"Skyboxes are one of the few profit items we have in that miserable stadium contract Bert signed," Ron said as he closed the door behind them. "This is actually two units turned into one."

She gazed through the cigar smoke at the luxurious gold and blue decor: thick pile carpeting, comfortable lounge chairs, a well-stocked mahogany bar. There were nine or ten men present, either cronies of her father's or owners of the fifteen percent of the Stars that Bert had sold several years ago when he'd needed to raise money.

"Ron, do you notice anything out of place here?"

"What do you mean?"

"Me. I'm the only woman. Don't any of these men have wives?"

"Bert didn't allow women in the owner's box during games." Mischievous lights twinkled in his eyes. "Too much chatter."

"You're kidding."

"The wives have box seats outside. It's not an unknown practice in the NFL."

"The boys' club."

"Exactly."

An overweight man she vaguely remembered having met at her father's funeral came toward her, his eyes bulging slightly as he stared at her. She was wearing what Simone called her "car-wash" dress because the clingy pink sheath was slit into wide ribbons from a point well above her knee to the mid-calf hem. With every step she took, her legs played peek-a-boo with the hot pink ribbons, while the sleeveless scoop-necked bodice clung to her breasts. The man held a cut glass tumbler filled to the brim with liquor, and his effusive greeting made her suspect it wasn't his first.

"I hope you're going to bring us good luck, little lady." He ogled her breasts. "We had a rough season last year, and a few of us aren't sure Calebow's the right man for the job. He was a great quarterback, but that doesn't mean he can coach. Why don't you use that pretty face of yours to get him to open up the offense more? With a receiver like Bobby Tom, you've got to throw deep. And he needs to start Bryzski instead of Reynolds. You tell him that, hear?"

The man was insufferable, and she lowered her voice until it was husky. "I'll whisper it right across his pillow this very night."

Ronald quickly drew her away from the startled man before she could do any more damage and introduced her to the others. Most of them had suggestions for adjustments they wanted Dan to make in his starting lineup and plays they wanted him to add. She wondered if all men secretly aspired to be football coaches.

She flirted with them until she could ease away, and then walked over to the windows to gaze down into the stadium. The kickoff was less than ten minutes away, and there were far too many empty seats, despite the fact that the Stars were playing their opening game against the popular Denver Broncos. No wonder the team was having so many financial problems. If something didn't change soon, those layoffs Dan had mentioned were going to become a reality.

The men in the skybox watched her legs while she watched a television commentator explain why the Broncos were going to beat the Stars. Ron appeared at her side. He shifted nervously from one foot to another, and she remembered that he'd seemed jumpy ever since he'd picked her up. "Is something wrong?"

"Would you mind very much coming with me?"

"Of course not." She picked up her small purse and followed him out of the skybox into the hallway. "Has something happened I should know about?"

"Not exactly. It's just . . ." He steered her toward one of the private elevators and pushed the button. "Phoebe, this is funny really." The doors slid open, and he drew her inside. "You've probably heard that athletes are notoriously superstitious. Some of them insist on wearing the same pair of socks all season or putting on their equipment in exactly the same order. A lot of them have developed elaborate pregame rituals over the years — which doors they use, how they approach the stadium. They tuck good luck charms in their uniforms. Silly stuff, really, but it gives them confidence, so there's no harm."

She regarded him suspiciously as the elevator began its descent. "What does this have to do with me?"

"Not you, exactly. Well, Bert, really. And certain members of the team." He glanced nervously at his watch. "It involves the Bears, too. And Mike McCaskey."

McCaskey was the grandson of George Halas, the legendary founder of the Chicago Bears. He was also the Bears' controversial president and CEO. But, unlike herself, McCaskey knew something about running a football team, so Phoebe didn't see the connection.

The doors slid open. As she and Ron stepped

out, she saw sunlight, despite the fact that she knew they were beneath the stadium. She realized they were in a hallway that ended in a large tunnel leading to the field. Ron turned her toward it.

"Ron, you're starting to make me very nervous."

He withdrew a white handkerchief from his breast pocket and pressed it to his forehead. "Mike McCaskey spends the first quarter of every Bears' game standing on the field by the bench. He doesn't interfere with the game, but he's always there, and it's become a ritual." He returned the handkerchief to his pocket. "Bert didn't like the fact that McCaskey was on the field while he was up in the Stars' skybox, so a few years back he started doing the same thing, and it's — uh — become part of the routine. The players have gotten superstitious about it."

A distinct uneasiness was creeping through her. "Ron —"

"You have to stand on the field with the team for the first quarter," he said in a rush.

"I can't do that! I don't even want to be in the skybox, let alone out on the field!"

"You have to. The men expect it. Jim Biederot is your starting quarterback, and he's one of the most superstitious athletes I've ever met. Quarterbacks are like tenors; they're easily upset. And Bobby Tom was quite vocal about it before the game. He doesn't want his karma disrupted."

"I don't care about his karma!"

"Then how about your $8 million?"

"I'm not going out there."

"If you don't, you're ducking your responsibilities and you're not the person I thought you were."

This last came out in a rush, and it gave her pause. But the idea of standing on the field filled her with a fear she didn't want to face. She searched her mind for a plausible excuse other than panic.

"My clothes aren't right."

His eyes shone with admiration as he studied her. "You look beautiful."

Her knee and a good portion of her thigh poked through the hot pink ribbons as she lifted one foot to show Ron a strappy sandal with a three-inch heel. "Mike McCaskey wouldn't go on the field dressed like this! Besides, I'll sink."

"It's Astroturf; Phoebe, you're grasping at straws. Frankly, I expect better of you."

"Some part of you is actually enjoying this, isn't it?"

"I must admit that when I saw you in that dress, it occurred to me that your appearance might spark ticket sales. Perhaps you could wave to the crowd."

Phoebe uttered a word she hardly ever used.

He regarded her with gentle reprimand. "Let me remind you of our initial partnership agreement. I was to supply the knowledge and you were to supply the guts. Right now, you're not holding up your end of the deal."

"I don't want to go out on the field!" she exclaimed in desperation.

159

"I understand that. Unfortunately, you have to." Gently clasping her arm at the elbow, he began steering her up the slight incline that led to the end of the tunnel.

She tried to hide her panic behind sarcasm. "Two weeks ago you were a nice guy with no leadership qualities."

"I'm still a nice guy." He led her out of the mouth of the tunnel into the blazing sunlight. "You're helping me develop my leadership qualities."

He escorted her down the concrete walkway, through the fence, and onto the field, guiding her behind the milling players to a spot just beyond the end of the bench. She knew she was perspiring, and a swell of anger toward her father swept through her. This team was his toy, not hers. As she gazed at the players, their bodies padded to superhuman size, she was so frightened she felt light-headed.

The sun streaming through the glass hexagon at the center of the dome shone on her hot pink dress and some of the people in the crowd called out her name. It surprised her that they knew who she was until she remembered that the story of Bert's will had become public. She'd already turned down dozens of requests for interviews with everyone from the local papers to NBC. She forced herself to fix a bright smile on her face, hoping no one would notice how unsteady it was.

She realized Ron was getting ready to leave her, and she grabbed his arm. "Don't go!"

"I have to. The players think I'm bad luck." He thrust something into her hand. "I'll be waiting for you in the skybox when the quarter's over. You'll do fine. And, uh — Bert always slapped Bobby Tom's butt."

Before she could absorb that unwelcome piece of information, he rushed off the field, leaving her alone with dozens of grunting, sweating, battle-hardened men, who were hell-bent on inflicting mayhem. She opened her fist and stared down at her hand in bewilderment. Why had Ron given her a pack of Wrigley's spearmint gum?

Dan appeared at her side, and she had to fight down a crazy desire to throw herself in his arms and ask him to protect her. The desire faded as he speared her with unfriendly eyes.

"Don't move from this spot till the end of the quarter. Got it?"

She could only nod.

"And don't screw up. I mean it, Phoebe. You have responsibilities, and you'd better carry out every single one of them. You and I might think the players' superstitions are ridiculous, but they don't." Without any further explanation, he stalked away from her.

The encounter had only lasted for a few seconds, but she felt as if she'd been broadsided by a bulldozer. Before she could recover, one of the men came charging toward her dangling his helmet by the face guard. Although she had kept herself away from the players, she recognized Bobby Tom Denton from his photograph: blond hair, broad cheek-

161

bones, wide mouth. He looked tense and edgy.

"Miz Somerville, we haven't met, but — I need you to slap my butt."

"You — uh — must be Bobby Tom." A very *rich* Bobby Tom.

"Yes, ma'am."

She absolutely could not do this. Maybe some women were born to be butt-slappers, but she wasn't one of them. Quickly lifting her hand, she kissed her fingertips and pressed them to his lips. "How about a new tradition, Bobby Tom?"

She waited with apprehension to see if she'd done something irreversible to his karma and, in the process, blown $8 million. He began to frown and the next thing she knew, hot pink ribbons whipped her legs as he snatched her up off the ground and planted a resounding smack on her lips.

He grinned and set her back down. "That's an even better tradition."

Hundreds of people in the crowd had caught the exchange and as he trotted away, she heard laughter. Dan had also observed the kiss, but he definitely wasn't laughing.

Another monster headed toward her. As he approached, he barked an order to someone behind him and she saw the name "Biederot" on the back of his sky blue jersey. This must be her temperamental quarterback.

When he finally came to a stop next to her, she took in his blue-black hair, meat-hook nose, and small, almost feminine mouth. "Miss Somerville, you gotta — Your father —" He stared at a point just beyond her left ear and lowered his voice. "Before every game, he always said, 'Eat shit, you big bozo.' "

Her heart sank. "Could I — Could I just slap your butt instead?"

He shook his head, his expression fierce.

She ducked and said the words as fast as she could.

The quarterback gave an audible sign of relief. "Thanks, Miss Somerville." He jogged away.

The Stars had won the coin toss, and both teams lined up for the kickoff. To her dismay, Dan began running toward her sideways while he kept his eyes firmly fixed on the field. He was tethered by the long cord on his headset, but it didn't seem to hinder his movements. He drew to a stop beside her, his eyes still glued to the field. "Do you have the gum?"

"The gum?"

"The gum!"

She suddenly remembered the Wrigley's Ron had thrust into her hand and unclenched her fingers, which were rigidly clasped around it. "It's right here."

"Pass it over when the kicker tees the ball. Use your right hand. Behind your back. You got it? Now don't screw up. Right hand. Behind your back. When the kicker tees the ball."

She stared at him. "Which one's the kicker?"

He began to look mildly crazed. "The little guy in the middle of the field! Don't you know anything? You're going to screw this up, aren't you?"

"I'm not going to screw it up!" Her eyes flew to the field as she frantically tried to identify the kicker. She picked the smallest of the players and hoped she was right. When he leaned over to position the ball, she shot her right hand behind her back and slapped the gum into Dan's open palm. He grunted, shoved it in his pocket, and rushed off without so much as a thank you. She reminded herself that only minutes earlier, he'd referred to the players' superstitions as ridiculous.

Seconds later, the ball arced into the air and pandemonium broke out before her. Nothing could have prepared her for the gruesome sounds of twenty-two male bodies in full battle gear trying to kill each other. Helmets cracked, shoulder pads slammed together, and the air was filled with curses, growls, and groans.

She pressed her hands to her ears and cried out as a platoon of uniformed men rushed toward her. She was frozen to the spot while the Stars' player carrying the ball charged toward her. She opened her mouth to scream, but no sound came out. The crowd went wild as he raced toward the sidelines pursued by a pack of white-and-orange-clad monsters from hell. She saw that he couldn't stop — he was going to run right over her — but she couldn't save herself because her knees had locked. At the last moment he swerved and charged into his teammates on the sidelines.

Her heart was in her throat, and she thought she was going to faint. Fumbling with the catch of her tiny shoulder bag, she groped inside for her rhinestone sunglasses, nearly dropping them as she clumsily slipped them on for protection.

The first quarter ticked by with agonizing slowness. She could smell the players sweat, see their sometimes dazed, sometimes crazed expressions, hear their shouted obscenities, one profanity after another until repetition had stripped even the filthiest of words of any meaning. At some point, she realized she was no longer standing there because she had been told to, but as a test of strength, her own private badge of courage. Maybe if she handled this challenge, she could begin to handle the rest of her life.

Never had seconds felt more like minutes, minutes more like hours. Through the corner of her eye, she watched the Star Girl cheerleaders in their sleazy gold costumes with blue spangles and applauded whenever they did. She dutifully clapped as Bobby Tom caught one pass after another against what she would later hear described as a strong Broncos' defense. And more frequently than she liked, she found her eyes straying to Dan Calebow.

He paced the sidelines, his dark blond hair glazed by the bright sunlight streaming through the center of the dome. His biceps stretched the short sleeves of his knit shirt and veins throbbed in his muscular neck as he shouted out instructions. He was never still. He paced, raged, bellowed, punched the air with his fist. When a call late in the quarter angered him, he yanked off his headset and began to charge the field. Three of his players leapt from the bench and physically restrained him, their response so well orchestrated she had the feeling they'd done it before. Even though this team was legally hers for the next few months, she knew that it belonged to him. He terrified her and fascinated her. She would have given anything to be that fearless.

The whistle finally blew, signaling the end of the quarter. To everyone's surprise, the Chicago Stars were tied with the Broncos, 7–7.

Bobby Tom dashed over to her, his expression so jubilant that she couldn't help smiling back. "I hope you're gonna be where I can get to you when we play the Chargers next week, Miz Somerville. You're bringin' me luck."

"I think your talent is bringing you luck."

Dan's voice rang out, his tone fierce. "Denton, get over here! We've got three more quarters to play, or have you forgotten that?"

Bobby Tom winked and trotted away.

9

Phoebe stood in the flickering shadows of the torches that had been placed at intervals around the pool at the Somerville estate and watched as five giggling women surrounded Bobby Tom Denton. None of the Stars' management or staff had regarded Bert's death or the fact that Phoebe would soon be moving out of the house as an excuse to cancel the party he had hosted each year after the season opener. While Phoebe had been at the game, her secretary had supervised the caterers setting up for the event. Phoebe had replaced her carwash dress with a slightly less conspicuous apricot knit tank dress.

The team's loss that afternoon to the Broncos had cast a pall over the early hours of the gathering, but as the liquor had begun to flow more freely, the mood had grown livelier. It was nearly midnight now, and the platters of steaks, ham, and lobster tails had been demolished. Phoebe had been introduced to all the players, their wives, and girlfriends as they arrived. The players were scrupulously polite to their new owner, but being around so many athletes had brought back too many bad memories, so she had removed herself to a wooden bench set by a clump of japonica bushes well off to the side of the pool.

She heard a familiar voice and felt a queer jolt as she looked toward the patio and saw Dan. Ron had told her that Sunday night was one of the busiest times for the coaches as they graded the players on their performances that afternoon and worked on the game plan for next week. Even so, she had found herself looking for him all evening.

She watched from the shadows as he moved from one group to another. Gradually, she realized he was drawing closer. She saw that he was wearing a pair of wire-rimmed glasses, and the contrast between those studious glasses and his rugged good looks did strange things to her insides.

She crossed her legs as he came up to her. "I've never seen you in glasses."

"My contacts bother me after about fourteen hours." He took a sip from the can of beer in his hand and propped his foot on the bench next to her.

This man really was a Tennessee Williams wet dream, she thought, as a film strip slowly unwound in her head. She could see him in the shabby library of a decaying plantation house, his white shirt damp with sweat from a lusty encounter with young Elizabeth in the brass bed upstairs. He had a cheroot clamped between his teeth as he thumbed impatiently through an old diary trying to discover where his great-grandmother had buried the family silver.

Her body felt warm and languid, and she had to suppress the urge to rub against him like a cat.

The burst of loud laughter that came from the pool pulled her back to reality. She looked over in time to see five of Bobby Tom's women shove him into the water fully dressed. When he didn't immediately come up for air, she gritted her teeth. "I'm forcing myself not to run over and pull him out."

Dan chuckled and took his foot down from the bench. "Relax. You have even more money invested in Jim Biederot than in Bobby Tom, and Jim's just lassoed one of the chimneys so he can climb the side of the house."

"I'm definitely not cut out for this job."

Bobby Tom rose to the surface, blowing water, and pulled two of the women in with him. She was glad Molly's bedroom looked out on the side of the house instead of the back.

"Tully told me Jim climbs the house every year," Dan said. "Apparently, the party wouldn't be the same without it."

"Couldn't he just put a lamp shade on his head like everybody else?"

"He prides himself on originality."

A burly defensive lineman lay down on the concrete at the side of the pool and began to bench press a shrieking young woman. Dan pointed his beer can toward them. "Now there's where your real trouble's gonna start."

She stood so she could get a better view and then wished she hadn't. "I hope he doesn't hurt her."

"That wouldn't matter so much as the fact

she's not his wife."

At that moment a tiny fireball with a shining mane of Diana Ross hair charged from the rear of the patio toward Webster Greer, a 294-pound All-Pro defensive tackle.

Dan chuckled. "Watch and learn, Phoebe."

The spitfire screeched to a stop on a pair of stiletto heels. "Webster Greer, you put that girl down right this minute or your ass is gonna be grass!"

"Aw, honey —" He dropped the redhead onto a chaise lounge.

"Don't you 'honey' me," the spitfire shrieked. "You want to find yourself sleeping in that bowling alley you built for yourself in our basement, that's just fine with me, 'cause you sure as hell won't be sleeping with me."

"Aw, honey —"

"And don't you come crying on my shoulder after I haul your ass to divorce court and take you for every penny you got."

"Krystal, honey, I was just foolin' around."

"Foolin' around! I'll show you foolin' around!" Drawing back her arm, she punched the tackle in the stomach with all her might.

He frowned. "Now, honey, why'd you have to go and do that? Last time you hit me, you hurt your hand."

Sure enough, Krystal was cradling her hand, but that didn't stop her sassy mouth. "Don't you worry about my hand. You worry about your ass! And whether or not I'm ever gonna let you see your kids again!"

"Come on, honey. Let's go put some ice on it."

"Go put some ice on your *dick!*"

With a dramatic flip of her hair, she stalked away from him and headed directly toward Phoebe and Dan. Phoebe wasn't certain she wanted a confrontation with this pint-sized termagant, but Dan didn't look all that unhappy about it.

As the woman came to a stop in front of him, he wrapped her injured hand around his beer can. "It's still cold, Krys. Maybe it'll keep the swelling down."

"Thanks."

"You've got to stop hitting him, honey. One of these days you're going to break your hand."

"He's got to stop making me mad," she retorted.

"That female's probably been after him all night. You know Webster's the last man on the team who'd fool around with another woman."

"That's 'cause I understand how to keep him in line."

Her tone was so smug that Phoebe couldn't hold back a bubble of laughter. Instead of being offended, Krystal smiled back at her.

"Don't ever let a man know he's got the upper hand if you want a happy marriage."

"I'll remember that."

Dan shook his head, then turned to Phoebe. "The scary thing is, Webster and Krystal have one of the best marriages on the team."

"I guess I'd better go settle him down before he picks a fight with somebody." Krystal rolled

171

the beer can in her injured hand. "Mind if I take this along as an ice pack?"

"Help yourself."

She smiled at Phoebe and then rose on tiptoe to plant a kiss on the corner of Dan's jaw. "Thanks, pal. Stop by the house sometime and I'll fry you up a hamburger."

"I'll do that."

As Krystal returned to her husband, Dan lowered himself to the bench. Phoebe sat next to him, keeping as much space between them as she could manage.

"Have you known Krystal for long?"

"Webster and I were teammates right before I retired, and all of us got to be pretty good friends. Neither of them liked much about my ex-wife except her politics, and Krystal used to show up at my door with milk and cookies when I was going through my divorce. We haven't been able to see a lot of each other socially since I joined the Stars."

"Why is that?"

"I'm Webster's coach now."

"Does that make a difference?"

"Rosters have to be cut, players traded. There has to be some distance."

"A strange way to conduct friendships."

"That's just the way it is. Everybody understands."

Although the others were in sight, the bench was tucked far enough into the shadows of the japonica bushes that she had begun to feel as if they were alone, and she was so aware of him that

172

her skin prickled. She welcomed the distraction of a female squeal, and, looking through a break in the hedges, saw a woman whip off the top of her bikini. The accompanying hoots and squeals were so loud she hoped they didn't awaken Molly and frighten her.

"The party's getting a little wild."

"Not really. Everybody's on their good behavior because the chaperons are here."

"What chaperons?"

"You and me. The boys aren't going to let their hair down with the owner and head coach hanging around, especially since we lost today. I remember a few parties during my playing days that lasted right through till Tuesday."

"You sound nostalgic."

"I had some fun."

"Getting tossed in swimming pools and judging wet T-shirt contests?"

"Don't tell me you've got something against wet T-shirt contests. That's the closest most football players ever come to a cultural event."

She laughed. But then her laughter faded as she saw the way he was looking at her. Through the lenses of his glasses, his sea-green eyes were enigmatic, yet something seemed to crackle between them, an electricity that shouldn't have been there. She was thrilled, frightened. Dipping her head, she took a quick sip of wine.

He spoke softly. "For somebody who flirts with everything in pants, you sure are nervous with me."

"I am not!"

"You're a liar, darlin'. I make you nervous as hell."

Despite the wine, her mouth felt dry. She forced her lips into a fox's smile. "Only in your dreams, lover." Leaning close enough to inhale his after-shave, she said huskily, "I devour men like you for breakfast and still eat a five-course lunch."

He gave a snort of laughter. "Damn, Phoebe, I wish we liked each other better, 'cause if we did, we could have ourselves a real good time."

She smiled, then tried to say something sexy and flippant only to discover that she couldn't think of a thing. In her mind the springs on the brass bed had begun to creak, only this time she was lying on it instead of young Elizabeth. She was the one in the lacy slip with the strap falling off her shoulder. She imagined herself watching him as he stood beneath the paddle wheel fan with his shirt unbuttoned.

"Damn." The curse was soft, hoarsely uttered, not part of the dream but slipping through the lips of the real man.

As he gazed into her eyes, her body felt as if it were shedding years of musty cobwebs to become moist and dewy. The sensation was so strange, she wanted to run from it, but at the same time, she wanted to stay here forever. She was overwhelmed by the temptation to lean forward and touch his lips with her own. And why not? He thought she was a champion man-killer. He didn't have any way of knowing how out of character such a gesture from her would be. Just this once, why didn't she take a chance?

"There you are, Phoebe."

Both their heads snapped around as Ron emerged through a break in the hedges. She took a quick, unsteady breath.

Since Ron had been rehired, he and Dan had kept their distance, and so far there had been no explosions. She hoped that wasn't about to change.

Ron nodded at Dan, then spoke to Phoebe. "I'm going to head home soon. The cleanup will be taken care of."

Dan glanced at his watch and stood. "I've got to go, too. Did Paul show up with those films for me yet?"

"I haven't seen him."

"Damn. He's got videotape I wanted to take a look at before I went to bed."

Ron smiled at Phoebe. "Dan's notorious for surviving on four hours of sleep a night. He's a real workhorse."

Phoebe's encounter with Dan had shaken her because she felt as if she'd exposed too much of herself. Standing, she ran her fingers through her hair. "It's nice to know I'm getting my money's worth."

"Do you want me to have him bring the tape over to your house as soon as he gets here?" Ron asked.

"No. Don't bother. But tell him to have it on my desk by seven tomorrow morning. I want to take a look at it before I meet with my staff." He turned to Phoebe. "I need to make a call. Is there a phone inside I can use?"

His manner was so businesslike that she wondered if she had imagined the crazy, charged
moment that had passed between them such a short
time ago. She didn't want him to know how he
had unsettled her, so she spoke flippantly. "Don't
you have one in that beat-up heap you drive?"

"There are two places I don't believe in keeping
phones. One's my car, and the other's my bedroom."

He'd won that round, and she tried to recover
with a lazy gesture toward a door on the far side
of the house. "The one in the family room is the
nearest."

"Thanks, baby cakes."

As he walked away, Ron frowned at her. "You
shouldn't let him address you so disrespectfully.
A team owner —"

"Exactly how am I supposed to make him stop?"
she retorted, turning her frustration onto Ron.
"And I don't want to hear about what Al Davis
would do or Eddie De— whatever."

"Edward DeBartolo, Jr.," he said patiently.
"The owner of the San Francisco 49ers."

"Isn't he the one who gives his players and their
wives all those lavish presents?"

"He's the one. Trips to Hawaii. Big, juicy Nie-
man Marcus gift certificates."

"I hate his guts."

He patted her arm. "It'll all work out, Phoebe.
See you in the morning."

As he left her alone, she stared toward the house

in the direction Dan had disappeared. Of all the men who had passed through her life, why did it have to be this one who attracted her? How ironic that she found herself so profoundly drawn to what she feared the most: a physically powerful man in superb condition. A man, she reminded herself, made all the more dangerous by his sharp mind and quirky sense of humor.

If only he hadn't left so soon. Ever since she had arrived in Chicago, she had felt as if she had been transported to an exotic land where she didn't know the language or understand the customs, and her encounter with him tonight had only intensified the sensation. She was confused but also filled with a strange sense of anticipation, a sense that — if only he'd stayed — something magical might have happened.

Molly drew up her knees and tucked them under her long blue cotton nightgown. She sat curled in the window seat of the cavernous family room looking out through the glass at what she could see of the party. Peg, the housekeeper, had sent her to bed an hour ago, but the noise had kept her from sleeping. She was also worried about Wednesday, when she would start public high school and all the kids would hate her.

Something cold and wet brushed against her bare leg. "Hello, Pooh." As Molly reached down to stroke the dog's soft topknot, Pooh reared up and placed her front paws on the teenager's thigh.

Molly lifted the dog into her lap and bent her

head to croon soft baby talk to her. "You're a good girl, aren't you, Pooh. A good, sweet doggy girl. Do you love Molly? Molly loves you, doggy girl."

Dark strands of her hair mingled with Pooh's white fur. As Molly laid her cheek on the powder-puff softness of her topknot, Pooh licked her chin. It had been a long time since anyone had kissed her, and she kept her face where it was so Pooh could do it again.

The door to her right opened. A large man entered, and she quickly set Pooh down. The room was dimly lit, and he didn't see Molly as he walked over to the telephone that sat on a table next to the sofa. Before he could dial, however, Pooh bounced over to greet him.

"Damn. Down, dawg!"

To avoid any social awkwardness, Molly politely cleared her throat and stood. "She won't bite you."

The man replaced the receiver and looked over at her. She saw that he had a nice smile.

"Are you sure about that? She seems pretty fierce to me."

"Her name is Pooh."

"As a matter of fact, she and I've already met, but I don't think the two of us have been introduced." He came toward her. "I'm Dan Calebow."

"How do you do. I'm Molly Somerville." She extended her hand, and he shook it solemnly.

"Hello, Miz Molly. You must be Phoebe's sister."

"I'm Phoebe's half sister," she stressed. "We

178

had different mothers, and we're not at all alike."

"I can see that. You're up kind of late, aren't you?"

"I couldn't sleep."

"It's pretty noisy. Did you get to meet the players and their families?"

"Phoebe wouldn't let me." She wasn't certain why she felt compelled to lie, but she didn't want to tell him she was the one who had refused to go outside.

"Why not?"

"She's very strict. Besides, I'm not fond of parties. Actually, I'm a solitary person. I'm planning to be a writer when I grow up."

"Is that so?"

"I'm currently reading Dostoyevski."

"You don't say."

She was running out of conversation, and she cast about for another topic to hold his attention. "I can't imagine they'll study Dostoyevski at my new school. I start there on Wednesday. It's a public school, you know. Boys go there."

"Haven't you ever gone to school with boys?"

"No."

"A pretty girl like you should get along just fine."

"Thank you, but I know I'm not really pretty. Not like Phoebe."

"Of course you're not pretty like Phoebe. You're pretty in your own way. That's the best thing about women. Each one has her own way about her."

He'd called her a woman! She tucked that thrilling compliment away to be savored when she was alone. "Thank you for being so nice, but I know my limitations."

"I'm pretty much an expert on the subject of females, Miz Molly. You should listen to me."

She wanted to believe him, but she couldn't. "Are you a football player, Mr. Calebow?"

"I used to be, but I'm the head coach of the Stars now."

"I'm afraid I don't know anything about football."

"That seems to run on the female side of your family." He crossed his arms. "Didn't your sister bring you to the game this afternoon?"

"No."

"That's a shame. She should have."

She thought she detected disapproval in his voice, and it occurred to her that he might not like Phoebe either. She decided to test the waters. "My half sister doesn't want to bother with me. She got stuck with me, you see, because both my parents are dead. But she doesn't really want me." That, at least, was true. She had his complete attention now, and since she didn't want to lose it, she began to fabricate. "She won't let me go back to my old school and she hides the letters I get from all my girlfriends."

"Why would she do something like that?"

Molly's active imagination took over. "A streak of cruelty, perhaps. Some people are born with it, you know. She never lets me leave the house,

180

and if she doesn't like what I've done, she feeds me bread and water." Inspiration struck. "And sometimes she slaps me."

"*What?*"

She was afraid she had gone too far, so she quickly added, "It doesn't hurt."

"It's hard to imagine your sister doing something like that."

She didn't like to hear him defending Phoebe. "You're a potent man, so her physical appearance has affected your judgment."

He made a funny choking sound. "Do you want to explain that?"

Her conscience told her not to say anything more, but he was being so nice and she wanted so much for him to like her that she couldn't help herself. "She acts differently around men than she does around me. She's like Rebecca, the first Mrs. de Winter. Men adore her, but she's quite vindictive underneath." Once again she thought she might have gone too far, so she tempered her statement. "Not that she's entirely evil, of course. Just mildly twisted."

He rubbed his chin. "I'll tell you what, Molly. The Stars are part of your family heritage, and you need to know something about the team. How about I ask Phoebe to bring you to practice some day after school next week? You can meet the players and learn a little bit about the game."

"You'd do that?"

"Sure."

The rush of gratitude she felt toward him

blocked out her guilt. "Thank you. I'd like that very much."

At that moment Peg stuck her head in the door and scolded Molly for not being in bed. She said good-bye to Dan and returned to her room. After Peg left, she retrieved Mr. Brown from his hiding place and snuggled beneath the covers with him, even though she was much too old to be sleeping with a stuffed animal.

Just as she was drifting off to sleep, she heard a soft scratching at her door and smiled into her pillow. She couldn't open the door because she didn't want Phoebe to discover that she'd let Pooh into her bedroom. But, still, it was nice to be wanted.

10

As Phoebe looked down at the videotape that lay on the passenger seat next to her, she knew that showing up unannounced at Dan Calebow's house was the stupidest thing she'd ever done. But instead of turning Bert's Cadillac around and going back home, she peered through the glare of the headlights toward the side of the road trying to find the wooden mailbox that Krystal Greer had told her to watch for. As she looked, she rehearsed what she would say when she got there.

She would be very casual, tell Dan that Paul had shown up with the videotape not long after he'd left the party. She'd known Dan wanted to see the tape before he went to bed, and she'd decided to deliver it since it was such a beautiful night for a drive. No trouble, really.

She frowned. It was one o'clock in the morning, so maybe she shouldn't say anything about it being a beautiful night for a drive. Maybe she'd simply say she hadn't been sleepy and had felt like taking a drive to relax.

The truth was, she wanted to see him again before she lost her nerve. She had been deeply shaken by that moment when she'd felt such an overpowering urge to kiss him. Now she needed to see him alone, where they wouldn't be interrupted, to try to discover what those feelings meant.

She could come up with a million reasons she shouldn't be attracted to him, but none of those reasons explained the way he had made her feel tonight, as if her body were slowly coming alive. The sensation was both terrifying and exhilarating. He hadn't made any secret of the fact that he disliked her, but at the same time, she sensed he was attracted to her.

Without warning, she felt tears gathering in her eyes. For years she hadn't even let herself dream that something like this could happen. Was she being a fool or was there a chance she might be ready to reclaim her womanhood?

Her headlights picked up the wooden mailbox, and she blinked her eyes. There was no name on it, but the number was right, and she braked as she turned into the narrow, graveled country lane. The night was cloudy, with barely enough moonlight to reveal an old orchard. She drove across a small wooden bridge and around a gentle curve before she saw the lights.

The rambling stone farmhouse wasn't anything like the sleek bachelor's pad she had imagined. Built of wood and stone, it had three chimneys and a wing off to one side. Steps led up to an old-fashioned front porch that was surrounded by a spindled railing. In the welcoming light that glowed through the front windows, she saw that the shutters and front door were painted a pearly gray.

Her tires crunched in the gravel as she pulled

up to the house and turned off the ignition. Abruptly, the exterior lights went out followed by the interior ones. She hesitated. She must have caught him just as he was going to bed. Still, he wasn't asleep yet.

Snatching the videotape up from the seat before she lost her nerve, she opened the car door and stepped out. An owl hooted in the distance, an eerie sound that made her even more uneasy. As she walked cautiously toward the front porch, she wished it weren't so dark.

Resting her hand on the railing, she gingerly climbed the four stone steps. In the thick darkness the chirp of the crickets sounded ominous instead of friendly, like creaking hinges in a haunted house. She couldn't find a doorbell, only a heavy iron knocker. She lifted it, then flinched as it hit with a dull thud.

Seconds ticked by, but no one answered. Growing increasingly nervous, she rapped again, then wished she hadn't because she knew she had made a terrible mistake. This was embarrassing. There was no way she could explain her presence. What had she been thinking of? She was going to slip away and —

She gasped as a hand clamped over her mouth. Before she could react, a powerful arm grabbed her around the waist from behind. All the blood drained from her head and her legs buckled as she found herself pinioned.

A menacing voice whispered in her ear. "I'm taking you into the woods."

She was paralyzed with fear. She tried to scream but she couldn't make a sound. It was just like the night when she was eighteen. Her feet left the ground, and he carried her down the steps as if she weighed nothing. Blackness and panic suffocated her. He dragged her toward the trees with his mouth pressed against her ear.

"Fight me," he whispered. "Fight hard, even though you know it won't do you any good."

The sound of that familiar accent penetrated her panic, and she realized it was Dan holding her captive! Her mind reeled. It was happening again! She had been attracted to him, flirted with him, and now he was going to rape her! Her paralysis unlocked. She couldn't let this happen to her a second time.

She began a desperate struggle for her freedom, kicking and trying to jab him with her elbows, but he was strong, so much stronger than she, with iron-hard muscles that had been shaped by years of physical conditioning. He hauled her into the woods as if she weighed no more than a child. She tried to scream, but the pressure of his hand on her mouth was merciless.

"That's good. You're putting up a good fight, sweetheart. You're making me work for it."

She bucked in his arms and tried to scream beneath his palm, but he held her fast. She could dimly make out a round wooden structure ahead, and as he dragged her closer, she saw that it was a gazebo.

"I'm going to give it to you good," he whispered.

186

"Just the way you like it. Give you that hurt you want so bad." He hauled her up the steps through an arched opening in the ivy-covered latticed walls. He wasn't even breathing hard.

"You're going to be helpless. I can do anything to you I want and you won't be able to stop me."

He dragged her into the darkness, and terror clawed at her the same way it had in that hot, dark pool shed so long ago. Keeping one hand clamped over her mouth, he shoved the other under her skirt and reached for the waistband of her panties.

"First I'm gonna rip these off."

The awful sounds coming from deep in her throat were garbled from the pressure of his palm. She hadn't wanted this. Please, God, don't let this happen to her again. Once again, she heard that horrible whisper at her ear.

"Maybe I should start here instead. Is that what you want me to do?"

He released her mouth and grabbed the bodice of her dress in his fist. With one hard jerk, he ripped.

Two things happened simultaneously. A violent scream erupted from her lips. And the hand cupping her breast froze.

"Val?"

He groped her breast. His entire body stiffened. And then he jumped away from her as if she were radioactive.

She began to sob. The amber glow from a yellow bug light mounted on a post suddenly flooded the interior of the small gazebo, illuminating outdoor furniture, a sisal rug, and the fact that he was staring at her in horror.

"Phoebe! Jesus . . . Jesus, Phoebe, I'm sorry, I — I didn't know it was you. I — Val was supposed to . . ."

Her teeth were chattering and her whole body had begun to shake. Where he had ripped her dress, the bodice gaped, revealing one of her breasts. She clawed at the material, while she backed away, tears running down her cheeks.

"Phoebe . . ." He rushed toward her.

She leapt back, frantically clutching her torn dress. "Don't touch me!" she sobbed.

He froze and backed away, holding up his hands. "I'm not going to hurt you. I can explain. It's all a mistake. I didn't know it was you. I — I thought you were my ex-wife. She was meeting me here."

"Is that supposed to make it better?" Her teeth wouldn't stop chattering, and her chest spasmed as she tried to swallow her sobs.

He took another step, and once again she backed away. He immediately stopped moving. "You don't understand."

"You bastard! You perverted bastard!"

"Dan!"

Phoebe froze as she heard the sound of a woman's voice.

"Dan! Where are you?"

Relief washed through her as she realized they were no longer alone. Then she saw the expression of entreaty in his eyes and watched as he pressed one finger to his lips, commanding her silence.

"Here!" she shouted. "In here!"

He dipped his head. "Shit."

"Dan?" A slim, attractive woman wearing a simple floral cotton dress stepped into the gazebo. "I heard a —"

She broke off as she saw Phoebe. Her gaze flew to Dan. "What's going on?"

"What we have here," he said unhappily, "is a case of mistaken identity."

The woman took in Phoebe's torn dress and mussed hair. Her eyes widened in consternation. "Oh, God."

As Phoebe's terror began to ease, she realized something was happening here that she didn't understand.

"It was dark," he told the woman, "and I thought she was you."

The woman pressed her fingertips to one temple. "Is she discreet?"

"Discreet, hell! She's scared to death! Can't you see what I've done to her?"

The woman's voice grew so cool and businesslike that Phoebe immediately hated her. "Who is she?"

"Phoebe Somerville," he replied, apparently realizing that Phoebe was in no condition to answer for herself.

"The Stars' owner?"

"One and the same." He turned back to Phoebe and, speaking softly, said, "This is Valerie Calebow, Phoebe. My ex-wife. She's also a mem-

189

ber of the United States Congress, but, despite that, you can trust her. Valerie is going to explain to you that I wasn't trying to hurt you, and she's going to tell you exactly what you walked into."

Valerie's forehead puckered in dismay. "Dan, I can hardly —"

"Do it!" he snapped, his expression murderous. "She's not in any state to listen to me right now."

She picked her words carefully, her expression stiff. "Miss Somerville, although Dan I are divorced, we have chosen to continue an intimate relationship. We are both rather adventurous lovers, and —"

"Speak for yourself, Val. I'd have been happy with a double bed and some Johnny Mathis tapes."

"Are you blaming me for what happened?"

"No," he sighed. "It was my fault. You both have light hair, and you're about the same height. It was dark."

"Dan and I had made arrangements to meet here tonight. I had an official function to attend so I was a bit late. Unfortunately, Miss Somerville, he mistook you for me."

Slowly, Phoebe began to comprehend what had happened, but she could only stare at the woman in bewilderment. "Are you telling me that you wanted him to treat you like that?"

Valerie refused to meet her eyes. "I'm afraid I have to go. I'm sorry you received such a fright. I only hope you understand how delicate this matter is. As an elected official, it would be extremely awkward for me if anyone were to find out."

"For chrissake, Val —"

She spun on him. "Shut up, Dan. This could put an end to my career. I want her assurance that she won't tell anyone."

"Who would I tell?" Phoebe said helplessly. "No one would believe me anyway."

"I'm sorry." Valerie gave her an awkward nod and quickly left the gazebo.

Phoebe didn't want to be alone with him. She was immediately conscious of his oppressive physical size, the muscles straining the too-tight sleeves of his knit shirt. Holding the front of her dress together, she began to move toward the vine-draped opening in the gazebo's latticework.

"Please sit down," he said quietly. "I promise I won't come near you, but we have to talk."

"It's all a game to the two of you, isn't it?" she whispered. "That's how you get your kicks."

"Yes."

"It wasn't a game to me."

"I know. I'm sorry."

"How could you do something like that?"

"It's what she likes."

"But why?"

"She's a strong woman. Powerful. Sometimes she gets tired of always being in control."

"She's sick, and so are you!"

"Don't judge, Phoebe. She's not sick, and until tonight, what went on between the two of us had nothing to do with anyone else."

She started to shake again. "You were going to — What if you hadn't stopped?"

"I'd have stopped. The minute I felt your —"
He cleared his throat. "Valerie's a little more flat-chested than you."

Her knees weren't going to hold her any longer, and she collapsed into the nearest chair. He came toward her cautiously, as if he were afraid she would start to scream again.

"What were you doing here?"

She took a shaky breath. "Paul showed up at the party not long after you left. I — I brought you the videotape you wanted." She made a helpless gesture as she realized she'd dropped it.

"But I told Ronald not to send it over tonight."

"I thought — I wasn't sleepy, and — Never mind, it was a stupid idea."

"You can say that again."

"I'm going." By bracing her hands on the arms of the chair, she managed to rise to her feet.

"You need a few minutes to settle down before you try to drive. I'll tell you what. I didn't get anything to eat at the party and I'm hungry. Let me make us some sandwiches. How about it?"

There was a boyish eagerness to please in his expression that alleviated some of her residual fear, but he was too large, too strong, and she hadn't recovered from those moments when the past seemed to be repeating itself. "I'd better be going."

"You're afraid to be alone with me, aren't you?"

"I'm just tired, that's all."

"You're scared."

"I was completely helpless. You're a strong man. You can't imagine what it's like."

"No, I can't. But it's over now. I won't hurt you. You know that, don't you?"

She nodded slowly. She did know it, but it was still hard for her to relax.

He smiled at her. "I know why you want to rush home. You're going to wake up your little sister so you can start slapping her around again."

Mystified, she stared at him. "What are you talking about?"

"Miz Molly and I had an interesting conversation tonight. But I'm not going to tell you about it unless you let me fix you something to eat."

She saw the spark of challenge in his eyes. He was the coach now, testing her mettle, just as he tested his men. She knew he wasn't going to hurt her. If she ran away this time, would she ever stop?

"All right. Just for a bit."

The unfamiliar path was difficult to maneuver in the dark. She stumbled once, but he didn't take her arm to help her, and she wondered if he knew that she would have fallen apart if he had touched her in the dark.

As they walked, he tried to put her at ease by telling her about the farmhouse. "I bought this place last year and had it renovated. There's an orchard and a stable where I can keep a couple of horses if I want. I've got trees on this place that are a hundred years old."

They reached the front porch. He bent down to retrieve the videotape she'd dropped, then opened the front door and flipped on a light before he let her in. She saw a staircase off to the left and an archway to the right that led to the side wing of the house. She followed him through it into a spacious open area that was rustic and welcoming.

The exposed stone on the longest wall glowed buttery in the light of the lamps he turned on. The room encompassed a comfortable two-story living area and a cozy, old-fashioned kitchen with a snug loft tucked above it under the eaves. The scrubbed pine floor held an assortment of furniture including a couch in a hunter green plaid with red and yellow accents, soft, oversized chairs, and an old pine cupboard. A wooden bench bearing decades of nicks and scars from tools served as a coffee table and held an old checkerboard sitting next to a pile of books. Chunky wooden candlesticks, stoneware crocks, and several antique metal banks rested on the mantel above the big stone fireplace. She had expected him to be surrounded by marble statues of naked women, not live in this comfortable rural haven that seemed so much a part of the Illinois prairie.

He handed her a soft blue chambray shirt. "You might want to put this on. There's a bathroom off the kitchen."

She realized she was still clutching the front of her dress. Taking the shirt from him, she excused herself and went into the bathroom. As she gazed at her reflection in the mirror, she saw that her eyes were large and vulnerable, windows into all her secrets. She straightened her hair with her fingers and rubbed at the mascara smudges with a tissue. Only when she felt calm did she leave the bathroom.

The shirt he had given her hung to mid-thigh, and she rolled up the sleeves as she came into the kitchen where he was pulling a loaf of whole wheat bread and a package of sandwich meat from the refrigerator.

"How about roast beef?"

"I'm not much of a beef eater."

"I've got some salami here, or turkey breast."

"Plain cheese would be fine."

"Grilled cheese? I'm real good at that."

He was so eager to please, she couldn't help smiling. "All right."

"Do you want wine or a beer? I've also got some iced tea."

"Iced tea, please." She took a seat at an old butternut drop leaf table.

He poured both of them a glass and then began fixing the sandwiches. A copy of Stephen Hawking's *A Brief History of Time* lay open on the table. She used it as an opportunity to restore some semblance of normality between them. "Pretty heavy reading for a jock."

"If I sound out all the words, it's not too bad."

She smiled.

He tossed the sandwiches into an iron skillet. "It's an interesting book. Gives you a lot to think about: quarks, gravity waves, black holes. I always liked science when I was in school."

"I think I'll wait for the movie." Taking a sip

of iced tea, she pushed the book aside. "Tell me what happened with Molly."

He braced his hip against the edge of the stove. "That kid's a crackerjack. I met her inside when I was making my phone call. She told me some pretty hair-raising things about you."

"Like what?"

"Like the fact that you're keeping her a prisoner in the house. You tear up her mail, put her on bread and water when you're mad at her. And you're slapping her around."

"*What!*" Phoebe nearly knocked over her iced tea.

"She told me it doesn't hurt."

Phoebe was flabbergasted. "Why would she say something like that?"

"She doesn't seem to like you too much."

"I know. She's like a fussy maiden aunt. She disapproves of the way I dress; she doesn't think my jokes are funny. She doesn't even like Pooh."

"That might be good judgment on her part."

She glared at him.

He smiled. "As a matter of fact, your dog was cuddled around her ankles most of the time we talked. They seemed to be old friends."

"I don't think so."

"Well, I might be wrong."

"She honestly told you I slap her?"

"Yes, ma'am. She said you weren't evil, just twisted. I believe she compared you with somebody named Rebecca. The first Mrs. de Winter."

"Rebecca?" Understanding dawned, and she

shook her head. "All that talk about Dostoyevski and the little stinker is reading Daphne du Maurier." For a moment she was thoughtful. "How do you know she wasn't telling you the truth? Adults slap children all the time."

"Phoebe, when you were standing on the sidelines at the game, you looked like you were going to faint whenever anybody took a hard hit. Besides, you just don't have the killer instinct." He turned to flip the sandwiches. "For example — correct me if I'm wrong here — but I'm guessing it's more than a fickle appetite that made you turn down Viktor's barbecue that day we ate in your kitchen, not to mention that good sandwich meat I've got in my refrigerator."

This man definitely saw too much. "All those nitrates aren't healthy."

"Uh-huh. Come on, sweetheart, you can tell Papa Dan your ugly little secret. You're a vegetarian, aren't you."

"Lots of people don't eat meat," she said defensively.

"Yeah, but most of them are on their soapbox about it. You don't say a thing."

"It's nobody's business. I simply happen to like unclogged arteries, that's all."

"Now, Phoebe, you're wiggling around the truth again. I have a feeling your eating habits don't have anything to do with your arteries."

"I don't know what you're talking about."

"Tell me the truth now."

"All right! I like animals. It's not a crime! Even

197

when I was a child I couldn't stand the idea of eating one of them."

"Why are you so secretive about it?"

"I don't mean to be secretive. It's just — I'm not philosophically pure. I won't wear fur, but I have a closet full of leather shoes and belts, and I hate all those hair-splitting discussions people try to push you into. Some of my reticence is habit, I guess. The housemother at my old boarding school used to make it rough on me."

"How was that?"

"We once had a showdown over a pork chop when I was eleven years old. I ended up sitting at the dinner table most of the night."

"Thinking about Piglet, I bet."

"How did you know?"

"It's pretty obvious you're a big A.A. Milne fan, honey." His eyes were warm with amusement. "Go on. What happened?"

"The housemother eventually called Bert. He yelled at me, but I couldn't eat it. After that, the other girls came to my rescue. They took turns sneaking my meat onto their plates."

"That doesn't entirely explain why you're so secretive about it now."

"Most people think vegetarianism is a little kooky, and my kook quotient is high enough as it is."

"I don't think I ever met anybody other than football players who invests so much energy in pretending to be tough."

"I am tough."

"Sure you are."

His grin annoyed her. "Just because I wasn't strong enough to fight you off tonight doesn't mean I'm not tough."

He immediately looked so stricken that she wished she'd held her tongue.

"I'm really sorry about that. I've never hurt a woman in my life. Well, except for Valerie, but that was —"

"I don't want to hear it."

He turned off the heat under the skillet and walked over to the table. "I've explained what happened, and I've apologized every way I know how. Will you accept my honest apology, or is this going to be lurking around every time we're together?"

His eyes were so full of concern she had a nearly uncontrollable urge to slip into his arms and ask him if he would just hold her for a few minutes. "I accept your apology."

"An honest acceptance or one of those female things where a woman tells a man she forgives him for something, but then spends all her spare time thinking up ways to make him feel guilty?"

"Does Valerie do that?"

"Honey, every woman I've been close to has done that."

She tried to slip back into her old role. "Life's tough when you're irresistible to the opposite sex."

"Spoken by someone who knows."

When she attempted to frame a retort, nothing came out, and she realized that she didn't have any resources left to play the part she had staked out for herself. "Those sandwiches must be just about done by now."

He went back to the stove, where he checked the bottoms of the sandwiches with a spatula, then lifted them out of the skillet. After neatly halving them, he returned to the table with two brown pottery plates and sat in one of the captain's chairs.

For several minutes they ate in silence. Finally, he broke it. "Don't you want to talk to me about the game today?"

"Not really."

"Aren't you going to second-guess me on that double reverse? The sportswriters are going to rake me over the coals for that one."

"What's a double reverse?"

He grinned. "I'm beginning to see that there are some definite advantages to working for you."

"You mean because I don't have any secret desire to coach the team myself?"

He nodded and bit into his sandwich.

"I'd never do that. Although I do think you might consider opening up the offense more and starting Bryzski instead of Reynolds."

He stared at her, and she smiled. "Some of Bert's cronies got to me in the skybox."

He smiled back. "The reporters were upset that you didn't show up at the postgame press conference. People are curious about you."

"They'll just have to stay that way. I've seen a few of those postgame interviews. A person would actually have to know something about football to answer the questions."

"You'll have to talk to the press sooner or later. Ronald can help you through it."

She remembered that Dan still thought she and the general manager were personally involved. "I wish you wouldn't be so negative about him. He's doing a good job, and I certainly couldn't function without him."

"Is that so?"

"He's a wonderful person."

He regarded her intently as he picked up a paper napkin and rubbed it over his mouth. "He must be. A woman like you has a lot to choose from."

She shrugged and listlessly picked at her sandwich.

"Damn. You're sitting there looking like a mule that's been kicked one too many times."

"Gee, thanks."

He balled his napkin and tossed it aside. "I can't stand to think that I did this to you. Where are your guts, Phoebe? Where's the woman who maneuvered me into taking Ronald back as GM?"

She stiffened. "I don't know what you're talking about."

"Like hell you don't. You conned me. It took me a couple of days to figure out your neat little scam. You and Ronald set me up. He actually had me convinced the two of you were lovers."

She was relieved to see that he seemed annoyed rather than angry, but she picked her words carefully. "I don't know why that's so hard to believe. He's a very attractive man."

"I'll have to take your word for it. But the fact

is, the two of you aren't lovers."

"How do you know?"

"I just do, that's all. I've seen the way you treat him when you think I'm watching: running your eyes all over him, nibbling on your bottom lip, cooing when you talk."

"Isn't that the way women behave with their lovers?"

"That's just it. You behave the same way with the janitor."

"I do not."

"You behave like that with almost every man you meet."

"So what?"

"Everybody but me."

He watched her push away her uneaten sandwich. "You try to tantalize me with that man-eater body of yours, but you can't pull it off very long, and the next thing I know, you're staring at your feet or foolin' around with your fingernails." He leaned back in his chair. "It hasn't escaped my notice that you stick your chest out for everybody in pants, but lately it seems I can hardly exchange two sentences with you before you're hunching your shoulders. Now, why is that?"

"You have an overactive imagination."

"I don't think so."

She stood. "It's late. I have to go."

He rose, too, and came around the end of the table to touch her for the first time since the incident in the gazebo. He was relieved when she didn't flinch, but his stomach still clenched when he thought about what he'd done to her.

As she stood before him in his old blue shirt, she looked both beautiful and fragile, and he couldn't remember ever meeting a woman so full of contradictions. He didn't want to like her, but it was getting increasingly difficult not to.

He closed his hand over her shoulder. "Are you still afraid of me?"

"Of course not."

She might not be afraid, but she was skittish, and his conscience couldn't tolerate that. Lowering his hand, he began very gently to rub her arm through the soft cotton sleeve. "I think you are. I think you're scared silly I'm going to turn into some kind of deviant and attack you again."

"I'm not."

"Are you sure?"

"Of course I am."

"Prove it."

"How do you suggest I do that?"

He didn't know what devil was prodding him; he only knew his teasing made her smile, and he loved the way her eyes crinkled at the corners when that happened. With a mischievous smile of his own, he pointed to his jaw. "Give me a kiss. Right here. A friendly little smacker like one friend gives to another."

"Don't be ridiculous."

Her eyes were crinkling, and he couldn't resist teasing her a bit more, although it wasn't exactly teasing since he kept thinking about how that incredible body would feel pressed up against his own, which, considering their earlier encounter, wasn't the best reflection on his character.

"Come on. I dare you. We're not talking about one of those unsanitary soul jobs. Just a friendly little peck on the cheek."

"I don't want to kiss you."

He noticed that she'd waited a few seconds too long to protest, and those golden brown eyes of hers were as soft as her lips. He was no longer in the mood to tease, and his voice sounded husky. "Liar. All this heat can't be coming just from me."

He dipped his head, and the next thing he knew, he was nuzzling the side of her neck, finding a soft spot just below her ear. He didn't draw her into his arms, but the tips of her breasts brushed his chest.

He heard her sigh. "We don't like each other."

"We don't have to like each other, honey. This isn't a permanent partnership. It's animal attraction." He kissed that alluring mole at the corner of her eye. "And it feels good. You feel good."

She moaned and leaned against him. He gently cupped her arms, and his kisses moved lower until he found her mouth.

Her lips were soft, neither parted nor sealed, just soft and right. She tasted good, smelled good, like baby powder and flowers. He felt like a randy sixteen-year-old, and as he slid his tongue over the plump curve of her bottom lip, he reminded himself that he'd outgrown her type of woman years ago. Unfortunately, his body seemed to have forgotten that fact.

He deepened the kiss, telling himself that he might be starting to like her, but he didn't respect her, he didn't trust her, and if he couldn't touch those breasts of hers soon, he was going to explode. Except after what had happened in the gazebo, he needed to move slow, but, God, she was driving him crazy.

She pressed against him and made a soft moaning sound that was like a shot of whiskey straight to his veins. He forgot about moving slow. He forgot about everything except this hot little, soft little, eat-me-up baby with the come-to-papa body.

Her lips parted and he plunged inside her warm mouth, but he wanted more. He caught her hard in his arms, felt those cream whip breasts spread against his chest while rockets shot off in his head. And then he had one hand on the sweetest curve of beautiful ass he'd ever touched in his life, and he deepened the thrust of his tongue, but even that wasn't good enough because he wanted to curl it around her nipples and slide it between her legs and lick the sugar right off her. He was hard and crazy and his hands were all over her, his lunacy fed by the throaty moans she was making and the frenzy of her movements against him.

He wanted her to touch him. He wanted her on her knees, on her back, straddled, spread, any way he could get at her, right here where the heat from their bodies would burn up the floorboards and send them plunging straight down to the fiery center of the earth.

He could feel her wildness matching his, her

maniac hands digging into his arms, her hips pushing and thrusting against him, grinding. She was crazy, as crazy as he was, and just as needy. And those sounds, almost like fear, almost like . . .

He went rigid as he realized that she was trying to get away from him, and he was holding her against her will.

"God *damn!*" He pushed himself away, knocking over a chair in his haste.

Her mouth was swollen and bruised from his kisses. Her breasts heaved and her hair was tousled, as if he'd plunged his hands through it, which maybe he had because he sure as hell didn't know what he was doing anymore. As he looked into her stricken eyes, he felt sick. He'd been with a lot of women, and this was the first time he'd ever had any trouble sorting out *no* from *yes*. The accusation in those tilty-up eyes made him feel like a criminal, and that wasn't right because they'd gone into this together.

"I'm not apologizing again, goddammit!" he shouted. "If you didn't want me to kiss you, all you had to do was say no!"

Instead of arguing with him, she lifted her hand in a small, helpless gesture that made him feel like the world's biggest bully. "I'm sorry," she whispered.

"Phoebe . . ."

She grabbed her purse and ran from the kitchen, from his house, from the dangerous heat of two bodies on fire.

11

Phoebe felt muzzy and depressed as she sipped her first cup of morning coffee. Slowly swiveling in her chair, she looked out through her office windows onto the empty practice fields. It was Monday, "Bumps and Bruises Day," when the players picked up the grade they had been given by the coaches for their performance during the game, had physical checkups, and looked at films. They didn't practice again until Wednesday, and she was grateful she wouldn't have to spend the day watching Dan run up and down the sidelines in a T-shirt and shorts, yelling and screaming and throwing clipboards as if he could propel his team to football glory through the sheer force of his will.

Why had she let him kiss her last night when she'd known that she wasn't woman enough to see it through? She couldn't blame him for his anger; both of them knew she had gone into his arms willingly. But when she had heard the hot rasp in his breathing, felt his strength, and known she couldn't control him, she had panicked.

She looked down at the body that made up the lie of who she was. If her outside matched her inside, she would be flat-chested, scrawny, brittle from lack of moisture. What good were curvy hips and full breasts if she couldn't let a man caress them, if they would never bring a baby into the world or nurture its new life?

She didn't want to be this way anymore. She wanted to go back to those moments before her fear had taken over, when Dan's kiss had sent fresh new blood pulsing through her body. She wanted to go back to those moments when she had felt young again and infinitely female.

She heard a knock and the door of her office opened. "Now, Phoebe, don't get upset." Ron crossed the carpet toward her, a stack of newspapers in his hands.

"An ominous beginning."

"Well, as to that . . . I suppose it depends on your outlook." He spread the newspapers in front of her.

"Oh, no."

Color photographs of Phoebe in her hot pink carwash dress and rhinestone sunglasses glittered on the pages of the assorted papers he spread in front of her. In one of the photographs, she had her knuckles pressed to her mouth. In another, her hand was resting on her waist and her breasts were outthrust so that she looked like a World War II pinup. Most of them, however, showed her kissing Bobby Tom Denton.

"That headline is my particular favorite." Ron pointed toward one of the papers.

STARS' OWNER COMPLETES
FORWARD PASS

"Although this one has a certain poetic quality."

BOBBY BUSSES BOMBSHELL BOSS

Phoebe groaned. "They've made me look like a fool."

"That's one way to interpret it. On the other hand —"

"It's good for ticket sales." She no longer had any trouble reading his mind.

He took a seat across from her. "Phoebe, I'm not certain you understand how dismal our financial picture is right now. This sort of publicity is going to fill seats, and we need to do everything possible to generate revenue immediately. With that brutal stadium contract we have —"

"You keep mentioning our stadium contract. Maybe you'd better fill me in."

"I suppose I should start at the beginning." He looked thoughtful. "You're aware that the days of the purely family-owned football team have just about disappeared?"

"How many are left?"

"Only two. The Pittsburgh Steelers, owned by the Rooney family, and the Phoenix Cardinals, owned by the Bidwells. Football has simply gotten too expensive for single-family ownership. Tim Mara sold off his half of the Giants in the late eighties, the McCaskeys got rid of a piece of the Bears, and, of course, Bert sold off fifteen percent of the Stars to some of his cronies."

"Those are the men who keep leaving me the

phone messages I'm not returning?"

"The same. For now, corporate ownership violates league rules, but that's probably where we're eventually headed. How can the Green Bay Packers, for example, which is a publicly owned team, compete with all the land barons, oil and gas men, and automobile fortunes that are pumping money into the Chiefs and the Cowboys, the Lions, the Saints, all the rest?"

He shook his head. "Teams have astronomical expenses and only limited ways of generating revenue: network television contracts, ticket sales, licensing agreements, and, for some of the teams, their stadium contracts. We don't get a penny from any food or liquor sold at the dome. We don't receive a cut from any of the advertising that's displayed, our rent is astronomical, and we have to pay for our own security as well as our cleanup."

"How could Bert allow something like that to happen?"

"He let his heart rule his head, I'm afraid. In the early eighties when the Stars' franchise became available, Bert wanted to buy it so badly that he didn't hang tough enough with the consortium of businessmen behind the sports dome. He also expected eventually to renegotiate the contract by making some threats and showing a little muscle."

"Apparently he thought wrong."

"The consortium that owns the stadium is headed by Jason Keane. He's a tough businessman."

"I've heard of him. He shows up at a lot of Manhattan clubs."

"Don't let his reputation as a playboy fool you. Keane's smart, and he had no intention of losing his sweetheart deal with the Stars. The contract comes up for renewal this December, and so far we've made no progress at all improving the terms."

Resting her elbow on her desk, she plowed one hand through her hair and swept it back from her cheek. The Stars had lost their final three exhibition games as well as their season opener, so there was little possibility of the team's qualifying for the AFC Championship game. All the sportswriters were predicting that the Portland Sabers would make it to the Super Bowl again this year, and she hadn't failed to note that the Sabers had won their opener against the Buffalo Bills 25–10.

The stadium contract was going to be Reed's problem, and there was no reason for her to waste time thinking about it except for an inescapable need to accomplish something her father hadn't been able to do. But how could she expect to remedy a situation Bert couldn't fix when she knew nothing at all about such things?

Reed had called her several times since the night he'd come to visit her. He'd even sent her flowers before the opener. Each time they'd spoken he'd been unfailingly polite, although he wasn't happy about the two-year contract she'd signed with Ron. She knew he was afraid that she was going to destroy the team before he could take it over.

He would never understand that her need to be more than the figurehead her father had envisioned outweighed any desire she might have to get back at him for his childhood bullying.

She gazed at the computer that sat idly on the corner of her desk. "Could you set me up with someone who can teach me how to use this thing?"

"You want to learn how to operate a computer?"

"Why not? I'm willing to try anything that's nonfattening. Besides, it might be fun to use my brain again."

"I'll send someone over." Ron got up to leave. "Phoebe, are you sure you don't want to move into Bert's office? I feel guilty having all that space to myself."

"You need it more than I do."

After Ron left, she looked around at the blue-gray walls, steel case desk, and football artwork. She'd decided she wasn't going to be here long enough to bother personalizing Ron's former office with her own belongings. The utilitarian furnishings provided a marked contrast to the luxurious condo she and Molly were moving into. One of Bert's mistresses had obviously been blessed with good taste in decorating, if not in men.

Peg Kowalski, Bert's former housekeeper, was spending the day supervising the transfer of Phoebe's and Molly's clothing and personal possessions. Peg, who was in her late fifties and tired of managing a large house, had immediately agreed to help out with cleaning, laundry, and grocery shopping as well as staying overnight with Molly if Phoebe needed to be out of town.

Molly had shown little interest in the move. She'd also turned down Phoebe's invitation to a shopping expedition so they could update her hopelessly drab wardrobe before she started school on Wednesday. Phoebe had decided there was no point in confronting Molly with the lies she had told Dan. It would only make a bad situation worse.

She had reports to read, phone calls to return, but, instead, she once again swiveled her chair so she could stare out the window. She had been playing games with men for so long she had no idea how to let one know she was honestly attracted to him. Mixed with her feelings of embarrassment and sadness was regret. If only she had been woman enough to let Dan Calebow make love to her, maybe she could have been healed.

Dan saw that Valerie was regarding him suspiciously as he entered the office she kept in one of Oak Brook's granite and glass commercial buildings. She gestured toward the nubby, rose-colored chairs that sat around the small conference table.

"Do you want coffee?"

"No, thanks."

He sat down, pushing the chair back on its wheels so he could stretch his legs out. As she rose from behind her desk and walked over to him, he took in her conservative navy business suit and white silk blouse buttoned to the neck.

213

Knowing Valerie, she probably had on a G-string underneath.

"I heard you lost again on Sunday," she said, as she sat next to him. "I'm sorry."

"Stuff happens." He'd wanted to do this right, so he'd told her they needed to talk and asked her to meet him downtown for dinner at Gordon, which was her favorite restaurant. When she'd refused and told him to come to her office instead, he'd figured she knew what was on his mind and just wanted to get it over with.

She snatched a pack of cigarettes from the middle of the conference table. "That incident at your house last night was appalling. I hope she keeps her mouth shut."

"She prob'ly will."

Valerie gave a cynical laugh. "My entire life flashed in front of me when I realized what had happened."

"I imagine hers flashed in front of her, too, when I was draggin' her into the woods. Unlike you, she didn't know I wasn't really going to hurt her."

"You did manage to calm her down?"

"We talked some."

She inhaled deeply on the cigarette she had just lit and made her first not-so-delicate probe. "It's going to put a damper on any seduction plans you have for her."

"Believe me, Val, the only plans I have for Phoebe are to stay as far away from her as I can."

He meant it, too. He was furious with himself for letting things go so far with Phoebe. He should never have kissed her, and he promised himself he wouldn't ever get carried away like that again. Finally, he had his priorities straight.

Val regarded him warily. "Then what's this about?"

He knew she wasn't going to like what he had to say, and he spoke softly. "I've met someone."

She was cool, he'd give her that, and if he hadn't known her better, he would have believed she was unaffected by his news. "Anyone I know?"

"No. She's a nursery school teacher." Val wouldn't understand if he told her he hadn't yet asked Sharon out for a formal date, but after last night's incident, he knew he couldn't indulge in any more sex games with his ex-wife, not when he was getting ready to launch a serious courtship.

"How long have you and this nursery school teacher been seeing each other?" She took a quick, angry drag.

"Not long."

"And she, of course, is everything I wasn't." Her mouth tightened as she stabbed out her cigarette in the ashtray.

Valerie had a good-sized ego and she didn't usually give in to petulance, but he understood that he was hurting her. "I'm sure she's not as smart as you, Valerie. Not as sexy, either. But the thing of it is, she's real good with kids."

"I see. She's passed your Mother Goose audition." She gave him a bright, hard smile. "Actually, Dan, I'm glad this came up because I've been wanting to talk to you about the same thing."

215

"What do you mean?"

"Our arrangement isn't working for me."

He feigned surprise. "You want to break it off?"

"I'm sorry, but, yes. I just didn't know how to bring it up without hurting you."

He jumped up from his chair and gave her a little of the outrage he knew she needed to hear. "Who is he? Have you got another man, Val?"

"It was inevitable, Dan. So let's not have any scenes."

He looked down. Shoved his foot around in the carpet pile for a little bit. "Damn, Valerie, you sure know how to cut a man down to size. I don't know why I even try to have the last word with you. Here I came over to break it off with you, and all the time you were getting ready to dump me."

She regarded him suspiciously, trying to see if he was putting her on, but he kept the same sincere expression on his face he'd used in Sunday's postgame interviews when he talked about how well the Broncos had played and how friggin' much they'd deserved to win.

She gave the conference table a brisk thump with her fingertips and stood. "Well, then, I guess there isn't anything more to say."

"I guess not."

As he looked down at her, the good times came back instead of the bad. Most of them had taken place in bed, but he supposed that was more than a lot of divorced couples could say. He wasn't sure who moved first, but the next thing he knew they had their arms around each other.

"Take care of yourself, y'hear?" he said.

"Have a good life," she whispered back.

Twenty minutes later as he pulled into the parking lot at the Sunny Days Nursery School, he was no longer thinking about Valerie. Instead, he was frowning into his rearview mirror. The gray van that had been following him looked like the same one he'd seen behind him a couple of times last week. It had a crumpled right fender. If he had a reporter on his tail, why the cloak-and-dagger stuff? He tried to see the driver as the van passed by the nursery school entrance, but the windows were tinted.

Shrugging off the incident, he parked his Ferrari and walked into the low brick building, smiling as he heard the various noises of the school: squeals of laughter, off-key singing, chairs scraping. He was due in Wheaton in half an hour to speak at a Rotary luncheon, but he couldn't resist stopping off for a few minutes. Maybe it would clear out his confusion over what had happened with Phoebe last night.

The doorway to Sharon's classroom was open, and as he looked inside, his chest swelled. They were baking cookies! Right then, he was ready to drop down on his knees and propose marriage. What he wouldn't have given when he was a kid to have baked cookies with his mother. Unfortunately, she had been too busy getting drunk. Not that he blamed her. Living with a bastard like his father would have driven anyone to drink.

Sharon glanced up from the big mixing bowl and dropped the spoon she had been holding as she spotted him. Her face flooded with color. He smiled as he saw what a mess she was.

Her curly red hair had flour in it, and a streak of blue food coloring decorated her cheek. If he owned *Cosmopolitan* magazine, he'd have put her on the cover, just like that. In his mind, Sharon, with her pixie's face and freckled nose, was a lot more alluring than those big-breasted blondes in sequins and Spandex.

An image of Phoebe Somerville flashed through his mind, but he pushed it away. He wasn't going to let lust interfere with a search for his children's mother.

Sharon fumbled for the wooden spoon she had dropped. "Oh, uh — Hi. Come in."

Her nervousness appealed to him. It was nice being with a woman who wasn't used to being with a man like him. "I just stopped by for a minute to see how my pal Robert was doing with his broken arm."

"Robert, somebody's here to see you."

A cute little black kid in shorts and a T-shirt came rushing over to show off his cast. Dan admired the signatures on it, including his own, which was somewhat the worse for wear.

"Do you know Michael?" the child finally said.

In a town like Chicago, there was no doubt which Michael he meant, not even when the question came from a four-year-old.

"Sure. He lets me play basketball with him at

218

his house sometimes."

"I bet he beats you real bad."

"Naw. He's afraid of me."

"Michael's not afraid of anybody," the child said solemnly.

So much for trying to make jokes about Jordan, even after his retirement. "You're right. He beats me real bad."

Robert led Dan over to the table to admire his cookies, and before long some of the other children had claimed his attention. They were so cute he couldn't get enough of them. Kids tickled him, maybe because he liked a lot of the same things they did: eating cookies, watching cartoons on TV, generally messin' around. Even though he was running late, he couldn't bring himself to leave.

Sharon, in the meantime, had spilled a measuring cup of sugar and just dropped an egg. He grabbed a paper towel to help her clean it up and saw that she was blushing again. He liked that curly red hair of hers and the way it was always flying all over the place.

"I seem to have the dropsies today," she stammered.

"That's one of those words you're not supposed to use around quarterbacks. Even retired ones."

It took her a few seconds to get the point, but then she smiled.

"You've got food coloring on your cheek."

"I'm such a mess." She dipped her head and rubbed her cheek with her shoulder, so that she ended up with food coloring in two places instead of one. "Honestly, I don't look like this all the time."

"Don't apologize. You look great."

"Ethan took my sprinkles," a little girl wailed.

Sharon immediately turned her attention to the child who was tugging on her slacks with messy fingers. This was something else he liked about her. Even when she was talking to an adult, the children were her first priority. He watched with admiration as she negotiated a settlement that would have done a diplomat proud.

"They could use you in the Middle East."

She smiled. "I think I'd better stick to sprinkles."

He glanced down at his watch. "I've got to go. I'm making a speech five minutes ago. My schedule's pretty crazy right now, but when things loosen up, let's go out to dinner. You like Italian?"

She had turned red again. "I — Yes, Italian's fine."

"Good. I'll call you."

"Okay." She seemed vaguely stunned.

Impulsively, he leaned forward and brushed her mouth with a quick kiss. On the way out to the parking lot, he smiled and licked his lips.

Maybe it was his imagination, but he thought he tasted vanilla.

12

Phoebe ran into Bobby Tom Denton in the hotel lobby at eight-thirty on Saturday evening. Although she had just arrived in Portland on a commercial flight from O'Hare, the Stars had been there since noon because NFL rules stated that visiting teams had to be in the city in which they were playing twenty-four hours before kickoff. She knew from an earlier glance at the schedule that the players had been in a meeting until 8:00 P.M. and were now free until their eleven o'clock curfew.

"Hey there, Miz Somerville." Her $8-million man gave her a grin that was nearly as wide as the black Stetson on his head. His stylishly frayed and faded jeans molded to his runner's legs, and his snakeskin cowboy boots had been perfectly broken in so that they were neither too new nor too run-down. Viktor would have been impressed.

Bobby Tom said, "I was worried you might not be here."

"I told you I'd come."

He pushed the brim of his hat back with his thumb. "You're going to be on the sidelines during the first quarter tomorrow, aren't you?"

She nibbled the corner of her lip. "Actually, Bobby Tom, I'm having some second thoughts."

"Hold on, now. I can see you and me need to

221

have a serious conversation." One of his nimble, receiver's hands clasped her arm and gently steered her toward the bar. She could have protested, but she wasn't looking forward to an evening in a strange hotel room without even Pooh to keep her company.

The hotel bar was quiet and dark, and they settled in a small banquette in the corner, where Bobby Tom ordered a beer. "You look like the white wine type," he said. "How 'bout one of those fancy chardonnays."

Phoebe would have loved a chardonnay but she wasn't sure she liked being classified as a "white wine type," so she requested a margarita. The waitress, who'd been gazing at Bobby Tom with hungry eyes, went off to fill their orders.

"Are you allowed to drink the night before a game?"

"We're allowed to do just about anything as long as we give the team all we've got the next day. Drinkin' and curfew are the only two things the coach isn't real strict about. We're supposed to be in our rooms by eleven, but Coach was pretty much a hell-raiser in his playing days, and he knows we all have our own ways of blowin' off steam." Bobby Tom chuckled. "He's sort of a legend."

Phoebe told herself not to ask, but when it came to Dan Calebow, her curiosity seemed to have no bounds. "What do you mean? What kind of legend?"

"Well, some of the stories about him aren't fit

for female ears, but I guess everybody knows how much he hated curfews. See, the coach only needs a couple of hours sleep at night, and when he was playin', he couldn't stand the idea of being cooped up in his room at eleven o'clock. Said it wound him up too tight for the game. So what he mostly did was slide in his room for bed check and then sneak out afterward for some serious partying. The coaches found out about it, of course. They fined him, benched him; none of it did any good, because he'd still be out closing down the bars. Finally, he told them if they didn't like it, they'd could either shoot him or trade him, but he wasn't gonna change. The only bad game he had his entire first season was when they put a guard outside his room. The next day, he threw five interceptions. After that, the coaches stopped bothering him about it. 'Course he settled down a little bit when he got older."

"Not much, I'll bet," she muttered as their drinks arrived.

Bobby Tom lifted his frosty mug. "Here's to whippin' some Saber butt."

"To butt whipping." She touched her glass to his, then licked a small space in the salty rim and took a sip of her margarita.

"Miz Somerville —"

"Phoebe's fine." She took another sip. Later, she would regret the calories, but not now.

"I guess when it's just the two of us first names are okay, but since you're the owner and all, I won't do it when we're in public."

223

"After those pictures in the newspaper, I don't think I have to worry too much about maintaining respectability."

"Weren't they great! Even got my best side." His grin faded. "You weren't serious when you said you wouldn't be on the sidelines tomorrow, were you?"

"I'm not sure it's a good idea. Not unless we can come up with a new good luck ritual."

"Oh, no. We can't do that. Even though we lost, I had one of the best games of my career against the Broncos last week. I've been playing football for a lot of years, and when something's working for me, I stick with it. See, as soon as I start making changes, then I'm thinking about the change instead of how the zone is lined up and whether or not I can get open. You understand what I'm saying?"

"Bobby Tom, I'm really not crazy about having photos in all the Monday morning newspapers of the two of us kissing."

"I'm surprised I have to remind you about this, Phoebe, but we're playing the Sabers tomorrow, and beating them is a lot more important than some newspaper pictures. They won the Super Bowl last year. The whole country thinks we're flushing this season down the toilet. We have to prove to them that we've got what it takes to be champions."

"Why?"

"Why what?"

"Why do you have to be champions? When you

224

think about it, what's the point? It's not like you're finding a cure for cancer."

"You're right," he said earnestly. "It's not like that. It's bigger. See, you've got good and you've got evil. That's what it is. That's how important it is."

"I'm having some trouble following you, Bobby Tom."

He lifted his arm for the waitress and jabbed two fingers toward their drinks for refills. That's when she realized that she'd nearly drained hers. She had no head for alcohol, and she knew she should refuse another, but Bobby Tom was good company, and she was enjoying herself. Besides, he was paying.

"The way I figure it is this," he went on. "Mankind is aggressive by nature, you agree with that?"

"Mankind maybe, but not necessarily womankind."

Bobby Tom obviously had no interest in sexual politics because he ignored her comment. "Football lets out man's natural aggression. If it weren't for the NFL, we'd probably have gone to war with Russia half a dozen times in the last forty years. See, that's the way Americans are. The minute we get crossed, we're natural shitkickers. Pardon my language, Phoebe, but everybody knows kickin' ass is part of our national conscience. Football gives us a — whadya-call? A safe outlet."

He was actually making a convoluted sort of sense, which was when she knew the first margarita had gone to her head. She picked up the second one, and licked another spot in the rim.

He clasped her arm and gave her a pleading look. "So, are you gonna be there for me or not tomorrow, 'cause I'll tell you God's truth — you're a fine woman, and I know you don't want a loss to the Sabers on your conscience."

"I'll be there," she sighed.

"I knew I could count on you." He gave her an engaging smile. "I like you, Phoebe. A lot. If we weren't business associates, I could really go for you."

He was so boyish and darling, she smiled right back at him. "Isn't life a bitch?"

"You said it."

Even without a margarita glow, Bobby Tom Denton was easy to be with. They talked about Mexican food, whether sports teams should be named after Native Americans, and Bobby Tom's resemblance to Christian Slater. She took more time with her second margarita, but even so, she was definitely feeling a buzz when he leaned over and brushed her mouth with his.

It was a light, friendly kiss. Respectful. A mark of comradeship and well-being. The kiss a twenty-five-year-old man gives to a thirty-three-year-old woman he'd like to go to bed with, but knows he won't, and doesn't want to spoil the friendship, but still wishes it could be more than a friendship.

Phoebe understood.

Unfortunately, Dan didn't.

"Denton!" His voice shot through the quiet of the bar like a Confederate cannon over a smoldering battlefield. "Doesn't that high-priced wristwatch of yours tell you you've got exactly three and half minutes to haul your butt up to your room or miss curfew?" He loomed over their table in his jeans and a denim shirt that was open at the throat.

"Howdy, Coach. You want to hear the funniest doggone thing? I was just explaining to Phoebe here how you've always been a little bit flexible about curfew. And then you show up. If that isn't —"

"Two minutes, forty-five seconds! And I'm fining you five hundred dollars for every minute you're not in your room."

Looking hurt, Bobby Tom got to his feet. "Dang, Coach, what's got you so riled?"

"You ran three bad patterns on Friday. How 'bout that for starters?"

Bobby Tom peeled some bills from a wad in his pocket and slapped them on the table. Then he gave Dan a long, shrewd gaze. "I don't think this has anything to do with bad patterns." He tipped the brim of his Stetson toward Phoebe. "See you on the sidelines tomorrow, Miss Somerville."

"See you, Bobby Tom."

As he disappeared, Dan barked at her like a drill sergeant. "My room! Now."

"Uh — I don't think so."

"When you start playing games with the best wide-out in the AFC, you've stepped clean over the line. Now unless you want our dirty linen aired in public, I suggest you start moving."

Phoebe reluctantly followed him out of the bar and into the lobby. She knew she should remind him that she was the boss, but as they stepped inside the elevator and began to travel in weighted silence up to the seventh floor, she found that she couldn't work up any steam.

He'd certainly worked up a full head, however, and the heat from it was burning right through her short, turquoise knit shift. Luckily for her, she didn't care. The two margaritas had left her with a cozy sense of well-being that made her want to puff out her lower lip and tell him not to be such an old fuddy-duddy.

She hadn't known their suites were so close until he stopped in front of the door across from her own. He unlocked it and gave her a none-too-gentle push inside. Then he shoved his fist, index finger extended, toward the brocade-covered sofa.

"Sit."

Although her brain had begun to issue the most alarming warnings, the warm tequila haze enveloping her made it impossible to take them seriously, so she gave him a mock salute as she followed orders.

"Yes, sir."

"Don't you get cute with me!" He splayed one big hand on his hip. "You stay away from my players, you hear me? These men are here to win football games; they're not your personal love toys, and I don't ever again want to see anything like I saw tonight!"

And that was just the beginning. He ranted and

228

raved, turning red in the face just as he did on the sidelines when he was yelling at a ref. Finally, he paused for breath.

She gave him a lopsided smile and slipped the tip of her index finger into her mouth. "What's the matter, puddin'? Didn't you ever kiss a girl in a bar?"

He seemed stunned, as if he'd never before been sassed by a woman. *God, he was cute. Cute and sexy and hunky and mean. Uhmm. Grrr. . . .* It would take a lot of woman to tame a man like him.

She uncrossed her legs.

It would take a bed, too. And the smell of jasmine drifting in through the open window. And the soft nighttime creak of a paddle wheel fan turning in the ceiling of the old plantation house.

She stood.

Young Elizabeth could tame him with her smoldering violet eyes, and her white breasts spilling like vanilla pudding over the lacy cups of her slip.

Yowl! He had come home to her, this moon-howling man. Drunk again. Dissolute. Smelling of whiskey and cheap perfume from a slut named Lulabelle. But he still wasn't sated, this hot-blooded, hot-cocked man. Only one woman could satisfy him.

Come to me, baby; I'll make you feel so good. I'm all woman, and I know how to tame my man.

She sauntered toward him, lips wet and parted, a lock of blond hair playing peek-a-boo with her lashes, every pore of her skin feeling his heat and getting ready to scorch him with her own. Why had she ever been afraid of him, a hot, dangerous cat like her? Let him see what kind of woman she was. Let him feel her sizzle.

"Phoebe?"

She stopped in front of him and cupped those hard fists hanging at his sides into the soft palms of her own hands. She gazed into his sea-green eyes and realized there was no need to be afraid of his strength when her own power was so much greater than his.

She arched her back and leaned into him. She was a cat in heat, and she kissed him with her lips parted, slanting her mouth over his, slipping out of one sandal to rub her hot pink toenails along the worn denim that sheathed his calf. As he accepted her tongue, a sense of exhilaration swept through her, fed by the knowledge of her own power. Why had she ever been afraid of sex when this was so easy, so natural?

He was making a soft, hoarse sound in his throat, or maybe it was her. Their mouths were joined, their hands clasped at his sides, and she wouldn't let the fear in. His tongue plundered. She told herself she was woman enough to meet his passion and liquor-relaxed enough to see it through to the end. Then, maybe she would be free.

"Phoebe . . ." He whispered her name into the warm, moist opening of her mouth, and he wasn't yelling anymore. His big hands slid up along her hips to her waist; his thumbs rose over her ribs. In a moment he would brush the undersides of her breasts, turning them into warm, living flesh.

They were already tingling, waiting.

"Don't stop," she pleaded against his lips. "No matter what I say, don't stop."

Stunned, he pulled back from her. "Do you mean it?"

"Yes."

Seconds ticked by as her words slowly registered in Dan's brain. Disappointment rushed through him, followed quickly by disgust and then cynicism. Why was he surprised? He should have learned his lesson from Valerie and realized what Phoebe had wanted all along. She was another woman who needed to play submission games. All of her *no*'s last Sunday night had meant *yes*. She had been manipulating him, and he'd been sucked right in.

Wearily, he gazed down at her lush curves, the soft sweep of the lashes framing those tilty-up amber eyes, the swollen lips of that wet, suck-me-up mouth. Was it too much to ask for a simple, uncomplicated romp in bed? No mind games. Nothing kinky. Just a few laughs and some good raunchy sex.

He was suddenly furious. As furious as he'd been when he'd found Bobby Tom drooling over her in the bar. She'd probably been feeling him up under the table. Rubbing against him with those long, bare legs. Brushing her centerfold tits against his arm. Hitting him with a whole load of shit. *Don't stop just because I say no, Bobby Tom. I really mean yes.*

Maybe Valerie had warped him, but it seemed as if the women in this country had gotten irredeemably screwed up when it came to sex. They either wanted to be stomping high heels into your chest or having you handcuff them to the bedposts. There didn't seem to be any middle ground.

He'd been down this path a hundred times, and he could play the tough guy without even thinking about it. After what she'd put him through, a little rough stuff with Phoebe Somerville might be just what he needed to get rid of those images of her that kept popping up in his mind at the worst times. Tonight, he would put an end to it.

"Whatever you say, baby."

Phoebe heard the edge of menace in Dan's voice, but she was feeling too good to let it frighten her. He lifted one hand to the back of her neck and plowed into her hair, catching it in his fist and tugging on her roots a bit too hard. With the other, he began to open the small covered buttons at the neck of her dress. The heel of his hand brushed her breasts, and the material fell open.

He gave a snort when he saw her plain white bra. Doubtless he was accustomed to sexier lingerie, but she'd never felt right in it. Her bare shoulders caught the chill of the air-conditioning as he pushed the bodice of the dress down to her elbows, trapping her arms in the sleeves. He worked the three heavy hooks that secured the wide elasticized strap of the bra in the back.

"You're big, baby, but you're not Dolly Parton. One of those sexy little underwires from Victoria's Secret would do the job."

The sneer in his voice penetrated her tequila

haze, diffusing some of her feeling of power. She tried to pull her arms from the constriction of her dress, but at that moment, her bra gave, and her breasts tumbled free.

"Damn." The softly uttered word sounded more like a tribute than a curse.

Before she knew what had happened, he had pulled her wrists behind her back and caught them in one hand. The rough movement thrust her breasts forward and up, and the helplessness she felt in that position produced little flutters of panic in the pit of her stomach. He bent his head. His warm breath touched her skin along with the light abrasion of his whiskers. He flicked one nipple with his tongue. It pebbled. He took it into his mouth and sucked on it.

Her bones began to feel as if they were buckling. The sensations were so exciting that she forgot about her pinioned arms. He moved to her other breast, licking and then sucking. She sagged against him.

When his hand slipped under the hem of her short dress and cupped her bare thigh, her panic returned, and she knew she had to get her arms free before she could let him go any farther. His fingers moved upward.

"Wait," she whispered. She tried to pull away, but his athlete's hands held her fast. "Let me go."

"I don't think so."

"I mean it."

"Sure you do."

"Dan!"

"Whatever the lady wants." He released her, but only long enough to yank her dress down over her hips. Her bra slipped off, leaving her standing there in one sandal, an ankle bracelet, and a pair of waist-high white cotton panties.

"You sure don't believe in spending your money on fancy underwear."

Her confidence dissolved and all the old ghosts were back. She grabbed for her dress to cover herself, but before she could reach it, he had picked her up and carried her into the bedroom. As he dropped her onto the bed, her lone sandal flew.

He loomed over her, and he was no longer a fantasy figure, but a real man stripping off his denim shirt, revealing an alarmingly well-developed chest with bulging pectorals, mountainous biceps, and veins standing out like ropes on his arms. A thick pelt of hair in the middle of his chest tapered into an arrow-straight line that disappeared along a hard, flat stomach into the waistband of his jeans.

She knew that he worked out in the weight room every day, and she'd seen him do laps around the field in the evening, but she still wasn't prepared for his powerfully muscled body. All thoughts of young Elizabeth fled from her mind. She felt like an eighteen-year-old virgin instead of a thirty-three-year-old woman who'd had both too many and too few lovers. She had set herself up to play with a pro when she couldn't even handle the amateurs.

His eyes were on her breasts as he unsnapped

his jeans. She grabbed for the edge of the bed-spread.

"Drop it."

"No, I'm not doing this." She drew the corner of the quilted fabric to her chin at the same time she slid to the opposite side of the bed.

"Right on schedule." Reaching down, he snared her ankle and sent her sprawling back against the pillows.

She let out a soft, strangled exclamation. The deadly sense of purpose in those ice green eyes sent fear rushing through her. She remembered his strength when he'd dragged her to the gazebo, and she clutched at the bedspread as her only protection.

"Please, Dan . . ." Her voice sounded helpless instead of strong, and she knew she had lost all control.

"You were the one who wanted fun and games."

"I didn't. I —"

"Shut up." He unzipped his jeans. "Now show me those tits again."

His rough vulgarity galvanized her. She spun away from him toward the opposite side of the bed, thrusting her legs out from under the twisted spread. She was off the bed and running toward the door. Dimly, she heard him grumbling from behind her.

"I'm getting too old for this."

She snatched up a damp towel he'd tossed on a chair after his shower and frantically raced into the living room for the door. Just as she yanked it open, he slapped it shut again with the palm of his hand.

"You're even crazier than Val!" He swung her around by her upper arm. "You don't have any clothes on. Do you want everybody to see you?"

"I don't care!" she cried, her heart pounding. "I told you to stop."

"You also told me not to listen, and that's just what I'm doing."

He whipped her up in his arms as if she weighed nothing, carried her back into the bedroom, and dropped her on the mattress.

"I'm not hitting you, so if that's what you're after, you'll have to find another stud." He knelt beside her, his big hand shackling her upper arm, and spoke almost indifferently. "How do you want it?"

She realized it was going to happen again. The liquor had made her let down her guard, and she was helpless.

That was when she screamed.

He was on her in a second, covering her mouth with his palm while he clamped her wrists above her head with his free hand. "Jesus," he hissed. "Not so loud." The denim of his jeans chafed her thighs as he glowered down at her, looking more disgusted than angry.

She went wild when she realized he actually expected her to keep quiet while he did this to her. Tears stung her eyes as she began to buck beneath him, twisting her hips and trying to free her legs. She bit hard into his hand and he released her with an angry exclamation.

"That's it!" He rolled off her, shaking his hand. "I've tried to be liberated and understanding, but I'm not doing this anymore!"

She was so startled she quit struggling.

He shot to his feet. "I'm hard as hell right now, but I'd rather disappear into that bathroom with a copy of *Penthouse* than keep on playing these caveman games. I don't care that you told me not to stop, because I'm stopping! I'm sick and tired of feeling like some slug who can only get laid if he beats up women." He loomed over her. "If you ask me, you've got enough notches on your bedpost to have a little more sensitivity when it comes to men." Bracing his hands on his hips, he glowered down at her. "From now on, when a woman tells me to stop, I'm stopping, even if she's already told me not to pay any attention when she tells me to stop."

Bewildered, she stared at him.

"Maybe I'd like to get strong-armed for a change!" he exclaimed. "Maybe I'd like to be so irresistibly sexy that *I* got tied to the bed for once! Would that be too much to ask?"

Understanding came slowly. She remembered what she had whispered to him, how she had told him not to stop no matter what she said. She remembered his twisted relationship with Valerie, and as it all came back to her, her relief was so sharp a bubble of hysteria rose in her throat.

He sank down on the corner of the bed, propped his forearms on his splayed knees, and gazed glumly out toward the living room. "Maybe it's divine justice. When I was in my twenties, I took part in so much kinky stuff with all those groupies that now I can't seem to manage something simple and uncomplicated."

She drew the spread to her chin. "Dan — uh — Could I say something?"

"Not if it involves whips and dog collars." He paused. "Or more than two people."

The bubble rose higher in throat. She gave a choked sound. "It doesn't."

"All right, then."

She spoke to his back, picking her words carefully. "I didn't mean what you thought I meant. When I told you not to stop no matter what I said, I was talking about kissing. You're really an — uh — an excellent kisser." She took a deep breath, pressing on even though she knew she was making a muddle of it. "I get — Well, I have a couple of hang-ups. Not hang-ups, really; hang-ups is too strong a word. More like — like an allergy. Anyway, sometimes when I'm kissing a man, I have this sort of reaction."

She knew she was babbling from the way he turned his head to stare at her. His chest distracted her. Cast in bronze and sitting in the front window at her old gallery, it would have made them a fortune.

She swallowed hard. "I was just trying to tell you that if I had it — this reaction — you could sort of . . ."

"Ignore it?"

"Right. But the other — When we weren't kissing. When you were touching me." The bubble dissolved. "When I said stop, I meant stop."

His eyes darkened with regret. "Phoebe . . ."

"If I ever say stop to you, I mean stop. Always." She drew a deep breath. "No questions. No second-guessing. I'm not your ex-wife, and sexual violence isn't a game I play. With me, stop means stop."

"I understand, and I'm sorry."

She knew she would burst into tears if she had to listen to another basket load of regrets from him that would only make her feel even more inept.

"About this kissing allergy." He rubbed his chin, and she thought she detected amusement in his eyes. "What if the two of us decide to kiss each other again. And you have this allergic reaction, and you say stop. Am I supposed to stop then?"

She looked down at the bedspread. "Even then, I guess. I'm not going to send out any more mixed signals."

Reaching forward, he brushed her cheek with the back of his knuckles. "Promise?"

"Promise."

She had intended to get up and put on her clothes, but now as he touched her so gently, she couldn't move. She felt his warmth as he came closer and knew he was going to kiss her again. She was no longer afraid. Instead, the slow heat of desire rekindled inside her — not a raging fire, but a small, cozy flame.

"You don't like my underwear," she whispered against his mouth.

"No." He nibbled at her bottom lip. "But I like what's inside it a whole lot." His fingertips trailed along the bumps of her spine as his mouth settled over hers.

The kiss was both gentle and passionate, full of sizzle and sweetness. At that moment she wanted to make love with him more than she'd ever wanted anything. His tongue invaded her mouth. Her hands slipped to his arms, but then she wished she hadn't touched him there because she didn't want to be reminded of his strength, only his gentleness. How did she know he would stay gentle?

"Dan?"

"Uhmm."

"I know you said you didn't want any — you know — any kinky stuff."

She could feel him stiffen, and she almost lost courage as he drew away. Sinking back against the pillows that bunched at the headboard, the spread still clutched to her chest, she spoke in a rush. "This isn't all that kinky. Really, it's not."

"Maybe I'd better be the judge of that. And I'm warning you — I'm getting more conservative every day."

Her courage left her. "Forget it."

"We've gone this far; you might as well get it off your chest."

"I was just — Never mind."

"Phoebe, if things keep progressing at their current rate, it's about eighty percent guaranteed we're going to be intimate before this night's over, so you'd better tell me what's on your mind. Otherwise, the whole time we're going at it, I'll be waiting for you to bark like a dog or tell me to call you Howard."

She gave him an unsteady smile. "I'm not that imaginative. I wanted to ask — I mean, would you mind very much if we —" She got stuck and tried again. "If we pretend I'm a —"

"Lion tamer? Prison guard?"

"A virgin," she whispered and felt her cheeks flush with embarrassment.

He gazed at her. "A virgin?"

She dropped her eyes, mortified at what she'd revealed. "Forget it. Forget I said anything. Let's just do it."

"Phoebe, darlin', what's going on here?" He brushed his index finger over her lips.

"There's nothing going on."

"You can tell me. I'm sort of like a bedroom priest; I've pretty much heard it all. Have you ground out so many miles between the bedposts that you want to turn back the odometer a little?"

"Something like that," she murmured.

"I don't have a whole lot of experience with virgins to draw on. Matter of fact, I don't recall that I have any. Still, I s'pose I could use my imagination." And then his eyes narrowed. "I don't have to pretend that you're sixteen or anything, do I, because that kiddie stuff turns me off."

"Thirty-three," she whispered.

"That old?"

He was teasing her, and she knew it, so she tried to sound offhand. "Why not? Maybe one of those dried-up women who's secretly afraid of men. Somebody like that."

"Now this is getting kinda interesting." His thumb brushed along the very top of her breasts, just above the edge of the bedspread. "I don't suppose a woman like you would let me have another look at what you've got hidden under here?"

"As long as you don't say anything nasty about them."

"I wouldn't do that."

"You did. You told me to show you my —"

He pressed his finger over her lips. "That wasn't me. Only a real jerk would talk like that."

She loosened her grip on the spread. Slowly, he lowered it, letting the cover fall to her waist.

"Now a man like *me* would appreciate a sight like this." Despite his words, he didn't even look. Instead, he was studying her face.

Before she knew it, she was the one touching him. She ran her palms over his arms and along his shoulders. She was entranced with the contrast between his iron-hard muscles and the gentle way he nuzzled her neck. He trailed kisses along her jaw, nibbled her chin, the corner of her mouth. Finally he drew back and looked down at her breasts.

They had been painted by Flores and viewed

by multitudes, but she felt as if they were being seen for the first time. He touched her. Just the pads of his thumbs on the very tips of her nipples, and the feeling was so exquisite that she sighed, an expression of desire and pleasure that spread all the way to her toes.

"Lean back," he whispered.

She sank into the pillows. He continued to touch her like that, just the very tips of her nipples, until she didn't think she could bear it any longer. She had never experienced desire like this, so warm and liquid with no place for fear. He slipped his hand farther into her panties.

"Stop."

He immediately withdrew.

She smiled. "I want to see you." Going up on her knees, she reached for his zipper, then found the courage to slide it down over the heavy bulge that strained the denim.

"Hold on a minute, darlin'." He stilled her hands before she could go further and got up from the bed to disappear into the bathroom. He reappeared a moment later.

Her lips curved as he tossed a handful of foil-wrapped condoms on the table at the side of the bed. "What an ego."

"How would a maiden lady like you even know what those are?"

"Public television."

Now he was the one with the grin, and she realized this was the first time she had ever laughed in bed with a man. Until this moment, she had never imagined that laughter and sex could go together.

"Where were we?"

She was amazed at her own boldness as she reached for the open V of his jeans. "Right here, as I remember." She couldn't believe how urgent her need was to see him. Instead of being afraid, she was experiencing a heady mixture of curiosity and lust.

"Don't faint on me."

"I'll try not to." She pushed the denim away and then swallowed hard as he sprang free from a pair of white cotton briefs.

"Oh, my." Her gasp wasn't feigned.

He chuckled. "Take deep breaths."

"Maybe it's just because your hips are so narrow. The contrast . . ."

"That's one way of looking at it." He smiled as he pulled off what was left of his clothing and stood naked before her.

She couldn't take her eyes off him. His shoulders were broad and powerful, his hips narrow with an almost concave abdomen. One of his knees was scarred, as was his opposite calf.

"This peep show works two ways, you know." He nodded toward the part of her still hidden beneath the spread that had settled in her lap.

"I'm too shy," she replied, sinking back on her heels.

"I guess I can understand that. Considering your inexperience and everything." The mattress sagged as he settled down on the edge. "What

I'm going to suggest is this. Since you're a maiden lady, you might be less embarrassed if you just reached under the cover, slipped off what you've got left, and handed it out."

Lowering her eyes, she leaned back into the pillows and did as he suggested. As she dropped her panties at the side of the bed, she could barely control her excitement over this crazy, unpredictable seduction.

He lay down next to her on a bent elbow, slipped his other arm under the cover and drew up her knee to play with her ankle bracelet. "You just tell me to stop any time you get nervous."

An overwhelming flood of emotion washed through her. Even though he was teasing, he would never know how much those words meant.

Leaning forward, he started kissing her again: lips, breasts, sweet, hot kisses burning her skin, while she kissed him back and his hand moved higher under the covers until he was stroking her inner thighs.

"Spread open just a little bit for me now," he whispered.

She moved her legs. The cover fell away except for a small corner between her thighs. He brushed it aside.

She waited for him to make some crack about her being a natural blonde, but he didn't say anything. She drew a deep, shuddering breath as he began to explore her.

"Does that feel good?"

"Yes. Oh, yes."

"I'm glad."

"Would you stop?"

He withdrew his hand.

Joy and lust swirled inside her when she realized he had done as she'd asked. His compliance gave her courage. She twisted her body so that she was above him, her breasts gently swaying, the nipples stirring the hair on his chest. She watched his expression as she began her own sensual mission, trailing her hand down over his chest to his belly, which was covered with a thin sheen of perspiration.

She slipped lower and touched him. He caught his breath. She felt him rigid and pulsing in her hand, straining for release, and once again, fear mingled with desire. This time, however, desire was stronger.

"We're getting close to the point of no return," he whispered hoarsely.

She shook her head. Fondled him. "You promised."

"Stop," he groaned.

She did.

He rolled over so that he was once again looking down at her. "Let's get you ready, virgin lady," he whispered, " 'cause I don't think I can hold off much longer."

It was so good.

He prepared her with his fingers as if she were brand-new. Emotions she couldn't name filled her heart while his deep stroking sent waves of fire surging through her. His breathing was heavy, his skin flushed. He stopped to reach for one of the foil packets and sheathed himself before he returned to his caresses.

"You're so tight," he whispered, as he shifted his hips and poised himself to enter her. "It's almost like —"

"Stop," she sobbed, even though she knew he had gone past the point where he would listen.

But he rolled off. Fell back. Sweat beaded his forehead. "You're killing me," he gasped, his chest heaving.

She couldn't believe he'd kept his promise, and in those moments she loved him. She told herself it wasn't a permanent emotion, not happily-ever-after, but an ephemeral love born of gratitude. Along with her heart, her whole body opened to him, demanding that he fill her and trusting him to do no damage. She clutched at his shoulders, drew him back.

He clasped her behind the knees and spread her thighs.

"Slow," she pleaded. "Don't hurt."

"Oh, I won't, darlin'," he said as he parted her. "I wouldn't hurt you for anything."

And he didn't. His entry was achingly slow, and he watched her the whole time, green eyes half-lidded, neck muscles rigid, skin damp. She could feel his iron control, even as her body stretched to take him. He began pumping inside her, and her own control slipped away.

"That's right," he whispered, as her head thrashed on the pillow and tiny moans slipped through her lips. "Make some noise for me, baby. Make all the noise you want."

He thrust deeply, and she moved with him. The sensation was wonderful and frightening. She began to spiral, and now it was not his loss of control that threatened her, but her own. Her fingers dug into the steely bands at his shoulders. Something was happening to her. Something wonderful. Something terrifying. If she lost control . . . She opened her mouth and sobbed, "Stop!"

The sound he made was barely human, a strangled exclamation deep in his throat. This time she knew he wouldn't listen. He had traveled too far and her request was no longer fair.

But he withdrew. This iron-willed man who could have overpowered her in an instant acceded to her wishes and fell back into the pillows, skin flushed, veins throbbing in his neck, chest heaving.

With his acquiescence, the shackles that had bound her for so long broke away, and joy took their place. She fell on him. Kissed him with her tongue. Took his hair in her fists as she reclaimed her womanhood and loved him with all her heart.

It seemed natural for her to mount him.

She slipped her leg over his hips and gradually took him into her body, his size forcing her to go more slowly than she wished so she could accommodate him. When she had completely impaled herself, she gazed down at him. His eyes were open, but glazed, his lips taut. She began to move, timing the strokes as little sobs slipped through her lips. He cupped her buttocks so she didn't lose him, his fingers soothing her where they were joined.

She splayed her hands in the hair on his chest, arched her back, and rode him higher and higher. Her hair began to fly. She had become a glittering blond amazon who had claimed the mightiest of men to service her. He bucked, but she stayed with him, her thighs gripping his powerful hips. She was in command. He was hers to take.

He was blowing now. His chest heaved as he emptied and filled his lungs, an athlete reaching for the limits of his endurance. She understood then that he was determined she would shatter first. He was a man who thrived on competition, and in this particular game, second place earned the trophy. He didn't know how it was with her. He didn't understand that she couldn't.

But there was something she didn't understand. To him, winning was everything. And he wasn't above cheating.

With his fingers, he found her most vulnerable spot. She gasped for air, her head fell forward. He deepened that thrilling, unfair touch. The room whirled around her, spinning faster and faster, and the boundaries between what was his and what was hers dissolved.

It couldn't be happening. It never happened. . . .

A great cry spilled from her very center. She heard a dim, answering roar and felt his fierce shudders. Spinning free of gravity, they hurtled into oblivion.

13

Phoebe's cheek was stuck to Dan's chest and her leg was twisted at an uncomfortable angle, but she didn't care. As she lay in his arms, her heart was filled with gratitude toward this tender warrior who had done so much to vanquish the enemies of her past.

The air conditioner hissed. In the hallway someone slammed a door. She waited for him to speak because she didn't know what to say.

He shifted his weight and rolled to the side. She felt chilly air on her bare back. He pulled his arm from beneath her and sat up on the edge of the bed, his back to her. She felt the first wisps of uneasiness.

"You were great, Phoebe."

He turned and gave her a fake, too-friendly smile. A chill shot through her as she wondered if it was the same one he'd given all the football groupies when he was done with them.

"I had a real good time. Really." He reached for his jeans. "Tomorrow's a big day. Got to get up early."

Every part of her had grown cold. She fumbled with the covers. "Of course. It's late, I —" She slipped out of bed on the opposite side. "Let me just —" She grabbed for her clothes.

"Phoebe —"

"Here. I've got it all." She made a dash for the bathroom. Her cheeks burned with shame, anger, and hurt as she pulled on her clothes. How could something that had been so earth-shattering for her have been so meaningless to him? She tried to force air past the knot in her throat. Her teeth began to chatter, and she clamped her jaw shut, determined not to let him know what he had done to her. She wouldn't fall apart until she was alone.

When she emerged, she saw that he had pulled on his jeans. He faced the bathroom door. His hair was tousled, his expression guilty. "You want a drink or something?"

Drawing on the same bravado that had kept her sane for so many years, she tossed her ugly white bra at his feet. "Add this to your souvenir collection, Coach. I don't want you to lose count."

Then she was gone.

As the door shut behind her, Dan cursed under his breath. No matter how much he wanted to rationalize, he knew he had just acted like a first-class heel. Even so, he rubbed his arm and tried to tell himself that what he'd done wasn't all that bad. Phoebe knew the score, so what was the big deal?

The big deal was the fact that, for the life of him, he couldn't remember the last time he'd experienced sex as good as what had just taken place in this room, and it scared him because it had been so unexpected. There'd been this crazy innocence about her that had excited him beyond belief. She'd been wild and sweet, and just thinking

251

about that curvy body of hers was making him hard again.

He kicked away the bra she had tossed at him and stalked over to the minibar, where he pulled out a bottle of beer. As he twisted off the cap, he acknowledged the real reason he'd acted so badly. It was because he'd felt guilty. From the time he'd seen Phoebe kissing Bobby Tom in the bar to the moment that beautiful blonde had shown him the stars in a million different colors, he'd forgotten all about Sharon Anderson.

Dammit! He'd told himself he wasn't going to do this kind of thing any more. He hadn't been with another woman since he'd met Valerie, and that had been almost five years ago. The first time should have been with Sharon, not with Phoebe. Now, when he and Sharon finally climbed into bed, that sweet little nursery school lady was going to be competing in his mind with a seasoned sexual tri-athlete.

Even so, he shouldn't have kicked Phoebe out like that. Guilt gnawed at him. Despite all her character defects, he couldn't help liking her, and he was almost certain he'd hurt her feelings, although she had so much sass, it was hard to know for sure. Damn, that woman had made him crazy from the first time they'd met. If he weren't careful, his lust for her would completely screw up his budding relationship with Sharon.

Right then he made a promise. No matter what he had to do, he wasn't going to let that gorgeous sex bomb sink her claws into him any deeper than she already had. Maybe he owed her an apology, but that was it. From now on, he was a one-woman man.

Phoebe was mad as hell as she got ready to go onto the field for the first quarter of the Stars-Sabers game. *Jerk! Idiot! Moron!* She stood at the mouth of the tunnel and called herself every name in the book. Of all the brainless, self-destructive, idiotic things she could have done, this one took the cake.

She still felt woozy from her crying jag last night. Sometime around four in the morning, she had finally taken a long, painful look inside herself and realized there was only one explanation for the depth of hurt she was feeling. She was letting herself fall in love with Dan Calebow.

Her chest spasmed in a short, painful hiccup. Afraid she would start crying all over again, she dug her fingernails into her palms and tried to find some rational explanation for how she had let such a disaster happen. She should have been the last woman in the world to have succumbed to a sexy Southern drawl and a gorgeous set of biceps. But there it was. Some hormonal imbalance, some reckless streak of self-destruction, had sent her flying too close to the sun.

And how hot that sun had burned last night. She had never imagined making love could be like that — funny and tender and wonderful. Her throat tightened as she reminded herself that *she* might have been making love, but *he* had been having sex.

She realized she was dangerously close to tears, and she couldn't afford to fall apart again. Fixing a blazing smile on her face, she walked out into the Oregon sunshine, where she planned to exact at least a small measure of revenge for every sweet second she'd spent last night lying in his treacherous arms.

The photographers spotted her before the crowd did. A prerecorded tape began playing the old standard, "Ain't She Sweet?" She realized this must be the surprise Ron had said he would have for her when she went on the field. She was going to be the only owner in the NFL with her personal theme song.

Accompanied by wolf whistles, she struck a pose, blew a kiss, and walked toward the bench, her hips wiggling to the beat. The photographers snapped away at the dazzling red and black python-printed leather jeans that hugged every curve of her lower body, and the fitted black silk man's vest cupping her bare breasts. The owner of the trendy boutique next to the hotel had been persuaded to open the door just for her at ten o'clock that morning after Phoebe had decided the conservative linen dress she'd brought with her would no longer do. The boutique owner had suggested a man's bow tie to accessorize the outfit, but Phoebe had chosen to loop a more feminine bit of black lace ribbon around her throat, while she showed her team spirit with clusters of silver stars dangling from her earlobes. The outfit was expensive, outrageous, and completely inappropriate, a flagrant in-your-face to Dan Calebow.

She had known how he would feel about it even before she saw him turn his head to see what all the fuss was about. At first he looked stunned, then murderous. For a moment their eyes locked. She wanted to blast him with her most smoldering gaze, but she couldn't manage it. Before he could sense her misery, she turned her attention to the photographers, who were calling her name. While they recorded her every curve, she knew she had never felt less womanly. Why had she ever thought a man like Dan could look at her as anything more than a body?

Bobby Tom came trotting up. "I got a feeling you're going to bring me luck today."

"I'll do my best."

She took her time giving him his kiss and then acknowledged the crowd's cheers with a wave. Jim Biederot appeared for his pregame insult. Several of the other players sidled up, and she wished them luck. Ron had pressed a pack of Wrigley's in her hand before the game, but Dan didn't approach her at the kickoff to claim it.

The ball arced into the air, and when the massive bodies of the players began to collide, she managed to avoid slapping her hands over her eyes. Although it was still terrifying to be near so much mayhem, she realized as the quarter progressed that she wasn't quite as panicked as she had been the week before. Ron had been teaching her the rudiments of the game, and more than once, she found herself caught up in the action.

Later, in the skybox, she had the satisfaction of watching Dan get ejected in the fourth quarter after insulting one of the refs. Inspired by her good luck kiss, Bobby Tom had caught five passes for 118 yards, but it wasn't enough to make up for his teammates' fumbles, especially against a powerhouse like the Sabers. With six turnovers, the Sabers beat the Stars by eighteen points.

She and Ron returned with the team on the charter flight back to O'Hare. She had changed from her python jeans into comfortable slacks and a red cotton sweater that hung to mid-thigh. As she approached Dan, who was sitting in the front row of first class and scowling over next week's game plan with Gary Hewitt, the offensive coordinator, she wished she could slip past him before he noticed her. Since that wasn't possible, she stopped momentarily beside his seat, arched her eyebrows, and flipped the pack of Wrigley's into his lap.

"You really should learn to control your temper, Coach."

He gave her a glare that could have scorched concrete. She quickly moved on.

After the plane took off, she left her seat in first class next to Ron and walked into the cabin to speak with the players. She was stunned to see how banged up they were. The team physician was giving one of the veterans a shot in the knee, while the trainer worked with another. Many of the men sported ice packs.

They seemed to appreciate the fact that she was willing to converse with them after an embarrassing loss. She noticed that there was a definite pecking order to the way in which they were seated. The coaches, GM, and important press occupied first class, while Stars staff members and the camera crew sat in the front of the coach section. The rookies occupied the next few rows, and the veterans took up the back of the plane. Later, when she asked Ron why the veterans chose the rear of the plane, he told her they liked to get as far away from the coaches as possible.

It was after one in the morning when they landed at O'Hare, and she was exhausted. Ron was taking her home since she hadn't driven to the airport. As she slid into the deep front seat of his Lincoln Town Car, she heard a brisk set of footsteps approaching.

"We need to talk, Phoebe. Let me drive you home."

She looked up to see Dan standing next to the car, his hand resting on the door as he leaned down to peer inside. He was wearing his wire-rimmed glasses, and he looked more like a stern-faced high school principal who was about to reach for his paddle than one of the gridiron's legendary hell-raisers.

She fumbled with her seat belt buckle as she snapped it together. "We can talk tomorrow. I'm going with Ron."

Ron, who was standing on the driver's side, had just finished placing their carry-on bags in the rear seat. He looked up as Dan came around the front of the car.

"I have some business I need to discuss with Phoebe, Ronald. I'll drive her home. We can trade cars at work tomorrow." He tossed over a set of keys and, ignoring her exclamation of protest, slid behind the wheel. While Dan adjusted the seat to accommodate his taller framer, Ron stared down at the keys in his hand.

"You're letting me drive your Ferrari?"

"Don't put any drool marks on the leather."

Ron snatched his carry-on bag from the back and handed over his own keys, so pleased at the prospect of driving "ICE 11" that he dashed off without telling Phoebe good-bye.

She sat in stony silence as Dan pulled out of the parking lot. Within minutes, they were heading south on the Tri State. In the gaudy lights of billboards advertising radio stations and beer, she could see that he was doing a slow burn, as if he were the wronged party instead of her. She made up her mind that she wasn't going to let him realize how much he'd hurt her.

"I suppose you know you disgraced yourself at the game today by showing up in that snake charmer outfit."

"*I* disgraced *myself*? Unless my memory's faulty, you were the one who got evicted."

"I got ejected, not evicted. That was a football game, not a damn landlords' convention." He glanced over at her. "What were you trying to prove, anyway? Don't you know that when you

258

wear clothes like that, you might as well have a For Sale sign plastered on your chest."

"Of course I know it," she cooed. "Why do you think I do it?"

His hands tightened on the wheel. "You're really pushing me, aren't you?"

"My clothing isn't any of your concern."

"It is when it reflects on the team."

"Don't you think those infantile temper tantrums you throw on the sidelines reflect on the team?"

"That's different. It's part of the game."

She hoped her refusal to respond told him exactly what she thought of his logic.

They drove for several miles in silence. Phoebe's misery settled in deeper. She was so tired of playing a part all the time, but she didn't know any other way to behave. Maybe if they'd met under different circumstances, they would have had a chance.

Dan's belligerence had faded when he finally spoke again. "Look, Phoebe. I feel bad about last night, and I want to apologize. I liked being with you and all, and I didn't mean to be so abrupt. It was just gettin' kind of late . . ." His apology trailed lamely into silence.

She could feel her throat closing, and she fought against it. Pulling the fragments of her willpower together, she spoke with the bored lockjaw drawl of a South Hampton socialite. "Really, Dan, if I'd known you would react in such an immature fashion, I would never have gone to bed with you."

259

His eyes narrowed. "Is that so?"

"You reminded me of a teenager who'd just done it in the backseat of the family car and was having an attack of guilty conscience. Frankly, I'm accustomed to a bit more sophistication on the part of my lovers. At the very least, I expected another round. It's hardly worth all that effort if you're only going to do it once, is it?"

He made a strange, choking sound and drifted into the right lane. She kept at him, prodded on by the pain of knowing he couldn't see through her, that this was the way he expected her to behave. "I don't think I'm terribly demanding, but I do have three requirements of my lovers: courtesy, endurance, and quick recovery for a repeat performance. I'm afraid you failed all three."

His voice grew dangerously low. "Aren't you going to criticize my technique, too?"

"Well, as to that. I found your technique to be quite . . . adequate."

"Adequate?"

"You've obviously read all the books, but . . ." She forced an exaggerated sigh. "Oh, I'm probably too picky."

"No. Go on. I wouldn't miss this for the world."

"I guess I hadn't imagined you'd have so many — Well, so many hang-ups. You're a very uptight lover, Daniel. You should relax more and not take sex so seriously. Of course you were operating at a disadvantage." She paused, then went in for the kill. "In all fairness, what man could be at his

260

best having sex with the woman who signs his paychecks?"

She was dismayed to hear a soft chuckle. "Phoebe, darlin', you're takin' my breath away."

"I wouldn't dwell on it too much. I'm certain it was just a temporary thing. Bad chemistry."

In the flash of headlights, she could see him grin. For a fraction of a second she almost forgot the sting of his rejection and smiled herself.

"Honey lamb, there are a lot of things in this world I feel insecure about. Religion. Our national economic policy. What color socks to wear with a blue suit. But, I've got to tell you that my performance in that hotel room last night isn't one of them."

"With that ego of yours, I'm not surprised."

"Phoebe, I said I was sorry."

"Apology accepted. Now if you don't mind, I'm exhausted." She rested her head against the window and closed her eyes.

He was just as good at nonverbal communication as she. Within seconds, he'd flipped on the radio and filled the interior of the car with the hostile music of Megadeth. Nothing had been settled between them.

Phoebe saw little of Dan during the week that followed. His days seemed to be spent in watching miles of film, attending an endless number of meetings with his coaches and players, and spending some time each day on the practice field. To her surprise, Molly agreed to accompany her to the

261

game on Sunday against the Detroit Lions, although when Phoebe suggested she bring a friend, she refused, saying that all the girls at her school were bitches.

The Stars beat the Lions by a narrow margin, but the following Sunday at Three Rivers Stadium in Pittsburgh, the team once again fell victim to a series of turnovers and lost a close game. They were now one and three for the season. She ran into Reed at the Pittsburgh airport. He was so cloyingly sympathetic, while at the same time subtly critical, that she couldn't wait to get away from him.

The next morning, when Phoebe arrived at her office, her secretary handed her a note from Ronald asking her to meet him immediately in the second-floor conference room. As she grabbed her coffee mug and made her way down the hall, she noticed that all the phones were ringing and wondered what new catastrophe had struck?

Dan was leaning against the paneled back wall, ankles and forearms crossed, a scowl on his face as he stared at the television that rested on a movable steel cart along with a VCR. Ron was seated in a swivel chair at the end of the table.

As she slid into the chair to his left, he leaned over and whispered, "This is a tape of 'Sports in Chicago,' a popular local program that aired last night while we were flying home. I'm afraid you need to hear this."

She turned her attention to the television and saw a good-looking, dark-haired announcer seated

262

in a tub chair against a backdrop of the Chicago skyline. He gazed into the camera with the intensity of Peter Jennings covering a major war.

"Through skillful trades and smart draft choices, Bert Somerville and Carl Pogue managed to assemble one of the most talented group of players in the league. But it takes more than talent to win victories, it takes leadership, something the Stars now sorely lack."

The screen began to show clips from Sunday's game, a series of fumbles and broken plays. "General manager Ronald McDermitt is not a football visionary — he's never even played the game — and he simply doesn't have the maturity to keep a maverick coach like Dan Calebow in line, a coach who needs to be concentrating more on the fundamentals his young players need and less on razzle-dazzle. The Stars are an organization verging on chaos, hampered by inept management, erratic coaching, shaky finances, and an owner who is an embarrassment to the NFL."

Phoebe stiffened as the camera began to display a montage of photos of her taken over the years. Briefly, the announcer sketched in the details of Bert's will.

"Socialite Phoebe Somerville's behavior is turning a serious and noble game into a circus. She doesn't understand the sport, and doesn't seem to have any experience managing anything more complicated than her checkbook. Her provocative clothing on the sidelines and her snubs to media requests for interviews make it clear how little respect she has for this talented team and the sport so many of us love."

The camera cut to an interview with Reed. "I'm certain that Phoebe is doing her best," he said earnestly. "She's more accustomed to moving in artistic circles than athletic ones and this is difficult for her. Once she's fulfilled the requirements of her father's will, I'm sure I'll be able to get the Stars back on track quickly."

She gritted her teeth as Reed went on, smiling into the camera and coming across as the perfect gentlemen to her wild-eyed party girl.

The moussed-up talking head came back on camera. "Despite Reed Chandler's chivalrous defense of his cousin, January is a long time away. In the meantime, when is Miss Somerville going to provide direction to her general manager? Even more troubling, how can she clamp down on her explosive head coach when a troubling rumor has surfaced. Normally, we would not report this sort of thing, but since it has a direct bearing on what's happening with the Stars, we feel it's in the public interest to reveal that a reliable source saw her emerging from Calebow's Portland hotel suite in the early hours of the morning two weeks ago."

Dan uttered a blistering obscenity. Phoebe gripped her hands together.

The announcer regarded the camera gravely. "Their meeting might have been innocent, but if it wasn't, it doesn't bode well for the Stars. We should also note that Miss Somerville's indiscre-

264

tions don't stop at a rumored fling with her head coach."

He picked up a copy of *Beau Monde* magazine, a glossy, upscale publication with a circulation nearly as large as *Vanity Fair*. Phoebe groaned inwardly. She'd had so much on her mind lately that she'd forgotten all about *Beau Monde.*

"Our new NFL Commissioner Boyd Randolph would be well-advised to take a look at the latest issue of popular *Beau Monde* magazine, which will be showing up tomorrow on area newsstands and features our own Miss Somerville in the buff. Perhaps these photographs, which FCC regulations prohibit me from showing on camera, will spur the commissioner to have a serious discussion with Miss Somerville about her responsibilities to the NFL."

His brows drew together in the studied outrage of a reporter trying to pump up his Nielsen's. "Professional football has worked hard at cleaning up its image after the drug and gambling scandals of the past. But now a young woman with no interest in the game wants to drag it right through the dirt again. Let's hope that Commissioner Randolph won't let that happen."

Dan pointed his finger toward the announcer. "Isn't that weasel one of Reed's buddies?"

"I believe so." The broadcast had come to an end, and Ron hit the switch on the remote control.

"Chandler's a real prince," Dan muttered in disgust. He snatched up the manila envelope that lay on the table, and Phoebe's outrage gave way to a sinking sense of dread.

"My secretary just gave it to me," Ron said. "I haven't had a chance to look at it yet."

Dan whipped out the magazine. Phoebe wanted to take it away from him, but she knew that would only postpone the inevitable. A page ripped as he began thumbing through it, searching for the offending photographs.

"Why bother?" she sighed. "You've already seen everything I've got."

Ron winced. "It's true then? You really were together in his hotel room."

Dan turned on her. "Why don't you just hire the Goodyear blimp so you can announce it to the whole world?"

Her fingers trembled as she cupped her now cold coffee mug. "It's not going to happen again, Ron, but you need to know the truth."

He looked at her like a worried father confronting a well-loved, but ill-behaved child. "I blame myself. It never occurred to me to talk to you about the impropriety of fraternizing with Dan. I should have realized — This, coupled with the photographs, is going to be a public relations nightmare. Didn't you realize that posing nude for a magazine, even a respectable one like *Beau Monde*, would embarrass the team?"

"I posed for those photographs in June, a month before I inherited the Stars. With everything that's happened, I'd forgotten about them."

Dan still hadn't found the photographs. He gritted his teeth. "I'm telling you this, Ronald. If we get any calls from *Playboy*, you'd better tie her down and gag her, because she'll be buck naked and airbrushed before you know it."

Abruptly, he stopped flipping and stared. Then he began to curse.

Phoebe hated the need she felt to defend herself. "Those photographs were done by Asha Belchoir, one of the most respected photographers in the world. She also happens to be a friend of mine."

Dan whapped the page with the back of his hand. "You're painted!"

Ron reached out. "May I?"

Dan tossed the magazine on the table as if it were a piece of garbage. It landed open, revealing a double page spread of Phoebe reclining in front of Flores's "Nude #28," a surrealistic portrait he had done of her not long before his death. Superimposed on Phoebe's naked body was an exact reproduction of the section of the painting that her reclining form covered. The effect was beautiful, eerie, and erotic.

Ron turned the page to reveal an enlarged photograph of Phoebe's breast, its nipple puckered beneath a coating of chalk white paint. Her skin had become a surrealistic canvas for miniature blue silhouettes of other breasts executed in Flores's characteristic style.

The final photograph was a full-length vertical nude taken from the rear. She was lifting her hair, knee bent, one hip slightly outthrust. Her unpainted skin formed a canvas for black and crimson handprints on her shoulder, the dip of her waist, the curve of her buttock, the back of her thigh.

Dan jabbed at the magazine photo with his index finger. "Some man must have had a good time doing that to you!"

Phoebe didn't take time to consider that his anger seemed out of proportion for someone who was trying so hard to distance himself from her. "*Men,* darling. One for each color." It was a lie. The body artist had been a pudgy, middle-aged woman, but he didn't have to know that.

Ron picked up his pen and tapped it on the tabletop. "Phoebe, I've scheduled a press conference for both of us at one o'clock. Wally Hampton in PR will brief you. Dan, I want you to stay out of sight until tomorrow. When the press finally catches up with you, don't comment on anything except the game. You know how to handle it. And unless you want the story to end up on the front page, keep your fists in your pockets if any reporter has the nerve to bring up the hotel room incident to your face."

She rose from her chair. "No press conference, Ron. I told you from the beginning that I won't do interviews."

Dan's lips twisted. "If you give her permission to strip first, I bet she'll do it."

"That's enough, Dan." Ron turned to Phoebe. "I apologize for the press conference."

Dan gave a snort of disgust. "That's tellin' her, Ronald. You sure do know how to crack the old whip."

Ron seemed not to have heard. "Unfortunately, you can't continue to snub the press without looking as if you have something to hide."

"I don't think there's much left that everybody hasn't already seen," Dan sneered.

Phoebe caught her breath. Ron rose slowly from the table and turned to face the coach. "Your comments are uncalled for. You owe Phoebe an apology."

Dan's expression was rigid with anger. "She's not going to get one."

"You're hardly innocent in all this. There were apparently two people in that hotel room. And if you hadn't lost so many games, we wouldn't be under attack. Instead of insulting Phoebe, perhaps you should consider doing something about all those turnovers."

Dan seemed to be having trouble believing what he was hearing. "Are you criticizing my coaching?"

Ron's Adam's apple bobbled as he swallowed hard before he spoke. "I believe I've made my point. You're being rude, belligerent, and insulting to Phoebe. Not only is she the owner of this team and your employer, but she is also a person deserving of respect."

Phoebe didn't have time to feel grateful for Ron's gallant defense. She was too alarmed by the vicious lines that had formed on each side of Dan's mouth. Too late, she remembered that this was a man who had been trained to meet all attacks with fierce counteraggression.

"Now listen here, you little pip-squeak. How I treat Phoebe isn't any of your business, and you know what you can do with your fucking etiquette lessons!"

"Stop right there," Ron warned.

But Dan was running on adrenaline and emotions he had no way to express except through anger. "I'll stop when I decide to stop! Unless you want to bring down an outhouse full of shit on your head, remember that I'm the one coaching this team. Looks to me like you've got more than you can handle just taking care of bimbo control!"

A heavy silence fell over the room.

All the blood drained from Phoebe's head. She felt sick and humiliated.

Dan's eyes dropped. His hand moved to his side in an ineffectual, almost helpless, gesture.

"I'm suspending you for one week," Ron said quietly.

Dan's head shot up and his lips tightened into a sneer. "You can't suspend me. I'm the coach, not one of the players."

"Nevertheless, you're suspended."

Alarmed, Phoebe took a quick step forward. "Ron . . ."

He put up his hand and said softly, "Please don't involve yourself in this, Phoebe. I have a job to do, and I need to do it my own way."

Dan closed the distance between them, hovering over the general manager in a manner that was so physically menacing Phoebe cringed. He spoke in a low, venomous drawl.

"I'm going to have your ass."

Ron's skin had assumed a faint greenish tone, but he kept his voice almost steady. "I want you to leave the building immediately. You're not to contact any of the other coaches or players until your suspension is up after the game next Sunday."

"I'll leave the building when I damn well please!"

"For Phoebe's sake, please don't make this any worse."

Seconds ticked by as Dan regarded him with tight-lipped fury. "You're going to regret this."

"I'm sure you're right. Nevertheless, I have to do what I think is best."

Dan gave him a long, hard glare and stalked from the room.

Phoebe pressed her hand to her mouth. Ron gave her arm a gentle squeeze.

"The press conference will take place on the practice field at one o'clock. I'll come to your office to get you."

"Ron, I really don't —"

"Excuse me, Phoebe, but I'm afraid I'm going to be sick."

Releasing her arm, he dashed from the room, while she stared after him in dismay.

Dan's feet slammed the stair treads as he stormed down to the first floor. When he hit the landing, he drew back his foot and kicked the metal door open. Once he was outside, the bright Indian summer day did nothing to soothe his rage.

As he stalked toward his car, he plotted what

he would do next. He was going to snap that little weasel's neck. Kick his weasel ass inside out. Any kind of suspension was in direct violation of his contract, and his lawyers were going to make mincemeat out of Phoebe and her GM. He didn't have to take shit like that. He was going to . . . He was going to . . .

He was going to stop acting like an ass.

He braced one hand on the roof of his car and took a deep, unsteady breath. He was embarrassed and furious, not at Phoebe but at himself. How could he have insulted her like that? He'd never in his life treated a woman so badly, not even Valerie. And Phoebe hadn't deserved it. She made him crazy, but she didn't have a mean bone in her body. She was funny and sexy and sweet in her own particular way.

He hated losing control like this, but when he'd heard that smug reporter telling the world that Phoebe had been in his hotel room, he'd been so full of rage at the violation of their privacy that he'd wanted to kick in the television screen. He knew enough about the press to realize that Phoebe would end up taking the heat for something that had been his fault. If only he'd talked to her about it instead of insulting her.

He knew he would have handled the whole thing a lot better if it hadn't been for those photographs. The idea of strangers looking at her body infuriated him. His reaction was completely illogical, considering the fact that her body had been on display in most of the major museums of the world, but

272

he couldn't help it. Besides, abstract paintings were different from brightly lit photographs. The photographs he'd seen in *Beau Monde* were works of art, but the world was filled with millions of horny assholes who weren't going to know that. Thinking about the way they would be drooling over those pages had made his temper snap.

His damned temper. When was he going to grow up and get it under control? It didn't take a degree in psychology to understand why he had such a hard time with it. Even when he was a little kid — four or five years old — his old man had beaten him up if he cried or complained because he was hurt or scared.

He could still hear his old man's drunken abuse. *Fetch my belt so I can give you something real to cry about, little girly.*

As he grew up, he'd discovered that the one emotion he could safely express around his old man was anger, whether on the football field or with his fists. Hell of a thing. A man thirty-seven years old still behaving like a playground bully. Except this time the bully had gotten what was coming to him. This time the bully had been cut down to size by the short little kid who couldn't even make the team.

Once again the anger came back to him, but now he was honest enough to admit it was a camouflage for shame. Shame that Ronald was the one who'd defended Phoebe. Shame that Ronald had been defending her against him.

If he hadn't been so mad at himself, he might

have been able to enjoy the fact that Ronald McDermitt had finally shown some gumption. If he hadn't been so mad at himself, he might have believed there was actually some hope for the team after all.

Ron cleared his throat. "Ms. Somerville posed for the *Beau Monde* photographs before she inherited the Stars. She certainly had no intention of embarrassing either the team or the NFL."

"Is it true that the commissioner has privately warned her about her behavior?" a female reporter asked.

"That is not true," Ron replied. "She hasn't spoken with the commissioner."

Only because she hadn't returned his phone calls, Phoebe thought unhappily as she sat in silence between Ron and Wally Hampton, the Stars' public relations director. The press conference was going even worse than she had anticipated. Not only had the local media shown up, but the national as well, hot on the trail of a terrific human interest story.

So many reporters had wanted to take part in the press conference that they had been forced to use the empty practice field. She, Ron, and Wally were seated near the fifty yard line behind a small table draped with a blue cloth bearing the Stars' logo. Some of the press members stood, while others had taken seats on wooden benches that had been set up for them.

At first all the questions had been centered

around Bert's will, but it hadn't taken them long to move on. So far, they had questioned Ron's management skills, Dan's coaching, and Phoebe's morals. Ron and Wally Hampton were answering all of the questions, even those addressed directly to her.

An overweight male reporter with bad skin and a scraggly beard stood. Wally Hampton whispered to her that he represented a sleazy tabloid. "Phoebe, are you going to do any more nudie shots?"

Wally interceded. "Ms. Somerville is much too busy with the Stars for any other outside activities."

The man scratched his chin beneath his beard. "This isn't the first time you've taken off your clothes for the public, is it?"

"Ms. Somerville's work for the great artist Arturo Flores is well-known," Ron said stiffly.

The tabloid reporter was interrupted by a local sports columnist. "There's been a lot of criticism of Coach Calebow recently, especially with so many turnovers every game. Some people think he's juggling his starters around too much. The players are starting to complain that they're being overworked and that he's taking the fun out of the game. For whatever reason, the team hasn't looked good yet this season. Any plans for changes?"

"None at all," Ron said. "It's still early and we're making adjustments." He went on to praise Dan's coaching abilities, and she wondered what would happen when the press learned that Dan had been suspended. Ron seemed to believe they could pass it off as a bad case of the flu, but she didn't think it would be that easy. What Ron had done was definitely illegal, and Dan was probably already on the phone to his lawyers.

She told herself not to think of his sneers and insults, but it was hard to put them out of her mind. Maybe it was all for the best that he had shown her so clearly what kind of person he was. Now she was forced to face the fact that she had been letting herself fall in love with the wrong man.

The obnoxious tabloid reporter was speaking again, an unpleasant leer on his face. "What about Coach Calebow's performance off the field, Phoebe? How's that?"

The other reporters shot him disgusted glances, but Phoebe wasn't fooled. Sooner or later they would have gotten around to asking the same thing. They would just have been more polite in their phrasing.

"Coach Calebow has a fine record —"

Phoebe couldn't take any more, and she put her hand on Ron's sleeve to stop him. "I'll answer this one." She leaned into the microphone. "Are you asking me to rate Coach Calebow's performance as a lover? Is that what your question means?"

For a moment the reporter looked taken aback by the directness of her attack, but then he gave an unctuous grin. "Sure, Phoebe. Tell it like it is."

"All right then. For the record, he's a terrific lover." She paused while the astonished reporters stared at her. "So is Coach Tully Archer, Bobby Tom Denton, Jim Biederot, Webster Greer, all of the running backs, and most of the offensive and defensive line. Now does that cover everyone in the organization I'm rumored to be sleeping with? I wouldn't want to leave anyone out."

The press corps laughed, but she wasn't done yet. Although she was shaking inside, she gazed directly at the obnoxious reporter and smiled. "By the way. If I remember correctly, you, sir, were a *small* disappointment."

The members of the press roared. If Phoebe hadn't won them over, she had at least proved that she wasn't quite as dumb as they thought.

The condominium Bert had kept for his mistresses was one of twenty luxury units set into a wooded area on the fringes of Naperville, which was located on the western edge of DuPage County. The attractive two-story beige brick unit was topped by a wood-shingled mansard roof. A pair of graceful Palladian windows sat on each side of an impressive set of double front doors inset with long ovals of leaded glass. Brass coach lamps glimmered in the six o'clock sun as Phoebe parked the car in the garage and walked into the house.

The interior was pleasantly decorated in soft shades of aqua, pearl gray, and white, giving the rooms a light, tropical feel. The kitchen opened out onto a sun room for informal eating, and a

278

cathedral ceiling made the small living room seem spacious.

"Molly? Peg?" Phoebe crouched down to pet Pooh, who was delirious with joy at her return. When there was no answer, she and the poodle went upstairs.

Her aqua and white bedroom held bleached oak furniture and a wide expanse of windows. She had been uncomfortable sleeping in the king-sized bed that dominated the room and had replaced it with a queen from the guest room at the estate. After tossing her linen jacket down on the puffy spread, she walked into the closet, where she changed into a pair of jeans and a Stars' T-shirt.

Neither Molly nor Peg had returned by the time Phoebe carried the whole wheat roll and pasta salad she found in the refrigerator out to the sun room. She padded across the pearl gray tiles in her sweat socks and sat on one of the white filigreed iron chairs that rested in front of a matching glass-topped table. A comfortable love seat upholstered in aqua and white peonies provided a cozy seating area at the end of the room.

She rubbed her toes along Pooh's back as she toyed with her salad. For once in her life she wasn't having any difficulty keeping off the extra five pounds that wanted to settle on her hips. Maybe because the blues were getting a firmer grip on her every day. She missed Viktor and her friends. She missed the gallery openings. She wanted a flat chest and a different childhood. She wanted a nice husband and a baby. She wanted Dan Calebow.

Not the real man who had verbally attacked her that morning, but the funny, tender man she had imagined him to be the night they had made love.

Her uncharacteristic plunge into self-pity was interrupted by the sound of the front door opening and closing. Pooh yipped and rushed out to investigate. Phoebe heard the rustle of packages, a soft greeting to Pooh, and then the sound of footsteps going upstairs. Pushing aside her salad, she made her way to the foyer in time to look through the sidelights and see Peg Kowalski's white Toyota pulling out of the drive.

She went upstairs and knocked on Molly's door. When there was no answer, she pushed it open anyway.

The bed was littered with sacks from the teenagers' dream stores: The Gap, Benetton, The Limited. Pooh, lying in the middle of the rubble, was watching as Molly pulled an assortment of clothes from the sacks.

Molly looked up at her, and for a few seconds, Phoebe thought she saw guilt reflected in her sister's small features. Then the old sullenness came back.

"Mrs. Kowalski took me shopping for school clothes. She has a teenage granddaughter, so she knew all the best stores."

Phoebe knew the best stores, too, but whenever she had suggested they shop, Molly had refused. "I can see that." Swallowing her disappointment, she took a seat on the side of the bed.

Molly reached out to stroke Pooh. Phoebe had

realized several weeks ago that Dan had been right about her sister's affection for the dog, but she hadn't commented on it. "Let me see what you bought."

For a while Molly behaved like a normal teenager. As she whipped out a denim jacket, ribbed sweaters, stonewashed jeans, and T-shirts, her eyes glowed with excitement. Phoebe couldn't fault Peg's taste. She'd helped Molly put together a perfect teenage girl's wardrobe.

"Have you thought about getting your ears pierced?"

"Could I?"

"I don't know why not. Think about it."

"I want to," Molly replied without hesitation.

"All right, then. We'll go on Friday." She refolded a pair of jeans and spoke carefully. "You haven't said much about school. How's it going?"

Each time Phoebe had asked the question in the past two weeks, Molly had refused to respond with anything more than monosyllables. Now her expression grew stony.

"How do you think? I hate it. Even the advanced classes are easy."

"Your classes were easy at Crayton, too."

"Public school is full of cretins."

"When you registered, your counselor mentioned that the English department uses student tutors in the writing lab. Why don't you volunteer?"

"Why should I?"

"Sometimes it feels good to help other people."

281

When Molly failed to respond, Phoebe continued her cautious probing. "At least you get to go to school with boys."

Molly became very busy picking at the tag on a pair of jeans. Phoebe tried again. "What's it like?"

"What do you mean?"

"Going to school with boys."

"They're big show-offs. And they're disgusting in the lunchroom."

"What about the boys in the advanced classes? Are they show-offs, too?"

"Some of them, I suppose. But a lot of them are nerds."

Phoebe suppressed a smile. "I've always liked nerds. There's nothing sexier in a man than intelligence. Of course, there is something to be said for dumb and cute."

Molly giggled, and for a few moments the barriers between them dissolved. "The boy who has a locker next to mine has long hair. He's really loud and obnoxious, always making guitar noises, but he's kind of cute, too."

"Is he?"

"He's in my advanced English class, but he's having trouble keeping up."

"Maybe you could offer to help him out."

"He doesn't even know who I am." Molly shoved a sack out of the way, her face clouding. "Nobody likes me. All the girls are bitches. If you're not a Pom Pom and you don't have the right clothes, they won't even talk to you."

Now Phoebe understood what had motivated the shopping spree. "I'm sure all the girls aren't that way. You just have to find the right group. It'll take time."

"I don't care about them! You told me that I only had to stay a semester, and then I'm leaving."

Defeated, Phoebe rose from the side of the bed. "Enjoy your new clothes. I wish we could have gone shopping together. I would have liked that."

Maybe she imagined it, but she thought she saw a flash of uncertainty cross her sister's face.

Just before bedtime that night, Phoebe clipped Pooh's fuchsia leash to her collar and led her outside for a walk. After the danger of Manhattan's streets, she loved this quiet residential area where she had the freedom to walk at night without worrying about becoming a statistic.

The town houses butted up against an area of wooded parkland. A paved bicycle path lit by an occasional streetlamp ran along the fringe. She loved the dense quiet, the loamy smell of the woods, and the crispness in the night air that announced the end of summer.

Pooh trotted ahead, sometimes stopping to poke her nose at a pile of acorns or beneath a clump of dry leaves, occasionally squatting to leave her mark on a particularly blissful spot. Phoebe's sneakers squeaked on the sidewalk, and the fleecy sweatshirt she wore was warm and cozy. For a few moments she let everything unpleasant slip away and enjoyed the night quiet.

Her sense of well-being was broken by the sound of a car turning into her court. She watched it slow down in front of her condo, then begin to pull into her driveway only to come to a stop as the headlights caught her. The driver immediately backed the car and drove toward her. Even before the vehicle stopped at the curb, she saw that it was a red Ferrari.

She tensed as Dan unfolded from the car and came toward her. He was wearing his glasses, and he'd thrown a Stars' windbreaker over a plum-colored shirt and jeans. Pooh began barking and straining at the end of her leash to get to him.

She tried to brace herself for what was certain to be another painful encounter, but it had been a difficult, exhausting day, and she didn't have many resources left.

He looked down at the fluffy white poodle trying to lasso his ankles with her leash. "Hey there, dawg."

"Her name is Pooh."

"Uh-huh. I guess it's just one of those words I don't like to use too often. Like 'snookums'." The breeze rumpled his dark blond hair as he took her in from sweatshirt to sneakers. "You look different. Cute."

She'd been called many things, but never cute. "What do you want?"

"How about a little meaningless chitchat for starters? Nice evening, isn't it?"

She couldn't let herself be pulled into whatever game he was playing, so she tugged on Pooh's leash and began walking. He fell into step next to her, adjusting his long stride to accommodate her shorter one.

"Weather's real nice. It's still hot during the day, but at night, you can tell fall's coming."

She said nothing.

"This is a real pretty area."

She continued walking.

"You know, you might think about contributing a little something to this conversation."

"We bimbos don't think."

He stuffed his hands into his pockets and said quietly, "Phoebe, I'm sorry. My temper got the best of me. That's no excuse, I know, but it's the truth. If anybody's a bimbo, it's me."

She had expected anger, not regret, but his attack that morning had wounded her too deeply, and she said nothing.

"It seems I'm always apologizing to you for something. It's been like that from the beginning, hasn't it?"

"I guess we're oil and water."

He ducked beneath a tree branch that dipped too low over the path. "I'd say we're more like gasoline and a blowtorch."

"Either way, I think we should try to avoid each other as much as possible." She stopped near one of the streetlamps. "I can't do anything about the suspension, you know. Ron refuses to lift it, and I won't countermand his orders."

"You know you're violating my contract."

"I know."

"The last thing you need right now is a lawsuit."

"I know that, too."

"How about we make a deal?"

"What kind of deal?"

"You keep me company next Saturday afternoon, and I keep my lawyers away from you."

That was the last thing she'd expected.

"I'm going to fly south for a couple of days to Gulf Shores. We call it the Redneck Riviera, and I have a place on the beach there. When I get back, I'll have some spare time on my hands. That big old house. Nothing to do. There's a local art show on Saturday, and since I know how much you like art, I thought we might check it out."

She stared at him. "Are you telling me you're not going to fight this suspension?"

"That's what I'm telling you."

"Why?"

"I've got my reasons, and they're private."

"I won't tell."

"Don't push it, Phoebe."

"Please. I want to know."

He sighed and she thought she saw something that looked very much like guilt flash across his features. "If you repeat this, I'll call you ten different kinds of a liar."

"I won't repeat it."

"The suspension is going to hurt the team, and I don't like that. It'll take a miracle for us to win this Sunday, and it'll be tough to recover from one and four. But I'm not fighting it because Ron finally did the right thing. I was way out of line.

I just never expected him to call me on it."

She finally smiled. "I don't believe it. You actually called him Ron."

"It slipped out, so don't count on it happening again." He began walking. "And don't think I've changed my opinion about him just because he finally showed some gumption. The jury's still out as far as I'm concerned. Now what about Saturday?"

She hesitated. "Why, Dan? We've already agreed that we don't mix well."

"I'm not siccing my lawyers on you. Isn't that a good enough reason?"

They had reached the end of the cul-de-sac. As they came around the curve, she gathered her courage. "I'm not a toy. You can't use me to amuse yourself and then toss me away when you're done."

His voice was surprisingly soft. "Then why do you act like one?"

Although he sounded more puzzled than accusatory, the hurt came back, and she picked up her stride.

He stayed with her. "You can't have it both ways. You can't flirt with everything in pants, wear clothes that look like they've been shrink-wrapped on your body, then expect people to treat you like you're Mother Teresa."

Because she knew there was truth in what he was saying, she stopped walking and turned to confront him. "I don't need a lecture from you. And since you're into personal assessment, maybe you should consider looking in the mirror and fig-uring out why you can't control your temper."

He stuffed his hands in his pockets. "I already know the answer to that one. And I'm not talking to you about it, so don't even let yourself get warmed up to ask."

"Then you shouldn't ask me why I act like a — The way I do."

He gave her a long, searching look. "I don't understand you. You're not like any woman I've ever met, except I keep thinking you're exactly like so many of the women I've met, and that's when I get into trouble."

Even as she gazed at him standing in a pool of golden light with the wind rustling his hair, she could hear the creak of the paddle wheel fan overhead. "I'm not going to bed with you again." She spoke softly. "That was a terrible mistake."

"I know."

She wished he hadn't agreed so quickly. "I don't think Saturday is a good idea."

He refused to be brushed off. "It's a great idea. You like art, and we'll be out in public, so we won't be able to paw each other."

"That's not what I meant!"

He grinned and chucked her under the chin, looking much too pleased with himself. "Pick you up at noon, hot stuff."

As he walked away from her toward his car, she raised her voice. "Don't you call me hot stuff!"

"Sorry." He opened the door and slid inside. "Hot stuff, *ma'am.*"

She stood beneath the streetlamp and watched him drive away. It was only an art show, she thought. What harm could there be?

Ray Hardesty could see Phoebe's blond hair shining in the streetlight from his vantage point on the hillside that ran behind the luxury condos. He had parked his van on a narrow road that led to a small residential development, and now he set the binoculars down on the seat. The rumors were true, he thought. Calebow had something personal going with the Stars' new owner.

He was storing up information about Dan Calebow like nuts for winter, ready to be drawn out if he had to use it, but so far Calebow was screwing himself over. The Stars had won only a single game since the season opener, and all their turnovers made them look like a college team. With each loss, Ray felt a little better. Maybe Calebow was going to get himself fired for incompetence.

He waited until the Stars' coach had driven away before he drove home himself. Ellen met him at the door and right away started fussing over him. He walked past her without a word, heading into the den, where he locked the door, slumped down in his favorite chair, and lit a cigarette.

The small room was paneled in knotty pine, although hardly any of it was visible because every foot of wall space was covered with memorabilia: action photographs of Ray Junior, trophies, jerseys tacked up with pushpins, framed certificates, and newspaper stories. When he was in here, Ray sometimes pretended all these honors belonged to him. For the past few months he'd even been sleeping on the old couch under the room's only window.

He sucked on his cigarette and coughed. The spasms were lasting longer all the time and his heart had been kicking up again, but he wasn't going to die yet. Not until he'd made Calebow pay. He wanted the Stars to lose every game. He wanted the whole world to know that bastard had made the biggest mistake of his life when he'd cut Ray Junior. Then maybe Ray could go back to some of his old hangouts and have a few drinks with his buddies. Just once before he died, he wanted to feel like a big shot again.

Ray got up from his chair and walked over to the built-in cupboards, where he pulled out the whiskey bottle he kept behind some boxes. He unscrewed the top and took a swig, then he carried the bottle over to the couch. As he sat, he picked up the gun he'd left on the end table when he'd gotten home from working the auto show at the Midwest Sports Dome yesterday.

The Dome's empty tonight, he thought, but tomorrow night they had a religious crusade coming in. The next night, it was some nigger rap group. He hated working concerts, but other than that, he liked being a security guard at the dome. Especially on Sunday afternoons when the Stars were losing.

Taking another swig, he stroked the gun in his lap and listened to the crowd call out his name.

Hardesty!

Hardesty!

Hardesty!

15

Phoebe slid back the curtain she had been peering through as Dan pulled his Ferrari into the drive at precisely noon on Saturday. Her stomach quivered like a teenager's on her first date. She went to the bottom of the stairs and called up to Molly. "Dan's here. Let's go."

"I don't want to."

"I understand that, but you're coming with us anyway. I need a dog sitter."

"That's just an excuse, and you know it. You could leave Pooh here with me."

"She needs some exercise. Stop stalling, Molly. Just give it a chance. It's a beautiful day, and we'll have fun." She wanted her words to come true, but she knew it was more likely that she and Dan would have an argument. She was hoping Molly's presence would act as a buffer.

The story of Dan's suspension had broken in Tuesday morning's papers, and both she and Ron had been hounded by reporters all week. Some of the press had even managed to locate Dan at his vacation home in Alabama. Dan and Ron had issued separate statements, neither of them substantive, and she had finally been forced to take the NFL commissioner's phone call. Needless to say, he wasn't happy with her. On the positive side, the suspension had squashed rumors about her affair with Dan.

Molly appeared at the top of the stairs wearing one of her new pairs of jeans, a plaid, oxford collar blouse, and a scowl. Phoebe had thought about calling Dan to let him know she was bringing Molly along, but something had held her back, maybe the intensity of her desire to hear his voice.

Molly had pulled her hair back to show off the small gold studs in her newly pierced earlobes. Phoebe was delighted that she had also somehow managed to talk Molly into a shorter, breezier cut, so that her hair no longer overpowered her small features. She thought Molly looked darling, but her sister refused to accept any of Phoebe's compliments.

"It's not fair," Molly complained. "I don't know why you're making me do this."

"Because I'm mean and heartless."

The day was warm, and Phoebe was wearing a pair of pleated khaki shorts with a daffodil yellow blouse, matching socks, and white canvas Keds. Just before she picked up Pooh, she plunked a floppy-brimmed straw hat on her head, positioning the sassy pink silk rose that held up the brim exactly in the center.

"That hat's stupid."

"Thanks for the vote of confidence, Molly. A lady always likes to know she's looking her best."

Molly's eyes dropped. "I just think you should look your age, that's all."

Ignoring that ego-booster, she opened the front

door. Dan was coming up the walk in a pair of faded jeans and white T-shirt, with a black and red Chicago Bulls' hat on his head. She reminded herself that she had met any number of men more physically beautiful. His nose wasn't entirely straight, his jaw was too square, and he was too muscular. But everything about him touched a hidden source of warmth inside her. She felt a connection with him that she couldn't explain, and she didn't like to remember how many times she'd thought of him during the week.

He greeted her with that drop-dead grin of his and stepped inside, while she busied herself scolding a yipping Pooh, who was twitching ecstatically in her arms in an effort to get to him.

"Quiet, Pooh, you're being obnoxious. Molly, would you get her leash?"

Pooh's pink tongue lapped and her eyes filled with adoration as she regarded Dan. He contemplated her warily.

"Tell me this is a bad dream, and you're not planning on bringing that major embarrassment with us."

"I've invited Molly along to watch her. We can take my car. I hope you don't mind."

He smiled at Molly. "Not at all."

Relieved, she stepped outside.

Molly's mulish expression made it obvious she wasn't happy, but Dan acted as if he didn't notice. "It's a good thing you could come with us, Miz Molly. You'll be able to keep that Chinese hors d'oeuvre away from me."

Molly forgot to look sullen. "Don't you like Pooh?"

"Can't stand her." He began leading both of them to the Cadillac Phoebe'd left at the curb.

Molly was so shocked that she quickened her steps to pull abreast of him. "Why? Don't you like dogs?"

" 'Course I do. Shepherds, labs, collies. Real dogs."

"Pooh is a real dog."

"She's a sissy dog, is what she is. A man spends too much time with a dog like that, next thing you know he's eating quiche and singing soprano."

Molly regarded him uncertainly. "That's a joke, isn't it?"

Dan's eyes twinkled. "Of course it's not a joke. You think I'd joke about something so serious." He turned to Phoebe and held out his hand. "Pass over the keys, honey lamb. There are certain things a man still does better than a woman, and driving a car is one of them."

Phoebe rolled her eyes as she gave him the keys to the Cadillac. "Today's going to be a living history lesson for you, Mol, on life in the fifties. You'll get to spend time with a man who's managed to miss an entire social movement."

Dan grinned as he unlocked the driver's door and reached inside to flip the automatic locks. "Climb in, ladies. I'd open the doors for you, but I don't want to be accused of holding back anybody's liberation."

Phoebe smiled as she passed Pooh to Molly, then

295

slid beneath the wheel to the passenger side of the front seat. As they pulled away from the curb, she turned toward the back. "If he takes us out to eat, Molly, order the most expensive thing on the menu. In the fifties, the men always paid."

"Dang," Dan grumbled. "Now you're playin' hardball."

Naperville was an old Illinois farm town that had grown into the largest city in DuPage County, with a population over ninety thousand. Intelligent city planning had made it into a showplace. There was plenty of parkland and a well-maintained historic district of shady streets, lovely gardens, and old homes. The town's small crown jewel was its Riverwalk, a park built along the section of the DuPage River that wound through the downtown area. It featured brick pathways, a covered bridge, a small amphitheater for outdoor concerts, and a fishing pond. At one end an old gravel quarry had been converted into a large public beach.

Dan left the car in a small lot on the edge of the festivities, and the three of them followed the brick sidewalk toward the crowd that had gathered beneath the trees. Every September the Riverwalk served as a picturesque setting for area artisans, a place where painters, sculptors, jewelers, and glassblowers could exhibit their work. Brightly colored pennants snapped in the warm breeze, and the beautifully mounted exhibits of paintings, ceramics, and glassware made splashes of color along the riverbank.

It was an affluent crowd. Young couples pushed

expensive strollers or carried well-fed babies in sturdy backpacks, while older adults in the brightly colored clothes they'd worn to the golf course that morning strolled between the exhibits. The teenagers' faces had been treated by expensive dermatologists, and thousands of dollars worth of orthodontics straightened their teeth. A sprinkling of African-Americans, Hispanics, and Asians, all well-dressed and prosperous looking, mingled with the crowd.

Phoebe felt as if she'd stumbled into the center of the American dream, a place where poverty and ethnic strife had been held at bay. She knew the city had its troubles, but for someone who had spent the last seven years in Manhattan, those troubles seemed small. There were full stomachs here and a sense of connection with others rare in a society that had become increasingly disconnected. Was it wrong, she wondered, to wish every community in America clean streets, unarmed citizens, families with 2.4 children, and a flotilla of Ford Broncos filling its parking lots?

She decided that Dan must have read her mind when his steps slowed beside her. "I guess this is just about as good as it gets."

"I guess so."

"Sure is different from the place where I grew up."

"Yes, I imagine it is."

Molly had gone ahead of them with Pooh, who was tossing her ears and prancing on her leash to show off for the crowd. Dan slipped on a pair

297

of Ray-Bans and pulled the Bulls' hat lower on his head. "This is about the best I can do for a disguise. Not that it's going to work. Especially with you in that hat."

"What's wrong with my hat?" Phoebe put her hand to the silk rose holding up the floppy brim.

"Not a thing. Matter of fact, I like it. It's just that we were going to have a pretty hard time looking anonymous anyway, and that hat makes it even harder."

She saw his point. "Maybe this outing wasn't such a good idea."

"It's a great idea. Now the press won't know what to think about us. I personally like the idea of thumbing our noses at all of them."

In front of them Molly tugged sharply on Pooh's leash and came to a sudden stop. "I want to go."

"We just got here," Phoebe pointed out.

"I don't care. I told you I didn't want to come."

Phoebe noticed Molly glancing toward a group of teenage girls sitting on the grassy slope just ahead. "Are those girls friends of yours?"

"They're bitches. They're all Pom Poms and they think they're better than everybody else. I hate them."

"All the more reason to hold up your head." Dan slipped off his sunglasses and studied the group for a moment. "Come on, Miz Molly. Let's show 'em what you're made of." He took Pooh's leash and passed it over. "Phoebe, hold on to your little rat. Miz Molly and me have a job to do."

Phoebe was too worried about Molly to take

298

Dan to task for calling Pooh a rat. She watched as he drew her sister toward the girls. It was obvious she didn't want to go any closer, but Dan wouldn't release her. Only when he pulled off his cap did she see what he was up to. Next to Bobby Tom and Jim Biederot, his was the most recognizable face in DuPage County, and he obviously intended to let Molly use him to impress the girls from her school.

But as Phoebe walked up the slope to get closer to the girls, she saw that Mr. Big Shot had overestimated himself. While males might recognize him, these teenage girls were definitely not football fans.

"Your daddy wouldn't happen to be Tim Reynolds, the realtor, would he?" she heard Dan ask a gum-chewing nymphet with long hair and mall bangs.

"Nuh-uh," the girl replied, more interested in the contents of her purse than exchanging pleasantries with the terror of the gridiron.

"Nice try," Phoebe murmured under her breath as she pulled up behind him. And then, more loudly, "Hi, girls. I'm Molly's sister."

The girls looked from Phoebe to Molly. "I thought she was your mother," an overly made-up redhead said.

Dan snickered.

Ignoring him, she searched her mind for a topic of conversation while Molly stared miserably at her feet. "How's school going so far this year?"

"Okay," one of them mumbled. Another slipped

the headset to her Walkman over her ears. The girls ignored Molly to scan the crowd for more worthy peers.

Phoebe tried again. "Molly said most of the teachers are nice."

"Yeah."

"I guess." The redhead got to her feet. "Let's go, Kelly. This is boring."

Phoebe glanced at Dan. This had been his idea, and it was a disaster. But instead of looking repentant, he seemed distinctly pleased with himself.

"It sure has been nice to meet you girls. Now y'all have a good time today, y'hear?"

The girls looked at him as if he were a Martian and began to move down the slope toward a group of boys coming along the path.

"You didn't exactly wow them," she pointed out.

He slipped his sunglasses in his T-shirt pocket. "Just you wait, honey lamb. I've been impressing females all my life, and I know what I'm doing."

Molly's face was crimson with embarrassment, and she looked as if she were ready to break into tears. "I told you I didn't want to come! I hate this! And I hate you!" She started to rush away, but before she could leave, Dan shot out his arm and pulled her to his side.

"Not so fast, Miz Molly. We're just getting to the good part."

Phoebe immediately saw the cause of Molly's increasing distress. Approaching the group of girls was a gang of four boys, their baseball hats turned backward, oversized T-shirts hanging nearly to the bottoms of their shorts, tongues flapping on big black sneakers.

"Dan, let her go. You've embarrassed her enough."

"I've got half a mind to leave the two of you to your own pitiful devices, except I'm not that cruel."

The girls were calling out the boys' names, and at the same time trying to look aloof. The boys jabbed each other in the ribs. One of them gave a loud belch that was obviously intended to impress.

And then they saw Dan.

Their mouths dropped, and for several moments they seemed to have lost the power of movement. The girls, chattering and tossing their hair, had surrounded them, but the boys paid no attention. Their eyes were riveted on the Stars' coach.

And Dan's eyes were riveted on Molly. He grinned at her and chucked her chin. "Now smile, Miz Molly, and act like you don't have a care in the world."

Molly saw what was happening. She swallowed hard as the boys all turned her way.

"Do you know any of them?" Dan asked quietly, keeping his eyes on her.

"The one with the long hair has the locker next to mine."

Phoebe remembered Molly's reference to the cute boy who made guitar noises.

"All right, now. You just lift your hand and

give him a little wave."

Molly looked panicked. "I can't do that."

"Right now he's a lot more nervous than you are. Do what I say."

Dan had been a leader of men since he'd thrown his first football, and an insecure teenage girl was no match for him. Molly gave a short, jerky wave before her arm dropped back to her side and her cheeks turned crimson.

It was all the encouragement the boys needed. Led by Molly's locker neighbor, they rushed forward.

"I stand in awe," Phoebe whispered to Dan.

"It's about time I got some respect."

Their leader's face was red with embarrassment as he came to a stop near Molly. He was tall, all knobby knees and bony elbows, well-scrubbed, well-fed, his long hair clean and shiny. The boys shuffled their feet as if they were stomping out ants. Dan still had his arm draped over Molly's shoulders, but he deliberately turned his head toward Phoebe, making it difficult for the boys to address him.

"Beautiful day, isn't it?" he said.

"Lovely," she replied, understanding immediately what he was doing. "I hope it doesn't rain."

"Weatherman said it was going to be nice all week."

"You don't say." She watched out of the corner of her eye as the long-haired boy's Adam's apple bobbed in his neck. The boys seemed to realize they could only get to Dan through Molly. Their eyes darted back and forth between him and her.

"I've seen you at school, haven't I?" their leader muttered.

"Uh-huh," Molly replied.

"Yeah, I guess I have the next locker."

"Yeah, I guess."

In Phoebe's opinion, someone with her sister's astronomical IQ could have come up with a more interesting reply. Where was that handy quote from Dostoyevski when it would do some good?

"My name's Jeff."

"I'm Molly."

While Jeff was introducing the other boys, Dan began pointing out the sights of the Riverwalk to Phoebe. He commented on the trees. The flowers. The ducks. But he never took his arm from around Molly's shoulders, and the warmth Phoebe had felt for him when she'd opened her front door turned into a soft melting.

The conversation between Molly and the boys was becoming a little less torturous. Phoebe saw the Pom Poms approaching, their mascaraed eyes alive with a wary curiosity.

"Lots of feathers on those critters, aren't there?" Dan kept his eyes on the river.

"Brown ones," Phoebe replied, "although the one in the lead seems to have a spot of blue."

"I believe that's green."

"Do you? Yes, I think you're right."

Dan's presence was like a magnet. Several other boys passing along saw who their friends were with and charged through the Pom Poms to approach.

"Hey, Jeff, how's it going, man?"

"Hi, Mark. Hi, Rob. This is Molly. She's new this year."

Dan and Phoebe traded a few more observations on duck plumage, before Dan finally turned his head to acknowledge the boys.

"Well, hi there, fellas. Are you guys friends of Molly's?"

They all enthusiastically agreed that they were very good friends. Responding to Dan's geniality, they gradually forgot their shyness and began asking questions about the team. The Pom Poms had joined the group and were regarding Molly with new interest. When several of the boys announced they were on their way to get ice cream, they invited Molly to go along.

She turned pleading eyes toward Phoebe. "May I?"

"Sure." Phoebe made arrangements to meet Molly at the Riverwalk's dandelion fountain in an hour.

But Dan wasn't done. As the kids began to move away, he called after them. "Molly, you should bring a few of your friends to a game one of these Sundays. You could introduce them to some of the players afterward."

The boys' jaws dropped. "Yeah, Molly!"

"Hey, that'd be neat!"

"Do you know Bobby Tom, Molly?"

"I've met him," she said.

"Boy, are you lucky!"

As the boisterous gang moved away, Phoebe

smiled at Dan. "That was blatant bribery."

He grinned. "I know."

"I'm not sure about some of those girls, though. A few of them looked as if they'd sell their best friend for lunch money."

"It doesn't matter. We just gave Molly an even playing field. Now she can make her own choices."

Pooh, impatient to strut her stuff, tugged on her leash. They walked down the slope of lawn and began to wander through the exhibits, but although Dan had once again donned his hat and sunglasses, too many people had noticed him as he'd talked with the teenagers, and some of them began to call his name, while they gazed at Phoebe with avid curiosity.

He nodded in response to their greetings and spoke to her under his breath. "Keep moving. Once you stop, it's all over." He glared at Pooh. "And would you mind either walking in front of me or behind me? I don't want people to think —"

"Your image as a macho man is more than a match for one small dog. Lord, if you're making this big a fuss over a poodle, I can't imagine what you'd do if Viktor were along."

"I like Viktor. It's that major embarrassment at the end of the leash I want to get rid of. Did you have to put that purple bow on her?"

"It's not purple, it's mauve. Have you been this insecure all your life, or does it go along with advancing middle age?"

"I'm not the one that girl thought was Molly's mother."

"Good thing. Considering how easily your masculinity is threatened, that might have pushed you over the edge."

The mutually pleasant volleying of insults continued for some time, each verbal serve immediately returned, but with no hard spikes and no balls hit out-of-bounds.

Dan bought her a handblown green and pink glass "witch's ball" to hang in a sunny window. She bought him a matted black-and-white photograph of the Chicago skyline with a fingernail moon high in the sky.

"I'm gonna hang this in my office. I've been looking for something special to put up."

As he admired her gift, another set of photographs came into her mind, and some of the pleasure she had been taking in the day faded. As they walked on, she realized she was mutilating the sack that held the glass witch's ball. She wondered if she had the courage, just once, to be honest with a man instead of playing games.

"Dan," she said softly, "I'm still upset about your reaction to the *Beau Monde* photographs. I'm proud of them."

"So much for our nice afternoon."

"I wish you wouldn't act as though they're pornographic. They're some of Asha Belchoir's best work."

"They're pictures of a naked woman, is what they are."

She felt like a fool for even trying to reason with him. "I can't believe how narrow-minded you are!"

"And I can't believe a die-hard exhibitionist has the gall to criticize me."

"I'm not an exhibitionist!"

"No offense, Phoebe, but you've taken your clothes off for more people than Gypsy Rose Lee ever did."

Her temper flared, and she came to a stop next to a clump of mock orange shrubs. "You redneck jerk! You wouldn't recognize art if it hit you in the head. You have the aesthetic judgment of a — a —"

"Football player?"

"No. A football!"

He whipped off his sunglasses and glared at her. "Just because I happen to think that nice women should keep their clothes on in public doesn't mean I can't appreciate art."

"Last week I was a bimbo and now I'm a nice woman. Maybe you'd better make up your mind."

She saw by his expression that she'd scored a hit, but that wasn't what she wanted. She wasn't interested in putting points on some imaginary scoreboard; she simply wanted him to understand. Her temper faded, and she slipped her hands into the pockets of her shorts. "It bothers me a lot that you're trying to make those photos into something sordid. They're not."

He looked out toward the river, and his voice lost its belligerent edge. "I can't help it."

She gazed at him, trying to understand the expression on his face. "Why? What does it matter to you?"

"I don't know. It just does."

"Because it reflects on the team?"

"You can't deny that."

"I'm sorry about the timing."

"I know that." He turned to her, and his expression was surprisingly gentle. "The photographs are beautiful, Phoebe. Both of us know that. But they're still not as pretty as you are."

They stood there without moving. She gazed into his eyes and felt as if he were pulling her into an embrace. She could feel herself leaning forward, see that he was doing the same. And then Pooh barked, breaking the mood.

He took her arm and propelled her forward. "Come on. I'm gonna buy you your very own hot dog bun. With a little mustard and pickle relish, you might not notice the best part is missing."

Taking his cue, she fell into step beside him. "Do you have any idea what goes into hot dogs?"

"No, and I don't want to know. Unless — Hey, Pooh, you interested in going into the meat industry?"

"That's not funny. Don't listen to him, Pooh." He chuckled.

Five minutes later, she was munching on a french fry, while Dan bit into his second hot dog. A wistful note crept into her voice. "There isn't any possibility, is there, that the Stars are going to win the AFC Championship?"

"I start every season planning to win the Super Bowl."

"I'm not talking about fantasies, I'm talking about reality."

"We're going to give it our best, Phoebe. A lot of it depends on whether or not we can stay healthy. Injuries always play a big part. Last year, for example, the Cowboys were a better team than the Sabers, but they lost the Super Bowl because so many of their starters were hurt. Right now we're not playing up to our potential, but things are going to start falling into place soon."

"This weekend?"

He gave her a rueful smile. "Probably not that soon."

"Everybody says the men are grumbling about how hard you're pushing them."

"That's my job."

She sighed. "I know you're looking forward to working for Reed, and I can't really blame you."

She expected a wisecrack, but instead, Dan looked thoughtful. "Frankly, I've never been too crazy about your cousin. I'm also getting the distinct impression he's behind some of our bad press. Over the years, he's cultivated a lot of friends in the media."

Phoebe had suspected the same thing. Still, she could hardly take Dan's statement as a vote of confidence. "At least he knows something about football."

"That's true." He slipped his arm around her shoulders and gave her a comforting squeeze. "But he sure is going to look funny kissing Bobby Tom."

309

16

Ron stared down at the field from the skybox window. "I knew what would happen when I suspended him, but I was hoping it wouldn't be this bad."

The Stars had been ineffectual against the bloodthirsty Los Angeles Raiders. Jim Biederot was intercepted four times, Bobby Tom couldn't keep his footing, and the defense didn't make the tackles that counted. Phoebe gave one last glance at the final score: *Raiders 34, Stars 3.*

"Never mind," she said. "It'll be better next week."

"We're playing the Giants next week. They only have one loss this season, and that was to the Sabers."

Before she could respond, one of Bert's cronies came up to talk to him.

The next morning, as she drove to work for the eight o'clock meeting Ron had requested, she once again found herself reliving Saturday afternoon. She couldn't remember the last time she'd had such a wonderful time. From the art fair, the three of them had gone to an area restaurant for an early dinner, and Dan had proved to be as good a listener as he was a storyteller. She'd invited him back to the condo, where he'd talked Molly

310

into modeling all her new clothes for him. His teasing compliments had done more for Molly's self-confidence than anything Phoebe had said. He'd left a little after eight, and she'd spent the rest of the night torturing herself with images of him in bed with his ex-wife.

Unusually heavy traffic on Naper Boulevard held her up, and she arrived at Ron's office a few minutes after eight. Dan was already there. She gave them both a cheerful smile as she took a seat around the conference table and hoped Dan couldn't see how skittish she felt being with him again.

As soon as she was settled, Ron began. "Now that your suspension is over, Dan, I wanted all of us to have a chance to clear the air. As you're both aware, we've taken some hard hits in the press these past few weeks. This morning's papers are the worst. I received a call at home from our new commissioner last night stating, in the strongest possible terms, that we have become an embarrassment to the League."

"Don't you think that's a little extreme," Dan said.

"He cited the *Beau Monde* photographs, your suspension, Phoebe's manner of dress on the sidelines, and, of course, the rumored romantic liaison between the two of you. He also mentioned a phone conversation he had with you last week, Phoebe. I wish I'd known about it. Is there any reason you didn't tell me you'd spoken with the commissioner?"

Phoebe shifted her weight in the chair and decided she'd liked Ron better when he was a wimp. "It slipped my mind."

Dan regarded her skeptically. "That's a little hard to believe."

"He's still rather upset about it," Ron said.

"I'm the one who should be upset."

"Would you like to tell us why?"

She tried to figure out how to present this so they wouldn't jump all over her. "He was actually sort of fatherly. He told me that sometimes a person can get in over her head — especially a pretty little thing like myself who is trying to do a man's job. He said I wasn't being fair to Reed. He mentioned all the things he spoke to you about, plus a rumor he'd picked up that I was also carrying on with Bobby Tom." Her mouth tightened. "He suggested that monthly hormonal fluctuations might be at the root of my troubles."

Ron knew her well enough to regard her warily. "What did you say?"

"I — uh —" She looked past him out the window. "Never mind."

"Phoebe . . ."

She bowed to the inevitable with a sigh. "I told him I had to get off the phone because *Playboy* was on the other line."

Ron winced, but Dan laughed.

"Don't encourage her." Ron was clearly annoyed. "You know that if the Stars were winning, we wouldn't be getting all this flak."

"I was suspended last week! It's real hard to

win a football game when you're not coaching the team."

"That's one of the reasons I wanted to talk to both of you." Ron toyed with his coffee mug. "As far as I'm concerned, what's past is past. We can't do anything about the photographs, and as for Phoebe's dress on the sidelines — Well, I believe the commissioner's wrong."

"I can just imagine how thrilled he was with that Stars' tattoo she had on her shoulder blade yesterday. It showed up real nice on TV."

"It's removable," she said. "And I was simply displaying my team spirit."

"You were displaying a lot more than team spirit."

"She's filling up some of the empty seats," Ron said. "Many of them with women, by the way." He looked at Dan. "Your suspension was my decision and I take full responsibility for yesterday's loss. I'm also giving you both a warning. I don't know what's going on between the two of you, but I don't want to get caught in the cross fire again. Is that understood?"

"Understood," Dan said brusquely.

"There's nothing going on," Phoebe said. Dan's steady gaze was making her uncomfortable. Once again she reminded herself that — temporarily, at least — these two worked for her. She stood. "Now, if you'll excuse me, I have work to do."

The corner of Dan's mouth kicked up. "Say howdy to your buddies over at *Playboy* for me."

She repressed a smile as she left the room and

headed for her office, where she spent the rest of the day reading reports and studying the spreadsheets on her computer screen that detailed the team's complex finances. As she jotted figures on the steno pad she kept next to the keyboard, she admitted to herself that it felt good to use her brain again.

Their next game was being played at Giants Stadium in the Meadowlands for ABC's "Monday Night Football." Since no team wanted to lose in front of such a sizable television audience, Monday night games were considered to be among the most important of the season. As the week advanced the already tense atmosphere at the Stars Complex grew so explosive that fights began to break out among the players, while the staff snapped at each other, and Dan snapped at everyone. The team's recent bad publicity had made it impossible for Phoebe to continue hiding from the media, and her dread of the upcoming game was compounded when she reluctantly agreed to ABC's request for a halftime interview.

The players were tightly strung, the chartered plane virtually silent as it left O'Hare on Sunday afternoon for Newark. "It's like a morgue back there," Phoebe said to Ron as the flight attendants handed them the drinks they had requested: beer for Ron, tomato juice for her. "I don't think it's good for the players to be so tense."

"Dan's worked them as hard as I've ever seen this week, and they know what's at stake. We have everything riding on this game."

She had done more than stare at spreadsheets this week; she had also read a year's worth of back issues of several well-regarded sports magazines, and she nibbled thoughtfully on her lower lip. "I still don't think they should be so uptight. Maybe that's why they're fumbling the ball so much."

"The only thing that will make them relax is finally having a win behind them."

"If they don't loosen up a little, that might not happen."

"I sincerely hope you're wrong."

He turned his attention back to *Forbes*. She hesitated for only a moment before she leaned down and surreptitiously lifted the latch on the small dog carrier she had stowed beneath her legs.

Seconds later, the interior of the plane was filled with shrill yips as Pooh tore down the center aisle.

In the row of seats ahead of her, Dan's head shot up, and he whirled around to face her. "Damn it, Phoebe! You brought that dog with you!"

"Oops." Her lips formed a small, pink oval as she stood and squeezed past Ron. "Excuse me. I seem to have misplaced my pooch."

Ignoring Dan, she made her way into the coach section of the plane, where she immediately heard the rumble of male laughter. As she had hoped, the players welcomed the distraction Pooh was providing. The poodle scooted between their feet, scrambled over their carryons, and licked any uncovered human part she could reach.

Bobby Tom reached down to snare her, but she dodged and crouched between Webster Greer's feet. Phoebe couldn't help but laugh at the sight of Pooh's fluffy little head with its perky periwinkle bow perched on top of Webster's size fourteen sneakers. She gazed warily up the aisle at her mistress and tried to figure out how much trouble she'd gotten herself into.

"I don't think she wants you to catch her," Webster observed.

"She's not too fond of her carrier."

Since Pooh seemed to be doing fine on her own, Phoebe began chatting with the players nearby, asking them about their families, the books they were reading, the music they were listening to on their Walkmans. Pooh had moved on to curl over the prized right foot of the team's placekicker, but as Phoebe came closer, the dog darted across the aisle only to have Darnell Pruitt, the Stars' largest offensive tackle, scoop her up.

"This what you're looking for, Miss Somerville?"

Phoebe hesitated. Of all the men on the team, Darnell Pruitt was the most intimidating. A gold tooth studded with a half-carat diamond glistened in the front of his mouth, and heavy gold chains draped his black leather vest. He was shirtless beneath the vest, revealing a huge chest and heavily muscled forearms displayed in all their polished ebony glory. His eyes were hidden behind menacing black sunglasses, his nose was broad and flat, and a heavy scar puckered one shoulder. An article she had read just the day before in *Sports Illustrated* had described Darnell as one of the five meanest men in the NFL, and as she studied him, she saw no reason to disagree. She noticed that his teammates had left the seat next to him empty.

Even Pooh was intimidated. The poodle crouched on Darnell's lap, muzzle down, peering up at him with wary eyes. With a flash of alarm, Phoebe saw that she definitely looked nervous.

She quickly moved along the aisle, absolutely certain that it was not a good idea for Pooh to get nervous while she was sitting on Darnell Pruitt's lap. When she reached his row, she regarded him anxiously.

"Maybe — uh — I'd better take her."

"Sit down," he barked.

It was a command, not a request, and she collapsed into the empty seat like an accordion.

Darnell's chains rattled.

Pooh began to tremble.

Phoebe chose that inopportune moment to recall the quote Darnell had given *Sports Illustrated*. *What I like most about football,* he had said, *is seeing my man being carried off the field.*

She cleared her throat. "It's — uh — not a good idea for her to get nervous."

"Is that so?" he said belligerently. Scooping up the dog in hands the size of stove mitts, he brought the animal to eye level.

They stared at each other. Darnell's menacing black sunglasses reflected Pooh's round brown eyes. Phoebe held her breath as she waited for catastrophe. The seconds ticked by.

Pooh stuck out her long pink tongue and licked Darnell's cheek.

The diamond in Darnell's gold tooth flashed as he grinned. "I like this dog."

"I can't tell you how happy that makes me," Phoebe said on a single rush of breath.

Pooh nuzzled through Darnell's chains to cuddle closer. He stroked the dog's topknot where the periwinkle bow had come undone as usual. "My mama wouldn't let me have a dog when I was growin' up. She said she didn't want fleas in the house."

"Not all dogs have fleas. Pooh doesn't."

"I'm gonna tell her that. Maybe she'll let me have one now."

Phoebe blinked. "You live with your mother, Darnell?"

He grinned. "Yes, ma'am. She keeps threatenin' to move out, but I know she won't do it till I get married. She says she doesn't trust me to take care of myself."

"I see. Are you getting married soon?"

"Oh, no, ma'am. Not sayin' I don't want to, but life can get complicated, you know."

"I certainly do."

"Sometimes the ladies you're attracted to might not be attracted to you or vice versa."

She regarded him curiously. "Which one is it?"

"Pardon me?"

"Vice? Or versa? Is the lady attracted to you, but you're not attracted to her, or —"

"The other way around. I'm attracted to her,

but she's not too crazy about me."

"That's hard for me to believe. I thought you football players could take your pick of women."

"You just try explainin' that to Miss Charmaine Dodd."

Phoebe adored hearing stories about people's love lives. Slipping off her loafers, she drew her legs beneath her. "Tell me about her. If you want to, that is."

"Well, she's a real stubborn lady. And stuck on herself. She's the organist at Mama's church, and the rest of the time she's a librarian. Shoot, she doesn't even dress right. Wears these prissy little skirts and blouses buttoned all the way up to her chin. Walks around with her nose in the air."

"But you like her anyway."

"Let's just say I can't seem to put her out of my mind. Unfortunately, the lady doesn't respect me in return because she's got a education, see, and I don't."

"You went to college."

For a moment he was silent. When he spoke, his tone was so quiet only she could hear him. "Do you know what college is like for somebody like me?"

"No, I don't."

"They take a kid like me, eighteen years old, never had much in life, and they say, 'Darnell, you play ball for us, and we'll take real good care of you. We'll give you a fine scholarship, and — You like cars, Darnell? 'Cause one of our alums got a big Chevy dealership, and he sure would like to give you a shiny new Corvette as a sign of his appreciation for choosing our fine university. We'll take good care of you, Darnell. We'll give you a high-payin' summer job, except — dig this — you won't even have to show up for work. And don't worry too much about your classes, 'cause we're gonna sign you up for some independent studies.' " He regarded her through the dark lenses of his sunglasses. "You know what independent study meant for somebody like me? It meant, I work my man over real good on Saturday afternoons, and I got an A when the grades came out."

He shrugged. "I never graduated, and now I got all kinds of money. But sometimes I think it don't matter. What good does money do when a lady like Charmaine Dodd starts talkin' to you 'bout some white dude wrote this famous poem she loves, and her eyes get all lit up, but you don't know jack about poetry, or literature, or anything else she thinks is important?"

Silence fell between them. Pooh had worked her muzzle into the crook of Darnell's neck and was snoring softly.

"What's stopping you from going back to school?"

"Me? Aw, no, I couldn't do that. Football takes up too much time."

"Maybe you could go during the off-season." She smiled. "Why don't you ask Miss Dodd what she thinks of the idea?"

"She'd laugh at me."

"If she laughs at you, then you've got the wrong woman for sure."

"I wasn't ever much of a student," he admitted with obvious reluctance.

"Probably because nobody expected you to be."

"I don't know."

"Come on, Darnell. You chicken?"

He glowered at her.

"Just kidding," she said hastily. "The fact that you're not a natural student could work to your advantage." She grinned. "You might have to request some private tutoring."

Darnell laughed, and half a dozen players swung their heads around to stare at him in disbelief.

Elvis Crenshaw stood up. "Hey, Darnell, you gonna hog that dog the whole trip? Pass it over. I like dogs, too."

Darnell scowled at him. "Why don't you go fuck — Er —"

The men hooted as Darnell ducked his head in embarrassment. And then their laughter abruptly snapped off.

Phoebe turned her head to determine what had caused the interruption and saw that Dan had entered the cabin. The men returned to their magazines and music, or closed their eyes and pretended to nap, acting as if they had been caught laughing at a funeral.

Dan's power over even the most hardened of these veterans amazed her. She knew from snatches of conversations she'd overheard that,

321

even though the men resented the relentless pressure he put on them, they still respected him. Ron said that one of the reasons Dan kept himself in such excellent physical shape was because he never asked the men to do anything he couldn't do himself.

His eyes had widened slightly at the sight of Pooh sound asleep on his star tackle's chest. He regarded Phoebe suspiciously, chatted for a few moments with the trainer, then, to everyone's obvious relief, disappeared back into the first-class cabin.

"That is one cranky man," Phoebe muttered as she stood.

"Coach has a lot on his mind," Darnell replied.

Pooh stirred and Darnell reluctantly passed her over to Elvis Crenshaw. Phoebe stopped for a few minutes to ask Webster about Krystal and his children, then Bobby Tom wanted to talk to her about an idea he had for marketing his own line of salsa. She asked Jim Biederot about his shoulder and talked to several of the rookies about Chicago nightlife.

When she finally reclaimed Pooh, the atmosphere in the cabin was considerably more relaxed, but she was certain Dan would reverse that tomorrow. She couldn't fault him for his dedication, but sometimes she wondered how much he knew about human nature. By the time the last team meeting was over, he'd have them all so tightly strung they'd be vibrating.

She spent the evening and much of the next

day with Viktor. He chatted enthusiastically about the game and was pleased that she had invited him to share her skybox. He took Pooh with him when they parted, promising to bring the poodle back with him for the game.

For the first time since she had taken over as owner, she joined the team for their pregame dinner at the hotel at five that evening. Instead of taking the chair next to Ron, she sat with Darnell and Elvis Crenshaw, where she bypassed the plate-sized sirloin that was set before her in favor of her baked potato and salad.

It was a grim, silent meal. Afterward, as the players filed out, she saw that a group of Giant fans had somehow gotten into the hotel lobby and draped it with red and blue signs that left no doubt about where their sentiments lay. Her quick flash of anger made her realize how much the Stars had come to matter to her. Instead of an anonymous sports team, they had become a group of people she cared about.

Lost in thought, she dressed automatically in the outfit Simone had made for her in a rush last week. After repacking her suitcase for the late-night return to O'Hare following the game, she met Ron in the lobby.

He smiled as he took in her clothing. "Perfect."

She looked doubtfully at her reflection in the mirrored tile on the lobby wall. "I knew this was no time to stage a retreat, but it's not exactly me."

She was wearing her own variation of a Stars' uniform: sky blue satin knickers with a sparkly gold stripe down the outside of each thigh. A pair of blue and gold socks were tucked into soft leather sneakers studded with rhinestones. Since the early October evenings were bound to be a bit chilly, Simone had put together a puffy blue and gold satin bomber jacket with an enormous sparkly star on the back and smaller ones scattered over the front. She wore her hair in curls with a wide ribbon threaded through and tied into a floppy blue bow on top of her head, just right of center.

"It's exactly you," Ron said. "The cameramen are going to go crazy."

They said little more to each other as they drove to the Meadowlands and Giants Stadium. Before it had been reclaimed, the Jersey Meadowlands had been a dumping ground for rusty automobiles and men who ran afoul of the mob. Rumors persisted that the stadium had been built on the bridge of Jimmy Hoffa's nose.

When they reached the owners' entrance forty-five minutes before kickoff, Ron volunteered to escort her up to the skybox before he made his regular pregame visit to the locker room, but she had already made up her mind what she needed to do and she shook her head.

"I'm going with you."

"To the locker room?"

She gave an abrupt nod. "To the locker room."

Ron regarded her uncertainly but made no comment as he led the way through the subterranean depths of the stadium. They entered a locker room that was ominously quiet. With the exception of their helmets, the players were fully dressed, and she felt as if she had stumbled into a land populated by titans. On the field, they were enormous, but trapped indoors wearing full battle gear, their size was truly awesome.

Some of them stood while others hunched on wooden benches with their knees splayed and hands dangling loosely from bent wrists. Bobby Tom and Jim Biederot sat on a long table at the side, their backs resting against the wall. All of their faces were grim as they listened to Dan speak.

". . . we're playing our own game out there tonight. We're not going to win with field goals. We've got to win in the red zone. We've got to win in short-yardage situations. . . ."

Dan was so intensely focused on his players that he didn't notice she and Ron had entered the locker room until he had finished.

Ron cleared his throat. "Uhm . . . Miss Somerville wanted to stop by and wish all of you luck tonight."

Dan's frown indicated that she was unwelcome. Forcing herself to ignore him, she pasted her brightest smile on her face and stepped into the middle of the locker room. She swallowed her self-consciousness and assumed a pinup pose that showed off her outfit. "Hi, guys. What do you think? Pretty nifty, huh?"

Several of the men smiled, but she knew it was going to take more than a fashion show to cut through their tension. Although she was the last person to consider herself an authority on football, several facts seemed clear to her. The Stars had superb players and excellent coaching, but for some reason, they couldn't manage to hold on to the football. To her mind, that was a mental problem, not a physical one, and ever since yesterday's plane ride, she couldn't shake the idea that they wouldn't fumble so much if they could just relax a little and have fun.

She stepped up on one of the benches near the front so she could see everybody. "Okay, guys, here goes. My first and — I sincerely hope — last locker room speech."

Several of them smiled.

"I have complete faith in Coach Calebow. Everybody tells me that he's a wonderful football strategist and a great motivator of men. Besides, he's s-o-o-o cute."

As she had hoped, they began to laugh. She didn't risk looking at Dan to see how he was receiving her teasing. Instead, she puckered her brow. "Not that the rest of you aren't cute, too. Except for Webster. I've seen Krystal in action, and, believe me, I'm not even looking in Webster's direction."

More laughter. Webster grinned and ducked his head in embarrassment.

Her own smile faded. "What I want to tell you is this. If you win tonight's game, you'll make my life easier as far as the press is concerned, but, to be totally honest, beating the Giants is more important to all of you than it is to me. I mean, I can only get so worked up about a football game, and —"

"Miss Somerville . . ." The warning note in Dan's voice was plain.

She hastily went on. "However, as incredible as it seems to me, I've actually gotten to like a few of you oversized bozos, and since all of you want to win so badly tonight, I'm going to tell you how to do it."

Even though she was deliberately avoiding looking at Dan, she could feel those fierce green eyes boring holes right through her skin. Regardless of her position as team owner, this was his turf, and she had invaded it. Still, she went on. "Coach Calebow has eons of experience, and I'm sure you should pay attention to everything he's told you. But if you'll do just this one little thing for me, I can practically promise you success."

She could feel the anger rolling off Dan's body. He had spent the entire week working the team into a killing frenzy, and she was blithely undoing all his efforts. She had to set aside her own survival instinct so she could concentrate on the men, not an easy feat when he was standing so close. "Tonight, gentlemen, when you line up on that field, I want you to do this." She paused. "I want you to pretend that the Giants are naked."

They were staring at her as if she had lost her mind, which probably wasn't all that far from the truth. She heard a few nervous chuckles, and regarded the offenders with mock gravity.

"I am absolutely serious. When the Giants are lined up, just pretend that guy across from you,

327

on the other side of the —" Her mind went blank, and she turned to Ron. "What's that thing called?"

"The line of scrimmage?" Ron offered.

"Right. Pretend the guy across the line of scrimmage from you is naked. It'll work. Really. I promise you. It's a trick I learned in school to overcome stage fright. I mean how can you be seriously worried about getting beat by some guy who has his — uh — stomach hanging out?" She smiled brightly. "So, for tonight . . . Think naked!"

For better or for worse, the tension in the locker room was gone. As the men's shoulder pads shook from their laughter, she knew she had accomplished her goal, and she finally allowed her own instinct for survival to kick in.

Jumping down from the bench, she made a dash for the door. "I'll see all of you on the field."

Unfortunately, Dan caught her before she could escape, and her courage flagged as she saw that his face was pale.

"You've gone too far, Phoebe. When the game is over, you and I are going to have it out for the last time."

She swallowed hard and slipped past him.

Ron found her twenty feet down the hallway, where she'd collapsed against the wall.

17

The Giants' defensive line was stunned the first time they took their positions at the line of scrimmage and found themselves staring through their masks at eleven grinning faces. None of them could figure out why a team with a one-and-four record was smiling unless they had a few dirty tricks tucked up their sleeves. The Giants didn't like surprises, and they definitely didn't like to see the opponents smiling.

Words were exchanged.

Unfortunately for the Giants' defense, several of those words reflected unfavorably on the morals of Darnell Pruitt's mother. On the next play, the infuriated Stars' offensive tackle took out two powerful linemen and an All-Pro linebacker to produce a first down.

It was beautiful.

By the time the first quarter had ended, the Stars were ahead by three, and Phoebe had nearly screamed herself hoarse. Although the violence on the field still made her flinch, she'd gotten so involved in the game she forgot she was supposed to return to the skybox until Ron appeared to escort her. As he led her through the gate that would take her from the field, she was so caught up in the excitement that she turned back toward the bench, cupped her hands around her mouth, and screamed, "Think naked!"

She realized too late that she was making even more of a spectacle of herself than usual, but the players who were nearby grinned. Fortunately, Dan was too engrossed in diagramming a play to notice.

During the second quarter, Biederot engineered a touchdown drive ending in a pass to the Stars' rookie halfback, while the Giants could manage only a field goal. When the whistle blew, the Stars were ahead by seven.

Phoebe had already decided that she would only make a fool of herself during the dreaded halftime interview with ABC's Al Michaels if she pretended knowledge that she didn't have, so she responded honestly to all of the questions directed at her and shared with the audience the difficulties her own ignorance of the game was giving her. She decided that she'd done as well as she could when, at the end of the halftime show, Michaels remarked to Frank Gifford that he thought Phoebe Somerville was trying to make the best of a difficult situation and that she deserved a chance to prove herself. Michaels also took a few pokes at her father's screwball will, expressing the opinion that Bert Somerville had done an injustice to Phoebe, Reed Chandler, and the Stars.

The second half was excruciating. Her neck muscles ached with tension as she twisted her head from the field below to the skybox television screen. Ron had stripped off his jacket and pulled down his necktie. Jim Biederot was only intercepted once, and put on a dazzling passing display. Bobby Tom performed flawlessly, and the defense was awesome. There were no Star fumbles.

When the game was finally over, Phoebe threw herself from Viktor to Ron, while Pooh yipped at her heels and the scoreboard flashed the outcome: *Stars 24, Giants 10.*

She declined Ron's request to come with him to the locker room. Instead, she and Viktor stayed in the skybox and watched the short postgame interviews that had recently been added to the Monday night game. Dan managed to be both modest and jubilant, heaping praise on his players. His words came to her in snatches.

"Great heads-up play by the defense . . . a lot of quarterbacks fancier than Jim Biederot, but no one's got more heart. . . . We got burned on the blitz a couple of times, but we came right back. . . ." He concluded the interview by saying, "You're not going to find a better ball club than the Giants. We're just glad we were ready for them."

Al Michaels congratulated Dan on the win, then moved to Bobby Tom, who had pulled his Stetson over his matted hair. "Bobby Tom, you were open all night. How do you account for that?"

Bobby Tom gave the camera his best Lone Star grin. "We worked hard this week. And, Al, I can't say enough good things about the way Jim threw the ball tonight. . . ."

After several more questions, Michaels turned

331

to Webster Greer. "What do you think made the difference for the Stars this week, Webster?"

Webster tugged on the towel that he'd hung around his neck, which was still glistening with sweat. "We've been a good ball club all season, but we've been tight. Miss Somerville talked to all of us before the game and helped us relax a little. We went out there and forced the Giants to play our game. It made a difference."

Al Michaels hadn't earned his reputation as one of the best sportscasters in the business by letting a tidbit like that slip by him. "Exactly what did she tell the team?"

Greer smiled and rubbed the towel over the back of his neck. "Nothing much. A couple of jokes. She's a nice lady."

Phoebe's cheeks flushed. She felt as if she'd been handed a valentine.

It was nearly two in the morning before the plane left Newark for O'Hare. Even though the victory was only a few hours old, Ron was already thinking about next week.

"We picked up momentum tonight," he said as the plane reached its cruising altitude and the seat belt light went off. "I hope we don't lose it."

"Try to relax and enjoy the victory. They're not worried." She tilted her head toward the back of the plane, where the raucous noise of the players celebrating could be clearly heard.

"I suppose you're right."

Three rows ahead of her, she heard Dan laugh at something Tully had said. So far, she'd managed to avoid him, but she hadn't forgotten his threat. She wanted to believe that he understood what she'd been trying to do before the game, but somehow she doubted that he'd be as gracious as Webster.

Almost as if he were reading her thoughts, he turned his head and scowled at her. She watched with alarm as he began to unfasten his seat belt. Jumping quickly to her feet, she slipped past Ron and escaped to the back of the plane, where the battered players greeted her boisterously. She visited with all of them, but when Darnell asked her to get Pooh, she declined. She was already living in the danger zone, and she saw no need to dig in any deeper.

Ron was asleep by the time she returned to the first-class cabin. He barely stirred when she slid past him into her seat. As soon as she was settled, she leaned against the window and shut her eyes, only to discover that all the diet soda she'd consumed had caught up with her. Easing back out into the aisle, she walked hastily past Dan's first row seat and slipped into the lavatory.

She hated using airplane toilets. She was always afraid the plane would choose the exact moment she was most defenseless to crash, and she'd spend her final seconds of life spiraling toward earth with her bottom bare to the world. As a result, she hurried through, washed her hands, and was just opening the bolt on the door when it flew out of her grasp. Before she could react, Dan squeezed in next to her and shot the bolt back into its locked position.

"What do you think you're doing!"

His massive body pressed her up against the washbowl. "I'm giving us a little privacy so we can talk."

The tiny cubicle was much too cramped for both of them. One of his knees wedged between her thighs and her breasts flattened against his chest. It was hard for her to catch her breath.

"I don't want to talk to you now. It's obvious you're going to lose your temper, and I don't happen to feel like being yelled at."

Anger crackled from him. "Maybe you should have thought of that before you stormed into my locker room tonight."

"I didn't storm in!"

"You came this close to sabotaging a whole season's work!" His eyes narrowed into the same fierce slits that had found the weakness in the most awesome defensive lines in professional football. "I want my players focused before the game, not distracted from the jobs they have to do with a lot of idiotic mumbo jumbo. If those men ever needed proof that you don't understand this game, they got it tonight. You don't have any idea what they're facing when they run onto the field. It's serious business out there, not some kind of joke."

She struggled to squeeze past him, but she didn't have a prayer. His body pressed harder against hers, and his voice was low and furious.

"I don't ever want you doing what you did tonight, you hear me? You stay out of the locker room before the game. You're just lucky they're

334

disciplined enough that your little exhibition didn't distract them so much it cost us a win!"

She stared at him. "You don't have a clue why I was there, do you? You have no idea what I was trying to accomplish. My God, you really do think I'm some brainless bimbo."

"After listening to your asinine theories about naked football players, I'm not going to argue with you there."

She'd never thought of herself as a short-tempered person, but now her fist shot up from her side, and she punched him in the ribs as hard as she could.

He gave a soft "oof" and stared at her incredulously. She stared back, unable to believe what had just happened. Even though she was too close to have put any real force behind the blow, she had still struck another human being, something she had never done in her life. This man was turning her inside out, and the fact that she had let herself be pushed so far made her even angrier. A red mist swirled before her eyes.

"You stupid, pigheaded, simple-minded *jock!* I'll tell you what's wrong with me! I'm saddled with a head coach who is not only an emotional six-year-old, but mentally deficient as well."

"Deficient!" he sputtered. "Now you listen to me —"

Her elbow hit the mirror behind her as common sense fled, and she jabbed him in the chest with her index finger. "No! You listen to *me,* buster, and you listen well. I was in that locker room —

335

not because I wanted to be there — but because *you've* managed to get *my* football team so tense that they haven't been able to hold on to the football."

"Are you actually suggesting —"

"*You*, Mr. Jock Strap, may be a brilliant strategist, but your knowledge of human nature is just about zero."

"You don't have the slightest idea —"

"Anytime —" She jabbed him again, punctuating the syllables with her index finger. "*A-ny-time*, do you hear me, that I want to address *my* players in *my* locker room, I will do it. Anytime I feel they're too tense, too jumpy, too uptight to do the job I am paying them a ridiculous amount of money to do, I'll stand in front of them and *strip*, if I want to. I'll do whatever I judge necessary to make certain that the Chicago Stars are able to do what they are supposed to do, which, in case you have forgotten, is what I helped them do tonight. That is, to win a football game! I, Mr. Pigskin-For-Brains, am the owner of this football team; not you. Do I make myself absolutely clear?"

There was a long pause. Her cheeks were flushed, her heart pounding. She was appalled at her loss of control, and she braced herself for his retaliation, but instead of exploding, he almost seemed distracted.

"Uh-huh."

She gulped. "That's all you have to say?"

The plane hit a patch of turbulence, pressing his hips more firmly against hers. Her eyes flew

336

open as she realized he was fully aroused.

Looking vaguely embarrassed, he held up both hands. "It's not intentional. I know you're trying to make a point and I heard every word you said. Honest. But you kept wiggling while you were talking, and the plane started to bounce, and — I don't know. It just happened."

Her temper rekindled. "I'm not in any mood for this."

"Neither am I. Not mentally, anyway. As for physically . . ."

"I don't want to hear it."

The jouncing continued, rocking their bodies together. Once again he shifted his hips, cleared his throat. "Are you — uh — seriously trying to tell me that you think you're — uh — responsible for us beating the Giants?"

The mildness of his tone, the hot friction between their bodies, took the starch out of her. "No. . . . Not exactly. . . . Of course not. Well, maybe a little bit. . . . Partly. Yes, definitely partly."

"I see." He ducked his head and braced both hands on each side of the counter behind her. His hair smelled of pine and spice from his postgame shower. She could feel his thumbs against her hips. The plane continued to bounce and she fought to ignore the thrilling abrasion of her breasts rubbing against his chest.

"You're a loose cannon," he said quietly, "and I don't like surprises." His jaw brushed her hair as he spoke. "If you thought there was a problem with my coaching, you should have talked to me about it."

"You're right. Theoretically." Her voice sounded as if it were coming from a distance. "But, you can be intimidating."

Once again, she felt the soft caress of his jaw against her hair. "So can you."

"Me?" Her mouth curled in a delighted smile. "Really?"

"Really."

Her smile faded as she saw the way he was looking at her. She licked her lips. "I'm . . ."

"Hot?" His molasses drawl made that short word last forever.

She swallowed. "Warm."

He smiled his Southern boy's crooked smile, slow and easy, conjuring up endless humid nights. "Not warm, darlin'. Hot."

"Maybe. . . ."

"Me, too."

She could feel every part of him through her clothes. He thrilled her, he scared her. He made her feel as if she'd only been half-alive before they'd met.

His hand settled around her waist. "You and me. We're . . ."

"Hot." The word slipped out.

"Yes." He dropped his head and took her mouth.

The lateness of the hour. The tension of the game. For whatever reason, the moment his lips touched hers, she lost all sense of restraint.

He scooped his big hands beneath her hips, and his elbow whacked the wall as he lifted her. Their bodies ground together. Her knee bumped into the door. She wrapped her arms around his shoulders and gloried in the feel of him pressed so hard against her.

Their kiss turned into a wild oral mating, something primitive and ungovernable, fed by a passion that had taken on a life of its own.

With a hoarse exclamation, he lowered her onto the edge of the small counter behind her and shoved up her sweater and bra. Gathering her breasts in his hands, he lifted them to his mouth. She gripped his belt buckle, while she pushed her other hand under his shirt so she could feel the hard muscles of his chest.

Her thighs were splayed wide to accommodate his legs, and his mouth dived to encompass one nipple. Sliding his hand down over her stomach, he cupped her.

"Don't ever . . ." he murmured against her moist nipple while he rubbed her through her slacks, ". . . wear these again."

"No . . ."

"Only dresses I can pull up." He unfastened her slacks, pushed down the zipper.

"Yes." She grappled with his belt buckle, shoved up his shirt.

"And no panties." His mouth left her breasts. He slipped his hand inside the cotton fabric.

Wet. Hot. He found her.

With a gasp, she pressed her open mouth against

his bare chest. The hair was silky under her tongue.

"Here," he murmured hoarsely. "Inside. . . ."

"Do. Yes. . . ." She worked at his zipper, but the fabric caught in the metal teeth halfway down. With a moan of frustration, she slid her hand inside, past the elastic band of his briefs to encircle him.

He made a strangled exclamation and lifted her while she stroked. His shoulder bumped into the wall. He braced his left foot on the platform that held the commode and worked at her slacks and panties, but their removal was difficult because of the confined space. She felt the wet cold of the basin on her buttocks and his heat in her hand. His upper arm hit one wall, his opposite elbow the other. He was finally forced to use the toe of his shoe to free her garments from their snare around her ankles. Kissing her deeply, he worked her with his fingers.

Her hand on him trembled. She had never done this to a man, but suddenly her hand wasn't enough. It was too distant from her heart. She pushed him as far away as she could manage and slipped from the edge of the basin. Turning her hips to the side, she bent into an impossibly awkward position and parted her lips. A shudder swept through her as she lost a new virginity to him.

It was thrilling. Deliciously sweet to do such a thing to this man.

Sweat broke out on his forehead as he felt the gentle tug of her mouth. He was abandoning all his principles, all his resolutions, and at that moment, he didn't care. The only commitment he'd made was to himself, and he could work that out later.

Through his raging excitement, he observed the tender, vulnerable curve of her neck. Many women had served him in this way, so why did this time seem so different? And it *was* different. There was a sweet ineptitude about that soft, warm suction that thrilled him even as it mystified him.

He caressed her hips, clenched her cheeks as his passion drove him higher. A dim internal voice pointed out to him that she wasn't doing it exactly right. Logic said she should be a pro at this, but the sweet awkwardness of that soft mouth defeated logic.

He stroked her hair, and a fierce wave of tenderness swept through him. Without planning it, he found himself drawing her up. Regardless of how she looked, how she dressed, how she behaved — regardless of his own raging need and every single damning thing he knew about her, he couldn't take her like this. She deserved something better from him than a mile-high pop in an airplane john.

"No," she whispered, and he saw something both bereft and bewildered in her amber eyes that tore his gut apart.

He kissed her lips and lost himself in that swollen mouth. She sobbed his name, shuddered, and he understood she had slipped past reason. Setting aside the violent demand of his own body, he stroked her with a deep and gentle movement of his hand. She dug her fingers into his shoulders, and the sound of those short, frenzied pants nearly drove him over the edge.

"Phoebe, darlin', you're killing me." With a hoarse exclamation, he plunged his tongue into the moist recesses of her mouth. When she shattered, he swallowed her cries.

She fell against him, her body limp and vulnerable, the nape of her neck moist with soft blond tendrils clinging to it. He felt her chest heave as she tried to draw breath. She attempted to slide her thighs together. At the same time, she shuddered, and he knew she wasn't done. He couldn't leave her like this, and he stroked her again.

She climaxed almost instantly. She gasped for breath and then began to tremble, signaling that her need still wasn't satisfied. He resumed his stroking.

"No. . . . Not without you."

At the sound of her soft, whispered wail, he ached to drive himself deep inside her. Nothing was holding him back. At that moment he couldn't even picture Sharon's face. And Phoebe was a curvy, buxom, good-time girl, custom-designed by God for just this kind of romp. Of all the women he'd ever been with, this one should have been the last to give him scruples. Instead, she seemed to be giving him the most.

He squeezed his eyes shut and forced himself to accept the fact that he couldn't finish this. Phoebe was too lost in passion to think straight, so he would have to do it for her.

"I don't have anything with me," he lied.

She slid her hand up his thigh, touched him. "Could I . . ." She tilted her head, looked at him, and the uncertainty in her eyes cut through him. "Maybe I could do the same thing to you."

Her throat spasmed as she swallowed, and those eyes, as uncertain as a fawn's, undid him. He simply couldn't let this go any farther. Painfully, he fastened his slacks.

"It's all right. I'm fine."

"But . . ."

He looked away from her wounded eyes. His hands weren't altogether steady as he slipped her sweater back down over her breasts. "Everybody in the front of the plane should be asleep by now, but maybe you'd better slip out first, as soon as you finish putting yourself back together."

She struggled with her slacks, rubbing against him with every movement. When all her clothing was back in place, she looked up at him. "How do you do it?" she asked quietly.

"Do what?"

"Act so hot, and then turn so cold."

She believed she'd been rejected. Even though he'd tried not to, he knew he'd hurt her. "Right now I'm about ready to explode," he said.

"I don't believe you. What is it Tully calls you? 'Ice'?"

He couldn't fight with her, not after he'd seen how vulnerable she was, and he could only think of one way to heal the hurt. He gave an elaborate sigh and managed to sound annoyed. "It's starting again, isn't it? The only time the two of us aren't arguing is when we're kissing. I don't know why I even try to be a good guy with you because it always backfires."

Her lips were still swollen from his mouth. "Is that what you were doing? Being a good guy."

"About as good as I've ever been. It doesn't come naturally, either. And you know what? You owe me for it."

"I *what?*" Those amber eyes weren't defenseless any longer. Just as he'd intended, they had begun to flash sparks.

"You owe me, Phoebe. I was trying to show a little respect for you."

"Respect? I don't think I've ever heard it called that."

The sarcasm in her voice didn't quite hide her hurt, so he kept pressing. "That's exactly what it is. And as far as I'm concerned, you just now threw that respect right back in my face. Which means you owe me what I didn't get in here, and I plan to collect."

"How do you plan to do that?"

"I'll tell you how. One day — Any day I happen to choose. Any hour. Any time. Any place. I'm going to look at you, and I'm going to say one word."

"One word?"

"I'm going to say *now.* Just that one word. Now. And when you hear that word, it means you stop doing whatever you're doing, and you follow me to wherever I choose to take you. And when we get there, that body of yours becomes my own personal playpen. Do you understand what I'm saying?"

He waited for her to explode, but he should have known she wouldn't let him off so easily. Phoebe knew almost as much about playing games as he did.

"I think so," she said thoughtfully. "Let me see if I've got this straight. You're telling me that, because you didn't make it to the mountaintop, so to speak, I owe you a debt. When you look at me and you say *now*, I'm supposed to turn into your love slave. Do I have it right?"

"Yep." The sadness had faded from his eyes, and he was definitely beginning to enjoy himself.

"No matter what I'm doing."

"No matter what."

"No matter where you choose to take me."

"A broom closet, if I've a mind to. It's completely up to me." He was playing with fire and actually anticipating the moment it would flame out of control.

"If I'm at work?" she inquired with remarkable calm.

"There's a fifty-fifty chance that's exactly where you'll be."

"In a meeting?"

"You lift that curvy little butt of yours right out of the chair and follow me."

"In a meeting with the commissioner?"

"You say, 'I'm sorry, Mr. Commissioner, but

I believe I have a case of the stomach flu coming on, so will you excuse me. And Coach Calebow, could you come with me just in case I happen to faint in the hall and need somebody to pick me up?' "

"I see." She looked thoughtful. "What if I'm doing an interview with — oh, let's say, Frank Gifford?"

"Frank's a good guy. I'm sure he'll understand."

The explosion was going to come any second now. He knew it.

She crinkled her forehead. "I just want to make absolutely certain I've got this right. You say *now*, and I'm supposed to turn into your — How was it you put it? Your personal playpen?"

"That's what I said." He braced himself.

"Playpen."

"Yep."

She took a deep breath and smiled. "Cool."

Stunned, he watched her slip through the door. When it shut, he threw back his head and laughed. She'd done it. She'd gotten him again.

18

Molly had just walked in the door from school the next afternoon when the phone rang. She heard Peg moving about in the laundry room as she set her book bag on the kitchen counter and picked up the receiver. "Hello."

"Hi there, Miz Molly. It's Dan Calebow."

She smiled. "Hello, Coach Calebow."

"Say, I've got a little problem here, and I thought you might like to help me out."

"If I can."

"Now that's exactly what I like about you, Miz Molly. You have a cooperative nature, in contrast with another woman I could name, whose entire mission in life seems to be making things tough for a guy."

Molly decided he was talking about Phoebe.

"I was thinking about dropping by your house for an hour or so tonight with a couple of gen-u-ine Chicago pizzas. But you know how Phoebe is. She'd probably refuse to let me in the door if I asked her straight out, and even if she said it was okay, you've seen how she likes to pick fights with me. So I figure things would go a lot better if you'd invite me over. That way Phoebe'd have to be polite."

"Well, I don't know. Phoebe and I . . . ."

"Is she still smackin' you? 'Cause if she is, I'm gonna have some words with her."

Molly caught her bottom lip between her teeth and murmured, "She doesn't hit me anymore."

"You don't say."

There was a long pause. Molly picked at the corner of a lavender spiral notebook that had fallen out of her book bag. "You know I wasn't telling the truth about that, don't you?"

"You weren't?"

"She wouldn't — Phoebe wouldn't ever hit anybody."

The coach murmured something that sounded like, "Don't count on it."

"Pardon me?"

"Nothing. You go on with what you were saying."

Molly wasn't ready to comment further about her relationship with Phoebe. It was too confusing. Sometimes Phoebe acted as if she really liked her, but how could that be when Molly wasn't even nice to her? More and more lately she'd wanted to be nice, but then she'd remember that her father had loved only Phoebe, and any good feelings she had toward her older sister evaporated. She did like Coach Calebow, however. He was funny and nice, and he'd made the kids at school notice her. She and Jeff talked every day at their lockers.

"I'd like it if you'd stop by tonight," she said. "But I don't want to be in the way."

"Now how could a sweet young lady like you be in the way?"

"Well, if you're sure."

"I certainly am. When Phoebe gets home, tell her that I'll be dropping by whenever I can get away. Will that be okay?"

"That'll be fine."

"And if she says she's not letting me in the door, you tell her you invited me and she can't weasel out. See you tonight, Miz Molly."

"See you."

Dan hung up Phoebe's telephone. He grinned down at her from his comfortable perch on the corner of her desk. "I'm coming over with pizza tonight. Your sister invited me."

Phoebe concealed her amusement. "Is it possible for you to do anything in a straightforward fashion? When you walked in my office less than three minutes ago, did it occur to you to simply ask me directly if you could stop by instead of telephoning Molly?"

"As a matter of fact, it didn't occur to me."

"Maybe I don't want to see you."

"Of course you do. Everybody knows I'm irresistible to women."

"In your dreams, Tonto."

"What are you so grouchy about?"

"You know what time the plane landed. I had to be here for an eight o'clock meeting, and I've only had a couple of hours of sleep."

"Sleep is highly overrated."

"For you, maybe, but not for those of us who are real human beings instead of cleverly designed androids programmed to stay awake all the time."

He chuckled, and she dug in her drawer for the bottle of aspirin she kept there. She still couldn't believe what had happened between them last night in the plane. When he'd issued that silly ultimatum at the end, she hadn't been able to resist sparring with him, despite the fact that she should know enough by now not to fall into his games, let alone try to beat him at them. Still, she couldn't suppress the hope that last night had changed things between them.

He would never know what a precious gift he had given her. She was no longer afraid of sexual intimacy, at least not with him. Somehow this good-looking, cocky, Alabama bruiser had helped her reclaim her womanhood. If only she weren't so afraid that he was also going to break her heart into a million pieces.

He transferred himself from the corner of her desk to the nearest chair. "We've got some unfinished business to take care of. If you'll remember, we got distracted last night before we completed our discussion."

She busied herself with the cap of the aspirin bottle. "Damn. I can never get these things off. I hate safety caps."

"Don't look at me. I can bench press 290, but I can't budge those suckers."

She fiddled with the cap and finally gave up. Dan was right. They needed to talk. Setting aside the bottle, she folded her hands on the desk in front of her. "Do you want to go first?"

"All right." He stretched out his legs and crossed

them at the ankles. "It's pretty simple, I guess. I'm the head coach, and you're the owner. I'd appreciate it if you didn't tell me how to do my job, just like I don't tell you how to do yours."

Phoebe stared at him. "In case it's slipped your mind, you've been telling me how to do my job since you broke into my apartment in August."

He looked injured. "I thought we were going to have a discussion, not an argument. Just once, Phoebe, make a little effort to hold on to that quick temper of yours."

Her hand crept toward the aspirin bottle. She spoke slowly, softly. "Go on, Coach Calebow."

Her formal mode of address didn't deter him. "I don't want you to interfere with the team again before the game."

"What do you consider interference?"

"Well, I guess it pretty much goes without saying that showing up in the locker room before the game would be at the top of my list. If you have something you want communicated to the players, tell me and I'll pass it on. I'd also appreciate it if you'd stay in the front of the plane when we're traveling. I guess the only exception to that would be on the flight home if we've won. Then it'd probably be appropriate for you to make a quick walk-through to congratulate the men. But I'd want you to do it in a dignified fashion. Shake some hands, and then leave them alone."

She slipped on her leopard-spot glasses and gazed at him steadily. "I'm afraid you're operating under the mistaken impression that I was having

351

an attack of female hysteria last night when I reminded you — quite forcefully as I remember — that the Stars are my team and not yours."

"You're not going to start that again, are you?"

"Dan, I've been doing my homework, and I know that a lot of people with some impressive credentials think you're on your way to being one of the finest coaches in the NFL. I know that the Stars are lucky to have you."

Despite the sincerity in her voice, he regarded her warily. "Keep talking."

"The Stars entered this season with a lot of high expectations from fans and the media, and when you didn't win the early games, the heat was turned up hard and fast. The stories about me didn't help, I'll admit. Everybody from the coaches to the rookies got understandably tense, and in the process, I think you may have forgotten one of the most basic lessons you learned when you were playing. You forgot to have fun."

"I'm not playing now. I'm coaching! And believe me, if I had a whole squad raising the kind of hell I used to raise, we'd be out of the game fast."

Judging from the stories she'd heard, that was undoubtedly true. She slipped off her glasses. "You're a tough disciplinarian, and I'm beginning to realize just how important that is. But I think you need to figure out when to turn up the heat and when to relax a little."

"Don't start this again."

"All right. You tell me why the Stars weren't able to hold on to the ball until last night's game."

"It's a cycle, that's all. Those things happen."

"Dan, the men were too tense. You've driven them hard for weeks, beaten up on them for the smallest mistake. You've chewed out everybody from the secretarial staff to Tully. You pushed too hard, and it was affecting everyone's performance."

She might as well have lit a keg of dynamite because he erupted from his chair. "I don't fucking believe this! I can't believe you're sitting there like John Fucking Madden and telling me how to coach a fucking football team! You don't know shit about football!"

Profanities exploded like firecrackers over her head, his anger so scorching she half expected the paint on the walls to blister. She was shaken, but at the same time, she had the weird sense he was putting her through some kind of a test, that his ranting and raving were a carefully staged ploy to see what she was made of. Leaning back in her chair, she began inspecting her nail polish for chips.

He went ballistic. The veins in his neck stood out like cords. "Look at you! You barely know the difference between a football and a fucking baseball! And now you think you can tell me how to coach! You think you can tell me my team's too tense, like you're some goddamn psychologist or something, when you don't know shit!" He paused for breath.

"You can shoot off that gutter mouth of yours all you want, Coach," she said softly, "but that doesn't change the fact that I'm still the boss. Now why don't you take yourself to the showers to cool off?"

For a moment she thought he was going to leap right over the desk and come after her. Instead, he gave her a furious look and stalked from her office.

Half an hour later, Ron found Dan behind the building slamming a basketball through the hoop near the outer locker room door. Dark patches of sweat soaked the front of his knit shirt, and he was breathing hard as he dribbled the ball to the center of the concrete slab and spun toward the hoop.

"Tully told me you were out here," Ron said. "I need some information about Zeke Claxton."

The hoop vibrated as Dan slammed the ball through. "Phoebe isn't happy with my coaching!" He spat out the words, then threw the ball at Ron's chest with so much force that the general manager stumbled backward.

"Take it in," Dan roared.

Ron looked down at the ball as if it were a grenade with the pin already pulled. He had observed Dan's murderous games of one-on-one when he was upset over something, and he had no intention of getting involved. Assuming an expression of deep regret, he gestured toward his newest navy suit. "I'm sorry, Dan, but I have a meeting, and I'm not dressed for —"

"Take it in, goddammit!"

Ron took it in.

354

Dan let him shoot, but Ron was so nervous that the ball bounced off the backboard well above the rim. Dan snatched the rebound and dribbled viciously to center court. Ron stood nervously on the sidelines trying to figure out how to get away.

"Guard me, for chrissake!"

"Actually, I was never too good at basketball."

"Guard me!"

Ron did his best, but Dan was nearly a foot taller and forty pounds heavier, as well as being a professional athlete instead of a born klutz.

"Move in closer! Use your elbows, for chrissake! Do what you friggin' have to to get the friggin' ball!"

"Uh — Elbows are illegal, Dan, and I —"

Dan stuck out his foot and deliberately tripped him.

As Ron sprawled to the concrete, he heard the knee of his new navy trousers rip. He felt the sting in the heels of his hands and looked up in outrage. "You did that on purpose!"

Dan's lip curled. "So what are you going to do about it, pussy?"

Furious, Ron scrambled to his feet and threw off his suit coat. "I'm going to shove that ball down your throat, you smug son of a bitch."

"Not if you play by the rules." Dan held the ball out, deliberately taunting him.

Ron went after him. He slammed his elbow into Dan's gut and punched the ball free with his opposite fist. It shot across the court. He raced after it, but Dan beat him there and snatched it up.

355

As the coach spun toward him with the ball, Ron punched him hard in the ribs then kicked at the back of his bad knee, knocking him off-balance. Before Dan could recover, Ron had the ball and drove to the basket, making a perfect shot.

"Now you're getting the idea." Dan grabbed the ball.

Ron moved in. Unfortunately, his violent bump didn't keep Dan from making his next shot. Ron took the ball, butted Dan with his head, and dribbled to the edge of the court, where he just missed.

The ensuing battle was vicious, fought with flying fists, jabbing elbows, illegal trips, and teeth. Dan, however, played clean.

When it was over, Ron examined the damage. He had destroyed his suit, bruised his hand, and only lost by three baskets. It was the proudest moment of his life.

The watery autumn sun came out from behind a cloud as the two of them collapsed on the grass next to the court to catch their breath. Ron propped his forearms on his bent knees, sucked in air, and gazed with deep satisfaction at the goose egg puffing up Dan's left eyebrow.

"I'm afraid you're going to have quite a shiner there." He tried, but couldn't quite hold back his glee.

Dan laughed and swiped at his dripping forehead with the sleeve of his knit shirt. "Once you stopped playing like a debutante, you came on strong. We'll have to do it again."

Yes! Ron wanted to throw his arms in the air

like Rocky on the museum steps but contented himself with a macho grunt.

Dan stretched out his legs, crossing them at the ankles as he leaned back on the heels of his hands. "Tell me something, Ron. Do you think I've been pushing the men too hard?"

Ron pulled off his ruined necktie. "Physically, no."

"That's not what I'm asking."

"If you want to know whether or not I approve of what Phoebe did in the locker room, I don't. She should have talked to you about her concerns first."

"She says I can't handle criticism."

He looked so outraged that Ron laughed.

"I don't see what's so damned funny."

"You *can't* handle criticism, and the fact is, you deserved some. Phoebe's right. You have been driving the men too hard, and it was affecting their mental attitude."

Ron probably wouldn't have been so blunt if he still weren't on an adrenaline high. To his amazement, Dan didn't explode. Instead, he managed to look injured.

"It seems to me that as the Stars' general manager, you might have worked up enough gumption to talk to me about the problem yourself instead of sending a woman who doesn't know a thing about football to do the job."

"That's exactly what she said to me this morning."

"She go after you, too, huh?"

"I don't think she's too crazy about either one of us right now."

The men stared at the empty basketball court. Dan shifted his weight and the dry leaves rustled beneath him. "That was some sweet win last night."

"It really was."

"Her locker room speech is gonna go down in football history."

"I'll never forget it."

"She sure doesn't know much about football."

"In the third quarter she cheered when we went offside."

Dan chuckled, then gave a long contented sigh. "I guess, all in all, Phoebe's working out better than either of us could've expected."

"Dan!" After their argument that afternoon, Phoebe was stunned to see the Stars' coach standing on her doorstep holding a deep-dish pizza box. It was nearly ten o'clock, and her makeup had long ago worn off. She was dressed for comfort in a faded pair of fake-Pucci leggings with a baggy purple sweater that barely covered her rear.

"I wasn't expecting you." She pushed her reading glasses to the top of her head and stepped aside to let him in.

"I can't imagine why not. I told you I'd be here."

"That was before our altercation."

"Altercation?" He looked annoyed. "That was nothing more than a business discussion, is what it was. You get riled about the strangest things."

He shut the door.

Phoebe was spared a response by Pooh, who scampered into the foyer, yapping and shivering with bliss when she saw who had come to call. Phoebe took the pizza box and watched with amusement as the dog circled Dan's legs so rapidly that she skidded on the floor.

He regarded the poodle warily. "She's not going to pee, is she?"

"Not if you kiss her and call her 'sugar pie'."

He chuckled and leaned down to give the dog a macho knuckle rub on her topknot. Pooh immediately flopped to her back so he could get to her tummy.

"Don't push it, dawg."

The poodle took his rejection good-naturedly and followed them through the living room to the kitchen.

"What happened to your eye?"

"What eye? Oh, this? Basketball game. Your GM plays dirty ball."

She stopped in her tracks. "Ron did that to you?"

"That boy's got a mean streak a mile wide. I'd advise you to stay clear of him when he gets riled."

She didn't believe for a minute that Ron had done that to him, but she knew from the glimmer in his eye that she wouldn't get any more out of him.

Molly's face lit up as they came into the kitchen, and she rose from the table where she had just been gathering up her homework. "Dan! Phoebe said you weren't coming."

"Well now, Phoebe doesn't know everything, does she? Sorry for arriving so late, but Mondays are long days for coaches."

Phoebe knew that Dan and his assistants generally worked till midnight on Mondays and she suspected that he would return to the Stars Complex as soon as he left here. She appreciated the fact that he was keeping his promise to Molly.

As she set plates and napkins on the table, he said, "I hope you ladies didn't eat so much dinner that you don't have room for a little bedtime snack."

"I do," Molly said.

"Me, too." Phoebe had already blown her fat intake for the day with a chocolate eclair, so what difference did a few hundred more grams make?

Dan took a seat at one end of the kitchen table, and as they all helped themselves to a gooey slab of the thick pie, he asked Molly about school. Without any more encouragement than that, she chattered on about her new best friend, Lizzie, her classes, and her teachers, effortlessly presenting him with all the information Phoebe had been trying to drag out of her for days.

Molly reached for her second piece of pizza. "And guess what else? Mrs. Genovese, our neighbor next door, hired me to baby-sit her twin boys for a few hours after school on Tuesdays and Fridays. They're three and a half years old, and they're so cute, but she says she needs a break sometimes because they wear her out. She's paying me three dollars an hour."

Phoebe set down her fork. "You didn't say any-thing to me about this."

Molly's expression grew mulish. "Peg said I could. Now I suppose you're going to tell me I can't."

"No. I think it will be a good experience for you. I just wish you'd talked to me about it."

Dan observed the exchange between the two of them, but didn't comment.

Half an hour later, Phoebe thanked him as she walked with him to the door. As she had suspected, he was returning to the Stars Complex for a late-night session to finalize the week's game plan against their crosstown rivals, the Bears.

He reached for the knob, but hesitated before he turned it. "Phoebe, I'm not saying you were right about what we discussed today, and I def-initely don't like the way you went about handling the problem, but I'm going to keep an open mind about what you said."

"Fair enough."

"In return, I want you to promise me that you'll tell me right out if you've got a problem with my coaching."

"Should I bring along a bodyguard, or do you think a loaded gun will be enough."

He sighed and dropped his hand from the knob. "You're really startin' to exasperate me. I don't know where you get this notion that I'm difficult. I'm about the most reasonable man in the world."

"I'm glad to hear that because there is something

else I wanted to discuss with you. I'd like you to put Jim Biederot on the bench next week so his backup can get some playing time."

He exploded. "*What!* Of all the *stupid, asinine* . . .*" The expression on Phoebe's face stopped him.

She lifted an eyebrow and grinned. "Just testing."

He paid her back by looking her over from head to toe and then speaking in a silky whisper that sent her shivering all the way to her toes. "Little girls who walk too close to the danger zone can find themselves in some real bad trouble."

He brushed her lips with a quick kiss, opened the door, and disappeared down the sidewalk.

As he climbed into his car and settled behind the wheel, he was already regretting both the kiss and his suggestive words. *No more,* he promised. He'd finally made up his mind how he was going to handle this relationship, and flirting wasn't part of it.

He'd spent the final leg of the plane trip home last night trying to figure out how he could have Phoebe in his bed while he was courting Sharon Anderson. He wanted Phoebe so much that he'd tried all kinds of arguments to convince himself it would be possible for them to have a brief affair, but even before they'd landed, he'd known he couldn't do it. His future with Sharon was too important for him to jeopardize just because he couldn't get his lust for Phoebe under control.

During a hasty dinner with Sharon last week,

he'd become even more convinced that she was the woman he wanted to marry. She'd been a little skittish around him, but that was to be expected, and she'd relaxed some by the time he'd taken her home. He'd given her a quick good-night kiss at the door, but that was all. Somewhere along the line, he'd gotten this old-fashioned notion that he and Sharon wouldn't make love until their wedding night.

As for Phoebe — He wanted her so much he ached, but he'd dealt with lust before, and he figured time would take care of that. He knew the safest thing for him to do would be to keep their relationship strictly professional, but the idea depressed the hell out of him. He'd grown to like her, dammit! If she'd been a man, she might very well have ended up in his inner circle of friends. Why should he cut her out of his personal life now, he asked himself, when she'd be going back to Manhattan at the end of the year and he'd probably never see her again?

It wasn't as if he planned to keep leading her on. All he had to do was treat her like a friend. There'd be no more slipups like that little kiss he'd given her tonight, no more sexual challenges issued in airplane johns. Right now, she might be interested in continuing the physical part of their relationship, but in his experience, women like Phoebe were philosophical about things like that. Once he showed her he was changing the rules between them, she'd follow along. She knew that sometimes things worked out and sometimes they didn't. Nobody'd have to spell it out for her.

He smiled to himself as he turned the key in the ignition. Phoebe was a crackerjack, all right. Without quite knowing how it had happened, she had managed to earn his respect. He'd never expected her to work so hard at her responsibilities as the Stars' owner, and her dedication was even more impressive because she was so far out of her element. She also had a way of standing up to him that he admired. Somehow she managed to hold her ground around him without being a bitch about it, in contrast to Valerie, who tore into him just for the pleasure of the kill.

His relationship with Phoebe had become important to him, and as long as he didn't give in to the powerful, but inconvenient, physical attraction between them, he didn't see what the harm was in enjoying each other as friends. Not that keeping his hands off her would be easy. It was a good thing he'd been sitting down most of the time he was with her tonight because watching her sashay around in those fancy tights with that sweater that barely made it over her rear had kept him in a constant state of arousal.

He grinned as he pulled away from the curb. If the Russians had been smart, they'd have taken Phoebe's radioactive body into account before they'd signed off on that nuclear proliferation agreement with the United States.

Which was all the more reason he needed to marry Sharon. He knew from painful experience that long-term relationships weren't built on lust.

They were built on mutual values, and that was what he and Sharon had in common.

So by the time the plane had landed, he had made up his mind. When Phoebe left town at the end of the year, he would pop the question to Sharon, but for the present, he was going to enjoy being with both women. As long as he kept his pants zipped, he wouldn't have a bit of trouble living with himself, and the fact that never again making love with Phoebe depressed the hell out of him was all the more reason to keep their relationship platonic. No matter what, he wasn't going to repeat the mistakes of his first marriage.

His thoughts were interrupted by a glimpse of a gray van parked on a narrow side street not three blocks from Phoebe's condo. Cursing, he shifted the Ferrari into reverse. The tires squealed as the car fishtailed. He shifted again. The powerful motor responded instantly and the car shot down the side street, reaching the van just as the driver began to pull forward. Dan spun the wheel so the van was trapped between the Ferrari and the parked car behind it.

He flung himself out of his car. In four long strides he had whipped open the driver's door and dragged the man out by the front of his jacket. "Why are you following me, you sorry son of a bitch?"

The man was heavy and he stumbled, barely righting himself before he fell. He drew back his arm to take a swing, but Dan slammed him against the side of the van. "Tell me!"

"Let me go, you bastard!"

"Not until —" He broke off as he realized there was something familiar about this man. Overweight, florid complexion, big nose, grizzled hair. At that moment he recognized him.

"Hardesty?"

"Yeah," he sneered. "So what's it to you, cocksucker?"

Dan wanted to slam his fist into the older man's gut, but he remembered Ray Senior's grief at the funeral and restrained himself. Instead, he eased the pressure he was keeping on his chest, although he didn't let him go.

"You've been following me for weeks. What's this all about?"

"It's a free country. I can drive wherever I want."

"The law has a different view. What you're doing is called stalking."

"So what? You got a guilty conscience about me tailing you?"

"Why should I have a guilty conscience?"

"Because you killed my son, you bastard! Ray Junior died because of you. If you hadn't cut him from the Stars, he'd be alive now."

Dan felt as if he'd been punched. He'd never quite buried his guilt, and he immediately released the man. "I didn't have a choice, Mr. Hardesty. We kept him on the squad as long as we could."

But he could see by the crazed expression in Hardesty's eyes that he was past reason. "You need him, you bastard! It was only luck that you won the Giants game without him. The Stars can't win for long without my boy. Without Ray Junior, you're a bunch of losers!"

Dan felt a wave of pity. Ray had been an only child, and his death must have pushed his father over the edge. "Ray was a great player," he said, trying to calm him.

"You're goddamn right he was. Because of him, I used to be able to walk anyplace in this town with my head high. Everybody knew who I was. Everybody wanted to talk to me. But now nobody knows my name, and it's all because of you. If you hadn't cut my son, people would still treat me with respect."

Bubbles of saliva had gathered at the corners of Hardesty's mouth, and Dan's pity faded. Hardesty didn't miss his son; he missed living in Ray's reflected limelight. His own father had been dead for fifteen years, but as he looked into Hardesty's small, mean eyes, he felt as if he were once again standing in front of Harry Calebow.

Harry had also used his son to pump up his own consequence. In high school Dan had squirmed under Harry's constant public bragging, all the more ironic since he never received anything but criticism in private. He remembered his sophomore year of high school when Harry had hit him with a bottle because he'd fumbled in the final thirty seconds of a game against Talladega.

He stepped back before he punished this man for something that had been another's fault. "Stay away from me, Hardesty. If I see that van of yours tailing me again, you're going to regret it."

"Big man," Hardesty sneered as Dan walked away. "Big fucking man! Let's see how big you are when your team loses again this week. Let's see how big you are when you finish in the bucket for this season. The Stars are nothing without my boy! They're nothin'!"

Dan slammed the car door against Hardesty's malice. As he drove away, it occurred to him that this might be why he wanted so much to be a father. Maybe he needed to prove to himself that he could do the job right.

19

Phoebe studied her reflection in the long, narrow mirror that occupied the end wall of the only ladies' rest room in the Stars Complex. The loose-fitting, gray cowl-necked sweater she had chosen to wear to work today covered her from neck to thigh. Below the sweater, a matching wool skirt fell in soft folds to mid-calf, where gray opaque hose and conservative pumps covered up the rest of her. She'd brushed her hair into a neat page boy held back from her face with a gray velvet headband, and only her enormous free-form silver earrings and wide cuff bracelets kept her from looking like the president of a suburban bridge club.

It was a good thing Viktor couldn't see her because he'd die laughing. She didn't care. For the first time in her life, she was enjoying dressing in different ways. Now when she donned her flashier clothes, it was because she enjoyed wearing them, not because she was trying to reshape who she was. Spandex and gold lamé would always be part of her wardrobe, but she was no longer afraid to dress in less conspicuous outfits.

She turned slightly and frowned as she ran her hands over her hips. They weren't boyishly slim by any stretch of the imagination. Maybe Dan thought she was fat and that was why he hadn't indicated any desire to make love to her since that night in the airplane rest room nearly two months ago. As she left the rest room, she wondered if he would ever cash in on that "now" he'd promised her.

Pooh trotted up to her, the red and green plaid bows Phoebe had just refastened at her ears dangling, untied. The staff had left an hour ago, and after the chaos of the day, the building seemed unnaturally quiet. She passed offices decorated with swags of gold tinsel and pots of red poinsettias in anticipation of Christmas, which was less than a week away. Pooh padded out to the lobby to claim one of her favorite spots near the door.

Dan chose the dinner hour to work out because he could have the weight room to himself, and Phoebe'd fallen into the habit of stopping by to talk with him before she left for home. She heard his rhythmic grunts even before she entered. He was lying on a padded bench with his knees bent, feet on the floor, and hoisting an alarmingly large set of weights over his chest. His muscles knotted and the veins in his forearms stood out like thick, dark cords as he extended the bar and slowly lowered it. She watched his pectorals bulge beneath the sweat-soaked cotton of his T-shirt and felt her mouth grow dry.

He hadn't seen her yet, so she didn't have to hide her longing as she gazed at him. The muscles in his thighs bunched, and her eyes moved upward to the leg openings of his baggy gray shorts. She treasured their growing friendship, even as it left her frustrated. She wanted to be his lover, not just his friend, but she was beginning to believe she might as well wish for the moon. A decade's worth of hang-ups about men was proving hard to overcome, and she was increasingly afraid that she couldn't give him whatever it was he wanted in a woman.

With a noisy grunt, he dropped the bar into the standards and sat up. His damp hair was rumpled, and sweat glistened on his neck as he smiled at her. "When are you going to get into some sweats and start working out yourself?"

"I'll get back to my aerobics classes one of these days," she said without much enthusiasm. "Besides, Pooh and I walk every night."

"I'll just bet that's a workout and a half."

"Don't be smug. Not all of us want world-class muscles."

He grinned. "So you think my muscles are world-class?"

"For a man of your age. Definitely."

He gave a hoot of laughter, rose, and made his way over to another bench, this one with a padded roller. While he turned his back to adjust the weights, she kicked off her pumps and stepped up on the elephant-sized Toledo scale at the end of the room. If she allowed nine pounds for her clothing, she was exactly where she wanted to be.

The dial was nearly the size of a stop sign, so she stepped off before he had a chance to read it. She walked over to the bench he'd vacated, and as she sat down on it, her soft wool skirt fell in decorous folds around her calves. At last Sunday's game, she'd worn an updated flapper dress that had been a big hit with the fans, but coming up with a new outfit every week was straining her living allowance.

"The front office was crazy today," she said. "Since the Bears are out of contention, the whole town's caught Stars fever."

He had hooked his ankles under the padded roller and was straightening his legs to lift an impressive stack of weights. "Chicago likes its sports."

Two more Stars' victories had followed their upset over the Giants, and then they'd lost to the Saints and the Buffalo Bills in the final weeks of November. They'd won three games against formidable opponents since then, however, and their record made them long shots for the AFC Central Division title.

The most surprising development had been in the AFC Western Division. Dan had told her what a devastating effect injuries could have on a team, and she'd seen it happen with the Portland Sabers. What had begun as a brilliant season for them had turned sour when they lost their talented quarterback and three other key players. After going undefeated for five straight games, they had lost every game but one. Their quarterback was healthy again, however, and the experts were expecting them to come back strong in the playoffs.

"Now let's see if I've got this right." She dangled one gray pump from her toes and let it swing back and forth. Her silver ankle bracelet, with its tiny crystal beads, glimmered in the light. "We can take the AFC Central title if we win this week and if Houston loses its game against the Redskins. Is that right?"

"Only if the Bengals beat the Steelers." He grunted from exertion. "And I have to remind you that we're playing the Chargers this weekend. The last time we went up against them, their defense held us to seven."

"Bobby Tom told me he's not afraid of the Chargers' defense."

"Bobby Tom'll tell you he's not afraid of nuclear war, so I wouldn't put too much stock in his opinion."

The ranking system was so complicated that it had taken Phoebe forever to get it straight. Although she still didn't completely grasp all the variables, she knew that if the Stars won the Central Division championship, they were in the running for the two AFC playoff games, which would culminate in the AFC Championship the third week of January. If they won that, she would be the undisputed owner of the Stars, and her father would roll in his grave.

She could no longer put her finger on the exact moment when the idea of keeping the Stars had begun to be far more appealing than returning to New York and opening a gallery. It was more than her attraction to Dan, more than achieving some sort of posthumous revenge against her father that lured her. Every workday presented new challenges. She loved turning on her computer and manipulating the numbers on the spreadsheets. She loved the meetings, the phone calls, the sheer, impossible task of trying to perform a job for which she was so woefully unqualified. Sometime in the past few months, she had begun to dread the idea of turning the team over to Reed.

"Frankly, I wish you'd act a little more confident. Where's all that jock talk I hear you giving the players."

"It's just the two of us now . . ." He gasped for breath. ". . . and you've got even more riding on this than they do. I don't want to give you false hopes. We've got a great football team, and we're getting better every game." He kept glancing over at her, and for some unfathomable reason, he seemed to be growing irritated. "Nobody gave us enough credit at the beginning of the season, but for all the heart our players have, they're still young and we still make too many mistakes. The Chargers have one hell of a football team, and with Murdrey coming off the injured list for the Sabers — *Would you mind not doing that?*" The weights fell with a clatter.

"Doing what?"

"What you're doing!"

He was glaring at the gray leather pump she was swinging back and forth from her toes. She stopped the movement. "What are you so grouchy about?"

He got up from the machine. "I'm trying to concentrate is all, and you're sitting there showing off your legs!"

Her skirt had ridden up until it was a scandalous three inches below her knee. "You're kidding. This is bothering you?"

"That's what I said, isn't it?"

He stood in front of her with his hands on his hips and that mulish expression on his face that told her he didn't intend to back down even though he must know he was well on the way to making a fool out of himself.

She forced herself not to smile, but a small bubble of happiness was expanding inside her. "I'm really sorry." Looking contrite, she stood. "I had no idea you were so sensitive."

"I'm not sensitive exactly."

She stepped a little nearer to him. "Of course you're not."

He looked wary. "Maybe you'd better not come any closer. I'm pretty sweaty."

"Gosh, I hardly notice anymore. I guess that's what comes from spending so much time around a football team."

"Yeah, well . . ."

With the courage of the desperate, she placed the palm of her hand on his damp T-shirt, directly over his heart. "You've been working hard."

He didn't move. She could feel the solid, fast thump of his heart and hoped it wasn't just a reaction to the workout. Their eyes locked, and she experienced a yearning so intense that she knew it must show in her face.

"This isn't a good idea." His words had a tight,

choked sound, but he made no attempt to back away.

She found her courage. "You didn't mind my touching you the night we were flying home from the Meadowlands."

"I wasn't thinking straight that night."

"Then don't think straight again." Closing her eyes, she wrapped her fingers around his upper arms and kissed him. When he didn't kiss her back, she brushed her lips over his, praying he would respond before she lost her courage.

With a groan, his lips parted and he thrust his tongue into her mouth. He splayed one of his hands over her bottom and caught the back of her head with the other, pulling her hard against him. Their mouths ground together, tongues probing. Her hands were all over him, she wanted him so badly. She felt him hard, throbbing. Maybe now.

He grasped her shoulders and gently set her away from him. She could see him struggling for control. "We shouldn't do this, Phoebe."

"Why not?" Numbly, she tried to absorb his rejection.

"There you are."

She whirled toward the door as Reed walked in. His black wool topcoat was unbuttoned and a white cashmere scarf showed inside his collar. How much had he seen?

As the Stars had begun to pile up victories, Reed's friendliness had developed cracks. He had never expected it to take so long for him to gain control of the team. Although he was still careful how he spoke to her when others were around, when they were alone, she caught glimpses of the young bully who had torn up her mother's picture.

He pulled off a pair of black leather gloves. "I'm glad I caught you, Dan. I want to get together soon to talk about the draft. I have a few ideas we need to discuss."

"It'd be real nice to chat with you, Reed," Dan said pleasantly. "But until we lose, I'm afraid I can only listen to Phoebe's ideas."

She could see that Reed didn't like being brushed off, but he was too smart to let Dan know it. Instead, he gave her that patronizing smile that made her want to claw his eyes out. "Phoebe doesn't know anything about the draft."

"Now you might be surprised what Phoebe knows. As a matter of fact, she was just now giving me her opinion about Rich Ferguson at Michigan State. Weren't you, Phoebe?"

"The kid's really something," she replied with remarkable confidence, considering the fact that she'd never heard of Rich Ferguson.

"It's amazing how much a smart woman can learn in just a few months. That doesn't mean I agree with you about that Jenkins kid, though."

"You may be right. I'll think it over." *Lord, don't strike me down for lying.* She appreciated Dan's defense of her, but it couldn't compensate for the undeniable fact that she had practically thrown herself at him, and he had rejected her.

Reed sensed an alliance and didn't like it. "You'll have to deal with me sooner or later," he said tightly. "And I'm afraid my management style is going to be more direct than Phoebe's."

"I'd expect you to do things your own way," Dan replied, refusing to take the bait.

Gary Hewitt, who was working nearly as many hours each week as Dan, poked his head through the door. "Sorry to interrupt, Dan, but we've got some new film I want you to look at. I think we may have an answer to the problem with Collier."

"Sure, Gary." He turned to Phoebe, and by the slight lift of his eyebrow asked if she wanted him to stay to lend moral support.

She smiled. "We can finish our discussion tomorrow."

He wrapped his towel around his neck and, with a nod to both of them, left.

Reed slapped his black leather gloves in his palm. "Let me take you out to dinner. It'll give us a chance to catch up."

"I'm sorry. I try to eat with Molly during the week."

His eyes narrowed slightly. "I haven't told you how much I admire the way you've taken over with her. You're hardly the maternal type, so I know it's been a sacrifice."

"I enjoy Molly. It hasn't been a sacrifice at all."

"I'm glad. Now that Bert is gone, I can't help but feel at least a little bit responsible for you. I guess that's only natural since I'm your only surviving male relative."

"Thank you for your concern, but I'm doing fine."

"I'm just grateful that you're a woman of the world. It's obvious from what I saw when I walked in here tonight that the sharks are circling."

"Sharks?"

He chuckled. "It's all right, Phoebe. You don't have to pretend with me. I'm sure you find Dan's courtship as amusing as I do. Nobody expected the Stars to get this far — not even their coach. I suppose it's natural that he'd hedge his bets, although I would have expected him to be more subtle about it."

"Reed, I have no idea what you're talking about," she said stiffly.

His forehead knit with concern. "Oh, God, Phoebe. I'm sorry. I thought — You're really serious about him, aren't you? God, I feel like an ass. I didn't mean to be so clumsy about this."

"Why don't you just say what's on your mind." Phoebe affected a calmness she didn't feel.

He gazed at her as if he were a kindly uncle. "Football is the most important thing in Dan's life. Both of us know that. Having even an outside chance of getting his hands on the Stars has to be driving him crazy. Now he's using you without any risk to himself. If the Stars lose, he can ease out of the relationship with no harm done. But if they don't lose —" His jaw tightened. "I think you can expect our head coach to hit you with a marriage proposal so fast your head will spin."

Dan wasn't without his faults, but he wouldn't use her to get the Stars, and she had never liked Reed less than she did at that moment. He was slick and oily, totally unprincipled and utterly self-ish. Even so, she knew he probably believed what he was saying since that was what he would have done had he been in Dan's shoes.

"Thank you for your concern, but I think you're taking my relationship with Dan more seriously than I am." *Liar!*

"I'm glad to hear that. I probably shouldn't have even mentioned it. This discussion will be pointless by Sunday evening anyway. The Stars are over-matched this weekend. I hope you're prepared for the team to lose."

"We'll see."

After Reed had left, she stood in the empty weight room and thought how ironic his suspicions about Dan were. If Dan was trying to get his hands on the Stars by romancing her, he was certainly botching the job.

Ron had to make a last-minute telephone call from his car phone, and Phoebe was alone as she entered the impressive silver and blue lobby of one of DuPage County's newest and most pres-tigious country clubs. It was three days after Christmas, and the lobby was still decorated with evergreen boughs and poofy silver bows. Since Jason Keane was the prime backer of the club, she wasn't surprised that he'd chosen its private dining room as the site of this meeting she had requested.

She was still trying to absorb the fact that the Stars' hopes were alive for at least one more week.

Contrary to Reed's prediction, the Stars had beaten the Chargers by a field goal in an unbearably suspenseful game on Sunday, managing to win the AFC Central Division title over the Steelers, who had lost to the Bengals in overtime. Now they would have another chance to keep her dream alive.

She was undoubtedly setting herself up for a fall. Bert had tried unsuccessfully for years to renegotiate the stadium contract with Jason Keane, and she had no reason to believe she could resolve a situation that had defeated her father. Her weeks of study had given her a fairly comprehensive understanding of the team's finances, but she had no experience with complex negotiations.

Logic dictated that she simply sign the new contract the lawyers had delivered last week. There would be no more last-minute reprieves for the Stars; their next defeat would put them permanently out of the running. If she somehow managed to improve the terms of the stadium contract, she would only be helping Reed. On the other hand, until the Stars lost their next game, she was still the owner, and she was going to do what was best for the organization.

Thinking about what lay ahead of her tonight had taken its toll, and her stomach was churning. The sensation escalated as the heavily etched glass door marked Members Only swung open on the far side of the country club lobby. She sucked in her breath as she identified the tall, well-built man in the tuxedo as Dan.

Planning for this evening had kept her mind too busy to dwell on his rejection of her kiss in the weight room last week. Now the hurt came back, and she stiffened as he walked toward her.

"What are you doing here?"

"I'm a member. Did you think I might be crashing your meeting with Keane?"

"How did you know about our meeting?"

"From Ron."

"It's supposed to be confidential."

"I haven't told anybody."

"You're deliberately missing the point. *You* weren't supposed to know about it."

"Now that doesn't half make sense, Phoebe. How could Ron invite me along if he didn't tell me you had a meeting?"

Tonight would be difficult enough without having Dan witness something that had every chance of turning into a disaster. "I'm afraid I have to withdraw Ron's invitation. We agreed this was to be a private meeting between the two of us, Jason Keane, and a few of his advisers."

"Sorry, Phoebe, but Ron gets vicious when I don't do what he tells me. I've been afraid to tangle with him ever since he gave me that shiner."

"He did not give you a shiner! You're being — That's the most ridiculous —"

As she sputtered, Dan had to force himself not to bend over and lick the scowl right off her mouth. A surge of hundred-percent pure lust had shot through him the moment he'd seen her. Instead of getting used to keeping his hands off her, not touching her had grown more difficult each day. Everything about her turned him on. Right now, for example. Most women's hair when they got dressed up looked all stiff and sprayed. Phoebe's looked bedroomy instead. It fell in soft blond waves nearly to her shoulders, curling a little bit at the ends as if he'd just run his fingers through it. And she had the prettiest neck he'd ever seen on a woman, long and graceful.

He told himself he should be thankful the rest of her was still covered up by that black evening coat. Even those loose-fitting clothes she wore to work sometimes lately didn't do much to conceal what was underneath. He knew he should be happy that she was dressing more like a conservative businesswoman, but the truth was, he found himself anticipating those days when she showed up looking like her old self. Not that he was going to admit that to her.

The hardest thing he'd done in his life was to stop kissing her that last time. Even though he'd been trying to do the honorable thing by backing away, the forlorn expression on her face had made him feel like a worm. Except for those few seconds when he'd lost control, he hadn't done anything in almost two months to lead her on. He should feel good about that, but instead he was miserable. He kept telling himself Phoebe would be going back to Manhattan soon and everything would be better, but instead of cheering him up, that made him even more depressed.

Phoebe was still going at him. Those tilty-up

eyes of hers had darkened to the color of old brandy as she did a slow simmer over his unanticipated presence tonight. He wished Sharon could stand up to him the way that Phoebe did, but Sharon was a sweet little thing without one ounce of Phoebe's sass, and he couldn't imagine it.

Even though he saw Sharon at least once a week, this was the first time he'd ever been involved with a timid woman, and he hadn't quite made the adjustment yet. A few times Sharon's mild nature had begun to irritate him, but then he'd reminded himself of the benefit. He'd never in his life have to worry about Sharon Anderson smacking his kids when she got upset. He'd never have to worry about her treating his kids the way his old lady had treated him.

Phoebe was tapping the toe of one of her high heels while her sparkly earrings swung back and forth through her hair. "Why did Ron want you here? He didn't say anything to me about it."

"You'll have to ask him that."

"Take a guess."

"Well, he did say something about maybe needing a backup quarterback. In case you went off the deep end or something."

"Is that so."

"You have a habit of doing that occasionally, you know."

"I do not!"

She yanked open her coat button, and as he saw what she was wearing beneath it, his amusement faded.

"Something wrong?" With a maddening smile, she allowed the coat to slip off her bare shoulders.

He felt as if he'd been poleaxed. How could she do something like this? He'd been strung tight for too long, and now he exploded.

"Dammit! Just when I start to think you might be learning a little common sense, you prove me wrong! Here I was actually believing you might be getting a faint glimmer of what this business is all about, but now I realize that you aren't even close!"

"My, my. Somebody certainly is grouchy this evening. Maybe you should mind your own business and go home." She finished removing her coat and carried it over to be checked, her hips swaying from side to side. As she turned back to him, he felt a pulse hammering in his temple. Just moments ago, he'd been thinking about how much he enjoyed Phoebe's exhibitionist clothes, but that was before he'd seen her current getup.

She was dressed like the head hooker in a bondage house. He took in the long, clingy black dress that looked more like an S&M harness than an article of clothing. The top half was made up of fishnet and black straps. One of the straps wrapped her neck like a collar, with a fan-shaped arrangement spreading down to a slightly wider strap that encircled the midpoint of her breasts and didn't do much more than cover her nipples. Through some black fishnet with holes the size of nickles he could see both the upper and lower swells straining against that narrow black strap.

At her waist the fishnet gave way to a slinky fabric that stuck like body paint to every curve of her hips. Near her thighs, the dress was ornamented with gold hardware that looked almost like garters, except garters should have been tucked away instead of hanging out where everybody could see. Adding insult to injury, the garment had a side slit that traveled all the way from here to kingdom come.

He yearned to bundle her up in his jacket and hide her from the world because he didn't want other people seeing so much of her body, which was a damned ridiculous notion considering her fondness for taking off her clothes. He grabbed her arm and led her toward an alcove off to the side of the lobby where he could hide her from public view and go at her in earnest.

"Is this your idea of how to dress for a business meeting? Is this your idea of what to wear when you want to negotiate a contract? Don't you understand that the only thing you're going to negotiate dressed like that is how much you can charge to crack a whip on some man's bare butt."

"What did *you* pay the last time?"

Before he could recover from that piece of impudence, she slipped right past him. Whirling around, he saw Ron walk in, and it was obvious from the stunned expression on his face that he was equally taken aback by Phoebe's getup. The men's eyes met, and Dan wondered if he looked as helpless as Ron did. Didn't she realize this was DuPage County? Women didn't dress like this in

DuPage County, for chrissake. They went to church and voted Republican, just as their husbands told them.

He stalked toward her with a vague idea of executing a low tackle and then carrying her out over his shoulder when one of Keane's lackeys appeared. Before Dan could stop her, she had set off with him.

He didn't have much choice but to follow. By unspoken agreement, he and Ron quickened their steps until they had pushed the lackey out of the way and positioned themselves on opposite sides of her. At the end of the mirrored hallway, they passed through the doorway into Jason Keane's private dining room.

Dan had known Keane for nearly ten years. They'd partied together a few times, played some golf. Once they'd spent a liquored-up weekend deep-sea fishing in the Grand Caymans with a couple of lingerie models. Keane had always attracted women and, from what Dan had heard, turning forty hadn't made him want to settle down.

The small dining room looked like the library of an English manor house, with Oriental rugs, leather club chairs, and dark wooden paneling. Heavy crown moldings framed an ornate ceiling of plasterwork medallions and vines that flickered with shadows cast by the burning logs in the fireplace. Heavy velvet draperies had been pulled shut at the window, hiding a view of the ninth green beyond. The damask-covered oblong table was set for six with ornate silver and china banded in deep burgundy and gold.

Jason Keane, along with two of his cronies, stood next to the fireplace with heavy crystal tumblers in their hands. The atmosphere was decidedly masculine, and as Dan entered the room with Phoebe dressed in her bondage clothes, the uncomfortable memory of one of Valerie's favorite pornographic books came back to him. He shied away from the ugly feeling that Phoebe was O, and that he was about to offer her up to the brotherhood.

Keane came toward them, hand extended. The multimillionaire developer was a cool customer, but he couldn't quite hide his astonishment at Phoebe's dress. That astonishment quickly changed to something more intimate, and Dan had all he could do not to shove himself in front of Phoebe and tell Jason to set his sights on somebody else's bimbo.

Keane shook Dan's hand. "How's the golf game coming, buddy? Able to sneak in eighteen on any road trips?"

"Afraid not."

"Why don't we play Pebble next month?"

"Sounds good."

Keane greeted Ron, who introduced him to Phoebe. To Dan's disgust, she went into her whole routine: breathy voice, come-hither eyes, centerfold breasts straining to break free of that narrow black band. While she was showing off her goods to Keane and his boys, she didn't once glance in Dan's direction.

Dan watched with a combination of disgust and

fury as Keane curled his palm over Phoebe's naked shoulder and drew her toward the fireplace. Keane was all millionaire playboy charm in his custom-made tux and white tucked shirt with its half-carat diamond studs. Of average height and build, he had dark, straight hair and a high forehead. Until that night Dan had considered Jason an okay-looking guy, but now he decided that his nose was too big and his eyes too weasely.

Dan took a drink from a waiter and exchanged greetings with the other men present — Jeff O'Brian, Jason's administrative assistant, and Chet Delahunty, his attorney. As soon as he could get away, he sauntered over toward the fireplace to eavesdrop. Ron obviously had the same idea because he trailed along.

Phoebe had her back to them, and he was almost certain he could make out her bottom-crack under that slinky dress material. She was licking Jason with her eyes and leaning into him as if he were a street corner lamppost. Dan's blood pressure shot into the stratosphere.

"I can call you Jason, can't I?" she cooed. "Especially since we have so many friends in common."

Dan waited for the drool to slide right out of Keane's mouth. "Like who?"

"Half of Manhattan." She rested her hand possessively on his sleeve, her red fingernails standing out like drops of blood drawn from the lash of the whip. "You know the Blackwells and Miles Greig, of course. Isn't Miles a scamp? And then there's Mitzi Wells, you devil."

Jason was obviously feeling the effects of all those gamma rays of adoration that were blasting away at him because his smile blossomed even wider. "You know Mitzi?"

"Of course I do. And you almost broke her heart."

"Not me."

She lowered her voice until it was a sultry whisper, then sucked on her bottom lip in a way that made Dan feel as if the top of his head were blowing off.

"If I confess something to you, will you promise you won't think I'm awful?"

"Cross my heart."

"I asked her to introduce us — this was before the two of you started to date seriously — and she refused. It nearly broke up our friendship, but now that I've met you, I can understand why she was so protective."

Dan could see Jason trying to spot the fastenings on Phoebe's cathouse dress, so he wouldn't waste any time getting her out of it later on. With a murmur of disgust, he tilted back his head and drained his glass. Keane would unfasten that dress over this ol' boy's dead body.

Dinner was ready and they took their places around the table, with Jason at the head and Ron and Phoebe on each side of him. Dan sat at the foot between Jeff O'Brian and Chet Delahunty. The meal seemed to drag on forever. By the time the main course was removed and dessert was served, the men at the bottom of the table had given up on even a desultory attempt at conversation so they could eavesdrop.

Dan watched Phoebe suck an out-of-season strawberry with her X-rated mouth. As she gazed into Keane's eyes, he told himself he was going to propose to Sharon Anderson that very weekend.

Ron had barely looked up from his dinner plate all evening, but as the coffee was poured, he finally seemed to come to life, about ninety minutes too late, as far as Dan was concerned.

"Excuse me for interrupting your conversation, Phoebe, but I think it might behoove us to discuss the reason for this meeting tonight."

Phoebe looked at him so blankly that Dan wanted to shake her. Was she so eager to add Keane to her scalp collection that she had forgotten why they were here?

"Reason?" she said.

"The stadium contract," Ron reminded her.

"Oh, pooh. I've changed my mind, Ronnie. I don't want to talk about that tonight. Why don't you just relax and enjoy yourself? Jason and I are friends now, and everybody knows you shouldn't do business with friends."

"A woman after my own heart," Jason chuckled.

"All Ronnie thinks about is business. It's so boring. There are more important things in life than some silly old contract."

Dan straightened in his seat. Something was wrong here. Phoebe did care about the contract, and she never called her GM Ronnie.

Keane gave Ron a smug smile. "Why don't you

have some more wine, McDermitt?"

"No, thank you."

"Don't pout, Ronnie. You can call Jason tomorrow and tell him what I've decided."

"What is there to decide?" Keane said smoothly. "Everything's pretty much cut-and-dried."

Once again, she curled her fingers around his sleeve. "Not exactly, but let's not spoil tonight by talking about business."

Keane grew almost imperceptibly more alert. "We've sent you a fair contract. The same one your father signed. I hope you're as satisfied."

"*I'm* not satisfied," Ron said with a forcefulness that earned Dan's admiration. He waited with interest to hear Phoebe's response.

"Oh, I'm not satisfied either," she giggled. "Ronnie made me so upset about the bad deal the Stars were getting that he convinced me I had to do something." Like a small child reciting a well-learned lesson, she said, "Ronnie keeps reminding me that I'm a businesswoman now, Jason. And even though I'll probably only have the team for a short time longer, I have to think like an owner."

Dan kept his expression carefully blank as he leaned back in his chair to watch the show. What was his brainy little bimbo up to now?

She rolled her eyes toward the ceiling. "I know what you're thinking. You're thinking that Phoebe Somerville isn't enough of a businesswoman to make the tough calls, but that just isn't true."

"I wasn't thinking that at all." Keane's lazy smile

392

was at odds with the hawklike intensity in his gaze. "What kind of tough calls do you have to make? Maybe I can help. I have a lot of experience with that sort of thing."

Ron's mouth twisted into something that, on any other man, would have been a sneer. "He's trying to manipulate you, Phoebe. Be careful."

Phoebe wrinkled her forehead. "Don't be rude, Ronnie. Jason wouldn't do anything like that."

Keane's eyes were boring holes through her skull, as if he were trying to see whether anything lurked between the air pockets. "Of course, I wouldn't. All of us have to make tough calls now and then."

Phoebe's pout turned into something closer to a whine. "But this one was really hard, Jason. Ronnie kept telling me you wouldn't be mad about it, but I'm not so sure. I don't see how you can be happy about the Stars moving."

Jason choked on the coffee he had been in the process of swallowing. *"Moving?"* His cup landed in his saucer with a clatter, and all his flirtatiousness disappeared. "What the hell are you talking about? Moving where?"

Dan watched as Phoebe's bottom lip actually began to quiver. "Don't be mad. Ronnie explained it to me, and everything'll be fine. We're going to exercise that one-year option we have with you for next season, so it's not as if we're moving immediately. You'll have lots of time to find another team to play in your stadium."

Keane spoke to Phoebe through gritted teeth.

"Exactly where are you thinking about taking the Stars?"

"Manhattan, maybe. Wouldn't that be a gas? I'm not absolutely sure, of course, that the other team owners will go along with it, but Ronnie hired these nerds to do this big market survey, and they told him the New York City area can definitely support another football team."

Keane, obviously having decided where the real power behind the Stars lay, shot Ron a look of pure fury. "That's ridiculous! The Stars won't be able to use Giants Stadium. There are already two teams playing there."

But Phoebe wasn't ready to turn over the stage to her GM yet, and once again she cupped Keane's arm. "Not Giants Stadium. That's in New Jersey, for goodness' sake, and I never go to New Jersey unless I'm on my way to Philadelphia. Just because I won't own the team anymore doesn't mean that I'm not planning on seeing every game. I'm crazy about football now that I know all the players."

"You can't move the team unless you have a stadium!" Keane was nearly shouting. "Didn't McDermitt tell you that?"

"But that's the best part! Donald has just about recovered from all those horrible things that happened to him a few years ago, and he wants to build a domed stadium on that West Side land he owns." Her eyebrows wiggled suggestively. "We're *close* friends, you know, and he told me he'd give me my very own skybox as a gift if I'd sign a contract with him before I turn over the team to Reed." She looked stricken. "Don't be mad, Jason. I have to do what Ronnie tells me. He gets all upset if I don't behave like a real businesswoman."

Dan was grateful no one was paying any attention to him because he'd gotten dizzy from the altitude. He had to hand it to the kid, however. Ron leaned back in his chair with the smug look of a mafioso who had controlling interest in a concrete block company.

Keane's attitude underwent a subtle transformation, and he regarded Phoebe in a manner that was both unfriendly and patronizing. The thought passed through Dan's mind that Keane, for all his smarts, had better take care. Dan knew from past experience how easy it was to get suckered by these two con artists.

"I have to warn you that the whole thing sounds much too tentative to me. It's extremely doubtful the League would agree to a third pro team in the New York City area. If I were you, I wouldn't set my heart on moving the Stars to Manhattan."

Phoebe gave the same giggle that only ten minutes earlier had set Dan's back teeth on edge. Now it sounded as musical as church bells. How could he ever have doubted her? Not only was she smart as a whip, but she had guts.

"That's exactly what Ronnie said," she chirped, "but I have a backup plan."

"You do?"

She leaned closer. "You wouldn't believe how much Baltimore wants its own NFL team. Ever since the —" She looked down the table at Dan, and he finally knew her well enough to recognize the glitter in her eyes. As he kept his expression inscrutable, his chest swelled with pride.

"What was the name of that team that left Baltimore?" she inquired.

"The Colts."

"Right. Ever since the Colts left, Baltimore's been dying to get another team. And then there's Orlando." An expression of pure bliss settled over her face. "Those men are the sweetest guys in the world. Last week when we talked, they presented me with the cutest little Montblanc pen with gold mouse ears on it." She gave a soft, Minnie-like squeal and sighed with pleasure. "Oh, I just love Orlando. Their stadium site is right next to Disney World."

Keane looked stunned.

"So you see, I do know how to be a tough businesswoman." She slipped her napkin from her lap and stood. "Now if you gentlemen will excuse me, I need to make a trip to the little girls' room. And, Ronnie, you be civil to Jason while I'm gone. You've gotten everything you want, so you can afford to be gracious."

As she walked away from the table, she took all of their eyes with her. The door shut.

Dan wanted to jump to his feet and give her a standing ovation. At that moment, he knew without doubt that he couldn't marry Sharon Anderson, and he felt as if a huge weight had been lifted from his shoulders. Phoebe filled his heart, not

Sharon, and he was going to have to rethink everything. The future he'd been so certain about was now murky, a fact that should have depressed him. Instead, he experienced a surge of exhilaration.

Jason threw his napkin on the table, jumped to his feet, and rounded on Dan. "I thought we were friends! What the hell is going on here?"

Dan concealed his elation with a shrug. "It's front office business. I don't get involved."

"Not even when your football team may end up wearing fucking *mouse ears* on their helmets!"

Dan set down his coffee cup and deliberately wiped the corner of his mouth with his napkin. "Considering her past history, I think Baltimore's more likely. It's closer to Manhattan."

Jason turned his anger on Ron. "This is all your doing, McDermitt. You've manipulated that fucking birdbrain! My God, you're leading her around by the fucking nose!"

Ron's smile revealed the teeth of a baby shark. "I've done what I had to, Keane. You've been screwing us over for years, and I finally found a way to stop you. Bert would never consider moving the team, but Phoebe doesn't have his sense of tradition, and it was quite easy to persuade her to look elsewhere. She has wonderful connections, you know, and I don't inquire too closely into how she's made them. One day she's on the phone with Trump. The next day with Disney. They've promised low rents, hefty concession percentages. They'll pick up the tab for security. I realize this

397

will leave you with an empty stadium, but perhaps the Bears —"

"Fuck the Bears!" Keane shouted. "Do you think I want McCaskey breathing down my ass?" His eyes traveled from Ron to Dan and back again. And then they narrowed suspiciously. He turned to his attorney. "Stand outside the door and keep Phoebe occupied if she comes back. O'Brian, get Trump on the phone."

Dan could see the flicker of alarm in Ron's eyes, and he couldn't suppress his own dismay. *You gave it your best shot, Phoebe,* he thought. Unfortunately, Keane wasn't as easily suckered in as he had been.

A heavy silence descended on the room as the men waited for the call to go through. After several moments of muted conversation, O'Brian passed the phone over to his employer.

Keane spoke into the receiver with false heartiness. "Donald, it's Jason Keane. Sorry to interrupt your evening, but I'm tracing down an interesting rumor." He walked over toward the fireplace. "The word here is that you're thinking about building a stadium on that West Side land you own. If it's true, I might be interested in getting in on the action. Provided you have a team lined up."

He gripped the receiver tighter in his hand as he listened. "Is that so? No, I understand. I thought maybe the Jets . . . Really? Well, those things happen. Yes, indeed. Oh, certainly."

There was a long pause.

"I'll do that. Of course. Good speaking with you, too."

His face was gray as he slammed the phone to the cradle. "The son of a bitch wants the Stars. He told me he's promised Phoebe a pink marble skybox. The bastard actually had the gall to laugh."

Silence fell over the room.

Ron cleared his throat. "Do you want me to get the names of the men she spoke with in Orlando and Baltimore?"

"Don't bother," he snapped. Dan could almost see the wheels turning in Keane's well-oiled mind. "Dan, I remember you admiring that antique George Low Wizard putter of mine. It's yours if you get Phoebe out of here."

"I'm always happy to help out a friend," Dan said slowly.

"And you." Keane jabbed his finger at Ron. "You're not going anywhere until we put together a new contract."

Ron took his time selecting a cigar from the humidor that had arrived at the table along with the brandy. He rolled it between his fingers like a miniature Daddy Warbucks. "It'll have to be an attractive offer, Jason. Very attractive. I rather like Orlando myself."

"It'll be plenty attractive, you slimy son of a bitch!"

"Then let's deal." Ron smiled as he slipped the cigar into the corner of his mouth. "And Keane — Don't forget who's holding Trump."

20

"Are you sure you've told me everything that happened after I left?" Since the Ferrari's heater was going full blast, Phoebe's teeth weren't chattering from cold, but from an overdose of adrenaline.

"As close as I can remember."

She still couldn't quite comprehend the amazing fact that right now, Ron and Jason Keane were in the process of renegotiating their stadium contract. She thought about her father and experienced an unfamiliar sensation of peace as she realized she'd never had anything to prove to him, only to herself.

The Ferrari bounced on a bump in the road and she suddenly became conscious of their rural surroundings. "I thought you were taking me home."

"I am. My home."

"Why?"

"Because the last time I stopped by your house, Miz Molly was there along with three of her girlfriends. I don't think I ever realized what high-pitched voices four teenage girls have." He glanced over at her. "It occurs to me that you and I need some privacy so we can talk a few things over."

Phoebe couldn't think of anything they had to talk about that wouldn't wait until the next day.

After what had happened last week in the weight room, she wasn't up to any more rejection, and she knew she shouldn't be alone with him. Since he was already driving down the lane that led to his house, however, it was a bit late to ask him to turn back.

"First we're going to talk," he said. "Then we're going to burn that dress of yours."

He was scowling, so she doubted that his remark was intended to be sexual, but as the Ferrari sped beneath the bare trees whose skeletal branches were silhouetted against the night sky, she realized her palms were damp. "It's Versace."

"Beg your pardon?"

"My dress. Versace. The designer. Or at least it's a Versace rip-off. I have this friend in Manhattan who can rip off any designer."

"What's wrong with your voice? It sounds funny."

"My teeth are chattering." The low-slung car bounced on a rut.

"I've got the heater on. It's warm."

"I'm not cold. I guess it's a delayed reaction. I was a little nervous this evening."

"You damn well should have been. Phoebe, in all my born days I never saw anything like what you did tonight. I'm a little disappointed in Ron, though, for not letting me in on your plans, especially since he invited me along."

"Ron didn't know exactly what I had in mind."

"Are you telling me he was winging it in there?"

"Not entirely. I told him the attitude I wanted

him to assume, but not the details of what I planned to do. He has this problem with heart arrhythmia. It kicks up when he gets too nervous, and I was afraid he'd give me away. But he's gotten very good at improvising, so I wasn't too worried."

"My respect for my good friend Ron grows by the day."

They stopped in front of the stone farmhouse, where faint puddles of golden light spilled through the living room windows onto the porch. The Dutchman's-pipe vine hung dry and withered on its trellis at the end of the porch, but it still somehow managed to be beautiful in the cold December night. She waited until he came around to open her door, and when he did, she was forced to swing her legs out first because her dress was so tight.

He extended his hand to help her. When his fingers closed around her own, she tried to repress a shiver of excitement. A leaf crunched under the toe of her beaded black heels as she and Dan climbed the front steps together.

He unlocked the door and held it open for her. "I thought it was all over when Keane placed that phone call to your close personal friend, Donald Trump."

"Donald has quite a sense of humor. It didn't take any persuasion on my part to convince him to back up my story."

The hallway was lit by a single brass library lamp with a black shade that sat on a small antique chest. She followed him into the living room, where he flicked on more lights until the interior was filled with a cozy glow. Once again, she was struck by how snug his house was. A discarded navy sweatshirt lay across the arm of the green and red plaid couch, while copies of the Chicago papers, along with the *Wall Street Journal*, were scattered on the floor near one of the overstuffed chairs. She smelled clove and cinnamon.

"This place is so homey," she said wistfully.

He followed the direction of her gaze toward a rush basket piled high with pinecones on the hearth. "I like outdoors things around me."

He shed his tuxedo jacket and, while he made his way across the rug to the fireplace, pulled at his bow tie. The ends dangled as he leaned forward to ignite the fire that had been laid. After it caught, he closed the screen and straightened.

"Are you going to take off your coat?"

Maybe it was the result of all those weeks of wearing pearls and headbands, but she didn't want to stand before him in the vulgar dress she'd used to disarm Jason Keane, not while they were enclosed by the cozy comfort of this wonderful old house. "I'm still a little cold."

If he knew she was lying, he gave no sign. "I'm going to have a beer. Do you want something to warm you up? Coffee? Tea?"

"No, thank you." As he moved into the open kitchen at the back, she slipped off her coat and replaced it with the zippered sweatshirt he'd left on the arm of the couch. It held the fresh scent of laundry detergent along with a fragrance that wasn't quite spice and wasn't quite citrus, but was indisputably Dan Calebow. She sat down at one end of the couch just as he came back into the room with a bottle of Old Style in his hand.

He settled at the other end, leaned back against the overstuffed arm, and propped one ankle over his knee. "You and Ron are getting good at pulling scams. Tonight was even better than the one you pulled on me. By the way, I'm a big enough man to admit you were right about him and I was wrong."

"Thank you."

"I'll even admit you might have been partially right about the team being too tense earlier in the season."

"Only partially right?"

"Mostly right," he conceded. "But that doesn't mean I'm not looking forward to living the remainder of my life without hearing any more speeches about naked football players." He shuddered. "Do you and Ron think you could let me in on your next scam ahead of time? I hope you realize I almost committed assault and battery tonight, although I'm not entirely sure whether I would have gone after Keane or you."

"Probably Keane. For all your yelling, I can't imagine you hitting a woman."

"You're forgetting about Valerie."

"You should introduce her to Jason. They're perfect for each other."

"How do you know that?"

"Instinct. That man would enjoy every kinky little game she could conjure up."

"I don't know. Some of them —"

"Never mind. I have a weak stomach." Even though Dan had told her he was no longer seeing Valerie, the thought of them together dug into her like sharp little spurs, and her voice was more waspish than she intended. "I'm sure other women must seem tame to you after being married to the kinky congresswoman."

He sighed. "You're determined to pick a fight with me, aren't you?"

"I'm not doing any such thing."

"Yes, you are, and I'm not in a fighting mood." He uncrossed his legs and set his beer bottle down on the hooked rug. "What I'm in a mood to do is fetch a pair of pliers and see if I can get you out of that dress."

She caught her breath and heat spread through her body, followed by uncertainty. "Dan, don't joke about this."

"I'm not joking." His expression was so solemn it almost scared her. "Believe me, I've tried to keep my hands off you. But I can't do it any longer."

"Is this *now?*" she asked quietly.

"Did I say *now?*"

"No."

"Then it's not *now*. It's just what I said."

"Oh." She moistened her dry lips.

"First I'd like you to take off my sweatshirt. I've got a good fire going, and it's plenty warm."

"I'd rather leave it on."

"Are you saying you don't want to make love?"

"No." She wished she hadn't protested so quickly, and she tried to speak more reasonably. "The minute you see this dress, you'll start yelling again."

"Phoebe, any woman with half a brain could figure out that yelling's about the last thing on my mind right now."

"That's what you say now, but your temper is unpredictable. It hasn't occurred to you that I did exactly what you expect the team to do."

"You want to come at that one again?"

"I put my body on the line for the good of the game. Isn't that what football's all about?"

"You're starting to make me crazy. You know that, don't you?"

She couldn't resist him when those little green lights of amusement were dancing in his eyes. "There's a small hook at the back of the collar."

"Slide over here and show me."

She did as he asked, and he gently pressed on her shoulders, indicating that he wanted her to lie facedown across his lap. She rested her cheek against his knee, her breast against his thigh.

He stroked her hair, freeing the strands that were tucked under the sweatshirt. "See, what I'm thinking is this. We'll start out here on the couch and sort of work our way from room to room."

"It sounds like spring housecleaning."

He gently drew the bulky garment off her shoulders, slid it out from beneath her, and dropped it on the floor. His fingertips stroked her back through the net fabric. "I suppose there might be a few parallels. I can think of some interesting things we could do with soap and water."

"Considering your past history, you probably know interesting things to do with just about everything." She caught her breath as he touched a particularly sensitive spot on the back of her neck.

He chuckled and cupped her rear with his palm. "You sure you're not into spankings?"

She smiled against his thigh. "I'm sure."

"That's another thing I like about you."

He stroked her bottom through the thin silky material of the dress, caressing the round slopes and then running his fingertip down the valley until she didn't think she could bear it any longer. She turned her head and pressed her lips against his zipper to find him fully aroused.

He groaned. "You're gonna do me in before we even get started."

He lifted her by the shoulders until he'd pulled her into his arms. For a moment their eyes met, and she was afraid he'd draw away from her as he had done before, but instead, his big, athlete's hands gathered her closer into his lap. Their lips met, open and seeking. She curled her arms around his neck, and they sank farther down on the couch.

Through the fishnet, she could feel his hands all over her. He shifted his weight, tugging at her dress to get at the rest of her, while she began pulling at his shirt studs. Both of them lost all sense of how precarious their perch was until they felt themselves rolling off the couch. Just as they hit the carpet, he turned his body so he wouldn't crush her with his weight.

Even after they had landed, they didn't immediately release each other's mouths. When she finally opened her eyes to look at him under her, he was smiling.

"Are you having as much fun as I am?"

"More." She couldn't resist kissing the small scar on his chin.

"Phoebe, darlin', I've got to get you out of that dress."

"Don't yell," she whispered.

"I thought I already explained to you —"

"I don't have anything on under it."

He blinked. "Nothing? I know you're wearing panty hose. I saw —"

She shook her head. "No panty hose. No garter belt. The dress is too tight."

"But, you've got black stockings —"

"The kind that hold themselves up at the thigh."

He rolled off her. "Phoebe Somerville, are you telling me that you don't even have on any underpants?"

"They leave a line."

"Just two black stockings?"

"And a spritz of White Diamonds."

He jumped up and pulled her none-too-gently to her feet. "We're headin' straight for the bedroom, darlin'. Since there's a good chance I'm going to have a heart attack before the night's over, I want to die in my own bed."

His silly banter made her feel like the most desirable woman in the world. He snuggled her against his side as they walked back out into the hallway and climbed the staircase. When they reached the landing at the top, he drew her through a doorway on the right into a spacious bedroom that looked as if it had been carved out of several smaller rooms. The ceiling sloped on both sides, and the wall on the right was stone. One end of the room held a comfortable sitting area, the other an old sleigh bed, which was covered in a beautiful Zuni Indian blanket of burnt orange, black, green, and cream.

He stopped in the center of the room and reached under her hair to open the hook at the back of the fabric collar that encircled her throat. His clever hands moved lower and found the fastenings on the strap that so cruelly bound her breasts. She sighed with relief as the pressure eased and the fishnet bodice fell to her hips.

"Hurt?"

"A little."

He reached around her from behind and gently caressed her breasts, soothing away the red marks with his thumbs. "Phoebe, promise me you won't show yourself off like this again."

She turned in his arms and kissed him so she didn't have to answer because she wasn't making any promises to him until she'd heard a few in return.

Dan's big hands slid up along her spine. He wanted to go on kissing her forever. He couldn't get enough of her mouth, the feel of her skin, the sweet woman's scent of her. But he hadn't waited this long to have it over so quickly, and he released her.

She gave a moan of disappointment as he stepped back. He loved the fact that she didn't want him to let her go. Pulling his shirttail from his pants, he sank down into a chair so he could look at her. A small pile of straps and fishnet had fallen in loops about her waist, and her breasts, round and swollen, were so beautiful he couldn't tear his eyes away from them. How could he even have imagined marrying Sharon when he felt like this about Phoebe? His heart had known the truth long before his mind had figured it out.

He lifted his gaze and was jarred by the uncertainty he saw in her expression. Those tiny little furrows between her brows, that hesitation in her manner, were completely at odds with her sinner's body. Having her look so vulnerable scared him. Some part of him wanted her aggressive and knowing, ready when it was over to raise her sharp-pointed fingernail file to the bedpost and add another slash mark next to his initials. But his heart didn't want that at all. He smiled to relieve the growing tension between them.

"You could make me a happy man, darlin', if you'd slide that dress off real slow, so I could see if you're lyin' to me about your underwear."

Her lips parted softly, and her eyes widened as if she had never taken off her clothes for a man in her life. That look of shy innocence combined with her nuclear reactor body nearly undid him.

410

When she didn't move, he cocked his head and inquired softly, "You don't want to do that virgin thing again tonight, do you, honey? Because I'm afraid you've put me in the mood for something a little spicier?"

"The virgin thing? Oh, no. No, I —" She clasped the wisps of fabric at her waist and began to peel.

"Not so fast now. Could we sort of pretend — now don't take this the wrong way because I don't mean anything disrespectful by it — but could we pretend that I'm planning to leave a hundred-dollar bill on the dresser after this is over, and I'm expecting to get my money's worth out of this striptease?"

Her smile was a little wobbly at the corners. "What's underneath this dress is definitely worth more than a hundred dollars."

"As long as you take American Express, you can name your price."

She toyed with the dress where it had fallen low on her waist. Although she had slipped her thumbs beneath the fabric as if she were getting ready to peel it down, she wasn't moving it any lower than her navel. "I thought you were a reformed man. You said you weren't into kinkiness any more."

"That was before I saw you in that damned dress."

"Would you take off your shirt first? I like looking at your chest."

"You do?" She was hardly the first woman who'd admired his body, but he still felt inexplicably pleased. He tossed his bow tie on the hassock and then his cummerbund. Without taking his eyes from her, he removed his onyx cuff links and slipped off his shirt.

Her eyes were all over him, which made him feel even better. "Your turn," he said.

She pulled the dress farther down on her hips, but stopped just before she got to the really good stuff and gave him that mischievous look he loved. "What's the credit limit on your American Express card?"

"You stop worrying about credit limits and start worrying about whether or not you're still going to be able to walk when I get done with you."

"I'm trembling, Mr. Tough Guy." She stuck out her lip — stuck out her front. Then she peeled that slinky black fabric down inch by inch over those full round hips, those shapely thighs, giving a performance so sexy he thought he was going to explode before he ever touched her. Even before she lifted first one high heel and then the other to step out of the puddle of net and straps at her feet, he saw that she hadn't lied about what she didn't have on.

Two black nylon stockings and a sexy pair of high, high heels were all that was left. She was wild and wicked, and for the rest of the night, she was his.

He wanted to run his hands over every inch of that body, slip his fingers into each crevice, but he'd have to get up to do that, which meant he'd lose this incredible view. Instead, he stayed where he was and stroked her with his eyes, sliding his gaze all the way down those incredible legs and back up to the spot between them.

The seconds ticked by, one after another, and as the silence lengthened, Phoebe's nervousness returned. Why didn't he say something? The longer he looked, the more certain she became that he had found something wrong with her. She had been bubbling with sexy confidence, but now she remembered that she wasn't even close to fashion model skinny. Her thighs weren't thin enough, her hips were definitely too round, and the only time her stomach had been truly concave was when she'd had the flu. When he showed no sign of breaking the silence, she lost her nerve and reached down to snatch the straps of her dress.

He was immediately on his feet, concern furrowing his brow. "Phoebe, honey, I was kidding about the hooker thing. You know that, don't you?" He pulled the dress from her fingers and took her in his arms.

His chest was warm against her breasts. She pressed her cheek to one of his hard pectorals. Her mind told her she wasn't safe in his arms, but her heart felt as if it had found a home.

"Tell me what's wrong, darlin'. Have I been teasing you too much? You know I didn't mean to hurt your feelings."

She could hide behind her old flirtatious evasions, or she could be honest. "I'm embarrassed to have you look at me like that."

"Like what?"

"I know I should lose ten pounds, but I can't

diet, and you're used to skinnier women. Valerie is —"

"What does Valerie have to do with this?"

"She's skinny, and I'm a little — I'm fat!"

"Man-oh-man. I'm giving up on women. I'm definitely giving up." As he grumbled, he began to caress her hips, and the skin at her temples tingled from the soft motion of his lips. "I know lots of women feel insecure about their bodies, and I know I should be sweet and understanding about this. But, Phoebe, honey, having you worry about being too fat is pretty much like having a billionaire worry about his money being too green."

"You were looking at me."

"You've got me there, but I've learned my lesson. From now on, I'm gonna shut my eyes." He lifted both her breasts in his palms, bent his head, and found the left nipple with his mouth. As he suckled her, liquid threads of pleasure, hot and tingling, spread through her. Her insecurities faded as she clung to his shoulders and offered herself up to him.

She didn't know how they got to the bed or what happened to her shoes, only that he was laying her on the soft, patterned blanket. She watched as he took off the rest of his clothes and came to lie beside her.

"I still have my stockings on."

"I know." He ran his hands over the sheer, black nylon and up to the soft, unprotected skin of her inner thigh, and she could see that the stockings excited him.

"Spread your legs for me, honey."

She did as he asked.

"Farther," he urged. "Pull up your knees."

She did that, too.

"You're looking again." She gazed down at the top of his head.

"And you're just as pretty here as you are everywhere else."

She could barely breathe as he did a moist tracing of her with the tip of his index finger. Taking his time. Looking his fill. Sometimes pressing his lips to the insides of her thighs. Murmuring little nonsense syllables against her skin.

His finger grew slippery as it pushed up a little and then withdrew, going round and round on its slow forever mission. She gasped for breath, taking short, quick pants. Her body was no longer part of the room, no longer lying on the bed, but spiraling toward some hot wet land.

He bent his head and took her with his mouth. She lost herself in pleasure. Then she felt not one finger, but two. Sliding. Pumping.

She knew he was watching her. Heard him praise her passion. "That's good, baby. So good. Let it go. Let it go, sweetheart."

"No," she gasped, barely able to speak. "No. I want you."

His fingers went deeper. "Do you, baby? Do you?"

"Yes, I . . ."

Her eyes flew open. Those fingers! They were everywhere. He knew no shame.

He laughed a devil's laugh, earthy and lusty. "Relax, baby. Relax and let me feel you."

She moaned and let him do what he wanted because nothing on earth could have made her tell him to stop, not even when he took her nipple in his mouth, suckled hard, and hurled her over the mountaintop.

She flew through space, end over end, spiraling, hitting the sun and then falling back to earth. He caught her safely before she hit the ground.

Long moments passed before her eyelids drifted open. "I couldn't wait for you," she finally whispered.

"I didn't let you." He settled between her legs.

She was slick and wet, but she still had trouble taking him. Feeling that sweet stretch, she tilted her hips to get more, then whimpered as he gave it to her.

He froze. "Am I hurting you?"

"No," she gasped in a thick whisper. "It's wonderful."

He arched his back like a great jungle cat, drove his hips, and she came again.

He laughed as he felt her shudders, then filled her mouth with his tongue and took her body away from her. It was his now. Sweet spoils won on a silken battlefield. Every inch belonged to him, and he would take it as he wished. Hard and deep, letting her feel the raw power of a strength so much greater than hers. Using her shamefully. Sensually. Making her cry out again and again in passion.

Sweat slicked his body but he wouldn't let himself climax because he wasn't done with her; he hadn't felt enough of her, not even when he had put her knees to her shoulders and driven so deeply he was blowing apart.

It wasn't enough! He wanted more. More of her sex. Her heart. Her soul.

She gave a soft cry that tore him apart, and something was unraveling inside him, something that should have remained coiled up tight and hard and safe. Frightened by instincts that had been developed in his childhood, instincts that warned him against the searing, unbearable pain of soft emotions, he turned her over like a rag doll. With one hand resting lightly on the back of her neck to hold her head down, he raised her hips, drawing her to her knees. Her blond hair swirled like a golden web on the pillow. He thrust into her from behind while he cupped the spilling bounty of her breasts in his hands and rolled the nipples between his fingers, taking her to that sweetest of all boundaries just this side of pain.

She was crying out his name, begging him to hurl her over the edge again, and this time he knew he couldn't send her alone.

Her face was hidden, her sex jutted up for his use. He was rutting like an animal, so he shouldn't have felt this all-encompassing tenderness, sensations so warm and soft they almost made him weep. He willed those gentle feelings away, cursed himself, but as she once again convulsed around him, he would have died for her.

His fierceness left him, and he turned her back so he could gaze down at that soft beautiful face, cheeks flushed, lips parted. Pulling her tight against him, he squeezed his eyes shut against the surge of an emotion he refused to name.

With a great cry, he flooded her.

21

Dan walked across the bedroom, unself-conscious about his nudity. As she lay in bed and gazed at the many scars on his body, she thought about all the hits he had taken over the years. He pulled a white terry cloth robe from the closet and slipped into it. "We've got to talk, Phoebe."

She had never seen him look so serious, and memories of what had happened the first time they'd made love in that Portland hotel room came rushing back.

He approached the bed and sat on the edge looking down at her. "I'm afraid we both got carried away tonight. I didn't use anything."

She gazed at him blankly.

"I don't know what happened. I've never been this careless, not even when I was a kid."

Understanding dawned, and with it an irrational sense of disappointment that the idea of getting her pregnant was so upsetting to him. "You don't have to worry. I'm on the pill." He'd never know how recently she'd gone on it, right after the night in the airplane.

"These are the nineties. I'm worried about a little more than birth control. It's been years since I've been with anyone but Valerie, and my contract with the Stars requires a regular physical. I know I'm healthy." He looked her right in the eye. "But I don't know the same about you."

She stared at him.

"You've led a full life," he said quietly. "I'm not passing judgment; I just want to know how careful you've been, and how much time has passed since you've had a blood test."

She finally understood what he meant. How could she admit to this worldly man that AIDS hadn't been a serious issue the last time she'd slept with another man? Stalling, she propped herself up on the pillow with one elbow and gazed at him through a lock of hair that had fallen over her eye. "You sure know how to make a girl feel good about herself."

"This isn't a joke."

"No, it isn't." She slipped her legs over the opposite side of the bed and went to the chair where he'd dropped his tuxedo shirt. She didn't want to have this conversation naked, and she couldn't bear the idea of struggling back into her dress while he watched. "You don't have anything to worry about. I'm clean as a whistle."

"How do you know?"

She slid her arms into the sleeves of his shirt. "I just do."

"I'm afraid that's not good enough."

"There's nothing to worry about. Take my word for it." There weren't any buttons on the shirt, so she wrapped his cummerbund twice around her waist and tied the ends.

"You're not even looking at me. Are you hiding something?"

"No," she lied.

"Then sit down so we can talk this through."

"I don't have anything else to say. Maybe you'd better take me home."

He stood. "Not until we have it out. You're scaring me."

He didn't sound scared. He sounded angry. She slipped into her heels. "I was fine at my last physical."

"When was that?"

"Spring."

"How many men have there been since then?"

His question was fair, but she still felt sick inside. "Dozens! Everybody knows I'll sleep with anybody who asks!"

In two long strides, he was at her side. "Dammit, don't do this! How many?"

"You want names and addresses?" She drew up her lip, trying to look hard and tough.

"Give me numbers first."

Her eyes began to sting. "You're going to have to trust me. I've told you that you don't have anything to worry about. My sexual history isn't any of your business."

"Right now, it's very much my business." He caught her arm, not hurting her, but letting her know she couldn't get away. "How many?"

"Don't do this to me!"

"How many, dammit?"

"There haven't been any! Just you."

"Right," he drawled.

His skepticism was the final drop in a night that had been an emotional roller coaster, and tears spilled over her lower lids. "Believe what you want to." She pulled away from him to head for the door.

His voice softened and he caught her before she could get away, turning her in his arms until she was pressed against his chest. "Don't cry on me. You don't have to cry, honey. Just tell me the truth."

"There hasn't been anybody for a long time," she said wearily. "A very long time."

He pulled back just far enough so he could gaze into her eyes, and she saw that his anger had been replaced by bewilderment. "You're telling the truth, aren't you?"

She nodded.

He slid his fingers into her hair and gathered her against the shoulder of his robe. "I don't understand you at all."

"I know you don't," she whispered.

He drew her over to a cozy arm chair and pulled her into his lap. "What are we going to do about this? You've turned me inside out ever since the day we met." He tucked her head under his chin. "When you said it's been a long time, are we talking more than a year?"

She nodded.

"More than two?"

She nodded again.

"A lot more?"

Another nod.

"I'm starting to get a glimmer here." He stroked her hair. "You really loved Flores, didn't you?"

"More than I've ever loved anyone." *Until now,* she thought.

"Are you trying to tell me there hasn't been anyone in your life since then? Is that what this is about? Phoebe, he must have died six or seven years ago?"

She was going to have to do this. They had no hope for a future together unless she had the guts to tell him the truth and let him see her as she was, scars and all. But revealing so much scared her to death.

He didn't try to restrain her as she rose from his lap and crossed to the bed. She sat on the edge so that she was facing him, with her knees pressed together and her hands clasped in the shirt folds that lay in her lap.

"Arturo was gay, Dan. He wasn't my lover. In every way that counted, he was my father."

She had never seen him look so bewildered. "Then I don't understand anything."

Placing so much trust in another human being was the most difficult thing she had ever done, but she loved him, and she could no longer live in the shadows. Gathering her courage, she told him about the rape, speaking in broken sentences and twisting her hands as she struggled to explain. She didn't realize until she saw the outrage on his face that she had been subconsciously preparing herself for disbelief, and the words came more quickly. As she spoke of those awful months in

Paris when she'd slept with so many men, he showed no condemnation, only a sympathy that relaxed the tough lines of his face and made her yearn to throw herself into his arms. But she stayed where she was, nearly faltering as she attempted to describe how frozen she had felt for years and how impossible it had been for her to be intimate with anyone.

When she was done, she fell silent, her muscles screaming with tension, while she waited for him to absorb the fact that he was the man with whom she had chosen to end so many years of celibacy. He had not made a commitment of any kind to her, yet she was letting him know without words what he meant to her. Never had she risked so much.

She sat stiffly on the edge of the bed and watched him rise from the chair. As he came toward her, she sensed his suppressed rage in the corded tension of his neck muscles, but, at the same time, the soft compassion in his eyes made her understand that his anger wasn't directed at her.

He gathered her into his arms, and when he spoke, his voice was thick with emotion. "I'm so sorry, sweetheart. I'm so very, very sorry."

Dropping his head, he began to kiss her, the warmth of healing in the touch of his lips. Right then, she wanted to tell him she loved him, but his kiss deepened and he began to caress her. Before long, she was lost to reason as he vanquished the shadows of the past with the sweet, deep stroking of his body.

It was nearly three in the morning before he drove her home. She'd put her bondage dress back on, along with his sweatshirt and her evening coat. After the emotional turmoil of the night, she felt very much at peace, and he, too, seemed relaxed.

"You're going to be exhausted tomorrow," she said as she leaned against his arm.

"I don't need much sleep. Even when I was a little kid, I'd crawl out of bed and sneak outside."

"You rascal."

"I was a stubborn little cuss. My mother took a switch to me whenever she caught me, but no matter how much she beat me, I kept doin' it."

His tone had been mild, but she lifted her head slightly. "Your mother beat you?"

A small muscle throbbed in his jaw. "My parents weren't exactly into modern child-raising techniques. They were backwoods people, teenagers when they had to get married. They both pretty much resented being stuck with a baby."

"I'm sorry."

"You don't have to look so sad. It got better when I was older. My father was real proud of me once I started to play ball."

She experienced a flash of rage toward a father who had needed a scoreboard to measure out love. "What about your mother?"

"She was an alcoholic. On her good days, she was proud of me, too. They were killed in an auto accident my freshman year in college." She understood what it was costing him to reveal so much

425

of himself to her, and she remained silent so he could tell this his own way.

"If you want to know the truth, I felt like I'd lost them a long time before that. It's strange. A couple of months ago, this guy was tailing me." He told her about Ray Hardesty, the Stars' player who had been cut from the team, and his father's apparent vendetta against Dan. "I haven't seen Hardesty since, so I assume he came to his senses. But when I had that man up against the side of his van, I felt like I was looking into my old man's eyes all over again. It was obvious that Hardesty had never made anything of himself, and he'd been living his life through his son. He wasn't grieving for Ray; he was grieving for himself. That's sick."

She shuddered at the idea of Dan's having someone stalking him.

His voice grew gruff. "That's why — It's a hard thing to explain, but family's important to me. A real family with kids and parents who care about each other."

"Was that why your marriage broke up?"

"Val never had any interest in kids. I'm not blaming her because things didn't work out, you understand. It was more my fault than hers. I should have gotten my priorities sorted out before I married her. She always said I was jealous of her career, but that wasn't it at all. Val's dedication to her work was one of the things I most admired about her. But I wanted her to care about family, too, and I can't ever let myself make a mistake like that again with a woman. I don't want my kids growing up with the kind of parents I had. I don't want to be the kind of father who makes his kid feel as if he has to score a touchdown before he can get any affection. And I want them to have a mother who's a real mother."

She gazed at him as he turned into her drive, trying to understand what he meant by that. Was he simply sharing his past with her because she'd told him about her own, or was there a deeper meaning behind this conversation? The intimacy between them was too new and fragile for her to ask.

He came around to help her out, and when they reached her door, he kissed her temple, then her lips. Long minutes passed before they drew apart. "I'm going to miss you."

"We see each other every day."

"I know, but it's not the same." He brushed a lock of hair back from her cheek with his thumb. "I'll be pretty busy the rest of the week getting ready for the Bills' game, so don't read anything into it if I don't stop by here."

She smiled. "I won't."

"You keep your chin up this week, hear?" He stroked her hair and gave her a gaze so tender she felt as if he were making love to her all over again. "Honey, I understand how much you've got riding on Saturday. We're gonna do our best."

"I know that."

For a moment she thought he was going to say more. Instead, he squeezed her hand, kissed her again, and began to walk away.

427

"Dan?" As he turned back, her voice dropped to a gentle whisper. "Kick some Buffalo butt for me, will you?"

His response was as soft as an Alabama breeze. "Sure enough, sweetheart."

Even though the pace was unbelievably hectic, Phoebe felt as if she danced through the rest of the week. She found herself laughing for no reason at all and flirting with everyone — male, female, young, old, it made no difference. She sailed through her interviews with the press and even managed to be polite to Reed when he called with good luck wishes that rang hollow because he couldn't quite hide his frustration at how long it was taking him to get his hands on the Stars.

The more she mulled over Dan's revelations about his childhood, the more she wanted to believe that he had been sounding her out to discover her feelings about having a family. His disclosures allowed her to unearth all those precious dreams she had kept locked away for years, dreams of a husband who loved her and of a house filled with children who would never know what it was like to grow up unloved.

The few times she and Dan passed each other in the hallway, she felt something warm and wonderful travel between them. Still, her love for him frightened her. How was she going to put herself back together if he didn't return that love? For so long she had lived in the shadows. Was it possible that she could finally walk in the sunshine?

The Stars-Bills game was scoreless at the end of the first quarter, and as Phoebe left the field and entered the skybox, she was so tense she wished she could spend the next three quarters hiding out with a VCR and an old Doris Day movie. She took a glass of tomato juice from the bartender and watched as the skybox's two television sets faded to a Nike commercial.

"You're always complaining about having to watch the game with men, so I've brought you a companion."

She turned to see Ron standing at her side accompanied by a young woman with curly red hair and a friendly, rather shy smile.

"My friend here was stuck in the VIP skybox next door, but the cigarette smoke was giving her trouble."

"I hope you don't mind," the woman said. "Smoke makes me wheeze, and Ron said you didn't allow it in here."

"I don't mind at all." There was something endearing about her small, almost elfin features and freckled nose. Phoebe decided she was a definite improvement over the tall socialites Ron had been dating lately and found herself automatically returning her smile.

One of Ron's assistants popped up at his side, and he excused himself.

"I feel like I'm barging in," the young woman said.

"Nonsense. I'm glad to have company. Maybe

you can distract me. I was just trying to figure out how I was going to get through the rest of the game without either throwing up or fainting." She extended her hand. "I'm Phoebe Somerville."

"Sharon Anderson." The woman returned her handshake.

"Let me get you something to drink." Phoebe led her over to the bar where Sharon requested a Diet Pepsi. "You're a two-fisted drinker like I am."

"Alcohol gives me a headache. I was voted the most boring girl in my college sorority."

Phoebe laughed. She had missed her female friends, and she liked this young woman's self-deprecating sense of humor.

The second quarter was beginning, and they took their drinks over to seats at the window. Phoebe gazed down at Dan and then turned to watch a close-up of him on the television screen as he barked orders into his headset while he kept his eyes riveted on the Stars' defense.

She flinched as the Bills' running back found a huge hole in the Stars' defensive line and made a fifteen-yard gain before Webster brought him down. "I don't think I can last three more quarters. I wish somebody would knock me out until this is over."

"It must be hard to watch the game when you have so much at stake."

"I used to hate football. It was —" She gasped with dismay and jumped up from her seat as the Bills completed a twenty-one-yard pass. "That's

430

it! I have to get out of here. Stay and enjoy yourself; I'm going to take a walk in the hallway to settle myself down."

Sharon stood. "I'll go with you."

"You don't have to. Really."

"I don't mind. To be honest, I'm not much of a football fan. Unless you'd rather be alone."

"I'd love the company."

The carpeted hallway outside was deserted but noisy with the sounds of blaring televisions, cheers, and groans coming from behind the doors of the other skyboxes. Phoebe crossed her arms tightly over her chest and began to walk. Hoping to distract herself, she asked, "How long have you and Ron been dating?"

"Oh, we're not dating. We just met today. He's really a nice guy, though."

"The best. The fact that he's gorgeous doesn't hurt, either."

"I must admit it's nice to be around a man who doesn't tower over me. I'm so short that most of them do. That's one of the best things about my job. Everybody's smaller than me."

"What do you do?"

"I'm a nursery school teacher."

"Do you like it?"

"I love it. Not that I don't look forward to the end of the day. Kids are cute, but exhausting."

They'd reached a bend in the hallway. As much as Phoebe didn't want to watch the action, neither did she want to be too far away, and she turned so they could retract their steps. "My sister Molly baby-sits for a set of twins who live next door. Sometimes she brings them over to our house when they've gotten cranky and she's having trouble controlling them. They're little stinkers, but I love playing with them."

Sharon regarded her curiously. "You don't look like the type of —" Breaking off, she dropped her eyes in embarrassment.

"I don't look like the type of woman who enjoys children?"

"I'm sorry. That sounds like an insult, and I didn't intend it that way. You're just so glamorous."

"Thank you, but you're not the first person to think that about me. Not even people with good imaginations seem to be able to see me as a mother." She bit her lip as all of her anxieties about her future with Dan crept back.

"Is something wrong?"

A collective groan echoed from the nearby skyboxes, all of them held by Star fans, and Phoebe picked up the pace. "Children are very important to the man I'm sort of involved with. They are to me, too, but he hasn't discovered that yet." She smiled ruefully. "I'm afraid it's easier for him to picture me popping out of a cake at a bachelor party than as his children's mother. Since he hasn't actually stated his intentions, it's tough figuring out how to let him know I feel the same way he does about having a family."

"Believe me, I understand from personal experience."

"Are you involved with someone?"

"Yes." She suddenly looked shy, and Phoebe gave her an encouraging smile. Sharon sighed. "It's a strange relationship. All my life I've attracted ordinary guys — brothers of my girlfriends, quiet, sweet men, not too exciting, but steady. And then this Greek god pops into my life out of nowhere, the kind of man who always passes up ordinary women like me for glamorous women like you. He's been subtly feeling me out about marriage and children for weeks, and I'm fairly certain he's going to get around to proposing any day now, but I still can't figure out what he sees in me."

"Maybe the same thing I do — a very nice woman who'd make a wonderful wife."

"Thanks, Phoebe. I wish I could believe that. He's making me crazy. In this day and age — I mean, if you were ready to propose marriage to somebody, wouldn't you expect —" Sharon turned red and blurted out, "He treats me like the Virgin Mary!"

"You're not sleeping together?"

Sharon tugged on her hair and looked embarrassed. "I can't believe we're having this conversation. I haven't even told my sister about this, and I tell her everything."

"We're meeting under a crisis situation. Like two strangers sitting next to each other on a doomed airplane." Another chorus of groans erupted from the nearby skyboxes, and Phoebe flinched. "Your secret's safe with me. To tell you the truth, I'm a little envious. At least you'll never

433

have to be afraid that he only wants you for sex."

"I suppose you're right. And to be honest, I haven't encouraged him at all. He's the most exciting man I've ever known, but I can't seem to relax with him. It's complicated."

Phoebe recalled Ron's saying that Sharon had been in the next skybox, the one the Stars used as an overflow for visiting VIPs. Sharon's suitor was obviously someone with a high profile, and she couldn't resist a gentle probe. "I haven't heard any unusual gossip, so you and your Greek god must be keeping this quiet."

"The local press had a field day with his divorce, so we've been careful about appearing together in public. This is the first game I've attended. As a matter of fact, there have been more rumors about the two of you than about us. Your friendship seems to mean a lot to him."

Phoebe looked at her quizzically, and then everything inside her went still. Wild cheering broke out in the skyboxes, but she didn't hear it. She didn't hear anything except the clamoring of her own heart.

Sharon failed to notice that anything was wrong. "I guess I shouldn't be surprised that Dan never mentioned me to you."

"No. No, he didn't." Her voice seemed to be coming from a great distance.

"He's a private person in a lot of ways. I'm not putting myself down when I say this — really, I'm not. But I just can't figure out what he sees in me."

Phoebe could figure it out. Sharon Anderson was the sweet, down-to-earth girl a man fell in love with and married. Phoebe was the sexy bimbo a man fucked and forgot.

Another round of cheering broke out. She didn't know how they got back into the skybox or how she managed to stumble through her halftime interview. Luckily, the wild cheering during the third and fourth quarters made conversation for the remainder of the game impossible. By the time it was over, she was barely able to register the Stars' decisive 24–10 victory over the Bills.

On the two televisions suspended from the ceiling, the commentator explained how it had happened. "The Bills began to lose their momentum during the second quarter, and they never regained it. You can't make that many critical mistakes against a team as talented and well coached as the Stars. This team has improved so much over the season. No doubt about it. The Stars are this season's Cinderella team."

Meanwhile, the Cinderella team's owner had been left with a broken heart and a glass slipper that had shattered into a million pieces. Hours later, as she stood at her bedroom window, her eyes swollen and her chest aching, she wondered how she was going to find the courage to go on. She had suffered a betrayal so deep and wrenching that she felt as if she had been ripped apart. For the first time in her life, she had dared to hope that she was worthy of love, only to discover, once again, that she was wrong.

She had no more tears left. Her insides were as empty as a broken vessel. *I loved you so, Dan. Why couldn't you have loved me back.*

The following Tuesday afternoon Sharon was putting the last of the poster paint away in the cupboard when Dan walked into the classroom. She was a mess, as usual, and she tried to tuck her shirttail back into her slacks. Why did she always have to look her worst when he came by?

"You missed the kids. They left almost an hour ago."

"I wish I could have gotten away earlier."

"I'm surprised you could get away at all." She fumbled nervously with her shirt cuffs as she rolled them down. "When are you leaving for Miami?"

"Tonight. We have our first practice Wednesday morning."

"One more win and you're in the AFC Championship."

"Too bad we have to beat the Dolphins to get there." He slipped his hands into his pockets. "I have to meet some reporters at five-thirty. Why don't we go grab a quick bite to eat?"

"I didn't know you were stopping by, and I promised my sister I'd go shopping with her." She saw that he looked edgy. "Is something wrong?"

"It can wait."

"Are you sure? I know how tight your schedule is. We didn't even get to see each other after the game on Sunday."

"I'd rather have some privacy. This probably

436

isn't the best place to talk."

She wasn't a naturally assertive person, especially around him, but she wanted to get this over with. Making her way to one of the small tables, she drew out a chair and sat down. "Everyone's left, so we won't be interrupted. Let's talk now."

He should have looked ridiculous as he lowered his large frame into the tiny chair next to her, but he accomplished the move as gracefully as he did everything else. Just looking at him made her feel awkward and unsure of herself. When would she feel comfortable with this man?

He picked up her hand and trapped it between his. "Sharon, you're one of the nicest people I've ever known."

Her heart began to pound in dread. She'd been waiting for this moment for weeks, but now that it was here, she wasn't ready.

"As soon as I met you, I realized that you were everything I admired in a woman. You're sweet tempered and kind . . ."

He listed her virtues, but instead of being flattered, she wanted him to let her hand go. Everything about him was too big for her — his size, his reputation. He was too good looking, too strong, too rich. Why couldn't he be ordinary like her?

He rubbed her hand. "For a long time now, I've been playing around with the idea that the two of us might have a future together. I suspect you know that."

He was going to propose, and she would have

to accept, because a woman would be insane to turn down a man like him. Life was getting ready to hand her the gold ring, so why did she feel as if she wanted to jump off the merry-go-round?

". . . that's why it's so hard for me to tell you I've made a mistake." He looked down at her hand.

"A mistake?"

"I've been leading you toward something I thought was right, but I've only recently realized that it's not."

She sat up straighter in the tiny chair and permitted herself the first flicker of hope. "It isn't?"

"Sharon, I'm sorry. I've been doing a lot of thinking about the two of us in the past few days. . . ."

"Yes?"

"This is all my fault. I'm old enough to know myself better and not make this kind of mistake."

She was afraid she'd expire from the suspense if he didn't get to the point soon.

"As special as you are, and you are special — As important as this relationship has been to me . . ." Once again, his voice trailed off.

"Dan, are you dumping me?"

He looked horrified. "God, no! It's nothing like that. We're friends. It's just —"

"You are! You're dumping me."

His face fell. "I feel like a heel for leading you on. I got caught up with you and the kids and everything. You'd think I would have figured out by now what I want out of life. I'm sorry I had to put you through my mid-life crisis."

"No, no, it's fine! Really. I understand." She could barely hold back her glee. "I guess I've known for a while that we weren't right for each other, but I didn't know how to talk to you about it. I'm glad you came to see me, and I appreciate you being honest with me. Most men wouldn't have put themselves through a confrontation. They would have just stopped calling."

"I couldn't do that."

"Of course you couldn't." She wasn't able to control the smile that was spreading over her face.

He began to look amused. "Don't you want to cry or hit me or something?"

She didn't always get his jokes, but she understood this one. "I guess you can tell that I'm a little bit relieved. I've been feeling sort of crazy these past few weeks. You're every woman's dream man, and I knew I should fall in love with you."

"But you didn't."

She shook her head.

"Sharon, I can't believe I'm going to do this, but I wasn't exactly expecting this conversation to turn out so well. Yesterday, a friend of mine asked me about you. At first I thought he was just curious because he knew you were my guest at the game on Sunday, but then I realized he wanted to ask you out himself."

"The one thing I've learned the past few months is that I'm not comfortable with athletes."

"Perfect."

She couldn't understand why he was smiling.

Still grinning, he rose from the small chair. "My friend's not much of an athlete. He plays basketball, but just between the two of us, he's pretty pathetic."

"I don't know."

"It's Ron McDermitt, our general manager."

"Ron?"

"Do you have a problem with me giving him your phone number?"

"Problem? Oh, no. No, I don't have a problem with that at all."

She must have sounded too eager because he started to chuckle. Leaning down, he gave her a peck on the cheek. "I have a feeling I'll be seeing you around."

He was still shaking his head with amusement as he walked out to his car. His life was starting all over again, and the future was no longer murky, but crystal clear. Now that he'd settled things with Sharon, he could tell Phoebe how much he loved her. The knowledge had been inside him for a long time, but he'd been too confused by the erotic smoke screen that surrounded her to realize it. His sweet, smart, gutsy little bimbo. He didn't think he'd ever forget the way she'd looked sitting on the side of his bed spilling out all her secrets. When she'd told him about her rape, he'd wanted to throw back his head and howl. She made him feel things that scared him to death.

He reached his car, and some of his euphoria faded. He'd survived childhood by learning not to love anyone too much, and the depth of emotion he felt for her terrified him a lot more than any defensive lineup he'd ever faced. He'd always held something back from women, but that wasn't going to be possible with her. Telling her how much he loved her would be the biggest risk he'd ever taken because there was always the chance that she'd throw those feelings right back in his face.

He reminded himself that beneath all of Phoebe's sassiness, she was the gentlest person he'd ever known. Surely there was no need for him to be afraid. Surely, his heart would be safe with her.

22

"Stop scowling, Darnell. You're scaring the photographers." Phoebe squeezed Darnell Pruitt's arm, a restraining action that was about as effective as trying to dent an iron bar. She nodded at one of the reporters. All week she'd been going through the motions of life, determined not to let anyone see her despair. Darnell had been good company tonight, and she was grateful he'd agreed to act as her escort on the tour of the corporate hospitality suites the night before the Dolphins game.

His eyes narrowed into vicious slits as he curled his lip at the Associated Press and spoke to her under his breath. "There's no way I'm letting anybody on the Dolphins' defense see a picture of me smilin'."

"Thank God there aren't any small children around."

"I don't know why you'd say that. I love kids."

It was approaching his eleven o'clock curfew as they left the last party and made their way to the elevator. Darnell's courtship of Miss Charmaine Dodd wasn't progressing quickly enough to suit him, and he was hoping one of the Chicago papers would print a shot of him with Phoebe that would stir Miss Dodd to jealousy.

Phoebe had minimized her contact with Dan by waiting until that afternoon to fly into Miami, and she'd barely had time to change into her gown, an old one she'd bought for a Christmas party several years ago. It was a high-necked, tight-fitting sheath of shimmering gold lace worn over a flesh-colored body stocking. Darnell was wearing his tuxedo with a black silk shirt and gold bow tie that matched his diamond embellished tooth.

The elevator was empty when they reached it, allowing Darnell to return to the discussion he'd been more or less carrying on by himself ever since he'd come to her room three hours earlier. "I don't see why everybody thinks Captain Ahab is evil. Damn, if it wasn't for his leg, I'd have that man on my team any day. He doesn't let anything stand in his way, dig? Those are the kind of men win football games."

Moby Dick was just one of the books she'd recommended that Darnell had devoured in the past few months on his quest for self-improvement. It hadn't taken her long to realize that football might have made Darnell rich in material things, but the game had robbed him of the opportunity to use his intellect. Because Darnell was big, black, and strong, no one had bothered to discover that he also had a fine brain.

Darnell continued his praise of Captain Ahab all the way to the door of her hotel suite. She dreaded being alone with her thoughts and wished he didn't have a curfew so she could invite him inside. Instead, she wished him good luck with a peck on the cheek. "Crunch some bones for me tomorrow, Darnell."

He grinned and took off down the hallway in his size fifteen dress shoes. She sighed as she shut the door. Charmaine Dodd was a fool if she didn't snatch him up.

The telephone rang. She unclipped one of her crystal earrings and sat down on the room's chintz couch to answer. "Hello."

"Where the hell have you been all week?"

The sharp crystal edges of her earring dug into her palm. She squeezed her eyes shut against the fresh wave of pain. "Hello to you, too, Coach."

"I stopped by the house on Tuesday night so we could see each other before I left, but Molly said you'd already gone to bed. You were giving interviews when I called the office on Thursday and Friday, and there was no answer at your house last night. I'm coming up to your room."

"No!" She bit her lip. "I'm tired. It's been a hard week."

"I need to see you."

It didn't take a crystal ball to figure out why. He wanted sex, a quick romp with the bimbo while his prospective bride remained untouched. "Not tonight."

He was clearly exasperated. "Look, give me your room number. We have to talk."

"Another time, Dan. I'm exhausted." She took a shaky breath. "Good luck tomorrow. I'll see you on the sidelines."

Her eyes glistened with tears as she set the receiver back on its cradle. She hung the "Do Not Disturb" sign on her door and walked over to the window where she stared out at the lights twinkling over Biscayne Bay.

She'd learned a lot from the players in the past few months. She'd learned that if you wanted to play the game, you had to be able to take the hits. That's what she was doing now. She was taking the hits. Dan had given her a killing blow, but she wasn't going to let him see the damage. Tomorrow, when she heard the music to "Ain't She Sweet?", she would hold her head high, wave to the crowd, and cheer on her team. No one would know that she was playing hurt.

The afternoon the Stars beat the Dolphins in the AFC semifinals, Ray Hardesty sat in the den with his .38 in his lap and wished he had enough whiskey left in the house to get drunk. In one week the Stars would be meeting the Portland Sabers in the AFC Championship. He tilted the bottle to his mouth and drained the last half inch, but even the fire in his throat didn't burn as hot as his rage. The Stars had never made it this far when Ray Junior was on the squad, and now they were going without him.

With a garbled, barely human sound, he flung the bottle across the room. It crashed into a trophy shelf and shattered, but he didn't worry about the noise because there was no one around to hear it. After a marriage that had lasted for three decades, Ellen had left him. She'd told him he'd been acting crazy and he needed to go to a psychiatrist or something. Fuck that. He didn't need to go to any psychiatrist. He just needed to get even with Dan Calebow.

After the Chargers game, he'd thought about killing Calebow. He'd eventually rejected the idea, not out of scruples, but because Calebow's death wouldn't necessarily guarantee a Stars' loss. He needed something foolproof. He wasn't rich enough to bribe anyone. Besides, the players made too much money these days to be susceptible, and most of the refs were honest. He wanted guarantees.

Phoebe Somerville appeared on the television screen. Last week he'd been hiding in the woods next to Calebow's house when the coach had brought her home. The bedroom lights had gone on less than half an hour later. He'd been spying on them for months now, borrowing cars so Calebow wouldn't spot him, and he knew their relationship was no longer casual. Although he'd filed the information away, until now he hadn't known what to do with it.

The idea that had been slowly taking shape in his mind was both complex and amazingly easy. He'd probably be caught, but by then it would be too late, and he didn't care what happened to him anyway. Only one thing mattered. Keeping the Stars from winning the AFC Championship.

On television, Phoebe Somerville's interview had ended and the cameras returned to the Stars' coach. Ray lifted his .38 and blew out the screen.

Dan had been through the media blitz that surrounds championship games as a player, but never as a coach, and he decided it was a good thing he'd learned to survive without sleep. Even so, by the time he freed up a few hours late Tuesday afternoon following the Stars' victory over the Dolphins, he was definitely punchy. He was also mad as hell at Phoebe.

As he pulled into her driveway and got out of his car, he decided the first thing he was going to do when he finally got hold of her was to kiss her. Then he was going to give her a piece of his mind. He knew exactly how busy she was, but so was he, and she could have squeezed in ten minutes sometime during the last two days to talk to him. Both of them had been under a lot of pressure, but that didn't mean they should shut each other out. She hadn't even flown home with the team Sunday night, something he'd been looking forward to. The last time he'd seen her was in the locker room after the game when Ron had brought her down to congratulate the team.

Phoebe's housekeeper, Peg, let him in as she was getting ready to leave for the day. He dropped his coat over the banister and heard high-pitched squeals coming from the back of the house. At first he didn't recognize the sounds, not because they were so unusual, but because they were so unexpected.

Pooh trotted out to greet him. With the dog at his heels, he made his way through the living room, then came to an abrupt stop as he reached the archway that led into the kitchen. What he saw there nearly knocked him off his feet.

"I want to do it, Phoebe!"

"It's my turn!"

"Mine!"

"Hush! You can both do it, you little stinkers. Here's a knife for each of you. That's the way, Jared. Good job, Jason. A little more icing on the side. No, Jared, don't lick it until we're — Oh, well, what are a few germs between friends? Right, pal?"

Jesus. He knew it wasn't just lack of sleep that was making his eyes sting, but emotion. He'd never seen anything more beautiful in his life than Phoebe icing that ugly-looking cake with those two little towheaded boys kneeling on chairs beside her.

She didn't look at all like the mother of his imagination. Her man-killer fingernails were painted vampire red. Big gypsy hoop earrings played peek-a-boo with her calendar girl hair, and at least three bracelets clinked on each of her wrists. She had on an oversized Stars' sweatshirt — she'd gotten that part right, at least — but instead of wearing it with some nice jeans like mothers were supposed to, she had on the tightest, slinkiest pair of gold stretch pants he'd ever seen in his life.

No, she didn't look like anybody's mother, but those two little boys with chocolate smeared all over their faces obviously adored her. And so did he, with all his heart. He pictured her showing up for their kids' PTA meetings decked out in red satin and rhinestones, but instead of dismaying him, the idea filled him with pleasure. She'd marry him. Of course, she would. As he watched her, he refused to let the shadows of his childhood give him any doubts. A woman didn't break a fifteen-year sexual fast with a man she didn't love.

"Sing that song again, Phoebe," one of the children demanded while Pooh licked up the chocolate crumbs on the floor beneath the table.

"Which song?"

"That one about monsters."

"The werewolf song?" As the boys nodded, Phoebe launched into a spirited rendition of Warren Zevon's "Werewolves of London," accenting the beat by swinging those amazing hips of hers. God, she was beautiful, and as he watched her, he felt an odd sense of peace. He couldn't imagine anything better than spending the rest of his life with her.

She swept the twins off their chairs to dance, her back still turned toward the doorway. He watched her wiggle to the rhythm, and he smiled when the boys tried to imitate her. She swung them around, then froze as she saw him.

"Don't let me stop the party," he said with a grin.

"What are you doing here?"

"Peg let me in as she was leaving."

The boys started to squirm and Phoebe released them. "I'm afraid you've got me at a bad time."

Jared tugged on her hand. "The cake's all frosty

now. Can me and Jason have a piece?"

"Of course. Let me get some plates."

Her hands were clumsy as she pulled the plates down. She saw that Dan had knelt in front of the boys so they were at eye level. Lines of fatigue were etched in his face, but she didn't permit herself to feel any sympathy. Keeping up with two women at the same time was undoubtedly exhausting. She blinked her eyes against a fresh flood of pain.

"That cake looks mighty good, fellas. You make it?"

"Peg maked it," Jared replied.

"But Phoebe let us put frosty on it," his twin added.

"Chocolate," Jared explained unnecessarily, since it was decorating most of his face.

Dan chuckled, and the sound ripped through Phoebe's heart. She quickly placed a wedge of cake on each of two plates and set them on the cluttered table.

Dan stood to watch the boys scramble for their chairs. "Yessirree, that cake sure does look good."

Jason didn't let the fact that his mouth was already full stop him from talking. "The man wants some, Phoebe."

She tried to keep her voice light. "Not such big bites, killer. You'll choke."

Molly burst into the kitchen. "I'm home! Hi, guys. Hi, Coach." She gave each twin a pat, leaned down to get a kiss from Pooh, who'd jumped up on her, then regarded Phoebe cautiously. "Did Peg

450

tell you what happened?"

"She said you had a meeting."

"There was a problem in the writing lab, and Mrs. Miller wanted to talk to us about it. Thanks for watching the boys." She made the statement begrudgingly.

Phoebe rinsed the frosting from her hands and dried them on a dish towel while Molly fussed over the twins. Dan came up behind her.

"Now that you can pass guard duty over to Miz Molly, what do you say we take a walk?"

"It's too cold outside."

"Shoot, that's good Chicago weather out there." Not giving her a chance to protest further, he grasped her wrist and pulled her from the kitchen. She couldn't engage in a struggling match with him in front of the children, so she went along with him until they had reached the foyer and were out of earshot.

"Let me go!"

For a moment he didn't say anything; he simply studied her with guarded eyes. "Seems like I've been a little slow to catch on. I just thought you were busy this past week, but you've been avoiding me."

"I've been busy."

"We need some privacy. Get your coat."

"I don't think so."

"Fine." He gripped her upper arm and pulled her up the stairs.

"Stop it!" she hissed. "I don't want to do this."

"Too bad." He led her into the bedroom and

shut the door. Only then did he let her go, bracing his hands on his hips just as he did when he was standing on the sidelines. He had the same fierce expression on his face that she'd seen when he was about to do battle.

"All right, let's have it. Why the deep freeze?"

She had tried to postpone this encounter, had even hoped to avoid it entirely, but she should have known that wouldn't be possible. Dan wasn't the type of person to avoid confrontations. She bit the inside of her cheek because, once she started to cry, she'd never be able to stop, and she couldn't bear to have him see her break down like that.

"Are you mad because I didn't call you right after we slept together? You know what's been going on this week. I thought you understood." He glanced at his watch. "Matter of fact, I'm short of time right now. We've got a coaches' meeting at six."

"You'd better hurry and get your clothes off, then." She tried to sound tough, but there was a painful rasp in her voice.

"What are you talking about?"

"Sex. Isn't that why you're here? To knock off a quickie before your meeting?" The words hurt her beyond bearing.

"Shit. This is going to be one of those woman things, isn't it? You're pissed off, and I'm going to ask you why you're pissed off, and you're going to say that if I can't figure it out for myself, you're not going to tell me. Dammit, I don't want to play games like this with you." She could feel his anger building.

"Pardon me!" She jerked the bangles from one wrist and threw them to the bed, knowing that rage was a safer emotion to express than grief. "Let's get to it, then." She kicked off her shoes, sending them flying across the room. "Hurry up, Coach. You've still got your pants on."

He closed the distance between them and caught her by the shoulders, his fingers digging into her flesh. "Stop it! I don't believe this. What's wrong with you?"

She had broken her resolution to get through this confrontation with dignity, and she grew still in his arms. Taking a shaky breath, she spoke quietly. "I'm not going to sleep with you anymore, Dan. It was a mistake, and I shouldn't have done it in the first place."

He drew back so they were no longer touching. Although his voice lost its belligerent edge, there was a dangerous wariness in his eyes. "I know you care for me. You wouldn't have slept with me if you hadn't."

"I met Sharon at the Bills game." The guilty look that flashed across his face told her everything. "She's very nice. You have good taste."

"Sharon doesn't have anything to do with the two of us. If you're thinking I was sleeping with both of you at the same time, you're wrong."

"That's what I understand. You had the best of both worlds, didn't you?" Her voice caught. "You could get your rocks off with the bimbo while you kept your future wife pristine."

Instead of being apologetic, he looked furious. "Is that the kind of man you think I am?"

"It's hard to think anything else."

She could see him struggling to hold on to his temper. "I'd made arrangements for Sharon to come to the Bills game weeks ago, and I couldn't call it off at the last minute. But I'm not seeing her any longer. I thought she was what I wanted in a woman, but then, after you and I were together last time, I knew I was kidding myself."

The knowledge that he and Sharon had separated should have made her happy, but it didn't. She needed to hear him say that he wanted more from her than sex, that he wanted love, and until he spoke the words, nothing could be right between them. Her voice was soft and unsteady. "Did you stop seeing her because she wasn't hot enough for you?"

The muscles in his throat worked as he swallowed hard. "Don't do this, Phoebe. Don't start saying all kinds of things that can't be taken back. I told you how screwed-up my own family was. For a long time I've been wanting to settle down to a real marriage — not just an ongoing orgy like I had with Valerie. I want kids."

"So you held auditions for your future children's mother, and Sharon won the baby ribbon."

"It's not hard to figure out why she appealed to me. I wanted somebody who liked kids, who wasn't going to be slapping them around whenever my back was turned."

"I see. Exactly whose mother was she supposed to be? Your children's or yours?"

He flinched, but she felt no satisfaction in knowing she'd hurt him. She didn't want that. She just wanted him to go away before she fell apart.

"That's a rotten thing to say."

"I guess it is. But I also suspect it's true."

His voice sounded hoarse. "Do you know that when I saw you with those kids downstairs, I was just about the happiest man in the world. For a few minutes today, I thought everything was coming together for us."

He hesitated, and she suddenly knew what was coming. It was as if he'd already spoken the words, and although the room was warm, she felt chilled. *Don't say it! Tell me you love me instead. Tell me love is what you want from me, not just children.*

He jammed his hands in his pockets. "I'd never seen you with kids. For all I knew, you felt the same way about them as Valerie. But I saw how you acted with those boys, and it wasn't hard to tell they're as crazy about you as you are about them."

Her whole body was aching. "Does this mean that I'm in the running now that Sharon's out of the picture?"

"I don't know why you're putting it like that, but, yes, I think you'd make a terrific mother."

She swallowed. "Am I in first place now or are there other women standing in line in front of me?"

He gritted his teeth. "There aren't any other women."

455

"So I'm the only candidate at the moment."

"I haven't had more than two hours of sleep a night for longer than I can remember," he said tightly. "I'm running on junk food and adrenaline, and I'm not going to apologize for wanting to marry you."

Of course he wanted to marry her. They were great together in bed, he knew she wouldn't abuse his children, and there was a possibility she'd give him the Stars as her dowry.

Until that moment, she had forgotten about Reed's sly insinuation, but now it came rushing back. The room began to spin. She struggled to speak. "This sudden desire of yours to marry me . . ." She cleared her throat. "Is it just because you saw me with the twins or does it have anything to do with the fact that I'm only one game away from owning the Stars?"

He went completely still, his face going pale. "Exactly what are you suggesting?"

"We've known each other for months, but this is the first time you've indicated that you want anything more than sex from me. Is that what today's all about? Are you laying the groundwork for a real marriage proposal in case the team wins on Sunday?"

"I can't believe you're saying this."

She gave a choked laugh. "I guess I hadn't really thought about what a catch I'd be. If the Stars win, whoever marries me will be getting big breasts and a great football team. I'm every man's fantasy."

His face was rigid. "Don't say another word."

"You'd be the envy of all the coaches in the league."

"I'm warning you. . . ."

"Will you still be this anxious to marry me if the Stars lose?"

A muscle jumped in his jaw. "What happens in that game on Sunday doesn't have anything to do with the two of us."

"But if you win, I'll never be sure of that, will I? The only way I'll know you're sincere is if you lose and you still want to marry me." *Say you love me, Dan. Say you want to marry me because you love me — not because I excite you in bed or you want me to have your children or you covet my football team. Say you love me, and push all this ugliness away.*

"I'm winning this football game."

"Then we don't have a chance," she whispered.

"What are you trying to say?"

She was bleeding inside and she wanted the pain to stop. Her throat had squeezed so tightly shut she could no longer speak.

He regarded her with a flat, cold stare. "I'm not throwing the game."

At first she didn't understand what he meant. But as she took in the bleak expression on his face, she felt sick inside.

His voice was hard and furious, and she remembered that he hid all his stronger emotions behind anger. "I've played hard all my life, but I've always played clean, no matter how much temptation I faced. I've been offered money. I've been offered drugs and women. But I don't throw games. Not for anybody. Not even for you."

"I didn't mean . . ."

His eyes flicked over her with contempt. Then he stalked out of the room.

She was only dimly aware of the passage of time as she sat on the edge of the bed with her hands clasped in her lap. She heard voices in the hallway when Molly took the twins home and then she heard her return a short time later. Pooh scratched at the door, but went away when she didn't open it. She sat in the room and tried to put the pieces of herself back together.

At ten o'clock, she heard water running in Molly's bathroom. She listlessly pulled off her own clothes, then slipped into her oldest bathrobe, finding comfort in its soft, worn fabric. There was a knock at her door.

"Are you all right, Phoebe?"

Under other circumstances, she would have been pleased that Molly had thought to inquire about her welfare, but now she merely felt empty. "I've got a headache. I'll see you tomorrow before you leave for school."

She wandered over to the window and pushed back the curtains to look down into the woods that ran behind the house. Tears clouded her eyes.

"Phoebe?"

She hadn't heard Molly come in, and she didn't want her here. Sooner or later she would have

458

to tell her sister they were leaving Chicago, but she couldn't do it tonight. "The door was closed."

"I know. But — Are you sure you're all right." The light in the room went on.

She continued to face the window because she didn't want Molly to see that she'd been crying. She heard the soft padding of Pooh's paws on the carpet. "It's just a headache."

"You and Dan had a fight, didn't you?"

"Dan and I are always fighting."

"You tease each other, but you don't really fight."

"This wasn't teasing, Molly. This was the real thing."

There was a long pause. "I'm sorry."

"I don't know why you would be. You hate my guts, remember?" She knew it wasn't fair to take out her unhappiness on Molly, but she was past caring. Pooh nudged at her ankles, almost as if she were reprimanding her.

"I don't hate you, Phoebe."

Fresh tears clouded her eyes. "I need to be alone, okay?"

"You're crying."

"Just a temporary weakness. I'll get over it."

"Don't cry. Dan would feel bad if he knew he'd made you so sad."

"I sincerely doubt that."

"I think you're in love with him."

She swallowed hard as tears rolled down her cheeks. "I'll get over that, too."

She felt a gentle hand on her arm. Her throat closed tight and something seemed to break apart inside her. Without quite knowing how it happened, she was in Molly's arms.

Molly patted her arm and rubbed her back. "Don't cry, Phoebe. Please, don't cry. It'll get better. Really, it will. Don't cry." Molly crooned to her just as she crooned to Pooh. Since she was several inches shorter than Phoebe, their position was awkward, but they held on to each other anyway.

Phoebe had no idea how long they stayed that way, but nothing on earth could have made her let her sister go. When she was finally cried out, Molly pulled away, only to return a few moments later with some tissues she'd fetched from the bathroom.

Phoebe sat down on the side of the bed and blew her nose. "It'll be better tomorrow. I'm just feeling sorry for myself."

The mattress sagged as Molly sat beside her. Several moments of silence ticked by. "Are you pregnant?"

Phoebe looked at her with startled eyes. "Why would you think that?"

"A girl in my ancient history class is pregnant. I know it can happen, even to older people who are supposed to know about birth control and everything. If you are, I'm sure Dan would want to marry you, but if he didn't — The two of us —" She spoke in a rush. "I'd help you take care of the baby. You wouldn't have to have an abortion, or give it away, or raise it by yourself or anything."

As Phoebe took in the intensity of her sister's expression, some of her numbness disappeared, and she gave a watery smile. "I'm not pregnant. But thanks. Thanks a lot."

"You're not going to start crying again, are you?"

Phoebe nodded and blew her nose. "I can't help it. That was the sweetest thing anybody's ever offered to do for me." She gave a small hiccup. "I love you, Mol. I really do."

"You do?"

"Yes." Phoebe wiped at her tears.

"Even though I've been a brat?"

Phoebe smiled weakly. "A real brat."

"Nobody's ever loved me before."

"Your mother did."

"Really?"

"She loved you a lot."

"I don't remember her. Bert said she was a bimbo."

Phoebe gave a choked laugh. "She was. So was my mother. Those were the only kind of women Bert married. He liked them blond, sexy, and not too smart. We got our brains from him, Mol, not from our mothers." She pulled at the tissue in her hands. "But your mother was one of the sweetest women I ever met, and she loved you so much. I ran away when you were just an infant, but I still remember how she'd hold you for hours, even when you were sleeping, just because she couldn't believe she had you."

"I wish I remembered her."

"She was a nice lady. She used to tell me stories about being a showgirl. So did Cooki, who was Bert's second wife. They were both sweethearts."

Molly was drinking in her every word. "Tell me about them."

She sniffed and dabbed her nose. "Well, Bert found all three of his wives in Las Vegas. None of them started out with anything except good looks, but they were exceptional women. Sometimes I think *bimbo* is just another word men made up so they could feel superior to women who are better at survival than they are." Pooh jumped up in her lap and she stroked her soft fur. "Instead of feeling sorry for themselves, all of Bert's wives worked hard to make something of their lives. They survived bad men, lousy working conditions, bouts of bronchitis from skimpy costumes, and they did it with a smile. Your mother wasn't bitter, not even when she figured out what kind of man Bert really was." She gave Molly an unsteady smile. "You've got sequins and fishnet tights in your heritage, Mol. Be proud of it."

Her sister, with her solemn face and splendid brain, was clearly entranced with the idea. As Phoebe watched her, a horrible thought flickered through her mind, driving out her own misery.

"You have photographs of her, don't you?"

"No. I asked Bert a couple of times, but he said he didn't have any."

"I can't believe I didn't think to ask you!" Getting up from the bed, Phoebe went into her closet and returned a few moments later with one of the cardboard boxes she'd had sent from New York. While Molly watched, she turned out the contents on the bed to search for what she wanted. "I know it's in here somewhere. Here it is." She drew out the gold dime-store frame with a photo of Lara sitting on a deck chair by the pool holding a new-born Molly in her lap. Lara's blond hair was tied back from her face with a floral scarf and she was smiling down at Molly, who was wrapped in a pink blanket.

She held her breath as she passed the photograph over to her sister.

Molly touched it gingerly, almost as if she were afraid it would dissolve in her hands, and stared down into her mother's face. An expression of awe came over her. "She's beautiful."

"I think you have her eyes," Phoebe said softly.

"I wish I'd known her."

"I wish you had, too."

"Can I have this?"

"Of course you can. I took it with me when I ran away. I used to pretend she was my mother."

Molly stared at her, and then a sob slipped through her lips. This time it was Phoebe who held her.

"I'm sorry I've been so awful. I was so jealous of you because Bert loved you and he hated me."

Phoebe patted her sister's hair. "He didn't hate you, and he didn't love me, either."

"Yes, he did. He was always comparing me to you." She slowly drew back so that Phoebe was looking into her tear-stained face. "He said that

I gave him the creeps, and that I looked like I was going to faint every time he talked to me. He told me you always stood up to him."

Phoebe drew her close again. "I didn't stand up to him until I was a grown woman. Believe me, when I was your age, all I tried to do was stay out of his way."

"You're saying that to make me feel better."

"Bert was a bully, Molly. He was a man's man, in the worst way. He had no use for any woman who wasn't either taking care of him or sleeping with him. That left out the two of us."

"I hate him."

"Of course you do. But when you're older, you may learn to pity him instead." As she spoke, she felt something let go inside her and she realized that her father's rejection had finally lost its power over her. "Bert had two of the best daughters in the world, and he didn't even care. I find that sad, don't you?"

Molly seemed to be thinking it over. "Yes, I guess it is."

As the winter moonlight made a pool on the carpet, their fingers met somewhere in the region of Pooh's topknot.

They squeezed tight.

23

The pep band struck up "Ain't She Sweet?" and the Star Girl cheerleaders formed a tunnel of blue and gold pom-poms for Phoebe to walk through. As she made her way onto the field for the AFC Championship game, she sparkled in a short velvet jacket encrusted with thousands of sky blue sequins, a matching metallic gold tank top and miniskirt, shimmery stockings, and square-heeled pumps with beaded gold stars twinkling on each toe. The crowd greeted her with wolf whistles and cheers while the Star Girls shook their pom-poms and wiggled their hips.

As she waved and blew kisses, she could feel the tension-charged atmosphere in the mood of the crowd and see it in the players' grim expressions as they huddled on the sideline. She avoided looking at Dan while she made her way to the end of the bench for her pregame rituals. Many of the players believed she brought them good luck, and she had been forced by necessity into a routine of thumping helmets, slapping shoulder pads, and slipping lucky pennies into shoes. Bobby Tom, however, refused to give up his good luck kiss.

"We're gonna do it today, Phoebe." He gave her a resounding smack and set her back down on the ground.

"I know you are. Good luck."

She watched as the Sabers joined the Stars on the field. Their starting quarterback had been reinjured in the last game, making the Stars a narrow favorite, but Ron had warned her that, even injured, the Sabers were a great ball club.

As the kickoff approached, she could no longer avoid looking at Dan. She saw the strained tendons in his neck as he spoke into the headset to the coaches' box and then said a few words to Jim Biederot, who stood at his side. Only when the players were in position for the kickoff did he turn in her direction. Their eyes locked, but his expression was blank, revealing nothing of his feelings. She fumbled for his gum in her jacket pocket as he came toward her.

It hadn't taken the fans long to grow familiar with the Stars' pregame rituals, and the crowd watched for the moment when the kicker would tee the ball and Phoebe would pass over the Wrigley's. As Dan drew up next to her, she tried to sound normal.

"I didn't forget your gum."

He studied her for a moment, his mouth set in a tight, hard line. "Bobby Tom gets soul-kissed and I get a pack of gum. I don't think so."

Her eyes widened as he whipped off his headset. Before she could react, he leaned down and gave her a long, punishing kiss.

Strobes flashed and the crowd roared with laughter, hoots, and cheers. When Dan pulled away, Phoebe forced herself to smile. The crowd thought

466

it was a joke, but she knew it wasn't. His kiss had been filled with anger and intended to hurt. He was letting her know that he hadn't forgiven her for insulting his honor.

He moved abruptly away and turned all his attention to the field as the ball soared through the air. The Sabers' return man caught it deep in the Stars' end zone.

Despite her own turbulent emotions, she was quickly wrapped up in the excitement of the game. She knew from Ron that part of Dan's strategy was to force Saber turnovers, and the defense's aggressive play did just that less than four minutes into the game, when Elvis Crenshaw knocked the ball loose from their tailback. The Stars quickly established control and by the end of the quarter, they had posted seven points and the Sabers were scoreless.

She made her way back up to the skybox, where the atmosphere was as tense as it had been on the field. The Stars were building momentum while the Sabers struggled to get into the game, but it was still far too early to relax. Ten minutes later, when the Stars intercepted a thirty-yard pass, Phoebe knew she couldn't stand the tension any longer. They were playing brilliantly, but what if they fell apart?

Muttering to Ron that she was going to take a walk, she slipped the chain of her purse over her shoulder and left the skybox. She nodded at the security officer outside, then began to pace in the otherwise deserted hallway. As another gale of cheers came from behind the closed doors, she rounded the bend at the end of the hall.

She wished Molly were with her instead of sitting outside with her friends. The last few days had been magic between the two of them as Molly had chattered away nonstop, determined to fill her older sister in on every detail of her life. Phoebe smiled. No matter what else she might regret about these past few months, she would never regret her decision to keep Molly with her.

She was so preoccupied with her thoughts that she barely noticed how far she'd walked until the door of one of the nearby skyboxes flew open, amplifying another round of cheers. Her fingers tightened over her purse as Reed came out. The last thing she wanted at this moment was to meet up with him, but he had already spotted her, so she couldn't retreat.

The Stars' last victory had put an end to his pretended affability, and now there was nothing left but hostility. When he reached her, he lit a cigarette with a gold lighter and squinted against the smoke.

"Bored with the game already?"

She had no desire for another confrontation, and she gave a casual shrug. "No. Just nervous. What about you?"

"I came out for a cigarette, that's all."

The cloud of smoke that had wafted into the hallway when he'd opened the skybox door still hadn't entirely dissipated. "You couldn't stand to watch either."

She immediately wished she'd kept her mouth shut. Although she hadn't meant her statement to be a challenge, that was how he took it.

"It's not even halftime. I wouldn't start celebrating yet."

"I'm not."

They heard another round of cheers, and he drew a quick, angry drag. "You've been lucky all your life. You're the only person I've ever met who could step into a pile of shit and have it turn into gold."

"I've always thought you were the lucky one."

He gave a snort.

She gripped the strap of her purse. "After all these years, you still hate me, don't you? When I was a kid, I could never figure out why. You had everything that I wanted."

"Sure I did," he scoffed. "I grew up in a run-down apartment with a neurotic mother and no father."

"You had a father. You had mine."

His lips drew tight in a sneer. "That's right, I did. Bert cared more about me than he ever cared about you, right up until the day he died. He just wanted to teach you a lesson. He kept saying that you were his only failure, and he thought you'd settle down if he could get you away from those faggots you were always running with." Reed jabbed his cigarette into one of the sand-filled ashtrays that stood against the wall. "Bert didn't mean for it to turn out like this. No one could have predicted all the flukes that happened this season.

469

The Sabers lose Simpson and McGuire, the Chargers lose Wyzak, the Bills and the Dolphins fall apart. Christ, if he'd had any idea the Stars would make it to the playoffs, he never would have let you get near the team, not even for a day!"

"The Stars did make it to the playoffs. And from the sound of the cheers, they're winning."

His face darkened with rage. The successful businessman had disappeared, leaving the cruel bully of her childhood in his place. "Goddammit, you're gloating, aren't you?"

"I'm not —"

But her denial came too late because he jammed her against the wall with his body. She winced as her shoulders hit and her purse dropped to the ground.

"You ruined everything for me! You always have!"

Frightened, she pushed against his chest with the heels of her hands. "Let me go or I'll scream!"

"Go ahead! If anybody sees us, they'll think you're coming on to me like you come on to everybody else."

"I mean it, Reed! Let me go."

She froze as she felt his hand move to her breast. He squeezed. "You were a hot little piece when you were eighteen, and you still are."

Shock held her immobile. "Get your hands off me."

"When I'm ready."

She struggled to back away from his obscene touch, but she was pinioned by his body. The expression on his face frightened her. She expected to see lust, but instead she saw something more dangerous. She saw hatred and the need to exert his power over her just as he always had.

"You may end up with the Stars, but before you start believing you've got the last laugh, there's something you should know."

The triumph in his expression made dread creep through her like poison. She was a child again, watching him hold a photograph of her mother just out of her reach. They might have been surrounded by eighty thousand people, but she had never felt more alone.

His lip curled. "That night in the pool shed . . ."

"No! I don't want to hear this!" All the old nightmares came rushing back. She could hear the thunder, feel the hot, sticky heat. Once again, she tried to pull away from him, but he wouldn't release her.

"Remember the storm? How dark it was?"

"Stop it!" She had begun to sob. He squeezed her breast tighter.

"So dark you couldn't see your hand in front of your face. . . ."

"Don't do this!"

"That night when Craig fucked you . . ."

"Please . . ."

"It wasn't Craig."

Her stomach heaved, and a whimper slipped through her lips as his words hit her like a blow. Her lungs felt as if they had collapsed and she was suffocating to death.

"I'm the one who found you in that shed."

She was going to vomit. Had she always suspected this in the deepest recesses of her subconscious or was it new knowledge? She gagged at the smell of his cologne.

He released her breast only to twist a lock of her hair around his fingers. She bit her lip to keep from crying out as he pulled hard.

"And the best part is, there's not a damned thing you can do about it, Miss High and Mighty, because it happened too long ago. It'd be your word against mine, and while you've been humping everything in pants, I've been Mister Clean. So whenever you start gloating about the Stars, know that I'll be remembering the way you screamed when I popped that sweet little cherry of yours."

"Are you all right, Miss Somerville?"

Reed jumped back as a security guard approached from the left. She pressed her fingers to her lips.

"Miss Somerville? Is everything okay here?

She struggled to speak. "No, I . . ."

"See you later, Phoebe." Reed straightened his tie, then crossed the hallway to the skybox. He turned and gave her a smirk. "Thanks for that cherry pie." Opening the door, he disappeared inside.

She pressed her hand to her stomach. The security guard took her arm.

"Everything's going to be all right, Miss. Let me help you."

She moved like a robot at his side as he drew

472

her down the hallway. The memories of that terrible night came crashing back. There had been no windows in the metal shed, and the heat trapped inside had been thick and heavy. When he'd opened the door, she'd seen only a hulking male silhouette against slick black sheets of rain. She'd assumed it was Craig, but she hadn't seen his face.

He'd been on her before she could move. He'd torn her blouse and bitten one of her breasts like an animal. She remembered the roughness of the uneven concrete floor scraping her bare buttocks as he had pushed up her skirt and ripped off her underpants. Her head had banged into a chemical drum when he'd spread her apart. He had made a guttural sound as he'd pushed into her, but after that, the only sounds she could remember were her own screams.

The floor gave out beneath her and her head shot up. For a moment she was disoriented, and then she realized the security guard had led her into an elevator. "Where are we going?"

"I'm taking you to first aid."

"I'm all right. I don't need first aid."

"You're white as a sheet. I don't know what that guy was trying to pull, but maybe you should lie down for a few minutes until you feel better."

She started to protest but realized she wasn't in any condition to go back to the skybox right then. A few minutes away from curious eyes would give her a chance to pull herself back together. "All right. Just for a bit."

As the elevator continued to descend, she

smelled cigarette smoke on the guard's uniform, and another wave of nausea came over her because it reminded her of Reed. She was overcome by a sense of helplessness. He was going to get away with this. He was right. Too much time had passed for her to be able to make accusations.

The security guard began to hack. He was overweight, probably in his early fifties, with grizzled hair and a florid complexion. Beads of sweat dotted his forehead. She read his name printed in block letters on his plastic tag. "You should give up those cigarettes, Mr. Hardesty."

"Yeah."

The elevator doors slid open. She saw the pipes overhead and realized they were in some sort of subbasement. "Where are we?"

"There's a first aid station for the employees down here. It'll keep you away from the crowds."

She followed him out of the elevator into a narrow corridor, which was painted a dull, battleship gray. Pipes hissed overhead and she heard a sound that reminded her of distant thunder. She realized that she was hearing the muffled roars of the crowd in the dome above them.

They rounded a sharp bend. "In here." He caught her elbow and turned the knob on an unmarked door.

Feeling her first quiver of uneasiness, she hesitated. With a hard push, he thrust her inside.

"What are you doing?" she gasped.

Her eyes widened with horror as she saw that he had drawn his gun and it was pointed directly

474

at her. A sense of unreality swept over her. Reed was her enemy, not this man she had never met. Above her the crowd roared like a beast in a padded cage, while she was trapped in a nightmare where she had escaped one terror only to be ensnared by another.

He pushed the door shut. "Get over there!"

"Why are you doing this?"

"Move!"

She stumbled backward, gradually becoming aware that he had pushed her into a room that seemed to be both a janitorial office and storage space. She saw a dented gray steel case desk, a file cabinet, and a wall of metal shelving holding cartons and machine parts.

He pointed the gun toward an armless secretarial chair that had a small V-shaped tear in the black vinyl seat. "Sit down."

Her legs trembled as she lowered herself into the chair. The oval-shaped back support squeaked and gave slightly as she leaned back. She stared with grim fascination at the ugly black gun that was trained on her heart. It didn't waver as he leaned down to pull a length of clothesline from behind a packing box that sat on a metal shelving unit across from the desk.

"Who are you?" she whispered.

Instead of answering, he pushed against the chair seat with his shoe, spinning it around so that she was facing the wall. She automatically reached out to brace herself, only to have him grab her arms and pull them behind her. She gave a cry of alarm.

He wheezed as he tied her wrists and secured them to the vertical metal bar that held the chair's back support. It rocked alarmingly on its spring hinge, pulling at her arms and making her wince. When she was bound, he gave the chair another push, sending it flying into the far corner of the cramped room. She stopped it with her feet before she banged into the wall and then, panic-stricken, pushed herself around so that she was facing him.

She tried to feel grateful that he hadn't tied her legs, but the cords were cutting into her wrists, sending shafts of pain shooting upward. He picked up the gun from one of the metal shelves where he had laid it while he tied her and returned it to the leather holster on his hip.

How long would it be before Ron noticed that she was missing? She fought down the hysteria rising inside her, knowing that no matter what happened, she had to keep her wits. She grew aware of the distant sound of music and realized that the halftime show had begun. Trying to ignore the pain in her arms and wrists, she forced herself to take in the details of the office.

The dented gray desk against the wall was cluttered with stacks of dog-eared manuals, cat-alogues, and a litter of papers. A small portable television, its tan case marred by greasy finger-prints, sat on top of a four-drawer file cabinet directly across from her. Clipboards hung from L-shaped hooks on the wall behind the desk, along with a calendar featuring a nude woman holding a brightly colored beach ball.

The guard lit a cigarette and held it between his stubby fingers, which were stained with nicotine. "Here's the way it's gonna be, lady. As long as your boyfriend does what I tell him, you don't have anything to worry about."

"I don't know what you're talking about."

"Yeah, well I guess that doesn't much matter." He walked over to the file cabinet and turned on the television set. The black-and-white picture showed the commentators in their network blazers sitting in the broadcast booth.

". . . the Stars played brilliantly in the first half. The offense mixed up their plays. They protected the ball well. The Sabers are going to have to be a lot more aggressive if they want to get back into this game." The display at the bottom of the screen showed the score: *Stars 14, Sabers 3.*

The guard gave a vile curse and turned down the volume. She looked at him more closely as he paced the narrow end of the office closest to the door, smoking furiously. Her eyes fell on his black plastic name tag.

HARDESTY

At that moment, it all came back. She remembered Dan's telling her about the man who had been stalking him, the father of one of the Stars' former players. His name was Hardesty.

A beer commercial blinked mutely on the television. She licked her dry lips. "My arms are hurting. The rope's too tight."

"I'm not untying you."

"Just loosen it."

"No."

She had to get him to talk. She would go crazy if she didn't find out what he had in mind. "This is about your son, isn't it?"

He pointed his cigarette at her. "I'll tell you something, lady. Ray Junior was the best defensive end to ever play for the Stars. There wasn't any reason for that bastard to cut him."

"Coach Calebow?"

"He had it in for Ray Junior. He didn't even give him a chance."

"Dan doesn't operate that way."

Clouds of gray smoke wreathed his head, and he barely seemed to have heard her. "I'll tell you what I think. I think he knew Ray Junior was a better player than he'd ever been. I think he was jealous. The press made a big thing about Calebow, but he was nothing, not compared to my Ray."

She realized that the man was insane. Maybe he'd been this way for a long time, or maybe his son's death had been the final blow. She tried to conceal her fear.

"Players get cut all the time. It's part of the game."

"You don't know what it's like! One day you're somebody special, and the next day nobody knows your name."

"Are you talking about your son or yourself?"

478

"Shut up!" His eyes bulged and his complexion took on a faint purplish hue.

She was afraid to push him any farther, and she fell silent.

He jabbed his finger at her. "Look, you don't mean anything to me. I don't want to hurt you, but I will if I have to. Because no matter what, I'm not going to let the Stars win this game."

Ron reached the tunnel just as the players were rushing back onto the field. He dreaded what he had to do. Dan had been a bear all week — temperamental, unreasonable, and impossible to pacify — and he had no idea how he'd react to this distressing piece of news.

Dan emerged from the locker room and Ron fell into step beside him. "I'm afraid we've got a problem."

"Handle it. In case you hadn't noticed, I'm trying to win a football game here, and —"

Ron pressed his folded handkerchief against his forehead. "Phoebe's missing."

Dan jerked to a stop, and his face went pale. "What are you talking about?"

"She left the skybox during the second quarter and never came back. Somebody found her purse in the hallway. I've called her house and her office. I've checked with first aid and sent someone to every skybox. She's gone, Dan, and at this point, I have to believe it's foul play."

Ron had seen Dan in pressure situations, but he'd never seen such raw panic in his eyes. "No!

She can't be — Christ. Did you call the police?"

"Yes, but since it's so early, they're not taking it as seriously as I am. I hate doing this to you in the middle of the game, but it occurred to me that you might be able to think of someplace else I could look. Do you have any ideas? Can you think of anyplace else she might be?"

He stood frozen, his eyes wild in the pallor of his face. "No." He grabbed Ron's arm. "Did you talk to Molly? Jesus! Talk to Molly! Maybe Phoebe's with her."

He'd never seen Dan like this, and he knew right then that there was more to the relationship between the Stars' owner and head coach than he had suspected. "Molly hasn't seen her since before the game. She's pretty upset. Tully's wife is with her now."

"If anything's happened to Phoebe —"

"Dan?" One of the assistant coaches had appeared at the mouth of the tunnel.

Dan rounded on him, the cords of his neck standing out like ropes. "Leave me the fuck alone!"

Ron could feel Dan's desperation, and he grabbed the head coach's other arm with an urgent grip. "You've got to get back on the field! There's nothing you can do for Phoebe right now. I'll let you know right away if we find her."

Dan regarded him with haunted eyes. "Don't let anything happen to her, Ron. For God's sake, find her!"

Ron wanted to reassure him, but he could only say, "I'll do my best."

One level below, Hardesty reached into his pocket for a fresh pack of cigarettes. Phoebe's eyes were stinging from the smoke, adding to the misery of the pain in her arms and wrists. The silence between them had strained her nerves to the point where she had to speak.

"Whose office is this?"

For a moment she didn't think he would reply. Then he shrugged. "One of the engineers. He has to stay with the generators until the gates close, so he won't be popping in for a visit, if that's what you're hoping."

The silent screen showed the Sabers kicking off. She flinched as he turned up the volume.

"You're not going to get away with this."

"You know something? I don't care. As long as the Stars lose the championship, I don't fucking care!"

Hardesty glanced at the TV, then moved to the desk, where he picked up the telephone and punched four buttons. Several seconds passed before he spoke into the receiver.

"This is Bob Smith with the Stars. I've got Phoebe Somerville here, and she wants to talk to Coach Calebow. Patch this call through to the sidelines, will you?" He paused, listening. "She doesn't give a shit about authorization. She says it's important, and she's the boss, but it's your ass, so you do what you want."

Whoever was on the other end must have decided to go along with the request because Hardesty slid the phone to the end of the desk closest to where she was sitting. The wheels squealed as he caught the back of her chair and pulled her to it. He waited silently, his hand clenching the receiver, and then he tensed.

"Calebow? I got somebody here wants to talk to you." He pushed the receiver to Phoebe's ear.

"Dan?" Her voice was thin with fear.

"Phoebe? Where are you? Jesus, are you all right?"

"No, I —" She cried out with pain as Hardesty dug his fingers into her hair and yanked hard.

On the sidelines, Dan went rigid. "Phoebe! What's happened? Are you there? Talk to me!"

His heart was banging against his ribs, and a cold sweat had broken out on his forehead. Phoebe was being terrorized, and there was nothing he could do about it. With blinding clarity, the strength of his fear peeled away all his self-protective layers, and he knew how deeply he loved her. If anything happened to her, he didn't want to go on living. He cried out her name, trying to convey everything he felt for her but had never been able to say.

A gravelly male voice traveled through his headset. "I've got her Calebow. If you don't want her hurt, you'll listen real hard to what I'm saying."

"Who is this?"

"The Stars lose today. Got me? Your fucking team loses or the lady dies."

Dan heard the wheeze in the man's voice and was gripped by a horrible suspicion. "Hardesty?

482

It's you, isn't it, you crazy son of a bitch!"

"Your team isn't going to win the championship without my boy."

The fact that Hardesty made no attempt to deny his identity magnified Dan's fear as nothing else could have. Only a man who didn't care if he lived or died would be so careless.

He knew he didn't have much time, and he spoke quickly, his voice commanding. "Listen to me. Ray wouldn't want you to do this."

"You were jealous of him. That's why you cut him."

"This is between you and me. Phoebe doesn't have anything to do with it. Let her go."

"Don't call the police." Hardesty coughed, a dry rattling sound. "I'm watching on TV, and if I see anything unusual going on, you'll be sorry."

"Think, Hardesty! You've got an innocent woman —"

"Any more points go on the scoreboard for the Stars, I'm gonna hurt your girlfriend."

"Hardesty!"

The line went dead.

Dan stood there, stunned. He heard the cheers of the crowd and everything inside him went numb as he remembered the series of plays he had just called. He spun toward the field. Standing in mute horror, he watched as the ball arced through the air and sailed directly between the uprights for a Stars' field goal.

The scoreboard flashed, and Dan Calebow felt a cold hand grip his heart.

In the subbasement of the dome, Ray cursed and slammed his foot into Phoebe's chair. She let out a cry as it flew across the slippery floor and crashed into the end wall. Her shoulder caught the impact and shards of pain shot through her body. She tasted blood in her mouth where she bit her tongue.

Afraid of what he would do to her next, she fought against the pain and forced the chair back around so that she was facing him. But he wasn't looking at her. Instead he was staring at the television and muttering to himself.

A close-up of Dan filled the small screen. He looked frantic, and since the score now favored the Stars 17–3, the commentators were making a joke about it. The sight of him made her feel as if she had been ripped open. She might die today. Was she going to be watching his face when it happened? The idea was unbearable and she forced her numb fingers to begin working at the knots that held her to the chair. As she bit back the pain her movements were causing her, she remembered their last conversation and the unshakable conviction in his voice when he had told her he would never throw a game.

I don't do that, Phoebe. Not for anybody. Not even for you.

24

On the sideline Dan called Jim Biederot over. He hoped the quarterback didn't notice the unsteadiness in his voice. "We're making some changes in the next series, Jim."

By the time he'd finished giving his instructions, Biederot's eyes had narrowed into indignant slits above the black smudges that angled across his cheekbones. "Those are goddamn running plays! I'm hitting every receiver I look at."

"Do what you're told or you'll sit!" Dan shot back.

Biederot gave him a glance of pure fury and stalked over to Charlie Cray, one of the assistants. Within seconds, he had grabbed Charlie's headset and was shouting into it.

Dan knew Jim was speaking with Gary Hewitt, his offensive coordinator, who sat with Tully in the coaches' box high in the dome. Before Hewitt could start giving him hell, too, he tried to swallow enough of his fear so he could sort out his thoughts.

Hardesty had said he was watching on television, which meant he'd be able to see any unusual movement on the sideline or in whatever part of the stadium was within camera range. As a consequence, Dan couldn't risk notifying the police. Once they knew that Phoebe truly had been kidnapped, they'd be all over the place, including right here on the sideline asking him questions. Even worse, they might decide to call the game, a circumstance that could very well push Hardesty right over the edge.

He briefly debated using his headset to contact Ron, but he was afraid Hardesty might be listening in. Although Dan didn't understand all the intricacies of the internal communications system, he knew Hardesty could only have accessed it from within the dome. That meant he might, even now, be eavesdropping on conversations between the sideline and the coaches' box. It also mean that Phoebe was tucked away somewhere nearby.

He swiped at his forehead with his sleeve as he tried to figure out what to do about Ron. Since he couldn't explain what had happened over the headset, he grabbed his clipboard and scribbled a quick note, making it cryptic enough so that it would be meaningless to anyone else who read it.

I spoke with the player we were discussing at halftime. Your negative assessment of the situation was correct. It is urgent that you take no further action. I'll explain after the game.

He slipped the note to one of the equipment men to deliver and told himself that Phoebe would come out of this unharmed. Anything else was unthinkable.

For the first time, he let himself consider how

his actions would affect her ownership of the Stars after all this was over and she was safe. Although there was no precedent for what was happening, he couldn't imagine the NFL would let this game stand — not unless the Stars won despite his coaching, which he wouldn't let happen. Once the NFL learned that he had deliberately thrown the game, ensuring a Stars' loss, they would schedule a rematch and she would still have a chance to keep the team.

And then an ugly thought struck him. What if the police didn't believe that she had been kidnapped? If Hardesty got away, there wouldn't be any tangible proof other than her own testimony. Dan was the only one who could back up her story, and his personal involvement with her would make his word suspect. She could very well be accused of fabricating the kidnapping simply because the Stars had lost and she wanted another shot at retaining ownership. There was no way the NFL would let this game be replayed.

He forced himself to face the painful fact that his failure to notify the police was going to cost Phoebe the Stars. Still, he couldn't do anything else. He wouldn't take a chance with her life, not for the world.

Gary Hewitt's voice crackled through his headset. "Dan, what the hell's going on? Why did you tell Jim to keep it on the ground? That's not our plan. He's never passed better."

"I'm making some changes," Dan snapped. "We've got the lead, so we're going to play smart."

"It's only the third quarter! It's too early to get conservative."

Dan couldn't have agreed more, so he simply removed his headset and glued his eyes to the field. No matter what he had to do, he was going to keep Phoebe safe.

By the middle of the quarter the Sabers had scored their first touchdown while the Stars' ground game had failed to move the ball, reducing their lead to seven points. The fans' booing had grown so loud that the offense was having a hard time hearing Biederot's signals. Dan's assistants were furious, the players livid, and, two minutes into the fourth quarter, when the Sabers evened the score at seventeen, the network's color man ran out of patience.

"Can you believe what you're seeing?" He was practically shouting into the cameras. "All season, Dan Calebow has been one of the most aggressive coaches in the NFL, and it's terrible to see him fold like this. This isn't the kind of football the fans came to watch!"

Phoebe tried to shut out the commentator's understandably harsh assessment of Dan's coaching, just as she'd been trying to ignore the sound of the crowd's jeers. She didn't want to think about what this public humiliation was doing to his pride, and she knew she had never loved him more.

Her wrists, chafed raw by her struggles to get free of the ropes, were bleeding. *Ignore the pain,* she told herself. *Play through it.* Everything she had heard the players say, she repeated to herself, but she was beginning to think the knots would never loosen.

Hardesty had tied her wrists in a figure eight of rope, then secured the free ends to the vertical post that supported the back of the chair. Although her fingers had become sticky with blood as she worked at that tight double knot that held her in the chair, it wouldn't give. *Play through the pain. Shake it off.*

Hardesty stared at the screen, took a drag on his cigarette, and coughed. The air was so thick with smoke that she could barely breathe. Sometimes she thought he had forgotten her, but then he would look at her with eyes so empty of any remorse that she didn't doubt he would kill her.

Five minutes into the fourth quarter, the Sabers pulled ahead. On the sideline the emotions of the players and assistants reflected everything from fury to despondency, while the crowd had begun to throw debris on Dan. He stood alone, isolated by the players and the coaches. Only his iron discipline was keeping a full revolt from breaking out on the bench.

Sabers 24, Stars 17.

As the Sabers kicked the extra point, Biederot slammed his helmet against the bench, hitting it with such force that the face mask cracked. Dan knew it was only a matter of time before Jim ignored the threat to bench him and began calling his own plays. With less than ten minutes left on the clock and the temper of the crowd growing uglier by the minute, he could no longer keep the game on the ground.

All his life Dan had been a team player and going it alone had become too risky. Praying that he wasn't making a fatal mistake, he called Jim and Bobby Tom over just before the offense took the field again.

Jim's face was ruddy with fury, Bobby Tom's rigid. Both of them started spewing obscenities.

"Bench me, you cocksucker! I don't give a shit because I don't want to be part of this."

"We didn't work this fucking hard to have you fuck us like this!"

A minicam zoomed in on them. Dan grabbed their arms and ducked his head. His voice was low and fierce. "Shut up and listen! Phoebe's been kidnapped. The man who has her is crazy. He says he's going to kill her if we win this game." He felt the muscles in their arms grow rigid, but he didn't glance up because he was certain the cameras were on him. "He's watching on television. I can't let the team score even a field goal because he's threatened to hurt her if we put any numbers on the board." He sucked in his breath and lifted his head. "I believe he'll do it."

Biederot swore softly, while Bobby Tom looked murderous.

Dan let every one of his emotions show in his eyes as he called the next series of plays. "Make it look good. Please. Phoebe's life depends on it."

He could see they had a dozen questions, but there was no time to ask them, and to their credit, neither man offered any argument.

In the subbasement below the dome, Phoebe heard the crowd cheer. Her bloody fingers grew still on the knot, and her eyes snapped to the television. She stopped breathing as Jim threw a long pass over the middle to Bobby Tom. Bobby Tom extended his body in the lean, graceful line that had been photographed so often, with his weight balanced only on the tips of his toes. How many times this season had she seen him snatch the ball out of the air from exactly that position, defying gravity as effortlessly as a ballet dancer?

But not this time. The crowd groaned as the ball bounced off his fingertips. Bobby Tom fell to the turf, and she remembered to breathe again.

It was the first long pass Biederot had thrown in the second half, and she wondered if Dan's control over the men had at last snapped. She refused to think about what that would mean. Not now. Not when the knot that held her to the chair had finally given way.

She had been so excited when it had shaken loose, but that small moment of triumph had evaporated when she realized she was still bound. Although she was no longer tied to the chair, her wrists were secured by a knot she hadn't previously discovered, this one holding together the figure eight of rope he had whipped around them. She was free of the chair, but that wasn't good enough when Hardesty had a gun and she couldn't use her arms.

The camera moved in for a close-up of Bobby Tom. Pain had dulled her senses, and several seconds ticked by before she noticed that something was wrong. When Bobby Tom missed one, his customary good humor always deserted him. He screwed up his face and cursed himself. But now, even on the small TV screen, she could see that his expression was devoid of any emotion.

He knows. Every one of her intuitive powers made her certain that Dan had told him what had happened. She knew how much this game meant to Bobby Tom, and she could only imagine what it had cost him to deliberately miss the ball. Her anger burned as she stared at Hardesty's back. He had no right to steal this day from them.

The Stars punted and the Sabers began their next series, while the scoreboard clock continued to tick.

7:14 . . . 7:13 . . . 7:12 . . .

The Sabers began a series of passing plays. She thought of the way the men looked after the games: dirty, limping, bloody. In her mind she saw them on the plane coming back from road games, with their knees wrapped in ice packs, their shoulders bandaged, while they popped pain killers so they could sleep. Not one of those men wouldn't do anything for the Stars.

6:21 . . . 6:20 . . . 6:19 . . .

With so little time left, she wasn't at all certain she could undo the last knot before the clock ran out. It was loosening, but not quickly enough. She had the awful feeling that she was letting down the team, that somehow she wasn't trying hard enough.

5:43 . . . 5:42 . . . 5:41 . . .

Portland scored another field goal. *Sabers 27, Stars 17.* She had to make a decision. She could play it safe and stay where she was, hoping he would let her go at the end of the game. Or she could risk everything to win her own freedom.

Dan's face came on the screen, and she made up her mind. She wasn't going to lose him or the Stars without a fight. Her mind raced. She would only have one chance, and she had to pick her moment.

5:07 . . . 5:06 . . . 5:05 . . .

Hardesty bent forward, racked by another of his hacking coughs. She planted her feet and shoved hard against the floor. The chair flew forward.

He spun awkwardly as he heard the wheels squeak. With a harsh exclamation, he lifted his fist to strike her. She drew up her legs and rammed her heel into his groin.

He gave a scream of pain and doubled forward. She shot up, drawing her arms over the back of the chair, her wrists still tied behind her. She stumbled for the door. Twisting the knob behind her back, she popped the lock and rushed out into the hallway.

She ran awkwardly in the direction of the elevator while she continued to tug at her wrists. But although the ropes were looser, she still couldn't slip free. She heard a groan from behind her and glanced back to see Hardesty staggering through the doorway.

She lurched toward a gray metal door marked "Stairs" and stumbled, barely righting herself before she fell. Once again precious seconds ticked by as she turned her back to pull on the door handle. A loop of rope slipped down over her fingers making the process even more difficult. Hardesty, still doubled over, moved forward.

"You bitch. . . ." he gasped.

Terror shot through her as he fumbled for the gun on his hip. The door into the stairwell swung open. She pushed herself inside, then screamed and hunched her shoulders as bits of concrete exploded from the wall in front of her, showering her with stinging debris.

She gave a choked cry. Before he could fire at her again, she began struggling up the stairs, frantically tugging at the tangled ropes that were making her movements so awkward. She had almost reached the landing when one of the loops finally slipped loose. She freed herself from the rest just as she heard that awful wheeze coming from below her, the sound amplified in the hollow stairwell.

"Bitch!"

She spun and saw him at the bottom of the stairwell, where his face was purple and he was gasping for air as if he were strangling. Paralyzed, she stared at the gun that was pointed directly at her.

"I'm not . . ." He sagged against the wall, clutching his heaving chest. "I'm not . . . going to let you . . ."

The gun wavered, releasing her from her paralysis. She raced around the bend of the landing.

Another shot rang out, hitting the wall behind her. She didn't dare stop to see if he was following as she flew up the remaining stairs. When she reached the door, she heard a cry of pain that was almost inhuman. She pulled on the handle just as the thud of a heavy weight hitting the floor echoed in the stairwell.

She dashed out into the hallway, trying desperately to orient herself. She heard the noise of the crowd and realized that she had stumbled into the far end of the corridor that led to the Stars' locker room. Wasting no time, she headed toward the field tunnel, throwing off her sequined blue jacket with its bloodstained cuffs as she ran.

A security guard stood at the mouth of the tunnel. He whipped around when he heard the clatter of her shoes. As she ran toward him, he gaped at her rumpled hair, torn stockings, and bloody wrists.

"One of the guards is lying at the bottom of the stairwell by the locker room!" She fought for breath. "I think he's had a heart attack. Be careful. He's crazy and he has a gun."

The man stared at her as if she'd lost her mind. Before he could question her, she ran past him toward the field. The guard stationed at the fence recognized her and jumped back from the gate. The Sabers' offense was on the field. She looked at the scoreboard.

2:58 . . .

And then, all she saw was the back of Dan's head.

The problems between them evaporated as she ran toward the bench. Players were blocking her way, and she shoved at their jerseys.

"Let me through! Let me by!"

One by one they stepped aside, clearly astonished to see her. Bobby Tom and Jim Biederot caught sight of her and began to rush forward.

"Dan!"

He whirled around as she called out his name. His face contorted with a depth of emotion she had never seen, and she leapt into his arms.

"Phoebe! Thank God! Oh, thank God, Phoebe . . ." Over and over he muttered her name as he held her tight against his chest.

The sideline minicam zeroed in on them, while in the owner's skybox, Ron shot to his feet and ran for the door. Meanwhile in the broadcasting booth, the announcers were stumbling all over each other trying to explain why the Stars' owner was embracing the coach who had spent the past two quarters of the game cold-bloodedly leading her team into disaster.

She wrapped her arms around his neck and kissed him hard. He returned the kiss and hugged her so tightly she could barely breathe.

"Can you still win?" she whispered.

"As long as you're safe, it doesn't matter. Nothing matters." His voice was gruff with emotion, and she drew back far enough to see that his eyes were filled with tears. "I thought I'd lost you," he said. "I love you so much. Oh, God, I love you."

She locked the words away like a treasure to be drawn out later. For now, she could only think of him and what he'd done for her.

"I want you to win. You've worked so hard."

"It's not important."

"Yes. Yes, it is." She realized she was crying.

He hugged her hard. "Don't cry, honey. Let's just be happy you're alive."

She realized he thought she wanted this for herself. "You don't understand. I don't want you to win for me! I want you to do it for yourself!"

"We're behind by ten, honey. There are less than three minutes on the clock."

"Then you'd better get to work."

He smoothed her hair back from her face, and his eyes were so full of love that all the doubts she'd had about his feelings evaporated.

"We'd have to score two touchdowns to win, and right now the men hate my guts."

"I'll talk to them."

"Phoebe . . ."

She cupped his cheek. "I love you, Coach. Now get to work. That's an order."

Leaving his arms took all her willpower, but she pulled away while he still looked dazed from her declaration. She'd barely taken two steps before Bobby Tom and Jim were at her side.

"Are you all right?" Bobby Tom's face was pale with concern. "Damn, Phoebe, you had us so scared."

"I'm fine." She grabbed their arms. "I want to win this game. I want Dan to be able to win it."

"If we had more time —"

Phoebe cut Jim off. "I don't care about that. I can't let this happen to him. Not to any of you."

She turned away and raced toward Darnell. Somehow she had to restore the players' faith in their coach, but she had so little time. He looked alarmed as he saw the state she was in, and he took a quick step forward.

"Phoebe, what happened to you?"

As quickly as possible, she explained. Attempting to catch her breath at the end, she said, "Dan was only trying to protect me. Tell the other linemen that. We're going to win this game."

Before he could question her, the players who were not on the field began to surround her, and she repeated her story. As they pelted her with questions, the Sabers punted.

Dan had his headset back on and was shouting instructions. Jim slapped his shoulder and dashed onto the field with the offense.

The two-minute warning sounded.

Dan hunched forward, his hands splayed on his thighs. The Stars were playing without a huddle. Phoebe dug her fingernails into her palms as the action on the field began to unfold.

Jim drilled a pass to his tight end for a completion. On the next play he just missed the tailback on a screen pass. And then on third down, he threw incomplete.

The Stars' trainer appeared at her side and began to wrap her wrists in gauze. Word of what had happened had spread through the team, and Webster Greer came up next to her like a bodyguard.

Jim connected for a first down at the thirty-eight yard line, and the dome reverberated with cheers.

The Sabers' defense was slow to adjust to the no-huddle passing attack. Dry-mouthed, Phoebe watched her team move to the seventeen.

1:10

Biederot connected with Collier Davis. Phoebe screamed as Davis took it in for the touchdown.

The fans went wild.

On the sideline Dan was huddled with the kick-off team and special teams' coordinator.

The Stars made the extra point. *Sabers 27, Stars 24.*

0:58

As the Stars' kickoff team lined up, the crowd anticipated the onside kick, knowing the Stars had to regain possession of the ball. The onside kick was a maneuver Dan had forced the players to practice hundreds of times during the season, until they could perform it flawlessly. But this wasn't a practice, and the other team knew that short, potentially lethal kick was coming.

Phoebe glanced over at Dan. He looked fierce and wonderful.

The ball rotated with a crazy spin as it came off the side of the kicker's foot. It barely traveled the required ten yards before it hit the hands of a Sabers' halfback. He tried to hold onto it, but couldn't. Elvis Crenshaw blasted him.

It was anybody's ball, and twenty-two men dived for it. Helmets cracked and the men's snarls

499

were audible on the sidelines even through the screams of the crowd.

The whistle blew and the refs began pulling off players. Phoebe dug her fingers into Webster's arm.

One by one the men got up — Stars, Sabers — until there were only two players left on the ground, one in a sky blue jersey and one wearing crimson.

Dan gave a jubilant yell.

The Sabers' player staggered up, leaving only Darnell Pruitt clasping the football.

The crowd noise was deafening. Darnell jumped up and threw his arms in the air. The Stars had recovered the ball on their own forty-eight yard line.

0:44

Dan slapped Biederot on the back as he ran onto the field. On the first play, Jim completed a pass to the forty-two.

0:38

The Sabers' defense, anticipating that the passing attack would continue, set up deep to protect against the bomb. Instead, they were suckered in by one of the sweetest running plays Dan had ever called. First and ten on the twenty-two.

0:25

The Stars' next two passes were incomplete, and Phoebe tried to prepare herself for defeat.

0:14

Biederot called for their remaining time-out and raced over to Dan on the sideline. They engaged in a furious dialogue. Jim ran back out.

The atmosphere in the dome was electric. As the teams lined up, Phoebe looked at the scoreboard. It was third down and they were twenty-two yards away.

Jim threw another incomplete pass.

0:08

Dan signaled wildly as the players rushed back into formation. But instead of the field goal that could bring them a tie and put them into sudden death, the Stars were going for a touchdown. Fourth down and twenty-two yards away.

Jim took the long snap from shotgun formation and searched for his favorite target, Phoebe's sweet-footed, nimble-fingered $8-million wideout from Telarosa, Texas.

Bobby Tom made a sharp cut at the seven to lose his man. The ball spiraled toward him. He leapt up and snatched it out of the air in a gesture so graceful it was almost feminine.

Defenders lunged for him.

He spun toward the goal line. He stumbled. Just as he righted himself, he got hit from the side. Once more he spun free.

But Brewer Gates, the Sabers' star safety, was barreling toward him.

Bobby Tom knew he was going to get hit, but he left his body unprotected as he stretched the ball out in front of him and threw himself at the goal line.

With bared teeth and a bone crusher's roar, Gates lunged to meet him at the two yard line.

And was blasted straight into the air by Darnell Pruitt.

Bobby Tom hit the ground hard, every muscle in his lean runner's body extended. His head was ringing and he tried to clear his vision.

0:01

Through his face mask, he followed the line of his arms to his hands. They cradled the ball directly on top of the goal line.

The ref's arms shot up in the air, signaling the touchdown. The screams of the crowd shook the curved walls of the dome.

Phoebe was laughing and crying. Webster hugged her, then Elvis Crenshaw. Pandemonium broke out on the field and in the stands as the final gun sounded.

She tried to get to Dan, but she couldn't move through the sea of blue jerseys that surrounded her. She scrambled up onto the bench and spotted him pushing through the men to reach her. His face was split by a huge grin and their eyes locked. She threw one arm up into the air and laughed. Behind him, she saw several of the players approaching with an enormous green plastic container held high. She laughed harder as they emptied it over his head.

A shower of Gatorade and ice sloshed over him. He hunched his shoulders and yelled as he received the victory baptism.

Some members of the crowd booed. They had no knowledge of the drama that had taken place behind the scenes, and they still wanted Dan's blood for forcing the game into such a desperate finish.

He shook his head, sending droplets flying everywhere as he cleared his eyes enough so that he could see Phoebe again.

Bobby Tom threw his arm around Dan's shoulder and shoved the game ball at him. "This one's for you, pardner."

The men hugged. Dan clutched the ball to his chest and once again turned toward Phoebe.

He swiped at his face with one dry cuff and saw that she was still standing on the bench. She looked like a goddess rising above the sea of swirling blue jerseys, her blond hair glittering in the lights. She was the most beautiful creature he had ever seen, and he loved her with all his heart. The strength of his feelings no longer frightened him. Having come so close to losing her, he would not take that risk again.

The men were getting ready to lift him to their shoulders, but he didn't want to go anywhere without her. He turned toward her as the players swept him off his feet and began to carry him through the crowd. She was laughing. He laughed back. And then everything inside him grew alert as something in the stands behind her caught his attention.

In a sea of screaming, shifting fans, Ray Hardesty stood in eerie stillness. Every muscle in his body was rigid with hatred as he glared at Dan from the front row. Dan saw the glint of a gun in his hand even before he lifted his arm.

Everything happened in a matter of seconds, but each fragment of time became a still photograph, an image of horror that would be frozen forever in his mind. Dan, bobbing high on the players' shoulders, had become an open target, but Hardesty, with a madman's insight, had found a better way to destroy the man he hated. Strobes flashed, reporters shouted questions at him, and Dan watched in impotent horror as Hardesty adjusted his aim so that the gun was pointed directly at the back of Phoebe's head.

A mass of security guards swarmed toward Hardesty. Those in the front saw his gun, but they couldn't use their own weapons in the middle of the teeming crowd.

In the foreground, Phoebe, unaware of the peril she was in, still laughed. Dan had no weapon, nothing to protect the woman he loved with all his heart. Nothing except the game ball cradled against his chest.

He was part of an exclusive fraternity of great quarterbacks, but as his hand closed around the football, he was no longer in his prime. Instinctively, his fingertips settled into the position that felt more familiar to him than the contours of his own face.

The names of the immortals flashed through his mind: Bart Starr, Len Dawson, Namath and Montana, the great Johnny U. himself. None of them had ever had this much at stake.

He drew back his arm and fired the ball. It shot above the heads of the crowd, low and hard, a fierce spiral, as perfectly thrown as any ball in the history of professional sports.

In the front row of the stands, Hardesty spun sideways as the ball slammed him in the shoulder. The force sent him sprawling into the seats, and the gun flew from his hand.

Phoebe, who had finally realized something was wrong, whirled around just in time to see a bevy of security guards converging directly behind her in the stands. Before she could see what had happened, Bobby Tom and Webster had grabbed her and she, too, was being carried toward the field tunnel.

25

Ron met Phoebe just inside the door of the locker room, and after assuring himself that she was unharmed, led her toward the small platform set up for the television cameras to record the postgame interviews and trophy presentation.

"I've spoken with the police," he said over the pandemonium surrounding them. "They'll talk with you as soon as the ceremonies are over. I've never been so frightened in my life."

"Is Molly all right?" The players were shaking up champagne bottles, and Phoebe ducked a frothy shower.

"She was upset, but she's fine now."

As they reached the platform, Phoebe saw Dan being interviewed on camera. He had pulled a Super Bowl cap on over his wet hair, and as Ron helped her up next to him, she heard him sidestepping questions about his second-half coaching by promising a full press conference as soon as the chaos had settled down. He didn't look at her, but as she drew near, he settled his hand comfortingly into the small of her back.

She ducked one champagne shower only to get drenched by another. Her hair dripped in her eyes and she dabbed at her cheeks as the president of the NFL came forward with the AFC Championship trophy. Standing between Dan and Phoebe, he began to speak. "On behalf of the —"

"Excuse me for one minute." Phoebe hurried to the side of the podium where she grabbed Ron's hand and pulled him up alongside Dan and herself.

Dan gave her an approving grin, grabbed a foaming champagne bottle from Collier Davis, and emptied it over Ron's head. While the GM sputtered, Phoebe laughed and turned back to the NFL official. "You can go on now."

He smiled. "On behalf of the National Football League, it is my great pleasure to present the AFC Championship trophy to owner Phoebe Somerville, Coach Dan Calebow, and the entire Stars' organization."

The players cheered wildly and released another shower of champagne. Phoebe tried to make a short speech, but got so choked up that Ron had to take over. The reporter, still trying to get answers to his questions about the strange progress of the game, turned to interview Jim Biederot, while Phoebe passed the trophy over to Ron.

Dan grabbed her hand, pulled her off the platform, and steered her behind a celebrating cluster of players so that they were hidden from the media. "Come on. We only have a few minutes."

He drew her around the corner toward the showers, through the equipment room, past a training room and into a hallway. The next thing she knew, he had hauled her into a small storage area, only a little bigger than a closet. No sooner had he pulled the door shut behind them than he gathered her into his arms and began to kiss her.

They clung fiercely to each other. Their bodies were wet and sticky from Gatorade and champagne. They tasted it on each other's mouths.

"I didn't know if I'd ever hold you like this again," he murmured hoarsely.

"I was so scared. . . ."

"I love you so much. Oh, God, I love you."

"I was afraid you didn't, and I couldn't bear it." She trembled in his arms. "Oh, Dan, it's been such a terrible day."

"You can say that again."

"Not just the kidnapping, but . . ." With a shudder, she told him about Reed.

She could feel his muscles grow taut as she spoke, and she waited for his explosion of rage. When he offered comfort instead, she loved him even more for understanding so clearly what she needed from him.

"I'm sorry," he said, his voice husky with emotion. "I'm so, so sorry, baby."

Just telling him about it somehow made it more bearable. She nuzzled deeper into the wet collar of his shirt. "I wish we could stay in here forever," she murmured.

"Me, too. All I want to do is take you home and make love to you."

"The police are waiting for me."

"I'll have to talk to them, too. And the press."

"And I need to see Molly."

He cupped her face in his hands and tenderly

stroked her cheeks. "Are you going to be all right?"

"I'm going to be fine. I just want to get all of this over with. We can meet at Ron's victory party tonight."

"Don't plan on spending too much time there." He gave her one last kiss, then held her hand as they slipped out into the hallway.

Inside the closet everything was still for a moment, and then there was a rustle in the farthest, darkest corner.

"Darnell?" The woman's voice was soft and ladylike, but clearly distressed. "Did you hear what she said? About Reed Chandler?"

"I heard."

Charmaine Dodd, who firmly believed in fair play, was indignant. "That rat! He shouldn't be able to get away with something like that."

"Oh, he won't, baby. I know the coach, and I can promise you Chandler won't get away with anything."

"I'm glad." She swatted Darnell's wandering hand, which had begun to massage her breast through her prim white blouse in the most delicious, although highly improper, manner. "Oh, no you don't. We're not married yet."

"But we're gonna be, and then I'll be touchin' you in places you didn't even know you had."

"I didn't say I'd marry you." The words were slightly muffled because she was trying to kiss him while she talked. Hugging a football player who was still wearing most of his equipment was very much like trying to cozy up to an armored tank. Even so, she wasn't ready to let him go. Not that she intended to make this easy for him by letting him know how much she'd grown to love him. Darnell was too full of himself as it was.

"Charmaine, baby, I just got off the field. I haven't been to the showers, but you still walked right into this closet with me. Now if that isn't a sign you're ready for marriage, I don't know what is."

"Maybe I just feel sorry for you."

He chuckled and slipped his hand under her skirt. His caress was so exquisite that, for several long moments, Miss Charmaine Dodd forgot her principles. Instead, she ran the tip of her tongue over the diamond embedded in his front tooth and told herself Darnell Pruitt was going to make one fine, fine husband.

It was eight that evening before Dan had finished with the police, the NFL commissioner, and the press. The lengthy and dramatic press conference had been especially difficult for Phoebe, but she had handled it like a trooper and was already being declared a heroine on the evening news. He didn't like the fact that the press was trying to make him into a hero, but he knew that stories like this died a natural death after a few weeks. Then their lives could return to normal.

Ray Hardesty had suffered a major heart attack and was under police guard at the hospital. As Dan gazed around the silent coaches' locker room where he'd finally been able to shower and change into clean clothes, he knew he would have no regrets if Hardesty didn't recover.

Everyone else had left long ago for the victory party. As he slipped into his parka, he was bone weary and all he could think about was getting to Phoebe. But there was something he had to do first.

He walked out into the silent corridor, then drew up short as he saw Jim, Darnell, Webster, and Bobby Tom leaning against the opposite wall. All of them were wearing street clothes.

He regarded them uneasily. "I thought you'd be at the party by now."

"We decided to wait for you," Jim said.

"I have to make a stop first. I'll meet you there."

Bobby Tom unfolded his lanky form from the wall. "We care about Phoebe, too."

"What are you talking about?"

Darnell took a step forward. "Me and my fiancée were sharing the same closet with you and Phoebe after the game. We overheard what she told you about Reed Chandler. I shared the information with my teammates here."

Long seconds ticked by as Dan studied them. "I can take care of Reed by myself."

"We know that. We're just planning to come along for moral support."

Dan began to argue, but fell silent when he realized that, in their minds, Phoebe had become their teammate today.

Twenty minutes later, they pulled up in front of Reed's brick and stone two-story house. Dan was relieved to see that the lights were on. Reed was home, so this wouldn't have to be postponed.

As they walked up the drive, he slipped his gloves into his pocket and regarded the men who had come with him. "Reed's mine. I don't want anybody else to touch him."

Bobby Tom nodded. "Just make sure there aren't any leftovers."

Reed answered the door himself. When he saw Dan, he looked puzzled, and then his eyes widened in alarm as he observed the platoon standing behind him. He immediately tried to slam the door, but he wasn't quick enough, and Dan drove his shoulder into it, sending him flying.

The men crashed into the hallway. Reed scrambled back against the archway that led to the living room. Dan could smell his fear.

"What do you want? Get out of here!"

Dan moved forward. "I think you know what I want. If you're a religious man, I suggest you start praying."

"I don't know what you're talking about! She lied to you about me, didn't she? She told you some kind of lie."

Dan took his first swing, a hard jab to the jaw, and Reed flew back against the couch. He gave a howl of pain and scrambled to his feet, panting with fear.

"You get out of here, Calebow. I'm going to

call the police. I'm going to —"

Webster calmly ripped the phone from the wall. "Too bad, Chandler. Phone's not working."

"If you touch me, I'll have you arrested!"

"Now how you gonna do that?" Bobby Tom stuck a toothpick in the corner of his mouth. "Right now the coach is having a drink with all four of us at my apartment. Anybody says different's a liar. Isn't that right?"

"That's right, Bobby Tom." Darnell wiped his shoe on one of the white damask chairs.

"You guys are crazy! You're fucking maniacs."

"We're not maniacs," Dan said. "We just don't think a slimeball like you should get away with rape."

"Is that what she told you? I didn't rape her! She's lying. She wanted it. She —"

Dan's next blow destroyed Reed's nose. He began to whimper and tried to push it back into place as blood poured down his face. "It wasn't my fault," he sobbed. "I was drunk. I didn't mean anything."

Dan dropped his parka on the back of the couch. "When I'm done with you tonight, you're gonna be hurt real bad."

Reed tried to scramble to his feet. "No! Stay away! Don't hurt me!"

Dan advanced on him. "You're gonna be hurt, but unless I miscalculate, you'll still be alive. If you want to keep it that way, don't ever come close to Phoebe again. If you threaten her in any way, you'd better be prepared to live the rest of your life in a wheelchair."

"No!"

It was the last word Reed uttered before Dan took him apart.

Phoebe didn't arrive at the victory party until nine o'clock. Her ordeal, combined with the lengthy press conference, had exhausted her. When she'd finally gotten home, Molly had clucked over her like a mother hen and insisted that she lie down. She'd been so exhausted that she'd immediately fallen asleep.

Several hours later, when she awakened, she was refreshed and eager to see Dan. She'd showered and chatted with Molly as she'd dressed. Her sister had been shaken by the events of the afternoon, but recovered her spirits when Phoebe suggested a last-minute slumber party. Peg consented to chaperone, and by the time Phoebe left, the girls were arriving.

The restaurant Ron had rented for the night had a cozy, rustic interior, complete with brick floor and copper pots hanging from open beams. As she entered, her hair was still a bit damp from her shower and it curled around her head. The temperature had been steadily dropping all evening, and she was wearing a loosely fitting fuchsia sweater over a matching skirt in soft, flowing wool. With the exception of a center slit that climbed to a point just above her knees, it was conservative attire, but it felt right with her curly hair and silver doorknocker earrings.

She had just checked her coat when she heard a group entering the restaurant behind her. She turned to see Dan walking in, along with Jim, Darnell, Webster, and Bobby Tom. Everything inside her grew soft and warm at the sight of him.

"I thought I'd be the last one here." Her voice sounded breathless.

His expression was so tender she could feel her chest swell. "We had a hard time getting away."

They stood in the middle of the entryway gazing at each other as the men began to move away to find their wives and girlfriends.

Bobby Tom coughed. "The two of you should probably breathe or something so nobody hangs a coat on you."

Dan didn't take his eyes from Phoebe. "Don't you have a playbook to study, Denton?"

"Yessir, Coach." Chuckling, he left them alone.

Phoebe could have looked at him forever, but they had duties to perform. Dan took her arm and began to lead her into the room. "Half an hour. And then you're all mine."

Ron met them just inside the door. To Phoebe's surprise, Sharon Anderson was at his side, and she greeted them both with a warm smile.

Dan didn't even attempt to hide his pleasure at seeing Sharon, and he immediately drew her into his arms for a bear hug. "Hi, sweetheart. How's Ron treating you? Has he proposed yet?"

Phoebe tried to work up a little jealousy, but his affection for Sharon was so open and honest she couldn't manage it. She realized he treated

Sharon exactly as he treated Molly and wondered how on earth he could ever have imagined that they would have been happy together as a married couple. Dan was one of the most intelligent men she had ever met, but he was definitely stupid about some things.

She took pity on Sharon, whose flush had spread out from the roots of her red hair to encompass every one of her freckles. "Don't let him tease you, Sharon. His idea of good manners is to mortify only those people he likes."

"I wasn't mortifying her," Dan protested. "This is my first serious attempt at matchmaking, and I want to know how it's working out."

"None of your business," Ron said mildly. "Now why don't you tend to your own love life and get Phoebe a drink?" He and Sharon smiled shyly at each other and moved away.

Phoebe giggled as Dan grabbed a beer for himself and a glass of wine for her from a passing waiter, but her smile faded as she saw that his knuckles were scraped and badly bruised. "What did you do to your hand?"

"I, uh —" He took a sip of beer. "I sure am glad Ron managed to keep the location of this party a secret from the press."

"Dan? What happened to your hand?"

He hesitated, and for a moment she thought he wasn't going to answer, but then he brushed a lock of hair from her cheek. "I went to see Reed. The two of us needed to come to an understanding about what he did to you."

Her eyes flew over him, but other than his hands, he didn't seem to be hurt. "What did you do?"

"Let's just say I practiced a little frontier justice. He won't bother you again, sweetheart."

Phoebe wanted to question him, but at the same time, the shuttered expression on his face told her she wouldn't get far. She decided she wasn't all that anxious to hear the details anyway.

Darnell approached and introduced his new fiancée. Phoebe liked Charmaine Dodd on sight, and she congratulated them. Other players approached with their wives, and she and Dan were separated. She moved from one group to another, greeting everyone and occasionally catching sight of Dan as he did the same.

She was chatting with Bobby Tom and the pair of shapely redheads draped over his arms when she heard someone yell.

"Quiet, people! Quiet!"

Everyone in the crowd was startled to realize that commanding voice was coming from Ron, and they all fell silent. He was standing at one end of the room holding a telephone, his hand cupped over the mouthpiece.

"Phoebe!" He thrust the receiver forward. "Phoebe, it's for you!"

She regarded him quizzically.

"It's the president!" He spoke the words in a stage whisper that could have been heard in the parking lot.

She had just spoken with the NFL president

a few hours earlier, and she didn't understand why Ron was so agitated. "I thought we had everything settled."

"The President! Of the United States! He's calling to congratulate you."

She gulped. Her hand fluttered to the neck of her sweater. The players laughed and then fell silent as she walked up to take the phone.

A woman's voice said, "Miss Somerville, I have the president on the line."

Just then someone tapped her on the shoulder. She turned to see Dan standing next to her, a grin the size of a football field spreading all over his face. "*Now*, Phoebe."

She regarded him blankly. "What?"

"*Now.*"

His meaning slowly penetrated her brain, and she stared at him in disbelief. He meant *now!* She pressed her hand over the mouth of the receiver. "Dan, it's the President! I can't —"

He crossed his arms over his chest, his expression unbearably smug. She realized that he had been waiting for a moment just like this. That rat! He had set her up, and now he was going to spend the rest of their lives teasing her unmercifully about not having the guts to take his dare. That cocky, infuriating *jock!* Somebody definitely had to take him down a peg or two.

The President's voice boomed over the wire. "Congratulations, Miss Somerville. It was an amazing game."

"Excuse me, sir." She gulped. "I have Miss

518

Somerville right here." She shoved the phone at an astonished Sharon Anderson.

Dan gave a hoot of laughter. She grabbed him and pulled him through the crowd. Just as they reached the door, she spoke.

"You'd better be worth it, studmuffin."

In the background, Sharon Anderson, after a stumbling start, had risen to the occasion. Much to Ron's bemusement, he heard her say, "I'm fine now, Mr. President. Yes, it was quite harrowing. By the way, sir, I want you to know that all of us in the Stars' organization share your concern about adequate funding for preschool education. . . ."

"*Studmuffin?*" Dan pulled out onto the highway. "You called me *studmuffin!*"

Phoebe was still trying to catch her breath. "This game can go two ways, Coach. Don't be surprised if you're in the final two minutes of the Super Bowl —"

"You wouldn't."

"I might."

He looked over at her and smiled. "Speaking of the Super Bowl. Will you marry me as soon as it's over?"

"How about Valentine's Day?"

"Too long."

"Groundhog Day?"

"Deal." The Ferrari raced down the ramp onto the Tollway. "You know that we've got a few problems we need to talk through before we get married."

"I'm not getting rid of Pooh."

"See, there you go being antagonistic. Marriage means learning to compromise."

"I didn't say I wouldn't compromise. I promise to take the ribbon out of her topknot before you walk her."

"You're all heart."

Phoebe's smile faded. "I want children, too. I always have. I just needed to know you loved me."

"I hope you know it by now. I never loved anybody in my life the way I love you. I want children, but not nearly as much as I want you."

"I'm glad." She caught her bottom lip between her teeth and then released it. "I don't want to send Molly away. I want her to stay with us."

He glanced over at her. "Of course she's going to stay with us. Where else would she go?"

"I thought you might want more privacy."

"Once that bedroom door is shut, we'll have plenty of privacy. Actually, when I mentioned problems we need to talk about, I was referring to the Stars."

"I know you're not marrying me for the Stars. I should never have said what I did. I was hurt."

"I'm glad you realize that. But you see, we still have a problem. Historically it's been women who've married the boss. As soon as they had a wedding ring on their finger, they quit their jobs and stayed home. Neither of us wants you to do that, but I have to tell you that I'm not all that comfortable with the idea of spending the rest of my life sleeping next to somebody who's got the power to fire me if my underwear doesn't make it all the way to the laundry hamper."

She repressed a smile. "I'm sympathetic to your problem, but I'm not selling the team just so you can be a slob."

"Somehow I didn't expect you would."

"It's a new world order. You men are going to have to figure out how to handle it."

"You're enjoyin' this, aren't you?"

"I'm mildly amused."

Despite her teasing, she had already been doing some thinking about how she might balance the enormous demands of owning the Stars with marriage and the children she hoped to have. "As a matter of fact, I have a few ideas on this subject. It's not completely worked out in my mind, but when it is, you'll be the first person I talk to about it."

"Then I'd better tell you that I'm not planning to coach the Stars the rest of my life."

"Dan, you can't go to work for another team! It would be an impossible situation."

"I'm not going anywhere for a while. But you've seen what this life is like during the season. I want to be around for you and for our kids, and I've been toying with this idea for a long time. I decided a while back that the day I wake up and realize I can't remember what my wife and kids look like is the day I get out of pro coaching. I'm going to find a Division III college nearby, and that's where I'm going to settle in for the rest of my coaching career."

"Division III? I don't know what that means."

"They're small colleges. They don't offer athletic scholarships, and the pros never scout them. The kids aren't the biggest, they aren't the fastest, and nobody's slipping them money under the table. They're only playing football for one reason, and that's because they love the game. So while you're off wheeling and dealing with all the high rollers, I'm going to tuck myself away on some nice little college campus and remember why I started playing the game in the first place."

"It sounds wonderful."

He shifted lanes. "That scarf you've got under your coat collar. Would you mind blindfolding yourself with it?"

"What?"

"*Now.*"

"Oh, for Pete's sake." She snatched the scarf from beneath her coat collar and tied it around her eyes. "This is ridiculous! You're not planning anything kinky, are you?"

There was a long silence.

"Dan?"

"Well, I suppose it all depends on how conservative your viewpoint is."

"You said you were putting all that behind you. That you wanted a nice, ordinary sex life."

"Uh-huh."

"You don't sound very certain."

"See, it's like this. After a lifetime of high living, it'd probably be best if I sort of tapered off gradually. That way it wouldn't be too big a shock to my system. And this is something I've been thinking about for a long time."

"You're making me very nervous."

"That's good, honey. That's real good." He then launched into the sweetest, softest dirty talk she had ever heard in her life until her skin was so flushed she had to unbutton her coat. But he still wouldn't tell her where he was taking her.

When he finally stopped the car, she realized that his monologue had distracted her so much that she'd forgotten to pay attention. Had the tires crunched on gravel? She listened hard, but although she couldn't hear any traffic noises, she wasn't absolutely certain whether or not he'd driven her to his house.

"You're going to have to wait here for a couple of minutes while I get a few things settled. I'll be right back, so don't get nervous." His lips brushed hers. "Promise me you won't spoil everything by sneaking a peek. That'd be a sign that you don't trust me, and what kind of marriage would we have then?"

"You're really pushing me. You know that, don't you?"

"I know, darlin'." He nibbled her bottom lip. "While you're waiting, why don't you just go over all those things I told you I was going to do to you. That way you won't be bored." His chuckle was definitely diabolical as he slipped his hand under her dress, squeezed her thigh, and then opened his door.

It was an absolutely rotten thing for him to have

said, because once he'd planted the idea, she couldn't think of anything else. By the time he returned to the car, she was quivering with sexual anticipation.

She felt a rush of cold air as he opened the door. "Everything's all taken care of. I'm going to carry you now." He caught her under her knees only to immediately set her back down on the seat. "Phoebe, honey, you're still wearing your underwear. I distinctly remember telling you I wanted it off by the time I got back."

"You did not."

"I'm sure I did. I guess I'll have to take it off myself." Sliding his hands under her dress, he pulled off her panty hose and her underpants.

"I'm going to freeze. It's not even twenty degrees."

"I don't think you'll have to worry too much about freezing. Where in the world did these panties come from?"

"I bought them."

"They're not much more than two little ribbons and a scrap of silk. Did you give up your industrial strength underwear just for me?"

"Just for you."

"That's sweet, honey, and I appreciate it. Now slip those high heels back on. I do like the way your legs look in high heels." As soon as she'd done what he said, he caught her under her knees and swept her out of the car. Her skirt fell free and cold air fanned her naked bottom, which was exposed for the entire world to see.

"Please tell me there aren't a dozen people standing around."

"Only half a dozen, sweetheart. But they're all too busy adjusting the carburetors on their motorcycles to look."

She buried her face in his collar and laughed. He was outrageous, impossible, and she was having the best time of her life. *But where was he taking her?*

He shifted her weight and opened some sort of door. She was relieved to feel warmer air on her bottom as they stepped inside.

"That blindfold still tight?"

"Uh huh."

"That's good. Don't pay any attention if you hear strange noises."

"What sort of noises?"

"Drunken laughter. Breaking glass. Jukebox. That sort of thing."

"I won't give it a thought."

"And if somebody named Bubba asks you what you're doing here, you just tell him you're with me."

"I'll do that."

He began kissing her, and by the time he stopped walking, she realized he'd once again distracted her from paying attention to where they were going. Had they traveled a short distance or a long one? He wasn't breathing hard, but he was in such good physical shape, that didn't mean anything. She couldn't even be certain whether he'd climbed a set of stairs or if they'd stayed on the same level.

"I'm going to set you down now. I don't want to get you too close to the bar. On account of fights breaking out."

"May I take the blindfold off yet?"

"I'm afraid not, honey. You've still got your clothes on."

"I have to take my clothes off?"

"I'm sorry, darlin'. I thought you'd figured out how this was going to work." He removed her coat. "Don't you worry, though. I'll help you."

"You're such a gentleman."

He slipped off her earrings, pulled her sweater over her head, and discarded it. "Phoebe, honey, I don't want to embarrass you, but did you know you can see right through this?"

"Can you now?"

"I'm afraid so. That means I'm going to have to ask you to stand real still for a minute."

Through the gossamer-thin silk of her bra, she felt his mouth settle over her nipple. The warm, moist suction sent torrents of excitement raging through her body. His sensual torture continued as he moved his mouth to the other breast, while the nipple he had abandoned pebbled beneath the damp, chilly spot he had left on the silk. Her knees were growing weak, and she wanted him inside her so badly she grasped his shoulders.

"Please. . . . You're making me crazy."

"Shhh. I'm just getting started here, and, frankly, I expect a little more stamina from you. Maybe you could recite some batting averages or something."

She laughed and then gasped as he gently nipped her with his teeth. A moment later, her bra fell away, and she was naked from the waist up.

"You are one beautiful woman, sweetheart. Isn't she, boys?"

He definitely needed to be put in his place. She began to lift her arms to remove the blindfold, but he caught her wrists and held them at her sides. "Not yet, honey. I'm real thirsty."

Releasing her, he cupped her breasts in his palms. Once again, he began to feast on her nipples, but this time, not even the frail barrier of silk was in his way. He suckled her until she was making soft, mewing sounds.

She reached out, desperate to touch him. At some point he had taken off his own coat, and she slipped her hands under his sweater, sliding them through the mat of hair on his chest to brush his nipples.

He groaned. She felt his touch at her waist, and then the light brush of wool as her skirt fell free. He spoke softly, his voice husky. "I don't want to scare you, honey, so I'd better tell you exactly what I'm going to do here."

She wasn't the slightest bit afraid and he knew it, but she decided it would be rude to interrupt.

"I've made a bed for us with our coats, and I'm going to lay you down on it. That's right. Now lean back. That's good; real good. Honey, I don't remember telling you that you could close up your legs like that. Uh-huh, now move that knee up so I can enjoy the view." His fingers found the sensitive skin of her inner thigh.

"Can I take the blindfold off yet?"

"Oh, I don't think so. No sense in gettin' you all riled up till I'm through with you."

She was definitely going to get even with him for this. But not until she had enjoyed every second of this exquisite, thrilling seduction.

She heard the rustle of his clothes as he discarded them, and her heart swelled with love. Six months ago she could never have imagined trusting any man enough to let him do this to her, let alone one with Dan's physical strength. Yet she lay here before him naked and open. Even though she had no idea where he had taken her, she had never felt safer and she realized that, along with his love, he had given her freedom from fear.

He lay down beside her on the bed of coats and drew her into his arms. "I'm going to kiss you a little bit. If you get bored, I can ask the band to play some music or something."

"I'm definitely not bored."

She breathed in his clean scent and touched the tip of her tongue to his shoulder. His muscles flexed and she felt his arousal pulsing hard against her thigh. His mouth closed over hers. Their tongues joined and everything else slipped from her mind until she was only aware of sensations. The sound of his groans, the dampness of his skin as he held himself back to pleasure her. His mouth traveled from her breasts to her waist. He kissed the insides of her thighs, then opened her to love her more deeply.

She had no idea when she lost the blindfold. She didn't know whether it had fallen off or one of them had removed it. She was only aware of the roar of blood in her ears, the ecstasy of being joined with this man she loved so very much, the fierce passion of his love words as he thrust so deeply into her body.

"All my life . . ."

"I know. My sweet . . ."

"Forever . . ."

"Oh, yes. Forever."

They pledged themselves with word and body, then cried out together as their love flowed warm and rich from one heart into the other.

When it was over, he held her against him as if he'd never let her go. His voice was thick with emotion. "I love you so much. I've been lonesome for you all my life."

Tears slipped from the corners of her eyes. "You're the most wonderful man in the entire world."

She could feel him smile against her forehead. "You're not mad?"

"Why would I be?"

"I wanted to drive out the bad memory, honey. I wanted to put a good one in its place."

She had no idea what he was talking about, and she was too lethargic to question him. Sighing with contentment, she snuggled her cheek into his neck and opened her eyes. She was aware of the gentle beating of his heart, the stars twinkling in the sky above, the soaring gridwork of steel. . . .

Her head shot up.

"Something wrong, sweetheart?"

"Oh, my God!"

They were lying naked on the fifty yard line in the very center of the Midwest Sports Dome.

EPILOGUE

Dan walked down the quiet lane and breathed in the fragrant evening air of late May. He caught the scent of rich, damp earth, along with the faint hint of lilacs from the bushes he and Phoebe had planted not long after they were married. Contentment seeped through every pore of his body even though his wife was in a snit, and he knew he was going to hear about it the minute she got him alone.

She got upset about the strangest things. Just because he'd asked a few perfectly innocent questions about that raging hormone who was taking Molly to her high school senior prom was no reason to accuse him of being overly protective. It had been odd starting out his marriage as a stand-in father for a teenage girl, but he knew he'd done a lot better job of it than Bert Somerville. He and Phoebe had secretly rejoiced when Molly had decided to go to Northwestern instead of one of the Ivy League schools. They didn't want her too far from home.

So much had happened these past three years. Ray Hardesty had suffered a fatal heart attack before he could go to trial. Reed Chandler had taken the hint about leaving town, and the last anybody'd heard, he was selling cheap condos on a run-down

Florida golf course. There had been weddings: Ron and Sharon, Darnell and Charmaine. He'd be surprised if Valerie and Jason Keane ever got married, but they certainly made an interesting couple. There had been a wrenching funeral when his friend Tully Archer had died of pneumonia. The Stars had lost their first two Super Bowls and failed to qualify the third year. This year, however, they'd finally won it, and the Lombardi trophy was sitting in the lobby of the Stars Complex to prove it. Best of all, he'd become a family man.

He smiled as he remembered that glare Phoebe had shot him over the dinner table tonight when he'd been grilling Molly about her love life. Although he tried to keep it a secret, having his wife in a snit was something he never failed to enjoy. He was a competitive person by nature, and the sheer challenge of seeing how long it took him from the time she started fussing at him to the time he got her naked appealed to his sportsman's nature. So far, his record was eight minutes, and that had been after a serious snit, too — the same night he and Ron had badgered her into signing Bobby Tom's new $10-million contract.

Phoebe loved Bobby Tom — he and Viktor were the twins' godfathers — but she was a real tightwad when it came to big-money contracts. The smartest thing he'd ever done was sic his lawyers on her right after they got married. That had been a battle and a half. Damn but he loved being married to Phoebe!

Not long before his twin daughters were born,

Phoebe and Ron had signed an agreement to reorganize the Stars. Unfortunately, that agreement had put an end to all kinds of enjoyable conflicts. Ron was now the Stars' president and the person in charge of day-to-day operations, while Phoebe was proving to be a real whiz at her new job as Director of Finance and Budget.

Under the terms of the agreement, only Ron had the authority to make personnel decisions. Signing over that responsibility had been a wise move on Phoebe's part. She loved crunching numbers, but she didn't have the stomach for the whole business of cutting and trading players. She still liked to poke her nose into Dan's coaching practices, however, especially when one of the players ran whining to her about being benched. On those occasions he took great pleasure in reminding her that he reported only to Ron.

Phoebe was so good-humored that everybody except the sports agents loved working with her. Only when salaries were being negotiated did she get prickly. The whole world knew by now how smart she was, so she couldn't pull off her bimbo scams anymore, and to Dan's embarrassment, she had rapidly earned a reputation as one of the most astute budget directors in the NFL, which didn't mean that he still wasn't planning to hit her with both barrels when his own contract expired this fall. Mrs. Phoebe Somerville Calebow was going to pay through the nose for that diamond choker he planned to slip around her beautiful neck when their next baby was born.

Although they hadn't talked too much about it, both of them knew it would be his last contract with the Stars. The girls were getting older and he was beginning to resent the brutal seven-day workweeks during the season. He already had his eye on a sweet little Division III college right here in DuPage County.

He smiled to himself as he remembered the way Phoebe had looked when he'd kissed her just before he'd slipped from the house for his nightly outing. She'd been sitting cross-legged in the middle of the living room floor, one of his old sweatshirts pulled tight over her big round belly while she played patty-cake with the girls, who kept trying to grab her charm bracelets and tug at her hair. Tonight he was going to pull that sweatshirt right up to her chin and whisper lots of girly things to her belly. He didn't care how much she teased him. He liked having girls, and he was hoping for another one.

He stopped walking and gazed at the farmhouse. The twins were two and a half now, mischievous little blond-haired cherubs who managed to get into nearly as much trouble as their mother. As he thought about them, he could feel his throat closing up, and he was glad nobody was around to witness the tears that gathered in his eyes. He'd always loved this place, but until Phoebe had settled in with her rhinestone sunglasses and glittery earrings, something had been missing.

Once again he drew a long, contented breath. He had everything he'd dreamed of. A wife he loved with all his heart. Beautiful children. A house in the country. And a dog.

He whistled softly. "Come on, Pooh. Let's go home."

The employees of G.K. HALL hope you have enjoyed this Large Print book. All our Large Print titles are designed for easy reading, and all our books are made to last. Other G.K. Hall Large Print books are available at your library, through selected bookstores, or directly from us. For more information about current and upcoming titles, please call or mail your name and address to:

G.K. HALL
PO Box 159
Thorndike, Maine 04986
800/223-6121
207/948-2962

C